The Lady Plays with Fire

The Lady Plays with Fire

Susanna Craig

ZEBRA BOOKS
Kensington Publishing Corp.
www.kensingtonbooks.com

ZEBRA BOOKS are published by

Kensington Publishing Corp.
900 Third Avenue
New York, NY 10022

All Kensington titles, imprints, and distributed lines are available at special quantity discounts for bulk purchases for sales promotion, premiums, fund-raising, educational, or institutional use.

Special book excerpts or customized printings can also be created to fit specific needs. For details, write or phone the office of the Kensington Sales Manager: Attn.: Sales Department. Kensington Publishing Corp., 900 Third Avenue, New York, NY 10022. Phone: 1-800-221-2647.

Zebra and the Z logo Reg. U.S. Pat. & TM Off.

First Printing: May 2024
ISBN: 978-1-4201-5481-8

ISBN: 1-4201-4404-9 5482-5 (e-book)

10 9 8 7 6 5 4 3 2 1

Printed in the United States of America

To my mom, with love

Acknowledgments

As always, I owe my thanks to the many people behind the scenes who make my books possible: Jill Marsal; the Kensington team and especially my editor, Liz May; the lovely authors of the Drawing Room historical romance group; Amy, for her endless store of encouragement; Anne, for letting me tap into her well of theater knowledge; and my family, for their patience and support. I couldn't keep doing this without you.

The Lady Plays with Fire

Prologue

Castle Dunstane, Scotland
June 1810

Graham McKay sat with his elbows propped on the scarred oak desk that had once belonged to the first Earl of Dunstane, his great-great-great . . . grandfather.

A more sentimental man would have known precisely how many *greats.*

Despite his present prayerful posture—eyes closed, palms together—Graham was not a man given to displays of sentiment. Or any other sign of weakness. Without looking up, he urged his secretary, Simon Keynes, "Go on."

"Aye, my lord." A burr scraped in Keynes's throat, and papers rustled. "'The scenery has been painted by a skillful hand, and the costumes are well-tailored,'" the man read, his voice flat and the words quick, as if he were hurrying through an unpleasant task. "'Very little more may be ventured as praise for Ransom Blackadder's latest desecration of the stage. Even the best performers of the day could not improve lines so obviously designed to offend and insult, with nothing of humor about them.'" A pause, followed by an audible swallow. "'Alas, Mr. Blackadder's reputation as a playwright does not attract the best performers of the day.'"

The crackle and hiss of a fire in the hearth would have filled the awful silence that followed. But it was at least nominally spring, no matter how damp and blustery the day. And coziness had never been Graham's way.

He ought, however, to take pity on poor Keynes. Bad enough to charge the man with scouring every two-bit, ink-wasting periodical in the British Isles—and they were legion, as it turned out—for any mention of Blackadder's scandalous, satirical work. To require him to read those words aloud—no matter how critical, no matter how cutting—bordered a little on cruel.

"'Nor,'" Keynes concluded, forcing the words over his reluctant tongue when Graham made no sign to desist, "'with so little attempt at decorum or civility, should *Vice Is Its Own Reward* attract the finest audience, or indeed, any audience at all.'"

Splotches of red—mortification, Graham supposed—mottled Keynes's face, only highlighting his pale, thin features. But really, the fellow ought to be used to it by now. In discussing Blackadder's plays, the papers always dripped with words like *shocking, offensive, disgraceful.*

Thanks to them, every seat in the theater was full, night after night.

For his part, Graham felt only relief. If people were daft enough to pay for the pleasure of being spat at and kicked, why shouldn't he profit from it?

A positive review could set the whole enterprise on its ear. Graham pressed the tips of his forefingers more firmly against his lips, the better to disguise the sardonic smile that had begun to curve them.

"Are there others, Mr. Keynes?" he murmured, once he felt certain of his ability to keep any hint of pleasure from his voice.

He had long since provided a reasonable excuse for his interest in how Blackadder got on. *Patron,* Graham had described himself. *Investor. Interested party.* Nonetheless, he wondered from time to time whether Keynes suspected the truth, whether he knew he was, in fact, delivering every scathing review to the playwright himself.

"Surely, my lord, what I've read is sufficient to—"

Graham opened his eyes and fixed his secretary with a look.

Briefly meeting Graham's gaze from behind smudged spectacles, Keynes gulped and began once more to rummage through his battered leather portfolio. Everything about Simon Keynes was thin: his gaunt frame clad in an earthy-gray woolen coat, the precise shade of which blended almost seamlessly into the stone wall behind him; his lips, perpetually pursed; his hair.

At long last, he retrieved what appeared to be a magazine from his satchel. "This is the final item I collected, my lord. Of a rather different character than most."

A different character? Had Keynes saved the best— or rather, the worst—for last? Graham dipped his chin once to signal the secretary to read it.

Keynes fumbled about for a moment, tucking the portfolio awkwardly beneath one arm and then drawing his thumbnail along the edge of the pages, a hurried attempt to find his place that did not reward his effort. He had to flip back and forth a few pages at a time, until he found what he was looking for. Once more, he cleared his throat sharply before he began.

"'*Vice Is Its Own Reward* presents a series of vignettes on society's hypocrisy and double dealing in matters of business, Acts of Parliament, and even marriage vows. One cannot shake the impression that Mr. Blackadder feels himself a man out of time. Perhaps, if he had written at the start of the last century instead of the start of this one, his wit would not have gone so unappreciated by the critics.'"

Something prickled along Graham's skin, a curious sort of agitation, and his pulse increased by a beat or two. The sensation was akin to the sort of wariness one felt when passing along an unfamiliar wooded path, where the crackle in the undergrowth might be something small and unthreatening . . . or something considerably more dangerous.

"'On the bawdy Restoration stage, or circulating in salons among the great Augustan satirists, Mr. Blackadder would surely have felt more at home—albeit humbled, one hopes, in the presence of their brilliance. Since his lot has fallen to us, however, rather than our great-great-grandparents' "—Graham had the distinct impression the reviewer knew precisely how many *greats*—" 'one might be forgiven for finding it curious that he persists in directing the jibes of an earlier age at the fashionable foibles of his present audience. If Mr. Blackadder wishes to mend our ways by making us laugh at ourselves, he might do better to let us in on the joke.' "

Graham could not contain a derisive snort. Every Ransom Blackadder play ridiculed its audience outrageously, duping people into mean-spirited mockery at their own expense. His work never hinted that he believed people might, in a moment of sober reflection, recognize their own flaws and fix them.

He made it perfectly obvious he felt them incapable of improvement.

"Thank you, Keynes. You may go," he said, with a dismissive flick of his hand.

But Keynes didn't move, didn't close the magazine, didn't even look up. "If it please your lordship, there's a bit more."

Again, the prickle of warning chased down Graham's spine, sharper this time.

Keynes adjusted his grip on the magazine, holding it farther from him, as if he struggled to bring the print into focus. Or couldn't quite believe what it said.

" 'This reviewer, however, doubts Mr. Blackadder's goals are so noble,' " he read. " 'And if I am right in my conjectures, what a pity to waste such a formidable talent on mere disdain for one's fellow creatures.' "

Graham dragged in a sharp breath through his nostrils. It wasn't exactly praise, at least—though *formidable talent* came dangerously close.

He had been even less prepared for pity.

"Who?" he demanded. "Where?"

Keynes jumped at the questions. "A newish publication, sir. *Mrs. Goode's Magazine for Misses.*"

"*Misses?*" Graham echoed, incredulous. "A *ladies'* magazine?"

"*Young* ladies, sir," Keynes clarified—a trifle gloatingly, to Graham's ear. "And as to who wrote it . . . Well, all the columns are anonymous, except for one by Mrs. Goode, and I suspect even that is an assumed name. This review is attributed to 'Miss on Scene.' "

" 'Miss on Scene,' " Graham repeated beneath his breath. " 'Miss on—' " In spite of himself, he broke off on a wry chuckle. "Ah. Clever."

He didn't intend the remark as a compliment.

Keynes didn't seem to get the joke.

"*Mise en scène,*" Graham said. "French for stagecraft." He thrust out his arm, palm upward. As Keynes approached the desk, he let the magazine fan closed before handing it to Graham.

The edges of the paper were soft and tattered, as if this particular copy had been read repeatedly and given up reluctantly. On the cover, two caryatids—columns in the shape of women—framed the title: *Mrs. Goode's Magazine for Misses.* Below, the magazine purported to "Promote Rational

Conduct and Improve Wisdom among Young Persons of the Fair Sex."

Someone had crossed out the word *Misses* and inked in another above it: *Mischief.*

Graham glanced up at Keynes for an explanation. "The content of the magazine is not necessarily what most would deem proper for young ladies," the secretary said.

Was it Graham's imagination, or was that a smile twitching at the corner of the man's mouth?

"Obviously," Graham shot back. "What would proper young ladies need with a review of *Vice?*"

To the extent that he wrote for such an audience at all, he certainly did not do so for their amusement. And he cared not at all for their opinions, good or otherwise.

"Some go so far as to call it *Mrs. Goode's Guide to Misconduct,*" the secretary continued, after dipping his head in acknowledgment—and perhaps to hide another smirk. "The associated scandal has only increased the publication's popularity . . . not unlike the work of a certain playwright. Forbidden by parents, governesses, and the like, the magazine mostly circulates surreptitiously, from hand to hand. Hence the rather battered appearance of this copy. I had to pay dearly to get it. From what I've been able to determine, every fashionable young lady in London knows what the *Magazine for Misses* has to say, even when they personally have not been fortunate enough to see the latest issue for themselves."

As Keynes spoke, Graham leafed through the well-read pages. At first glance, nothing struck him as remarkable: sketches of the latest fashions; gossip passed off as news; advice.

But when he attended more closely, he discovered the advice columnist urged the shocking step of breaking off an engagement with a notorious rake ("better a contented spinster than a miserable wife," opined someone calling herself Miss Busy B.), and the fashion plates were satirical renderings of the fashionable nearly worthy of one of Ransom Blackadder's plays.

And speaking of . . .

The paper crinkled beneath his fingertips as he sought and found the review by Miss on Scene. Settling in to read, he was interrupted by Keynes's shadow falling across the page.

"The estate business will wait until tomorrow," Graham said. He did not look up but twitched his fingertips in a dismissive wave. "You may go."

He heard Keynes's intake of breath, the prelude to some objection or rebuttal. The estate business was surely more important than some silly review; his secretary had been away for a fortnight, during which time correspondence had been piling up. Graham knew it all too well.

But in the end, Keynes said nothing, merely turned and walked away, closing the heavy door with a soft *click*. Graham wasn't even sure the man had bothered with the customary courtesy of a bow.

He was too absorbed in his reading to care.

What a pity to waste such a formidable talent . . .

Slapping the magazine shut, he moved as if to fling it in the direction of the empty hearth. But at the last second, he caught himself, dropping the magazine on his desktop instead and smoothing the wrinkled cover with his palm.

What a pity . . .

With automatic movements, he drew a stack of clean foolscap from a drawer and fished a pencil from a tarnished silver tray, touching the tip to his tongue. Ransom Blackadder was going to have to teach Mrs. Goode's Misses a lesson. The author of that ridiculous review would soon understand the misery that befell a young lady foolish enough to play with fire.

Chapter 1

London, September 1810

As the carriage crept along crowded West End streets, Julia Addison's anticipation grew, until the butterflies dancing and fluttering inside her might have been mistaken for a herd of dashing, leaping stags. Tonight marked the official start of her second London Season.

But it wasn't a ball or a rout or a dinner party that had set her nineteen-year-old heart racing. *That* part of the Season was yet to come, and nothing she, as a lady's companion, was likely to participate in. What marked the true beginning of the Season in Julia's mind was not even the opening of Parliament. It was the fresh bill of operas and ballets and, most important of all, plays to be performed each autumn and winter at the Theatre Royal, Covent Garden, this year to be observed from Mrs. Mildred Hayes's reserved box on the second tier, overlooking stage left.

Mrs. Hayes sat on the carriage's forward-facing seat, the tip of her cane planted on the floor between her feet, both hands resting on its polished silver handle, her relaxed body swaying easily with the vehicle's desultory progress. Her eyes were closed.

Julia marveled that anyone could sleep at a time like this. The noise surrounding them was terrific: the clatter of hooves and harness, the rattle of iron-rimmed wheels over cobblestones; men, women, and children along the pavement hawking goods and services ranging from the practical to the profane; and the shouted oaths of carriage drivers—occasionally including their own.

As she peered out the window, a sedan chair hurried by, easily threading its way through the snarl of traffic. Julia envied its occupant. No matter how burly the men hoisting the poles, Mrs. Hayes could never consent to put her trust in such a contraption. So, they lumbered through the crowded streets in Mrs. Hayes's old-fashioned barouche, traveling at a snail's pace, even as the minutes flew by.

They would be late. At half past six, the curtains would rise on the celebrated Mrs. Siddons acting the part of Desdemona in *Othello*, and Julia might as well be back in the little stone rectory in Oxfordshire, where she had had grown up, for all she would see of it.

No, *there!* The head of Bow Street, just visible in the distance. If she hopped down now—she wouldn't even need to signal the driver to stop, they were moving so slowly—she could make it the rest of the way on foot in a matter of moments.

"Settle yourself, my dear. We'll only be fashion-ably late."

Julia had reached for the door handle without realizing it. Now a spasm of guilt drew her primly back into her seat. Of course, Mrs. Hayes couldn't be expected to walk so far. The staircase to the boxes would be trial enough. And even aside from her rheumatism, such bustle did not suit her no-tions of either propriety or consequence.

Mrs. Hayes had spoken those words of reassur-ance without even opening her eyes, Julia realized. The jewel-handled lorgnette Julia had long known to be an unnecessary aid to Mrs. Hayes's vision, not quite an affectation. But surely she was not possessed of the gift of second sight?

"I do beg your pardon, ma'am." Julia folded her hands in her lap and refused even to glance to-ward the window, though the increasing gloom of the carriage's interior was a telltale sign of the late-ness of the hour. "I must learn to curb my impa-tience."

A smile carved Mrs. Hayes's wrinkled cheeks, her round face a pale circle against the leather squabs, rising above her black bombazine gown. "I understand your eagerness—though when I was your age, I fear the audience would have held at least as much of my attention as the actors. Well . . . *most* of the actors." A twinkle revealed that her eyes were not as tightly closed as Julia had thought.

Mrs. Hayes, who had been a widow far longer than she had been wife, was rumored to have had an affair with Mr. Garrick, one of the leading actors of her day. Most of the time, Julia found the story impossible to believe. But at the moment—her fancy helped along by the magic of the evening and Mrs. Hayes's mischievous expression—she wondered whether it might not be true after all.

"One cannot avoid looking at the audience, ma'am," Julia conceded, try though she might to focus all her attention on the stage. Enormous chandeliers lit the house throughout the performance, and most people—dripping with jewels and swathed in showy silks and sparkling taffetas—attended the theater less to see than to be seen.

"Surely even you will agree that sometimes it is the more interesting show."

Grudgingly, Julia dipped her chin. "Sometimes." Not every item on the bill could be equally entertaining.

Though, truth be told, she had never seen a gentleman in the audience who could hold her attention, who made her breath catch and her pulse quicken, like the actors who trod the boards. From the first time she had seen a traveling troupe spout their lines from a makeshift stage on the village green, she had wished for some way to join them—an impossible dream for almost every woman, but most especially the daughter of a clergyman.

The sharp turn onto Bow Street caught her off guard, so absorbed had she been by the image in her mind's eye: a fantastical vision of herself as a celebrated actress, the audience in her thrall. "Nearly there now," she said to Mrs. Hayes, who surely knew the route at least as well as Julia.

A moment before, everything had seemed to

stand in the way of their pleasure. But now, every
lurch brought them closer, as each carriage in line
ahead of them disgorged its passengers, and the
distance between Julia and the theater doors dwindled, measurable now in mere yards, in feet, in
inches.

With her eyes raised to the theater's grand
façade, Julia descended first, the better to assist
Mrs. Hayes. She turned back just as Mrs. Hayes appeared in the carriage's opening, reaching for the
cane with one hand and wrapping her other securely around the older woman's left arm as a liveried footman took her right. Together they
helped Mrs. Hayes down the two steps and onto
the pavement. Once she had shaken the creases
from her skirt and straightened herself, she gestured for her ebony walking stick and Julia restored
it to its rightful owner. The usual *clickity-clack* of its
silver tip against the ground was inaudible over the
noise of the crowd as they made their way inside.

True to her word, Julia spared no more than a
glance for the crush of patrons surrounding them
on every side. Once through the doors, they made
their careful way up the sweeping staircase to the
elegant saloon that ran behind the private boxes,
decorated with marble sculptures in the Grecian
style and tufted benches upholstered in crimson
velvet. Cologne was thick on the air, not quite
masking the lingering scent of tobacco, the che-
roots the gentlemen had extinguished outside,
just a moment or two before. Conversation buf-
feted them like waves, a greeting here, an exclama-
tion there. The plumes on Mrs. Hayes's turban

nodded to her left and to her right, but she never paused for more than a moment, nearly as eager now as Julia to reach their seats.

Every indication gave her hope that they had not missed the start of the performance, though it must surely be nearing a quarter of seven. Heavy crimson velvet draperies guarded the entrances to the individual boxes, giving the occupants some degree of privacy and muffling the incessant noise from the saloon. A good number of them still stood open, awaiting the occupants' arrival. As no usher stood nearby to assist, Julia stepped ahead to sweep aside the curtain to their box for Mrs. Hayes.

Curious. The cord that fastened the curtain shut during the play had been secured from the inside. She supposed it had accidentally fallen into place, somehow. She would have to slip her hand around the corner of the door frame to release it.

As her gloved fingertips found the curved metal hook and fumbled to slide the silken loop over it, the curtain was wrenched open by someone unseen, and a strong, warm hand encircled her wrist.

"And just what do you think you're doing?" demanded a man's voice in an unmistakable, though not unpleasant, Scottish accent.

Against the glare of light from the theater beyond, she could make out little of the man's appearance beyond the fact that he was tall, with brownish-red hair the color of burnished copper. She was still trying to blink him into focus, and to rein in her clattering pulse, when Mrs. Hayes spoke.

"We are trying to enter our box, good sir," she

said in a firm voice, accompanied by a sharp rap of her cane against the floor. "And I will thank you to unhand my niece."

Mildred Hayes was not Julia's aunt. At best, she was Julia's aunt-in-law, if such a relationship could even be said to exist. Not quite two years ago, Mrs. Hayes's actual niece, Laura, had married Julia's brother, Jeremy, Viscount Sterling, and moved with him to Wiltshire. Mrs. Hayes, however, had been determined to remain in London. Not wishing to abandon her elderly aunt, Laura had suggested her new sister-in-law might take her place as Aunt Mildred's companion.

Relatively few young ladies of seventeen would have jumped at the chance to serve at the whim of a widow who, in spite of her professed Town habits, actually lived quite retired in Clapham. But Julia, faced with the prospect of returning to quiet country life at her brother's estate, had readily accepted Mrs. Hayes's offer. Mrs. Hayes had a reputation for being liberal-minded and good-natured.

Most important of all, she loved the theater almost as much as Julia herself.

Julia's brother had taken her to plays now and again, when he could spare the time and the coin. She had treasured the memories of those evenings in Haymarket and Drury Lane: straining for a view of the lavish costumes and fancying she could still catch a whiff of greasepaint, even from the cheapest seats in the house. Then, she had never dared to dream of what Mrs. Hayes had since provided: tickets for the Season, every performance within her grasp.

And speaking of grasps . . .

The unknown gentleman released her reluctantly, as if she were a thief he had fully intended to turn over to the authorities.

Once freed, she longed to rub her wrist, not because it hurt—he had been neither rough nor careless, despite the quickness of his movement—but to rid herself of the sensation of his unwelcome touch.

The impatient tap of Mrs. Hayes's cane had given way to a sniff of derision as the widow snapped open her lorgnette and eyed the gentleman suspiciously through it. "Who the devil are you? And what are you doing in my box?"

"*Your* box, madam?" The words were punctuated with a mocking laugh. "I think you'll find you're mistaken."

All of Julia's blinking had managed to bring the man into better focus, though his features were still cast in shadow by the glare of light behind. He was not quite thirty, she guessed, impeccably but not ostentatiously dressed, with surprisingly broad shoulders that seemed somehow in contradiction to his aristocratic bearing.

Julia turned and began to murmur to Mrs. Hayes. But before she could request to be allowed to fetch an usher, Mr. Pope, the box manager, appeared beside them as if summoned by the imperious snap of someone's fingers. Someone's strong, warm fingers.

Despite her earlier resolve, she wrapped her other hand around the wrist he had held, however briefly, in his implacable grip, hoping her movement was disguised by the folds of her skirt.

Mr. Pope bowed to the gentleman, as if Mrs.

Hayes were suddenly beneath his notice, however respectable she might be. "May I be of some assistance, my lord?"

My lord.

Julia narrowly managed to avoid rolling her eyes. She had no good opinion of noblemen—her brother excepted, and then only because he had inherited the title unexpectedly, without the encumbrance and expectations of a fortune to go with it, and not until he had been almost a grown man, past the age of spoiling.

"Yes," said Mrs. Hayes. "You may explain to this"—she tossed another dismissive glance toward him, her lorgnette only half-raised to her eyes—"*gentleman* that he is in my box, and then do me the kindness of escorting him from it to his proper seat."

The color that flushed into Mr. Pope's cheeks was visible, despite the uncertain light in the area between the saloon and the rear of the box, still half-shielded by the curtain. "I, er . . ."

"Aye, Mr. Pope." She heard a thread of humor in Lord Scottish's voice now, as he widened his stance and crossed his arms behind his back. "Why don't you explain matters? I confess I'm most eager to hear what you have to say for yourself."

"I, er . . ." he stammered again, glancing downward before turning toward Mrs. Hayes. "This is Lord Dunstane's box and always has been. But as he comes to Town so rarely—almost never—I, uh, I took the liberty of selling the tickets again to you, ma'am."

The reselling of tickets was a common enough practice. When those with a private box had already seen a performance, or were unable to attend, the box manager was employed to sell the tickets again to another interested party. But what Mr. Pope had done was a clear violation of both theater policy and good manners.

"Pocketed the double profit yourself, I daresay," added Lord Dunstane. To Julia's astonishment, he now sounded not angry, but almost amused.

The pink in Mr. Pope's cheeks darkened to crimson. He did not refute the accusation.

Mrs. Hayes gripped the handle of her cane more firmly. "I see. Then you must forgive us for the intrusion, my lord. We, of course, had no idea."

She had taken a box this year with every intention of asking friends to join them throughout the Season; thankfully she had not done so tonight. Now Julia thought with some embarrassment of the invitations that would have to be rescinded: Lady Clearwater and her daughters next week; later, Mama and her husband, Mr. Remington, and Mr. Remington's particular friends, General and Mrs. Scott.

"Perhaps Mr. Pope can find us another box," Julia suggested.

"Unfortunately, the performance for the next several evenings is . . ." the box manager began. Julia could guess what he was hesitant to say.

Sold out!

She had seen the placard, plastered over the playbill displayed outside the theater. Even if she had not, she might have guessed the state of things from the crush of carriages on Bow Street and the noisy crowd mingling in the vestibule. The size of the audience, the chaos of getting everyone properly seated, no doubt explained the delay in starting the performance.

"I paid for tickets for tonight, Mr. Pope," Mrs. Hayes reminded him, holding up the thin ivory disk that was marked with Lord Dunstane's box number. "Tickets you *will* find some means of honoring."

Mr. Pope glanced downward into the pit, where patrons seated on long benches could be squeezed together to accommodate another person or two.

This silent suggestion was met with a *harumph* of displeasure. "Oh, I think not, sir."

"I could easily find you places for next week," Mr. Pope suggested.

Next week? Julia gulped. Not that she had grown so spoiled she imagined she would suffer some irreparable harm by waiting a few days to see *Othello*. It was not her own disappointment she was struggling to swallow.

Under the name "Miss on Scene," she wrote reviews of theatrical performances for *Mrs. Goode's Magazine for Misses*, and this month's deadline was tomorrow. Lady Stalbridge, the magazine's editor, was expecting Julia's contribution by midday at the latest. Lady Stalbridge, the readers, and the magazine would all lose by Mr. Pope's double-dealing.

A sudden hush had fallen across the theater, which caused the noise in her throat to be surprisingly audible, easily mistaken for a soft sob. Lord Dunstane settled his light eyes on her, taking in every detail of her appearance, her age, the modest quality of her sprigged muslin gown. *A poor rela-*

tion, his sardonic gaze said clearly, *doomed to a future as a lady's companion.*

And yet, he did not immediately look away—at least, not until Mrs. Hayes's pronouncement: "Unacceptable. We shall simply have to join Lord Dunstane here. As he's alone, I'm sure he won't mind."

With that, she began to move deeper into the box, her cane clearing the path ahead of her, both Mr. Pope and Lord Dunstane looking on, dumbfounded.

When neither of the men made as if either to assist or prevent her, Julia stepped forward and laid a hand on her arm. "We mustn't presume, ma'am . . ." she began.

But Mrs. Hayes kept going. "*Hmph.* Can't see that *we* are the presumptuous ones. Now, help me to that seat, child." She pointed with the tip of her cane.

Though well-positioned, the box—*their* box, as Julia had been thinking of it until a few moments ago—was one of the smaller ones in the theater, holding just six seats in two rows of three. Lord Scottish was evidently not the sort who reserved a box with the intention of inviting a dozen of his closest friends to chatter their way through the performance.

After Mrs. Hayes was seated in the front row closest to the stage, Julia moved to take one of the blue-upholstered chairs in the back. Lord Dunstane spoke from behind her. "You'll be more comfortable—see better—from the seat beside your aunt."

With a mute nod, more surprise than acquiescence, she accepted the middle chair. In another moment, he had taken the spot to her right. Of course he would expect to have the best view—or at least, the best remaining view—from his own box. She refused to turn her head in his direction, not even when a wry laugh gusted from his lips, as if he were incredulous at his own misfortune.

She wanted, uncharacteristically, to fidget. But why should Lord Dunstane make her agitated? After tonight, he would doubtless never give her another thought. *Sooner, in fact,* she thought, when she recollected his glance of disdain and pity. Once the performance began and gave them all something else to think about, he would forget her existence entirely.

Nevertheless, she could not remember ever having been so aware of the strange intimacy of a theater box, where people sat, almost shoulder to shoulder, snug within their private world and yet on display to anyone who cared to look.

And people *would* look, from below or across the way, everyone eager for a glimpse of something new or unexpected.

Lord Dunstane—a striking-looking Scotsman who came to London so infrequently that Mr. Pope had believed his deception would go undiscovered, but who nonetheless reserved a box at Covent Garden for performances he would never see—certainly fit the bill.

For just a moment, Julia considered slipping into one of the empty seats at the back of the box after all. But before she could make her move, the curtain rose.

Chapter 2

Determined not to look, Graham could still see the young woman out of the corner of his eye. The shell of her ear, the velvet curve of her cheek, the tilt of her nose . . . she was a shadow in his peripheral vision, a distraction, a constant reminder that he was not spending the evening as he had intended: alone.

It had not been the act of a gentleman to catch the young woman by the wrist and restrain her, as if she were some mere pickpocket. But the appearance of that slender hand beyond the curtain of his box had startled him, and he'd reacted instinctively to guard his solitude.

Rather than succeeding at warding off an impertinent thief of his privacy, he now found himself in the intolerable situation of sharing his box with perfect strangers. If he had not been certain the old lady would cause an unpleasant scene—and more important, if the play had not been about to start—he would have insisted upon their removal. Churlish of him? Yes, of course.

No one who knew him would have expected anything less.

Well, at least he could not be expected to socialize with them. Watching the performance was a silent activity. And they had not even been introduced.

The lack of an introduction proved something of an inconvenience as the play went on, however. Beside him, the young lady began to lean forward, evidently enraptured by what he would have called a mediocre performance. He shifted slightly in his own chair and sighed.

But his sigh fell on deaf ears. Or its meaning was misunderstood.

Rather than disappearing, her profile inserted itself more insistently into his line of sight. She had a long neck he supposed some fool would describe as swan-like. And a pert chin to go with her pert nose, entirely inappropriate for a meek lady's companion. And a thoroughly unfashionable abundance of dark brown hair that would surely fall to her waist when unbound . . .

"Ahem." He cleared his throat once, softly, hoping as much to disrupt his own reverie as hers. He had no business thinking about a young lady's unbound hair, how it would caress her shoulders and cling provocatively to the curve of her full breasts. Most ungentlemanly of him. He was churlish, yes, but not a cad.

"Ahem." More loudly the second time, when his first effort did not have the desired effect—either on her posture or his thoughts.

When she had intruded so thoroughly into his line of vision that he could focus on little else, could hardly even see the stage, he was driven to lean forward himself, lay a hand on the front railing of the box, and say, "I beg your pardon, miss—"

"Addison," she supplied without ceremony. Without fully turning her head. And then added for good measure, "Shhh."

Unaccountably, her reprimand made a laugh rise in his chest. Surely a reaction to the absurdity of his predicament.

She had shushed him! This . . . this *girl*, really— she couldn't be more than twenty—whose lot in life no doubt meant her experience with the theater was that of an occasional sweetmeat, a luxury doled out in dribs and drabs by her crotchety aunt. That would explain her despair when it had seemed the outing would be denied. Her single-minded focus on the stage. Her . . . *enthusiasm*.

The word sent a shiver of distaste through him. He could not remember the last time he had been so enthusiastic about anything.

And perhaps that was part of the problem. Perhaps that was why he was finding it all too difficult to ignore Miss Addison's intrusion into his box, his view, his thoughts. If he let himself, he could still recall the softness of her skin, the scant half inch between the top of her kid glove and the hem of her sleeve, where he had touched her.

Good God. He shook off the tingle of memory with a flick of his fingers and tucked that hand against his ribs as he folded his arms across his chest. Evidently, he needed to work off a bit of, er, *enthusiasm* himself.

The remote situation of Castle Dunstane, combined with the sparse population of the Highlands generally, meant that female companionship could be difficult to come by.

And what an outrageous euphemism that was. As if he required *companionship* from anyone, especially a woman.

But he was still a man, with a man's needs.

Fortunately, London was an excellent place to slake them. He'd simply waited too long to visit the metropolis and then let himself be diverted by the first tolerably pretty young woman to fall beneath his gaze.

Now, however, he was well-positioned to find a more suitable object of attention. If he sat up a bit straighter and leaned away from Miss Addison, rather than toward her, he could see the stage well enough.

Well enough, for example, to recognize the charms of the actress playing Emilia. When the performance was over, he would go to the green room and introduce himself. She would know why he had sought her out, and when he offered to take her to supper, she would not refuse—unless she had a protector already. But perhaps not even then. Infrequent though his forays into Town might be, Graham still had a certain reputation as a . . . well, call it *a patron of the arts*.

In a few hours, he would have forgotten all about the thin, silky skin of Miss Addison's wrist, against which her pulse had thrummed so insistently, making him all too aware that he was the cause of its precipitate rhythm. He would forget about the length of her hair, or the turn of her throat. About the saucy tilt to her nose.

She would be—*was*—nothing to him, the merest nobody, her presence a minor inconvenience of the sort one ought to expect when one was foolhardy enough to venture amongst people again.

Furrowing his brow, he focused all his attention on the stage. Emilia was even more beautiful than he had first realized, with perfectly symmetrical features and gleaming golden hair.

Not, however, a particularly good actress. Her gestures lacked subtlety. And more time ought to have been spent sanding the sharpest edges from her voice before giving her a speaking role. She hailed, quite obviously, from Plymouth—somewhere very near the docks.

Time was when he would have been delighted by the girl's performance. Lord, how particular he had grown—a consequence he supposed, of having learned to school the contours of his own speech. Just as well that Miss Addison was not privy to his thoughts. She would think worse of him than she already must—not that he cared one jot for her good opinion.

A murmur of annoyance must have passed his lips. Or else the grinding of his teeth had been audible. Miss Addison twisted her head over her shoulder to fix him with a look of mild irritation that slid almost imperceptibly into concern. Or perhaps alarm. He was probably scowling, the expression common enough with him that he was not always aware of doing it. And given their relative positions, it must look for all the world as if he were scowling at her.

Which, in a way, he was.

"Are you well, my lord?" she mouthed. Despite her evident apprehension, the excitement of the evening—or at least, the light of the chandelier— twinkled in her blue eyes.

"Perfectly," he replied with a brusque nod.

But the word itself was drowned out by the sudden clamor of applause as the curtain fell, and her gaze snapped back to the stage without seeming to notice his dismissive gesture, as if she were startled to discover the performance was at intermission.

The noise made her aunt jerk a little in her seat. He wondered whether she had been dozing—an understandable response to the uninspiring performance, in his opinion. Miss Addison, he noted, did not clap.

Perhaps they were better judges of the theater than he had given them credit for being.

Below, the rustle of the crowd rose to a dull roar as people began to look about themselves and converse with acquaintances across the aisle or a few rows away. Some got to their feet and began to mill about. Others lifted their faces to study the occupants of the boxes, to see which scions of society could be spotted, and with whom.

Graham wished, not for the first time, that he had taken a seat at the back of the box. Though even there, he would hardly have been unobservable. Particularly not to Miss Addison, who had once more turned toward him, her expression now almost expectant.

"Well, my lord? I take it you were displeased by

the performance so far." Again, that mischievous blue sparkle—not merely an effect of the light, then. The chandelier was behind her. "Either that, or our intrusion on your box has soured your enjoyment of the evening."

May not both things be true?

It was precisely the sort of quelling retort he would ordinarily make—although there was nothing ordinary about the present situation. But for the first time in many, many years, he did not speak the taunting words that rose effortlessly to his lips. He did not have to.

Miss Addison did it for him.

"*Both,*" she supplied in a slightly deeper voice, a vaguely Northern accent. Mocking him.

"Julia," scolded her aunt, who was giving the exchange far more attention than she had given the performance.

"I only said aloud what his lordship was clearly thinking," Miss Addison defended herself.

But Graham's thoughts had already taken another turn. Or rather, returned to their previous, forbidden track.

Julia. Julia Addison.

"Forgive me," he said, rising. The rail at the front of the box was too low to give a man of his height much security. He rounded his chair and stepped into the narrow channel between the two rows of seats, closer to the older woman, before making his bow. "Since the worthless Mr. Pope did not think to do the honors, allow me to introduce myself. Dunstane, at your service, ma'am."

She snapped open a jeweled lorgnette and looked

him up and down before answering, with a surprisingly regal nod, "Mrs. Hayes."

Mrs. Hayes did not apologize for barging into his box. He had not really expected it of her. After all, she had been wronged, just as he had. Graham intended to see that the box manager regretted his double-dealing.

"My niece, Miss Addison," Mrs. Hayes added with a wave of her hand.

Miss Addison unhurriedly came to her feet. "My lord." Her curtsy was graceful, despite the confined space. But also grudging. Whatever timidity and deference she had exhibited—or he had fancied her exhibiting—upon entering the box had flown. If she had said as much, it could not have been clearer that she suspected him of arrogance.

Perceptive chit.

"May I fetch you some refreshment, Mrs. Hayes?" he offered, intending not to prove Miss Addison wrong about him—she wasn't wrong, after all—but to rattle her certainty. To put her off balance, so to speak. Metaphorically, of course. He was not quite awful enough to wish her to take a tumble into the pit and break that lovely neck.

"Thank you, my lord," Mrs. Hayes said, the gracious dip of her head pairing rather incongruously with a poke of her now-folded lorgnette at her niece. "Go on, then."

Miss Addison's—Julia's—eyes widened, and for just a moment, he thought she meant to refuse to accompany him.

Not, of course, that he would have minded one whit if she had. He had made the offer as much to

garner himself a temporary reprieve from their
company as out of any sense of gentlemanly oblig-
ation.

But after a momentary hesitation and with an
almost imperceptible squaring of her shoulders, as
if it required effort to comply with her aunt's request, she moved to leave the box. He did not
offer her his arm.

The long saloon was every bit as crowded as one
might expect, and Graham hated crowds. At the
edge of the room, he hesitated, anticipating with a
shudder the feel of strangers jostling against him.
Again, he sighed, the sound lost beneath the rumble of conversation surrounding them.

Undaunted by the throngs, Miss Addison stepped
forward, prepared to thread her way through. She
would have been lost to him in a moment if he had
not reached out to touch her elbow.

She stopped, a stone to trouble the stream of
humanity flowing around her, and looked up at
him. "Yes, my lord?"

How had she been so certain the fingertips
pressed briefly against her arm had belonged to
him, and not the hand of some careless passerby?

"Wait here." He jerked his chin toward the nearest statue and then set about the task of procuring
Mrs. Hayes's refreshments on his own. Despite his
reluctance to enter the fray, he made his way with
relative ease; his size was an advantage, and he was
not above using it.

When he returned a few moments later, two
glasses of wine in hand, he scanned the top of the
crowd for the familiar statue. A quasi-Greek figure
of a woman, half-clothed in her marble—or more

likely, plaster—drapery. It put him in mind of one of the caryatids on the cover of that damned ladies' magazine, which had occupied a larger share of his thoughts over the last few months than the publication had any right to do.

Beneath the statue stood Miss Addison—right where he had left her, much to his surprise. She glanced about her, taking in the spectacle without seeming to be much affected by it. As if she were one of the rare sort who came to the theater to do something other than ogle the other theatergoers.

Her hands were folded primly in front of her, but the plain hem of her muslin gown rippled tellingly where she tapped her toe.

"Impatient to return to the play?" he asked when he had made his way unnoticed to her side.

She started. Evidently, she had not been awaiting his return with bated breath. Her bright eyes looked him up and down. He noted the exaggerated sweep of her gaze, as if she had not before realized how he towered over her. She darted a glance over her shoulder, toward the curtained entrance to his box. "I don't want Mrs. Hayes to worry."

He took no step in the direction she so obviously wanted to go. "Are you enjoying the performance?"

She paused before replying. "The role of Iago is creditably done." He had the distinct impression even that partial answer had required careful weighing. "I suppose on the whole, I find it generally entertaining."

Damning with faint praise. He hadn't expected it of her—or rather, he hadn't expected it of the girl who had sat beside him not half an hour ago, to all appearances riveted by everything that passed before her on the stage.

But perhaps he had misread her enthusiasm. Misread her.

Perhaps she, too, had been determined to ignore the distraction posed by her unexpected companion for the evening.

"Interesting," he replied with a sage nod. "I would have described it as insipid."

The flare of her eyes reflected surprise but not, he thought, disagreement with his assessment.

"It happens sometimes," he went on, leaning slightly toward her so as to be heard when he lowered his voice. "Even the great actors are affected by opening night jitters."

Miss Addison glanced again toward the boxes. "Then perhaps Mrs. Hayes should have accepted Mr. Pope's offer to find us tickets for another night."

He recalled Miss Addison's quiet noise of displeasure at the prospect. She must have been looking forward to this evening for some time. Now she was disappointed by how things had unfolded. Disconcerted.

Well, tonight had not gone as he had planned, either.

In the distance, a jangle of bells signaled the end of intermission. He held out a glass of cloyingly sweet ratafia. "For your aunt."

Some indefinable reaction wrinkled across her brow and was gone. "Mrs. Hayes is not my aunt," she said, though she accepted the glass. He expected some further explanation—he had quite plainly heard the older woman call Miss Addison her niece—but none came. She turned toward the entrance to the box, then glanced back over her shoulder when she realized he had not followed. "You do not intend to watch the rest of the play?"

He contemplated another hour of sitting beside her, her profile inserting itself into his view of the stage, the soft scent of her soap intruding on his senses. He shook his head. "Another night may be better, as you say."

She seemed to sense his reluctance was not based solely on the mediocre performances. Swallowing back whatever retort she had been about to make, she curtsied rather stiffly instead. "You have that liberty, I suppose. It is your box."

The crowd divided them as people made their noisy way once more into the theater. He watched Julia's retreating form until it was lost to him among the throng.

Alone at last, he glanced down at the remaining glass with a grimace. He had intended it for her.

Placing it untasted on the pedestal of the statue, he hurried down the staircase to the exit.

Chapter 3

Insipid.

She had been trying for half an hour to finish her review of *Othello* for the *Magazine for Misses*. Every word had been a struggle. Too frequently, the words that suggested themselves to her mind had belonged first to Lord Dunstane.

Not that two people mightn't choose to describe a play in similar terms. Particularly not a shared experience of a performance. Or part of one, anyway.

Oh, but she was glad he had left at intermission. His presence in the box had been a weight on the evening, a looming shadow. The mere memory of him sitting beside her sent a prickle down her spine, forcing her to sit up a little straighter.

~~*Insipid.*~~

She dragged her pen through the word, pressing the tip so firmly into the paper that it tore.

"Oh, drat!"

Mrs. Hayes, who was seated by the parlor's large window overlooking Clapham Common, glanced up from the letter she had been reading. "What's that you're working on, my dear?"

"A letter to Daphne," Julia fibbed.

Daphne, Lady Deveraux, was also Miss Busy B., the *Magazine for Misses'* advice columnist—a role she continued to fulfill even after marrying the very rake she'd infamously advised a reader against. She was quick spoken, bordering on impetuous, and Julia had liked her instantly.

Julia did write to Daphne often. But this morning's missive was, in fact, intended for Lady Stalbridge, an elegant older woman with whom Julia could have no plausible reason for corresponding. Hence the lie. The countess was the editor of the magazine, about which Mrs. Hayes—thank God—knew nothing at all.

"A frustrating letter, it would seem," Mrs. Hayes acknowledged, before returning to her reading.

"Yes, ma'am," Julia agreed, sliding a fresh sheet of foolscap from the shallow drawer of the escritoire. Fortunately, Mrs. Hayes never stinted with the supply of paper and ink. "I have been attempting to describe the play last night, but I cannot seem to find the words this morning."

"Dull," Mrs. Hayes suggested without looking up. "Spiritless. Wooden. I have rarely been so disappointed by an opening night. I almost regret insisting that we stay." She paused to murmur over something she read, shaking her head as she refolded the letter and laid it aside before turning to

the next. "At least the farce was tolerably amusing.
A pity Lord Dunstane missed it, don't you agree?"

She could picture the scorn with which Lord
Scottish would have viewed such silliness, the disdain with which he would have listened to her
laughter.

Oh, his hauteur was unsufferable. Unforgive-
able.

Or ought to be.

"Really, ma'am, I hadn't given him a moment's
thought."

Julia didn't like to lie to Mrs. Hayes. Not least
because it was so easy to do that it was impossible
not to feel guilty afterward. She was such a trusting, oblivious soul. Why, her niece Laura—now
Julia's sister-in-law—had got up to no end of antics
while living under this very roof, and Mrs. Hayes
had never been the wiser.

Though occasionally, there was a moment, like
last night in the carriage, or when the older
woman would lift her lorgnette halfway to her eyes
and fix Julia with a look, that made her wonder
whether she knew more than she let on.

Thankfully, this morning was not one of those
times.

Mrs. Hayes was fully absorbed in her letters.
Later, Julia would be expected to go through that
same stack of correspondence, answering the invitations as directed. But for now, for another half
hour at most, she was at leisure to finish writing
her own.

She could not afford to be frittering that time
away, mulling over the contrast between icy eyes
and fiery hair, between cool words and the peat-

smoke-and-whisky warmth of the voice in which
those words had been spoken.

Dipping her pen, she began again.

> *When one is tasked with reviewing a
> performance of* Othello, *one is not permitted to
> fault the playwright. When the stage is graced by
> such luminaries as Mrs. Siddons, one is not ex-
> pected to fault the acting. How, then, to explain a
> staging of the Moor of Venice so dull as to have
> made Miss on Scene wish she might find some way
> of hurrying the action along to its inevitable end-
> ing—its tragic ending, I had almost written.*
>
> *But is it a tragedy to put a thing out of its mis-
> ery?*
>
> *With all due respect to both Mr. Shakespeare
> and Mrs. Siddons, Desdemona ought to be* angry.
> *Emilia too. How are such vapid playthings as I
> saw last night, women who can respond only by
> whispering and whimpering at their betrayal,
> meant to have attracted men of such vigor and
> supposed valor?*

Julia paused to reread what she had written so
far and gave a self-satisfied smile. Lord Dunstane
could have his *insipid*. She had done him one better.

> *Perhaps Mr. Shakespeare's genius was
> hampered by the knowledge that the impassioned
> words of his great tragic heroines would be—could
> only be, in those dark days—mouthed by mere
> boys. Perhaps Mrs. Shakespeare was the forgiving,
> accommodating sort, willing to overlook her hus-*

band's misdeeds, and so he had no true notion of how a woman in Desdemona's situation might feel.

If my readers attend the theater to have their passions stirred, I fear they will leave this performance unmoved.

If a young lady attends with other motives, she may feel secure in regarding the scenes passing before her as a harmless backdrop to the various amusements which an evening at Covent Garden may afford.

The farce—perennial favorite "A Scandalous Marriage"—was at least tolerably amusing,

"Something's got into you," Mrs. Hayes remarked, with a pointed glance.

"Ma'am?"

She nodded toward the half-filled sheet. "You seem to have found some words."

A laugh eased from Julia. "Oh, yes. I did. I was trying to be delicate at first, you see. Rather than honest."

"I thought perhaps you had moved on to pleasanter subjects than the play." The hand holding her letter dropped into her lap, and a sharp sigh burst from her. "I'm still quite vexed about the box. How *could* Mr. Pope—? And Lord Dunstane . . . such a lonely-looking gentleman, didn't you think? I felt certain he would offer—"

"Now, Mrs. Hayes," Julia soothed. She wanted nothing from haughty Lord Scottish.

After transforming her last comma into a point, she waved the sheet back and forth a few times before folding it. Lady Stalbridge abhorred smudged ink. Julia had had every intention of writing more, but the clock on the mantel warned her that she was already past her time.

Rising, she stepped toward Mrs. Hayes. "If I may, ma'am, I'll post my letter and then go to the bookshop and find something interesting to help us pass the next few evenings."

Surely, once the rush of opening night was over and the excitement at seeing Mrs. Siddons had abated, there would be seats to be had. They had managed well enough last year without a reserved box.

"A new novel, dear?" Mrs. Hayes sounded intrigued. "But rest assured, I haven't given up on the theater. When you return, I intend to write to Mr. Pope and give him a piece of my mind."

Which meant, of course, that Julia was to write and find the words to convey Mrs. Hayes's displeasure.

She donned her pelisse, tucked her review into her reticule, and was tying the ribbons on her bonnet when Mrs. Hayes added, "And then a note of thanks to Lord Dunstane, of course."

Julia's fingers fumbled. It was one thing to chastise Mr. Pope. Or even Shakespeare.

Words of gratitude would be far more difficult to come by.

In her mind's eye, she saw Lord Scottish clutching two glasses of wine. *For your aunt,* he had said, and then kept the other for himself.

Of course, a man like him had not thought of getting a glass for her.

Mere companions, or poor relations, or whatever part he imagined she played, evidently did not require—or perhaps deserve—refreshments.

"Perhaps he will yet do the polite thing," Mrs. Hayes went on, "and agree to share the box with us."

Julia dipped her head to hide the incredulous laugh that rose to her lips. *Polite?* She doubted the man even knew the meaning of the word.

Besides, having to spend an hour or two in company last night had likely confirmed Lord Dunstane in his reclusive ways.

With any luck, he was already on his way back to Scotland.

Then at least they might be left to enjoy his—*their*—box in peace.

Porter's Antiquarian Bookshop was not the sort of place that stocked titles to amuse Mrs. Hayes on a dull autumn evening. It was, however, the location of the makeshift editorial office for *Mrs. Goode's Magazine for Misses.* Once each month, any of the writers who happened to be in Town met in the room at the back of the shop to discuss matters of business and plan future issues. The rest of the time, the space was used for storage, which explained its perpetually disheveled state.

Behind the counter near the front of the shop were three things of interest to Julia: a pigeonhole in which messages could be left for "Mrs. Goode," a key to the back room, and a clerk who knew enough to look the other way when Julia slipped a folded note from her reticule and reached across into the cubby.

With the tip of her finger, she could feel that the little box was half full of paper. Lady Stalbridge's servant had not yet come to collect her messages, then. Miss on Scene's column might be the last one in, but once it was shuffled in between Miss N.'s News and Miss R.'s Arts and Accomplishments, no one need be the wiser.

It was something of a stretch to reach the pigeonhole, and its rounded opening required her to refold her column to make it fit. On her second attempt, she turned her head, the better to extend her arm, and made two discoveries.

The first was that the hook from which the key to the back room ordinarily hung was empty.

That, in and of itself, was not surprising, though today was not a meeting day. Miss Cooper, the artist behind the magazine's regular cartoon, "What Miss C. Saw"—a satirical look at people and places about Town, which readers had instantly dubbed the "Unfashionable Plates"—often worked in the back room, though in Julia's estimation, the light was rather poor for drawing.

Constantia Cooper had not taken any of the staff members into her confidence, so no one, with the possible exception of Lady Stalbridge, knew where she lived or anything about her family. It required no great stretch of imagination to guess that someone at home disapproved of her sketching hobby. But that begged the question of how she then got away to spend hours at Porter's, evidently unchaperoned.

Neck twisted, shoulder strained, Julia was weighing whether to investigate after—or rather, *if*—she managed to get her blasted letter into the blasted box, when she made the second discovery.

Lord Dunstane was headed her way, a curious— well, it might be more accurate to describe it as *disapproving*—expression on his face.

"Miss Addison?"

Yes, definitely a note of disapproval, though she could not seem to help liking the way her name sounded on his lips, the way his slight brogue made the vowels curve in unexpected ways.

"My lord," she answered, sliding slowly down the counter on which she had been half-propped as if it were the most natural posture in the world. *Should I drop the note? Or—?* Her hand brushed against the binding of a book, and without a second thought, she snatched it up. In the half a moment it took for him to close the gap between them, she managed to slip her column between the book's pages and now dipped into a curtsy.

When she looked up again, he was watching her expectantly, obviously awaiting an explanation for her odd behavior. Were his eyes gray? Or possibly green? Even the midday light streaming through Porter's front window was not bright enough for her to determine. And she was certainly not going to stare.

"I, er—" she began, then giggled, then despised herself for giggling. "I came in to fetch a book they were holding for Mrs. Hayes, but I couldn't get the clerk to help me, so I had to reach it myself."

At that, the clerk—who had been standing a few feet away, leafing through a stack of orders and steadfastly not looking in her direction as he had no doubt been instructed—glanced down at her over the top rim of his spectacles, gave a little *harumph* of irritation, and strode off toward another customer.

With a triumphant smile, Julia held up the small, battered volume, bound in dull brown leather. "I've managed it, you see," she said, belatedly tugging on the sleeve of her spencer to straighten it.

Surely this little display would send the man scurrying through the shop door behind her.

"May I?" he asked instead, and held out his hand, palm upward, for the book.

"May you . . . Oh. You wanted to see . . . oh, yes, of course." As she rambled, she surreptitiously tucked the folded letter more securely between the book's pages before surrendering it.

Lord Dunstane was, objectively speaking, a handsome man. More handsome than any man with red hair had a right to be, as far as Julia was concerned. If it had been the pale red shade, tending toward blond, that Constantia Cooper sported, Julia could have dismissed him more easily. But his hair was darker, not quite auburn. And he wore it unfashionably long, the better to frame a collection of sculpted features, the sort of face that made her curious what it would take to soften his expression, why he never smiled.

Not, she supposed, that their two encounters had been especially pleasant from his perspective either. Though her appearance today might at least be worth another sardonic curl of the lips, as she had glimpsed last night.

But a real smile? Coaxing one of those would be a challenge, indeed.

And absolutely *not* a challenge to which she intended to rise.

He turned the book over in his hands, ran a fingertip down its spine, opened to the title page, and gave a *hum* of surprise. "Mr. Hume, eh? I had thought Mrs. Hayes—and you—more likely to prefer novels."

Julia bristled. "And why shouldn't we read history? Or philosophy," she hastily added. She hadn't looked at the book before giving it to him, and Mr. Hume had been too prolific for her to assume the nature of the volume Lord Dunstane now held.

"No reason," he replied, the thread of amusement in his voice undoing whatever attempt at mollification he had intended to make with his words. "But very few young ladies do, or so I'm given to understand."

As he spoke, he continued to examine the book, and her mind raced.

Please don't let him thumb through it. Please don't let him—

Beneath his fingertips, the pages, slightly yellowed with age, fanned open, leaving Julia's now-mangled sheet of paler foolscap standing up in the center.

"What's this?" he exclaimed. "Looks like whoever sold the book to Porter's left a letter behind—"

"Merely a receipt, I'm sure." She snatched it from between the pages before he could investigate further. "And of course young ladies read history," she insisted, though in truth, she rarely did. All the battles and masculine posturing, hardly any women. "All the drama, those invented speeches—it's very little different from a night at the theater."

His eyebrows lifted. "I could argue—"

Of course he could. He was exactly the sort of person who would take pleasure in picking apart anything and everything others said.

He held out the book, returning it to her. "But I won't."

Why did his refusal deflate her? She had neither the time nor inclination to spar with Lord Dunstane. She had come to Porter's for one purpose, and she certainly did not intend to let a handsome, insufferable, insufferably handsome Scotsman interfere with—

Out of the corner of her eye, she glimpsed the purposeful stride of someone approaching: Lady Stalbridge, with the key to the back room dangling from her left hand.

Lord Dunstane did not appear to notice her. Or, if he did, he had no interest in an introduction. "I'll wish you a good day, Miss Addison," he said, with a dip of his head, and before she could reply, the bell above the shop door jangled to signal his departure.

"And who was that?" asked Lady Stalbridge, following him with her gaze—which, when his retreating form had disappeared, she then turned on Julia. No mistaking, in any light, that the countess's eyes were blue, and sharp enough to see right through a fib.

"Lord Dunstane," Julia said and paused to draw

breath before launching into an explanation of how they had come to be acquainted.

But Lady Stalbridge did not require an explanation. "The Earl of Dunstane?" she echoed, glancing once more toward the window, though he was no longer visible. "The theater patron?"

"P-patron?" Was that Lady Stalbridge's discreet way of describing a gentleman who flirted with actresses?

"Yes. His name is well known among those seeking support for various productions and playwrights, though the man himself almost never comes to London to see the results. I suppose he has other ways of knowing whether his investment paid off," she added, with the sort of sly smile that made Julia think her surmise about the actresses wasn't entirely wrong.

"Which playwrights?" Difficult to imagine whose work would please surly Lord Scottish.

"Most famously—or infamously—a fellow Scot, Ransom Blackadder."

Julia could not entirely contain her reaction, though she knew Lady Stalbridge was watching her and no doubt thinking of the same thing: Julia's pointed review of Blackadder's latest in the *Magazine for Misses* last spring.

"Speaking of," she said, though neither of them had expressed their thoughts aloud. Into Lady Stalbridge's hand, she pressed her review of *Othello*, the state of which had not been improved by being clutched in Julia's too-warm palm. "I have to go. Mrs. Hayes will be wondering what became of me."

Turning, she laid the dull little volume she had no intention of purchasing on the counter. With her fingertips, she pushed it a few inches in the direction of the harried clerk. She would send Daniel, Mrs. Hayes's errand boy, out later to fetch some horrid novel the whole household would enjoy. Lord Dunstane had left Porter's empty-handed, and she did not intend to risk being confronted by him in yet another bookshop, particularly not in the midst of making such a frivolous purchase.

Really, it ought not to have come as such a surprise to her, the connection between the *ton*'s favorite misanthrope and the supposed gentleman so ready to dismiss the intellectual capability of young women, the feelings of a lady's companion, and the respect due an elderly widow.

Unfortunately, the notion of Lord Dunstane as a patron of the theater did not make him any less intriguing to her.

Or any less attractive.

Chapter 4

Graham's study in the house in Half Moon Street was a square, modern room, with painted woodwork, papered walls, and upholstered furniture, everything light and bright and as unlike Castle Dunstane as it was possible for a room to be. Two large windows faced the street, framed by blue silk curtains edged with gold fringe. Shepherdesses frolicked across the toile-covered walls.

If he hadn't been so absorbed in his reading, their vacant smiles—at the sheep, at the occasional bumpkin leaning against a stile, at one another—would have set his teeth on edge.

"Have you seen this?" he demanded, slapping the back of his hand against the page open before him.

At the noise, Simon Keynes started, sending the tip of his pen juddering across the letterbook in which he had been recording Graham's correspondence. He was seated at a delicate Chippendale table beneath the nearer of the two windows, and when he turned toward Graham, the light behind him made his scalp gleam through the wisps of gray-brown hair that still clung to his crown. "I beg your pardon, my lord. To what do you refer?"

"Miss on Scene's new review." He gestured with the latest issue of the *Magazine for Misses*.

That very morning, the housekeeper, Mrs. Beatty, had overheard a gaggle of housemaids chattering over something other than their work, swatted each of them with the rolled-up periodical when it had been produced, and then been on her way to dispose of the trash in the nearest fire when Graham had happened upon her and relieved her of the duty.

"In *Mrs. Goode's Guide to Misconduct?*" Keynes pushed his spectacles a fraction of an inch higher on his nose; if Graham hadn't known better, he would have suspected his secretary of attempting to hide a smirk. "No, my lord. I haven't had the pleasure."

Graham wasn't exactly sure that reading the review had been pleasurable—or rather, he was quite sure it *wouldn't* have been, if he were not the kind of man who took occasional delight in others' misfortunes.

For the first time in his life, he had been glad *not* to be Shakespeare.

Rising, he stepped across to Keynes and laid the open magazine atop the letterbook, jabbing at the page with his forefinger. "Find out who wrote this."

Keynes glanced upward and askance, sighed as he laid aside his pen, but did not offer any other

protest. As unpleasant tasks went, Graham had demanded worse. "Any leads as to the reviewer's
identity, my lord?"

"Judging from both the harshness of the review
and the timing of its publication, it would have to
be someone who was in the audience for opening
night."

One of, oh, three thousand or so people, then.

Mentally, Graham scanned the crowds, wondering which of those who had been present wielded
such a sharp pen. A grande dame, perhaps, someone with a lifetime's practice in issuing cuts both
direct and indirect. Or more likely, a man, despite
the alias. Periodical work wasn't terribly lucrative,
but if a writer cobbled together enough bits and
pieces, he might keep his creditors at bay, eking
out a sort of living in some frigid garret, with the
manuscript of his magnum opus stuffed beneath
his lumpy bed. Few writers in such a position
would turn down an opportunity to write for a
popular magazine.

"Personally, I've come to doubt whether it's written by a young lady," Graham added, "regardless
of the magazine's claims to be written by, as well as
for, *misses*."

"You don't think a young woman would produce such a scathing review?"

"Heaven knows they've opinions enough," Graham admitted, "and saucy tongues eager to share
them. But they lack the necessary . . . *experience*, I
suppose, is the kindest way of putting it." Not that
he generally concerned himself overmuch with
kindness. "They have too little knowledge of the
world." Sheltered and shielded, kept from educa-

tion, they could hardly be expected to judge well. "Now, if *I* had sisters—"

Keynes, who had been attempting to read the review as instructed, darted another glance in his direction, this one pointedly delivered over the top rim of his spectacles.

Graham knew that look, knew it was meant to conjure a memory. And it did, though perhaps not the memory Keynes intended. Graham thought of the enormous family portrait in oils that hung over the fireplace in the drawing room at Castle Dunstane and then turned his head, wishing he could avert his mind's eye as easily. But the subjects followed him. A husband and wife, stiff, unsmiling, posed with four of their children: the eldest, a boy of eight or nine; a babe in arms; and between their ages, standing beside their mother's chair, two little girls. He had no recollection of those towheaded girls, save the painting. They had died that very winter, snatched away by a ruthless fever that had, for reasons unknown, spared their baby brother—spared him.

"Very well," he snapped at Keynes, who had returned his attention to the review. "I *had* sisters."

And *if* they had lived, and *if* he would have had some say in the management of their education, he chose to believe they would have been rational creatures, not like the silly things who read . . .

At that moment, Keynes closed the magazine. The cover's claim that the pages within would *promote rational conduct and improve wisdom among young persons of the fair sex* presented themselves to Graham's eyes. Before he could snarl over the unfortunate convergence of his thoughts and those of Mrs. Goode, whoever she might be, Keynes held the magazine out to him and said, "I presume Ransom Blackadder will have something to say in response?"

Graham shifted his gaze to the gray London scene outside the window. Why hadn't he thought of that himself? He'd written a whole play to squelch presumptuous reviewers—and what could be more presumptuous than this?

"Though it would seem from the latest invoices to cross my desk that *The Poison Pen* is already in rehearsal," Keynes continued, laying aside the magazine when Graham made no move to take it from him.

"Well, it's hardly unheard of for a playwright to make an eleventh-hour revision to a script," Graham answered gruffly, though at the moment, he wasn't sure what form that revision ought to take. "But the review—did anything strike you as peculiar? A turn of phrase, for example. Something you could use to figure out who writes the blasted column?"

"To be quite honest, my lord . . ." Here Keynes paused to dip his pen and resumed his recording of the day's correspondence in the letterbook. "I thought it sounded not unlike something *you* would say."

Graham had seen the performance of *Othello* twice through in its entirety since opening night and found it improved each time from what it had been at first. Nevertheless, like Miss on Scene, he still judged Mrs. Siddons ill-cast in the role of Desdemona, far better suited to the power and determination of a Lady Macbeth or a Queen

Catherine—or even the philosophizing indecision of Hamlet, a part she had performed many times, though always away from London.

Miss on Scene's idea of an angry Desdemona struck him as too simple, however. Too primitive. But he agreed that the production as a whole had lacked some spark. Each subsequent viewing, he had felt the absence of *something*, something missing from the performances or the costumes. Something missing . . .

"Do you still happen to have Mrs. Hayes's note to hand, Keynes?" he asked, peering over the man's shoulder at his work.

"Mrs. Hayes? Mrs. Hayes . . ." Once more, Keynes laid aside his quill. He ran a finger swiftly down a column of names, then turned back a page, to those letters received earlier in the week, and began again at the top. "Ah. Here we are." He paused, and his fingertip tracked across a single entry. "Oh, yes. The unfortunate mix-up with your box at Covent Garden." With his other hand, he tugged off his spectacles and looked at Graham. "I'm afraid not, my lord. It did not seem to be a matter of great importance, so once I recorded its receipt, I disposed of it."

Julia had written that note. Graham had been sure of it—and not just because the handwriting had obviously not belonged to an elderly woman. If Keynes had not been looming over his desk as he'd perused it, he might have given in to the temptation to trace the elegant swoop of the *D* in the salutation. Curved and pretty, yet bold—just like Miss Addison.

But it had been something more than pen and

ink that had revealed its author to him. Something about the style, the—the turn of phrase, just as he'd said earlier about the anonymous reviewer.

Of course, Mrs. Hayes might well have dictated the thing, word for word. In which case, he was still at liberty to imagine the spark in Miss Addison's eye as she was made to express sentiments she would rather not, to express regret and humble thanks—to him. The irritation she must hide behind her mask of good cheer.

It's very little different from a night at the theater.

The memory of her words gave him an idea . . .

At Graham's expression, a trace of apprehension slipped across Keynes's features, as if he sensed he'd made a mistake in tossing out the letter. Graham flicked his hand to wave it away.

"No matter. You still have her direction?"

Keynes squinted at the information underlined by his ink-stained nail. "She lives in Clapham, my lord."

Clapham? Good God. Poor Miss Addison. No wonder she had not wanted to miss a night out.

Graham reached across the table, picked up the discarded magazine, and tucked it under his arm. "Write and tell her that upon further consideration, I—no, no. That sounds too much like a letter of business. Just say—you'll know best how to do it—that she is welcome to my box whenever I'm not using it. Aye, that's right," he said in answer to the unsubtle lift of Keynes's brows. But it wasn't mere generosity on Graham's part—or, really, generosity at all. An empty box, night after night, was an affront to the men and women on the stage. "And to hell with Mr. Pope."

If anything, Keynes's eyebrows rose a notch higher. "The, uh . . . the *poet*, sir?"

"What? No. The box manager at the Theatre Royal, Covent Garden. You needn't involve him."

A sharp nod, though not quite a nod of understanding. "Of course, my lord. And will you—?"

"No time, Keynes. I want to catch today's rehearsal of *The Poison Pen*." Graham spoke over the other man as he moved toward the door. "I must fig—er, find out what Blackadder means to do about this." He shook the *Magazine for Misses* in the air. "Once you've sent off that letter, set your mind to uncovering the identity of this reviewer, Keynes. I need to know before opening night, because I intend to issue 'Miss on Scene' a personal invitation to the show."

With a benevolent smile, Mrs. Hayes poured Julia a second cup of chocolate; that smile turned almost guilty as she filled her own cup for a third time, then added a dollop of cream.

Julia would have preferred tea. Her throat was parched with reading aloud the French romance Daniel had procured for them, a wonderfully ridiculous tale set in a distant castle, where Veronique, obligatory damsel in distress, awaited rescue by her knight, who was taking his own sweet time about the business.

Practicing her French was the only remotely edifying aspect of the experience, and as far as Julia was concerned, that was just as it should be. She preferred novels to more serious fare and often

enjoyed the farce far more than the play that pre-
ceded it.

As she laid aside the book and reached for her
chocolate, Daniel entered, bearing a letter on a
salver.

"Bit early for the post, isn't it?" Mrs. Hayes asked
as he approached.

He offered the letter first to Mrs. Hayes, as was
proper, and when she fluttered her fingers to wave
him away, he turned to Julia. "Came by messenger,
this did."

At that, Mrs. Hayes sat up a bit straighter and returned her cup to its saucer. "Oh? Well, go on,
then. See what it says."

As she fished the letter from the tray, Julia nodded at Daniel to indicate that he could go. A lad of
fourteen or so, handsome but not yet tall enough
to live out his ambition of becoming a liveried and
powdered footman, he backed his way out of the
room—but lingered just beyond the doorway to
listen. She suspected he would do quite well in one
of the grand houses in Mayfair, when the time
came.

She slipped a fingernail beneath the seal, absently noting the Latin motto surrounding a rather
scraggly-looking flower. No, not a flower, she realized belatedly as she unfolded the note. A thistle.

"It's from Lord Dunstane," she said to Mrs. Hayes.

He hadn't written it himself. Highly unlikely
that such a man would have copperplate handwriting flawless enough to do a law clerk credit. Nevertheless, it must express his wishes. It was signed
with his name and sealed with his seal. She ran the

pad of her first finger over its imprint in the circle of scarlet wax.

"He's offering the use of his box. On the nights he's not there, of course."

That strange, hollow sort of feeling in her chest at the news they would not only have the box, but also have it all to themselves, must be elation.

Yes. Yes, of course, she was thrilled to think that she and Mrs. Hayes would be viewing every performance from a private box at stage left, just as planned. How marvelous to be able to invite their friends, to enjoy even the farces without a grumpy Scotsman leaning over her shoulder, puncturing her happiness with his little grunts of disapproval.

Only a ninny like Veronique would be disappointed at the thought of being spared the company of the villain of the piece.

"Oh, excellent," declared Mrs. Hayes, clapping her plump hands, the sound muffled slightly by her crocheted lace mitts. "Didn't I tell you? Does he say when we may take advantage of his generosity?"

Generosity? A scoffing noise nearly escaped Julia's dry throat. Was it not a gentleman's duty to right the wrong perpetrated against a poor, old widow and her innocent companion?

Oh, dear. That sounded like a line from the last chapter she'd read. She glanced toward the thick volume lying beside her on the damasked sofa. Perhaps Lord Dunstane had been right. Perhaps she ought sometimes to read better books.

"He doesn't," she explained to Mrs. Hayes. "At least, not directly. We'll need his ticket, of course."

Mrs. Hayes's ticket to the box, being an unauthorized duplication, was little better than counterfeit. "There's a bit here about dealing with Mr. Pope, or rather . . ." She squinted at the sentence again; it was written rather awkwardly, despite the flowing handwriting. "Anyway, I suppose the box office knows when it is to be free."

"I'd rather not have to speak with Mr. Pope," Mrs. Hayes said, a sour expression wrinkling her lips. "Particularly not after that letter I sent."

Generally, she left the details of her less personal correspondence to Julia, concerned only with the substance of the matter at hand. But on the occasion of dressing down the box manager, she had chosen every harsh word herself.

"I'll take care of it, ma'am. Why, if I go now," Julia offered, rising, "we might be able to attend the theater tonight."

A visit to the playhouse would be the perfect opportunity to plan out the subject of her next column. It would also provide welcome cover for her absence when she slipped out to the magazine meeting at half past two. She would simply tell Mrs. Hayes she had been delayed.

With Mrs. Hayes's permission secured, she donned her pelisse and bonnet and set out for Covent Garden. Daniel called her a hackney. As far as Mrs. Hayes knew, he accompanied her on every outing, an acknowledgment of her status as the younger sister of a viscount. But in general, Julia preferred to give him an hour's freedom, his silence purchased with a portion of her wages from the magazine. She considered it proper preparation for his future career, when the young ladies of whatever grand house at which he was eventually employed begged him to look the other way when they got up to mischief.

"I'm only a lady's companion," she reminded Daniel when he looked askance at the destination she gave the cabbie. Little more than a servant in the world's eyes, in other words, and perfectly capable of moving about independently.

A damp morning had given way to a marvelous October midday, sunny and crisp. The leaves on the trees were mostly still green, though here and there a hint of gold could be seen. She felt fortunate that Mrs. Hayes insisted on staying in Clapham, where, despite its sleepy appearance, radicals and freethinkers congregated. Together they attended the most interesting lectures and heard the most stirring sermons. Julia had heard it said this was the only part of Town where one could speak the phrase *Rights of Woman* without being mocked. Occasionally, she wondered whether Mrs. Hayes would even disapprove of her involvement with the *Magazine for Misses* if it were discovered.

As the cab rattled over the bridge, she glanced out the window with what most certainly was *not* a wistful sigh. She had an extraordinary degree of freedom for a well-bred young lady of almost twenty. She had work she enjoyed and the friendship of intelligent women.

And very soon, she would have tickets to the theater, to be enjoyed without ever again having to cross paths with Lord Dunstane.

Really, what more could she want?

Chapter 5

Once a play took the stage before an audience, there was very little left for a playwright to do but wait for reviews. What was done, was done. Now, during rehearsals, was the moment to make adjustments, to improve things.

Graham's aversion to London meant he didn't often take such an opportunity, however. And even from his current position in the pit, a few rows back from the stage, he couldn't quite see how to pull it off.

For one thing, he was reminded—as he had been reminded twice during *Othello*'s run—that sitting alone, while congenial to his mood, was not the ideal vantage point from which to view a performance. With no hint from another person's expression, no sound of someone's murmuring or laughter or even breath, he was having a great deal of trouble imagining how theatergoers would react to his reviewer character's first victim—a poet, because a playwright had seemed . . . too scornful, somehow. Or at least, too on the nose.

He was not a sympathetic character, particularly given George Fanshawe's rather limp depiction of him. Then again, people did not go into a Ransom Blackadder play expecting anyone in it to be genuinely likeable.

But it went against Graham's purpose for writing the damn thing if everyone wished a bad review really might be capable of killing a man.

When Fanshawe called a stop to the day's rehearsal, an audible sigh eased from Graham's lungs. Not that anyone was nearby enough to hear it.

"I hope you'll give Mr. Blackadder a good report, my lord," said the actor as he swung down from the stage and hustled toward Graham, who had explained his presence by claiming to observe on the playwright's behalf.

The tattered state of Fanshawe's script put Graham in mind of the first issue of the *Magazine for Misses* he had seen. In the wake of that memory came the recollection of his reaction to the reviewer's audacious pity. And then his subsequent concern that if more people began to see through his gambit, Ransom Blackadder's popularity would fade.

The profits from his first play, modest though they had been, had saved Castle Dunstane from toppling over a precipice, quite literally. The second and third had allowed Graham to claw his way out of most of the debts his elder brother had left behind. And the fourth, had it arrived a few weeks earlier, would have—

He shook all of it away with a visible shudder that the other man clearly misinterpreted. Graham didn't correct the misunderstanding. He wanted this play to do well, to draw crowds, even if they came—as the majority always had—to jeer.

He did not intend to let Miss on Scene have the last word.

"I'll give Blackadder an *honest* report, Mr. Fanshawe," Graham told him, his tone cool. "And you can expect he will be equally forthright in his reply. He'll want to see some changes, I have no doubt. And if my support of your work here is to continue—" He raised his voice enough that all the actors still milling about the stage could hear, though he needn't have bothered. The mention of money always made people's ears perk up. "You'll want to do as he says."

Fanshawe blanched. "Of course, my lord. Tell him—if you please—tell him it's early days yet, sir. We're all just getting a feel for the thing. No need to fret."

Graham arched one brow. *Fret?*

At his expression, Fanshawe began to babble more excuses, new regrets, the incoherent sounds of which followed Graham as he turned on one heel and strode out of the theater via a less-public door nearer the stage.

Absorbed in his thoughts, he paid little attention to the handful of people who crossed his path: scene painters and carpenters daubed and dusty with the marks of their trades; actors half out of costume; a wiry lad sent to fetch a pot of coffee or, more likely, a bottle of gin. The comingled odors of greasepaint and sweat hung heavy on the stale air.

Behind the scenes, and especially at midday, Covent Garden was a different world entirely, stripped of illusion, devoid of magic. Nothing fit to be consumed by most patrons of the theater, to be sure. The stomach that craved a well-prepared roast or even a simple chop would inevitably be turned by a visit to the knacker's yard.

For Graham, the pockmarks and perils of the theater had always been inseparable from its pleasures. He had made his first trip backstage at the ripe old age of eleven, despite his elder brother, Iain, having forbidden him to tag along. He had peered through the narrow crack of a door left ajar, the door through which his brother had disappeared, bouquet in hand. He had goggled as the lead actress—too old for Iain and positively ancient in Graham's eyes, which was to say perhaps thirty—had tossed aside the flowers with a wicked laugh, pushed the fresh-faced Earl of Dunstane into a chair with just the tips of her fingers pressed against his chest, and then hiked up her skirts to straddle—

Graham had looked away, then. Or else had scrubbed his mind of the memory. But he knew perfectly well what had transpired between his brother and the actress. If he had been innocent before the curtain had risen on *Tartuffe*, he was innocent no longer.

Whether he loved the world of the theater or hated it had long since ceased to be a relevant question. He was transfixed by it, from that day forward, first pinned on the edge of his seat in the balcony as the action unfolded below, and later trapped in that dingy corridor, where he'd waited . . . well, it had seemed at the time like hours. But knowing now what he did about the prowess of green lads when presented with a willing woman, it had probably been all of five minutes. Long enough, in any case.

Long enough for the theater to get in his blood.

Like blood poisoning from a dirty knife.

He'd earned prizes for his recitations in school when he'd otherwise been too shy to speak. Penned impassioned monologues he'd never shown to another soul. Dabbled with acting at university . . . and dabbled with the occasional actress too.

So, when Iain had died—young by any measure; too soon, according to some—and Graham had become the earl and been forced to confront the state of things, was it any wonder he had turned once more to the theater to find a solution, a way out?

"The play's the thing," and all that.

"I beg your pardon?"

He'd been unaware of having passed from the underworld into the open, out of the warren of corridors backstage into the large, elegant vestibule, where theatergoers congregated before a play. And he had been unaware of speaking his thoughts aloud . . . until the young woman spoke to him, though without looking in his direction.

"Miss Addison?"

Julia jerked up her head, and whatever she had been studying so intently fluttered from her fingers to the floor. Until the sound of his voice had intruded, she must have been equally oblivious to her surroundings. Another step or two and they might have collided.

Her cheeks flushed an appealing shade of rose that greasepaint could never hope to capture. Then again, such delicate color would be lost on anyone more than a few feet away.

He took a step closer and retrieved the paper that had fallen: a leaflet advertising the next run of plays, concluding with *The Poison Pen* in the last week of November.

As he handed it back to her, he glimpsed a thin circle of ivory, his box ticket, clutched in her hand. He nodded toward her curled fingers. "You had my letter, I take it."

"I, er—Mrs. Hayes did, yes." The pink in her cheeks darkened a shade. "Thank you."

Either rehearsal had run longer than he'd thought, or Mrs. Hayes had dispatched her companion with some haste. Surely no more than a few hours had passed since he had told Keynes to write.

Julia seemed to anticipate his thoughts. "You did not specify for which performances the box would be free, my lord, but I knew *The Iron Chest* was to be next, and I could not imagine *that* would be of much interest to a gentleman of your"—a mischievous smile twitched up one corner of her mouth—"discriminating tastes."

Even Graham could not be displeased by such a sally. In the decade since its debut, *The Iron Chest; or, the Mysterious Murder* had become a playhouse staple, both in Town and in the provinces. Anyone with a passing familiarity with the theater might have seen the thing a dozen times at least by now. And indeed, Julia had the right of it. He had had no intention of sitting through it again.

Curiously, however, he now found himself wondering whether all the seats in his box had been claimed for the evening. Surely Mrs. Hayes could not have invited guests to join her on such short notice.

Mightn't there be a seat to spare?

"So, I offered to come straightaway," Julia continued, "and see if we might have the box for tonight. Imagine my surprise at learning that Mr. Pope has been dismissed!"

Graham ruthlessly ironed his answering smile—a response more to her previous expression, to her teasing words, than to the news about the duplicitous box manager, about whose fate he cared very little, hardly enough to bother expressing pleasure. "Shouldn't selling others' places without their permission have cost him his?"

"I—I suppose," she agreed, though her eyes were round. Then she dipped into a shallow curtsy. "Thank you again, your lordship." Was it his imagination, or was that a hint of disdain in her voice? "I had best be on my way."

Once more, he let her walk away from him, taking undisguised enjoyment in the opportunity to observe the lightness of her step, the slight sway of her hips. But when the door was opened not by the accompanying manservant he had expected, but by one of the passel of lads who crowded around doorways and crossings to wheedle a few ha'pennies for performing such services, and he heard Julia ask the boy to call for a hackney, Gra-

ham stepped forward, closing the distance between them with long strides.

"Won't you allow me to deliver you to your destination, Miss Addison?" Before she could reply,
he tossed the lad a coin and ordered him to
bring 'round his curricle, which Graham had entrusted to a similarly eager lad a couple of hours
before.

As the boy trotted off, she lifted her eyes to him.
"You needn't trouble yourself, Lord Dunstane."
Her posture had suddenly stiffened, and her voice
had cooled by several degrees. *Pride*, he supposed.
A determined independence.

He found her unexpected prickliness almost as
appealing as her warmth.

He made no answer, and a few minutes later, a
pair of gleaming chestnuts rounded the corner,
drawing an emerald-lacquered curricle, trimmed
in gold. He thought of it as Blackadder's equipage,
slick and a trifle showy. He heard Julia suck in a
breath.

"It's no trouble," he insisted as he held out a
hand to help her up, though, in fact, he had been
looking forward to the solitary drive and the
chance to sort his thoughts about the play.

After a moment, she laid her fist on his palm,
her fingers still curled around the ticket, as if it
were some precious treasure. As she clambered
into the carriage, he dipped his head to hide another smile.

When he swung up beside her, the carriage
swayed, forcing another gasp from her lips.

"Are you nervous, Miss Addison?"

"Of course not, my lord." She spoke primly,

though her tone did not convey the confidence she evidently intended. "It's only that I—well, I've never—"

"Ridden in a racing curricle?"

"No, my lord. The daughters of country clergymen are rarely afforded such opportunities."

Ah. A clergyman's daughter. That explained much—her clothing, her present position, the forbidden allure of an evening at the theater.

"Well, there's no getting up to speed on these London streets," he reassured her as he took up the reins.

Though he suspected it might not be the speed that concerned her, but rather the discovery that the curricle had a seat for two, with nary an inch to spare. She could not help but be aware—as he certainly was—of how their legs pressed against one another at hip and thigh and knee.

Then she tilted her chin just enough that he could see the twinkle in her eyes and said, "What a pity."

Fallon, the near horse, gave his head a shake, rattling the harness and alerting Graham to the sudden tautness of his grip. He forced himself to relax his hold on the reins. "Perhaps another day, Miss Addison."

"I know you do not mean that as a sincere offer, Lord Dunstane," she said. "But I believe I would thoroughly enjoy such an outing."

As would I.

He nearly spoke the words aloud, though he could hardly comprehend how they had risen to his tongue. He had purchased this curricle for the promise, the momentary pleasure, of outrunning his problems. Alone. He certainly had not purchased it for the prospect of taking young ladies on long country drives.

He didn't take young ladies *anywhere*.

"Does Mrs. Hayes know that you go about without a servant to accompany you?"

It wasn't concern that motivated the question. Not really. Graham made a point of not concerning himself with other people's affairs, unless he could skewer them in a play. But a country miss, alone in London?

Innocence and enthusiasm were a dangerous combination, as he knew firsthand.

"I *am* a servant," she reminded him. "I'm Mrs. Hayes's companion."

It wasn't an answer to his question. "She calls herself your aunt."

Ah, that pricked Julia's conscience. He felt her shift on the narrow seat.

"Out of habit, I imagine," she answered after a moment. "Her previous companion was her niece, who left when she married my brother, which is how I came by the post."

"You went into service rather than live with your brother?" She likely thought him astonished by her decision, but his feelings were otherwise— something more akin to empathy and, at the very notion of having such a choice, spiked with a dash of envy.

"Jeremy has a taste for country living," she said, turning to take in the bustle that surrounded them, the unbroken rows of shops and carts with their wares on display, the throngs of people along the pavement, and the tangle of conveyances in the street ahead. "I do not."

"A clergyman like his father, I suppose." To that, she made no answer at all. "To Clapham, then?" he asked after a moment, even as he longed, quite unaccountably, to choose another route, a dash to Brighton perhaps, some stretch of open roadway where he could let the horses have their heads.

"You needn't go so far out of your way," she said, though he'd given no indication as to where he was headed. "I have business to transact in Bond Street. At Porter's Bookshop."

At those last words, she looked away, as if she regretted having revealed so much.

"Again?" he said. "I confess myself astonished that you would require another volume of Hume so soon."

As he'd hoped, his taunt brought her bright eyes back to his face. Stripes of color flushed across her cheekbones as she laughed, though a trifle self-consciously. "Did you doubt me when I told you that I find history excessively diverting?"

At that moment, an unhitched delivery cart rolled into the roadway, a grizzled man with an eye patch chasing after it. Graham's horses started and shied, demanding all his attention and preempting his answering laugh.

By the time he had matters under control and the obstruction had been cleared, the moment for a clever retort was long past. Uncertain how to pick up the dropped thread of their conversation—*banter*, the playwright in him wanted to call it—he opted instead for comfortable silence for the remainder of the journey.

But when the curricle at last rolled to a stop in front of Porter's, he discovered the sense of comfortableness had been his alone.

Julia hurried down, refusing to await his assistance. "No need, my lord," she insisted, her feet already on the ground. From the pavement, she looked up at him, her color still high, though now he saw that the bright spots in her cheeks hinted at embarrassment. "I've clearly delayed you long enough. I thank you for—" She paused, then laughed again, and this time he heard a certain wryness in it. Perhaps there had been no banter between them after all. "I was about to thank you for your kindness, but I have a notion you would protest if I did."

"Protest your thanks?"

"No." Her eyes met his again. They still sparked, but with something other than merriment. "Being thought kind."

If she meant to tease him again, this time the remark was just barbed enough to sting.

He nodded once and touched the brim of his hat. "Take care, Miss Addison." The habitual gruffness of his voice transformed those words of leave-taking into a warning.

Not that she required one. She had the right of things already. He *wasn't* kind . . . even if he had been on the point of offering to wait while she made her purchase and then drive her home.

She dipped her head in acknowledgment and turned to go into the bookshop, wiggling her fingers in greeting to another young lady headed in the same direction. Her other hand was still clamped around the theater ticket, he noted.

He had forgotten all about Covent Garden.

As she reached the door, Graham shook the reins, unwilling to wait and see whether she glanced over her shoulder at him.

He should be thinking about how to transform George Fanshawe into a more worthy adversary for Perpetua Philpot's poison pen. How, in other words, to ensure Ransom Blackadder's triumph.

Julia Addison was no concern of his.

And he would remind himself of that fact as many times as necessary, until it stuck in his brain—or wherever the lesson most needed to be learned.

Chapter 6

Julia reached the door to Porter's at the same time as Miss Theodosia Nelson, a West Indian heiress whose fashionable bonnet trimmed with yellow ribbon perfectly set off her brown skin and eyes. She wrote the magazine's news columns, foreign and domestic, which provided young ladies with the latest information about politics and the war with France, topics that supposedly lay far outside their interest.

As if the state of the world, the risks being taken by fathers and brothers and lovers, concerned them not at all.

Theodosia reached for Julia's hand to squeeze it in greeting, but stopped short when she discovered her clenched fist. "What's that?" she asked, a curious tilt to her head. "In your hand?"

"Oh." Julia uncurled her fingers to reveal the

circle of ivory. "The ticket to Mrs. Hayes's box. She sent me to fetch it."

"And was that—?" Theo looked past Julia with narrowed eyes, prompting her to turn.

The curricle was already spinning away, twinkling like a gem in the sunshine. *A gaudy gem,* she tried to convince herself, but the sour words left behind a bitter tang. In truth, she'd never seen anything quite so splendid.

A pity it belonged to such an unpleasant, humorless man.

"Lord Dunstane is a friend of Mrs. Hayes," she replied, at last dropping the ticket into her reticule—what a goose she had been, carrying it about in her hand, like something she couldn't bear to part with.

Theodosia sent her a speculative glance but said nothing.

Inside the shop, Julia and Theo parted ways, as Lady Stalbridge had advised. A gaggle of young ladies descending all at once on the back room might have attracted undue attention, though from whom wasn't entirely clear. As always, the bookshop was almost empty. The same clerk stood behind the counter, the one who had refused to help Julia out of her predicament a fortnight earlier, still shuffling through what she suspected might be the same set of receipts. Even he did not look up when the bell above the door jangled to announce their arrival.

Theo strode past a wall of bookshelves and gave a passing glance to a few volumes of sermons before disappearing. Julia stayed longer, looking at row upon row of history, a good deal of it in languages she couldn't read, about wars long past and kings whose triumphs had dwindled into dusty myth.

Still, she was absorbed enough that when Lady Stalbridge spoke low in her ear, she started.

"Did I see you arrive in Lord Dunstane's company?"

She was standing shoulder to shoulder with Julia in the narrow aisle between two rows of towering shelves, though Lady Stalbridge had positioned herself facing opposite, toward the mathematics section.

"I went to the theater to retrieve Mrs. Hayes's ticket for tonight, and our paths happened to cross" was Julia's murmured explanation.

"Your paths seem to cross quite often, Miss Addison."

Julia couldn't decide whether the countess sounded disapproving or intrigued.

"He offered to convey me where I was going. I thought it would be rude to refuse."

"And I'm sure the prospect of a ride in a curricle, cozied up to a dashing gentleman, had no bearing on your decision."

Cozy? Dashing? Julia twisted her head to face Lady Stalbridge, though she knew she was meant to keep looking at the books. "I assure you, ma'am, I—"

Lady Stalbridge's lips were pressed together, poorly disguising a smile. "Say nothing more, my dear. But if your paths should cross again, may I suggest directing his steps somewhere other than Porter's? Else he might begin to suspect you're up to something here."

"Yes, ma'am." Julia snatched back her fingers,

which had been resting momentarily on the edge
of a shelf, near a volume with the name HUME em-
bossed on its spine in faded gold.

With that, Lady Stalbridge glided away.

Julia was the last to arrive at the meeting table,
though Lady Stalbridge was still settling herself
and drawing a stack of papers from her leather
satchel when Julia slid into the seat next to Theo.
Because the room was used for storage, sorting,
and sometimes repair of damaged volumes, it was
in a shifting state of disorder, with stacks of old
books scattered about, last time on the little desk
tucked into the corner, today on the floor surrounding the oval worktable.

The magazine's artist, Constantia Cooper, was
also already there. Then again, she seemed almost
to be a permanent fixture in the room, a handful
of half-completed sketches perpetually spread before her and a pencil tucked into her rather frizzy
red-blond coiffure.

Equally unsurprising was Miss Busy B.'s absence.
Since Lord Deveraux had married Daphne Burke,
the former rake had settled quite nicely into life as
a country gentleman and had very little difficulty
persuading his wife to stay by his side.

Lady Clarissa Sutliffe, whose golden ringlets
gleamed even in the meager light that passed
through the room's single, grimy window, was the
unexpected addition to the meeting. The talented
young pianist who wrote the Domestic Arts and
Accomplishments column under the name "Miss
R."—"*my mama has always called me 'Rissa*," she had
explained when she chose it—would be presented
to the queen in the course of the coming Season

and would surely take the *ton* by storm. But she must have had some difficulty in coaxing either her mother or her father or both to leave their seaside estate in Hampshire to come up to Town in autumn.

Together with Julia, they made up the *Magazine for Misses'* regular columnists, under the editorial guidance of Lady Stalbridge. In each issue, their work was supplemented by excerpts from important works of the day, poems and entertaining short stories, occasional essays on a variety of interesting subjects, and usually a letter from their figurehead, the famed author of *Mrs. Goode's Guide to Homekeeping*—who was really Lady Stalbridge's stepson, Lord Manwaring.

Lady Stalbridge cleared her throat to call the meeting to order. "I begin with good news, ladies," she said, lifting the uppermost sheets from the stack before her. "This is an essay by the esteemed botanist, the Duchess of Raynham, which she has agreed to let us publish in our next issue. It will, I believe, not only inform our readers but also provide them with a sensible answer for those who still insist that botany is too scandalous a subject for young ladies."

Julia wondered whether Daphne had had a hand in procuring it, since the duchess was a former Miss Burke and Daphne's elder sister. But, of course, Lady Stalbridge was also well-connected and had ways of getting what she wanted for the magazine, all while managing never to reveal her own connection to it.

"That should do very nicely," Constantia chimed in.

"Will it be too much trouble for you to come up with a picture for it, Miss Cooper?" Lady Stalbridge asked, extending the sheet of paper to her. "Something to set it off."

Constantia flushed with pride, right to the roots of her hair, where the two shades of red met and clashed. "Not at all."

"And sadly, Bonaparte's rapaciousness means you never lack subjects to cover, Miss Nelson." She handed the next several pages in her stack to Theodosia. "I've had a look at your plans for your next column, and I believe your approach is sound, as always. The young ladies in this country may be better informed about political and economic matters than their brothers, at this rate."

Theo's pleasure in Lady Stalbridge's praise was evident, though she only dipped her head in acknowledgment.

Lady Stalbridge turned to the next in line. "I wasn't expecting you to be here today, Lady Clarissa, though, of course, I am always pleased when you can join us."

"Mama persuaded Papa that she and I must return to Town a few weeks early, on account of all the visits to the dressmakers and such. But I intend to make the most of it. We have tickets to Covent Garden tonight," she added with a shy smile at Julia.

"How delightful! Yes, you must do all you can to enjoy yourself." Lady Stalbridge's first marriage had been the sort of miserable society match that Clarissa, the daughter of a marquess, might well be expected to make—though one hoped that Lord and Lady Estley, rumored to be very much in love with one another, would look for more than a title and a fortune for their own child. "There's nothing more for the next issue that you need concern yourself with. I already received the sheet music you sent to be included." Lady Stalbridge tapped the page now uppermost, and even at a distance, Julia could see musical notes scattered gaily across the paper. "If I'm not mistaken, this must be something of your own." Clarissa's demure nod hardly moved a ringlet out of place. "Does your mama suspect you've turned your hand to composing?"

"If she does, she's said nothing, for which I'm grateful, because Papa would insist on my playing it for him."

"He would be displeased by the discovery?" Lady Stalbridge's question was sharp. He might be a doting father in every other respect, but everyone knew that Lord Estley had not yet warmed to his daughter's great ambition to be a concert pianist. Public performances, especially for money, were considered improper for young ladies of her rank.

"Oh, no. He would praise it far beyond its deserts," Clarissa explained. She paused for a private laugh. "And then, if he ever chanced to hear the same tune coming from some other young lady's instrument—someone who reads the magazine, I mean—I'm certain he'd make a fuss and try to say they'd stolen it from me."

Lady Stalbridge's features softened into a gentle smile, and she patted the girl's hand, a more maternal gesture than she was usually wont to give any of them. Then again, Lady Clarissa was the youngest member of the magazine staff, not quite seventeen years of age.

For the next few moments, silence hung over the meeting table, marked only by the quiet sounds of Lady Stalbridge leafing through the next set of pages and the scratch of two pencils: Theo making notes on Lady Stalbridge's editorial suggestions, and Constantia already working on a sketch to accompany the duchess's botanical essay.

Lady Clarissa's dainty fingertips danced silently across the edge of the table in front of her, as if she were seated at a pianoforte. Julia watched the movement absently, waiting for Lady Stalbridge to turn her attention to the latest from Miss on Scene.

She had reviewed *The Iron Chest* once already in the magazine, and though each performance was something new and she looked forward to attending tonight, she couldn't muster much enthusiasm for devoting another column to a play everyone had seen. Nothing new to interest those with . . . *discriminating tastes.*

Good heavens, had she really spoken so saucily to Lord Dunstane?

Evidently, possession of the ticket to his box had made her bold—or relieved her of her good sense.

But it had seemed, just for a moment, as if her daring would be rewarded with an elusive smile. She would swear she had glimpsed a hint of one playing about his lips.

Not that she had been staring at his mouth, of course.

Though it *was* as sharply sculpted as the rest of

his features, and so firm she was beginning to doubt there was any hidden softness within. Perhaps he was simply hard everywhere.

Warmth rose to her cheeks. A ready blush was a curse she shared with her brother, though she had always considered that he, with his slightly darker coloring and brighter eyes, wore the color better.

This was more than a blush, though. This was heat in unexpected places and a quickened pulse and—

"Miss Addison?" Lady Stalbridge's piercing look had no difficulty traversing the length of the scarred oak table and pinning Julia squarely in her straight-backed chair. "Are you feeling quite well?"

"Perfectly, ma'am."

Painful though it might be, she *would* remember Lord Scottish's caustic comment about her taste in reading, his gravel-voiced dismissal, the speed with which his curricle had spun away. *Those* were sufficient cures for whatever ailed her.

At her reply, Lady Stalbridge looked skeptical, as well she might. But Julia could sense something more than skepticism in her expression. Was she disappointed? Displeased?

She had begun the meeting with good news. Did she have bad news to report, as well? To Julia in particular?

Constantia paused in her sketching and lifted her head to glance between them. Whatever it was, she sensed it too.

"I—I apologize if my latest column is not up to my usual standards," Julia stammered. "There's been no new play at Covent Garden since my last, so my only option was to review the opera I attended with Mrs. Hayes at the Haymarket a few nights ago." There had been nothing severe about her assessment this time, because her thoughts had been elsewhere during the performance, such that she could hardly distinguish one part from the next.

"I am aware that the theater's bill does not always coincide neatly with the magazine's publication schedule." With the tip of her index finger, Lady Stalbridge separated a half-dozen sheets from the top of her stack and laid them aside, face-down. "The problem is not with your *next* column, Miss Addison."

The stress she placed on the word *next* made it a clear she intended to imply a contrast with *last.*

"Is it—were readers unhappy with my review of *Othello?*"

Lady Stalbridge fixed her with another assessing look, and the others fell perfectly silent. Clarissa's hands slid from the edge of the table and into her lap.

"Our regular readers? No, I don't believe so." Three more sheets joined the smaller stack. "However, Mrs. Goode has had the honor of receiving correspondence from two noted scholars of Shakespeare's tragedies, the manager of the recent production, and someone purporting to be a close personal friend of Mrs. Siddons."

Silence reigned once more, broken after an interminable moment by Theo's wry laugh. "I hope they wrote to praise Miss Addison's honesty. She had the right of it." A shudder passed through her. "Oh, I despise that play."

At that, Lady Stalbridge's lips twitched in a sort of bemused smile.

Julia's breath eased from her. "But if you weren't intending to speak to me about my last review, ma'am, or my next, then—?" Clearly, the countess had something on her mind.

"Much as I agree with Miss Nelson, I am concerned about the convergence of the *Othello* review and another matter of which I have recently been apprised." And then, she pushed away from the table, rose to her feet, and began to pace. Though her steps were measured, as always, it was nonetheless a hint of agitation none of them had ever seen her exhibit. "This morning, I had the pleasure of breakfasting with my stepson, who is always full of . . . interesting information."

Gossip, Julia translated in her thoughts. *Innuendo. Rumor.* And the subject might be anything, for Lord Manwaring sometimes moved in less-than-refined circles.

"By chance, have you heard about that new poet, Lord Byron? Most particularly, his *English Bards and Scotch Reviewers*?"

Baffled, Julia shook her head.

"Well, it was meant to be anonymous, though of course everyone now knows." Constantia had returned to her sketch and did not look up as she spoke. "He took issue with what the *Edinburgh Review* had to say about his first book of poems. So, he wrote a . . . well, I suppose you could call it a scathing review of reviewers, in verse. And savaged a number of his fellow poets, too, for good measure."

"Oh," Julia said. Another bad-tempered noble-man. But she was no less baffled as to what this Lord Byron character had to do with her. She didn't review poetry, after all. Or aspire to write it.

But Lady Stalbridge said, "Precisely," as if Constantia's explanation had clarified everything. "Ransom Blackadder's new play, *The Poison Pen*, has begun rehearsal, and the few who know anything about it have taken to calling it . . ." Speaking the epithet seemed to require an unusual degree of fortitude. She paused to draw breath and moistened her lips, but did not break her nervous stride, though the room only permitted a few steps in any direction. "An English Reviewess and the Scots Bard."

"I don't—" Julia began, then broke off. *I don't understand*, she had started to say. But she was beginning to. What had Constantia said of the poem? A "scathing review of reviewers"? "Am *I* meant to be the English 'reviewess'?" she asked, incredulous.

"So it would seem," Lady Stalbridge answered with a sigh. "Evidently, Mr. Blackadder has decided to use his next play to respond to Miss on Scene's review of his last."

Julia thought back to what she had written, to that night last spring when she had sat in the crowded theater and listened to those around her who could not seem to make up their minds to be affronted or amused. She had been neither. She could not fathom why Mr. Blackadder wished so clearly to waste his talent to no good end. And she had said as much in her review.

But Miss Cooper was right. Other reviewers had

been far more scathing, even going so far as to call for his plays to be banned.

"Perhaps," offered Theo, "it's less a matter of *what* she said than *where*."

"What do you mean?" asked Clarissa.

"It's quite one thing to be excoriated by a highly regarded reviewer," explained Miss Nelson. "But I, for one, have no difficulty imagining that Ransom Blackadder would regard criticism launched by a young lady, in a magazine for young ladies, rather differently."

"You may well have the right of it," said Lady Stalbridge. "According to Oliver"—her stepson— "other reviewers come in for their share of criticism, but the lion's share seems to belong to a woman meant to suggest Miss on Scene and the ladies' magazine for which she writes." Here she turned toward Julia. "I fear that the play, combined with the furor over your review of *Othello*, may renew interest in discovering your identity." Her gaze then traveled around the table. "*All* our identities."

Clarissa's eyes were wide; she looked more girlish than ever. "That would put an end to the *Magazine for Misses*."

"No."

Inside, Julia was trembling. But she spoke with conviction enough that Lady Stalbridge stopped pacing.

"What will you do?" Constantia's pencil was poised, as if she were prepared to take down whatever answer Julia gave.

The trouble was, Julia had no answer.

Theo flicked the corner of her notes with her

fingernail, refusing to look at Julia as she asked in an unusually quiet voice, "What about Lord Dunstane?"

"What about him?"

"Well, he is known to have influence in the theater."

"Over Ransom Blackadder, in particular," Lady Stalbridge added.

"And you are obviously acquainted," Theo pointed out, a knowing lift to her brow.

"Only slightly," Julia protested. "I could hardly presume . . ."

But hadn't her presumptuousness got her into this mess?

As she looked around at the faces of her fellow staff members—her *friends*—and watched their fear give way to cautious hope, she knew she had no choice.

Without revealing her secret identity, she was going to have to find a way to persuade surly Lord Scottish to intervene on Miss on Scene's behalf with Ransom Blackadder.

Chapter 7

After dismissing his valet, Graham stood a moment longer before the pier glass, eyes narrowed, assessing.

As a lad, he'd come in for his fair share of mockery for his red hair. At the fine English public school to which his father's will had ordered he be sent, some had seen it as the mark of a peasant, not the son of a nobleman. *Did your mother lift her skirts for every stableboy, McKay? Or just the ugly ones?*

He had responded with a flail of fists and a fine assortment of Gaelic oaths that none of them had been able to understand, not even the headmaster—though he'd nevertheless caned Graham for his foul mouth. Graham hadn't been able to sit at table for a week.

Eventually, he'd learned to confine his replies to paper. Poems and dialogues tucked into his copybook, hidden beneath his blotter or in the locked wooden box beneath his bed. No one ever saw them. Those English boys fancied they'd triumphed.

At least, until Ransom Blackadder's work had begun to appear onstage.

In the years since, Graham had had more than ample reassurance that, in spite of his schoolmates' claims to the contrary, women did not think him ugly. Apparently, they couldn't see the ugliness inside. How bitterness and fear had tainted his blood and eaten away at his soul like a canker.

Or if they did see it, they were willing to overlook it in favor of his chiseled jaw.

He ran one hand over his chin, feeling the growth of a three days' beard. When he was a younger man, his beard had been little more than a golden gleam. Now, at almost thirty, he bore an auburn shadow. He considered calling back Harcourt, his valet, to scrape it away.

But no, his present appearance would have to do. The curtain rose promptly at half-past six. It waited for no man—not even the king.

Though pressed for time, once outside his chambers, he paused again. Rather than descend, he followed the staircase up another flight and stopped before the door to a room at the back of the house, relieved to see a narrow seam of light beneath it.

"Keynes?" He rapped with the knuckle of his first finger.

A moment's bustle within, and then the door swung open and his secretary bowed. "My lord. May I be of some assistance?"

Keynes had been given, or more likely had chosen, the smallest, most spartan chamber. Though both were narrow, the bed and writing table together hardly left room for a comfortable chair.

Yet Keynes looked comfortable, enviably so, with his spectacles perched on his forehead, his cravat loosened, and the top buttons of his waistcoat undone. Rather than being littered by Graham's correspondence and bills, as in the study below, the table here contained only half a glass of claret and a thick volume lying face down and open. The book bore all the signs of having come from a circulating library. A novel, then, and evidently of the page-turning variety.

Graham felt a slight pang. Guilt at having intruded on the man's quiet hours. But also, even more unexpectedly, envy. Such a peaceful, pleasant means of escape, so unlike the various routes Graham had chosen.

He waved off Keynes's flustered attempt to put his clothes to rights. "I'm sorry to interrupt."

The other man's hands fell slack, along with his jaw. Graham's apology appeared to have struck him dumb.

Good God. It was almost enough to make Graham regret having been such a bastard to his secretary all these years.

But not enough to keep him from saying, "I came to find out what you've learned about the identity of Miss on Scene."

Keynes quickly pulled himself together. "Verra little, my lord. I calculated the proportion of nouns and adjectives in the review, to determine if there is anything distinctive about the author's style. And I made note of uncommon diction. I had nae time for more. I didnae think you would want the matter to take priority over my usual tasks. But if you wish it, I will—"

He moved as if intending to go down to the study immediately and resume his work.

Graham squared himself in the doorway and shook his head. "Nay, Mr. Keynes. That'll do for now."

Keynes dipped his head once in acknowledgment. The movement did not disguise the flare of astonishment in his eyes. Clearly, he had not been expecting a reprieve.

In fact, Graham had come tonight, planning on adding to the man's assignment. Oh, nothing too taxing. A few simple inquiries, nothing more. But enough to further delay progress on the important undertaking of discovering Miss on Scene's identity.

So instead, Graham said, "Enjoy your evening, Mr. Keynes," as he turned away from the door.

"Thank you, my lord." The slightest pause. "From the hour, I ken you're bound for the theater?"

Graham did not glance over his shoulder. "Aye."

"Are you quite certain, after your letter this morning, that Mrs. Hayes will nae have claimed the box already for the night?"

He thought of Julia's small, gloved hand wrapped around the ticket, the way the ivory disc must have absorbed the warmth of her touch.

"In fact, Keynes, I'm certain she has."

He could also picture how the groove between Keynes's brows, etched there by years of care and consternation, must have deepened at that reply.

He hadn't yet been reduced to explaining himself to his secretary, however.

Graham had repeated one simple phrase—*Julia Addison is no concern of yours*—often enough that afternoon that it had almost become an incantation. He was fully persuaded he spoke the truth. He *wasn't* concerned. Merely . . . *curious.*

And surely a man was entitled to assuage his curiosity.

Graham arrived at Covent Garden with little time to spare before the curtain rose. Fortunately, he faced no obstacles in gaining admittance, though he was not in possession of the ticket to his box. It had required no more than his name, which had elicited a few whispers and nudges among the staff—those who presumably knew what had become of the box manager—and he had been ushered inside with alacrity.

He found his box full to overflowing with fashionable females, and none of them the women he had expected to find within. Convinced he had taken a wrong turn and pulled aside the wrong velvet drapery, he began a slow, strategic retreat.

Too late. His presence had been observed. Around him, the ladies' alarmed expressions told him his own face had settled into its habitual scowl, a mask he had found far more effective at hiding its wearer's true feelings than even Melpomene or Thalia, the familiar masks of tragedy and comedy. When these women reported on the evening to their friends, they would describe him as angry or irritated or unhappy.

Better that than the truth: surrounded by so many strangers, discomfort had shot shards of ice into his veins and struck up an ominous thudding in his chest. The longer he hesitated, the greater the risk of him turning to stone.

But at the sight of him, the sea of occupants parted to reveal Mrs. Hayes. The widow, already seated in the center of the back row, expressed her delight that he should join them.

And then, over her shoulder, Miss Addison appeared, and his pulse, already rapid, ratcheted another notch upward. She blinked at him twice in evident astonishment before sinking into her seat.

With curtsies, sidelong glances, and a great deal of whispering behind fans, several of the women departed for their own boxes, leaving just five behind: Mrs. Hayes; her friend Lady Clearwater; Lady Clearwater's two daughters, whose dark-blond hair and elegant dresses were, he suspected, too often mistaken for prettiness; and Julia.

The two Misses Clearwater joined Julia in the front of the box; "the better to be observed," remarked their mother slyly. Her daughters tittered at the insinuation, while Julia slumped lower in her chair. Or was it his imagination? Was he ascribing his own preference for the shadows to her? Certainly she was every bit as deserving of society's notice as the Misses Clearwater. Whether she wanted the attention was a question yet to be answered.

Mrs. Hayes gestured him to the chair on her right as Lady Clearwater settled into the chair to her left, behind Miss Addison. He and Julia were thus seated as far apart as the small box made possible, which was, of course, irrelevant to his mission. Perhaps even an advantage. Less of a distraction.

He was more than usually annoyed, however, by the two other young ladies, who—in addition to chattering and fluttering their fans and waving to friends on the opposite side of the theater even after the curtain had risen—dared to send him the occasional simpering glance.

Oh, it was hardly surprising behavior, no matter how often he scolded audiences for it in his plays. Even when the production was something new and exciting—and *The Iron Chest* did not qualify as either—people came to the theater to be seen and to socialize, to flirt and to fawn, not to listen and learn.

Still, must they continually disrupt his view of the stage, perfectly situated as it was past the end of Julia's tilt-tipped nose?

Not that he had come to watch the play either. Tonight, he would be among the guilty parties. He had come intending to give most of his attention to Mrs. Hayes.

He began well enough, with a leading question about how often she and her companion attended the theater. But he hadn't considered just how much of his research would involve listening to Mrs. Hayes rattle on about everything *but* Julia. By the second act he had accomplished nothing more than confirming what Julia herself had already revealed: she was the daughter of a clergyman, now deceased.

Eventually, Mrs. Hayes added that Julia had been born and humbly raised in Oxfordshire—"just out of reach of everything a girl could truly want, though she never complains, of course."

Throughout, Julia had remained devoted entirely to what passed on the boards below, indifferent to the noise around her. He supposed, in her time with Mrs. Hayes, she had determined how much of that lady's flowing stream of conversation could safely be ignored. But at those last words— *everything a girl could truly want*—her shoulders gave the slightest twitch, as if she were fighting the impulse to twist around in her chair and send Mrs. Hayes a quelling glance.

Just what had the woman inadvertently revealed about her companion's desires?

Before he could begin to speculate, Mrs. Hayes was on to the next bit of gossip. Buried among a number of far less interesting anecdotes was the information that Julia's mother had recently remarried and was now Mrs. Remington. And Julia's brother had not, in fact, followed in his father's footsteps, but had instead joined the army. "I suppose," Mrs. Hayes reflected, raising her lorgnette to peer at the occupants of the pit, "he must have thought it a surer route to being able to support his mother and sister, after inheriting more debts than devoirs."

That was a detail uniquely suited to pique Graham's attention. He knew firsthand about troublesome inheritances. Something tied up in Chancery, perhaps, or an entailed piece of property that cost more to maintain than it brought in.

"Imagine," Mrs. Hayes went on, "waking up one morning to find yourself a viscount!"

Better or worse, Graham wondered, *than being*

roused with the news of my brother's death and realizing I was the earl?

"The title was worth so little that to this day, he still prefers to be called *Captain Addison* among his friends," exclaimed Mrs. Hayes, returning his thoughts to the present moment. "Though I believe that's also to protect my niece," she added in a softer tone. "My Laura has a stout heart, but after all that nonsense two years ago, what young woman wouldn't shy away from the prospect of being addressed as Lady Sterling?"

"Forgive me, ma'am. But I—"

I don't particularly care.

It was Julia he wanted to understand, not her brother—though the information that she was sister to a viscount was a not unpleasant surprise.

Mrs. Hayes, however, was too ready to offer an explanation, whether or not he had expressed a need for one. "It was in all the papers, about that pickpocket who styled herself *Lady Sterling,*" she told him, openly incredulous that anyone would not remember such a tale. "But I'm glad to know some people have begun to forget the scandal. For all the good Captain Addison and my niece have done, I should like to hear them addressed as they ought to be."

Mrs. Hayes told the rest of the story with numerous detours and interruptions, but Graham eventually deduced that Lord and Lady Sterling had established some sort of philanthropic endeavor on his estate in Wiltshire—the *taste for country living* of which Julia had spoken that afternoon— made possible by the substantial dowry Mrs. Hayes's niece had brought to the match. And they were assisted in the work by Lord Sterling's mother and stepfather.

Instead of joining them, Julia had elected to put herself at the beck and call of the garrulous Mrs. Hayes. What kept her connected to London? Something more than the prospect of an occasional outing to Covent Garden with her employer, whatever she might claim. And he thought he could guess what it might be.

He had some familiarity with a longing for independence, even to the point of recklessness. But he had never had to battle against the sort of restrictions society placed on young ladies. Here, she had no family nearby to check her, to watch over her. He doubted whether Mrs. Hayes knew that her companion went gallivanting about London on her own. To say nothing of what she might get up to while she was out.

Not that he was *concerned* about Julia. Merely *curious.*

If anything, more curious than he had been an hour ago.

Well, as Mr. Pope—the poet, not the box manager—had so succinctly phrased it nearly a century before, "A little learning is a dangerous thing." *Dangerous,* not because one should wish to remain ignorant, but because those first sips of new information could be intoxicating, without truly slaking one's thirst.

Fortunately, Graham knew the rest of that pithy couplet, the admonition to drink deep from the wellspring of knowledge. Better to learn as much as one could.

At long last, intermission put an end to the pretense that any of them, except possibly Julia, was there to watch a play. Perhaps he could get more information straight from the source.

"Tell me," he said, speaking over the fading applause and the rising conversation as all but Mrs. Hayes stood. "What is your impression of the performance, Miss A—?"

Before he could complete the sentence, both Miss Anna Clearwater and Miss Agatha Clearwater—he had not paid enough attention to know which was which—whirled to face him, their expressions eager. Julia turned too, albeit more slowly.

"My daughters know so little of the theater," said Lady Clearwater, with a warning glance to silence them before they could venture an opinion. "I'm sure they would benefit more from hearing *your* thoughts on the play, Lord Dunstane."

So, Lady Clearwater meant to give him an opportunity to pontificate. Hardly surprising. In the world of fashionable society, a young lady was expected to shape her sentiments to match the gentleman's, no matter what.

Julia dropped her gaze to the floor, as if trying to hide her face, though not before he thought he glimpsed a smile. Was she recalling her own jibe about his *discriminating tastes*?

"I assure you, ma'am," he replied to Lady Clearwater, thinking about the shocking things he could reveal to innocent young ladies about the theatrical world, "they would not."

Lady Clearwater was undeterred, however. "You are right, of course. This is no place for serious conversation. I wonder, my lord, whether you might join us one evening—say, the day after tomorrow—for a small entertainment at home among friends: supper, cards—"

"And dancing, Mama?" added one of the Misses Clearwater, sounding hopeful.

Lady Clearwater smiled warmly at her daughter before turning the expression on him. "Whatever would most amuse our guests."

He knew just the sort of *small entertainment* to which Lady Clearwater referred, neither small enough for a man of his solitary disposition, nor entertaining to a man of his understanding.

When he did not immediately answer, she coaxed him with a playful tap of her folded fan against his shoulder. "Surely, my lord, you have not returned to London after all these years merely to attend a few plays?"

Perhaps not. But neither had he come to Town to put himself at the service of a matchmaking mama.

If and when he became convinced of the necessity of a wife—or, more accurately, the necessity of an heir—he would look elsewhere than among the English beau monde.

Out of the corner of his eye, he saw a movement, the slightest shrug of Julia's shoulders. As if she might now be suppressing not just a smile, but a laugh. As if she found his predicament amusing.

"Mrs. Hayes will be among the company, I hope?" he asked archly. If the answer was no, Lady Clearwater was being unpardonably rude to her friend. "And Miss Addison—her niece?"

Lady Clearwater's smile faltered, but she caught it before it fell away from her lips entirely. He could not blame her for wanting to avoid the possibility of Julia competing for suitors with her daughters. Absent exceptional dowries, the Misses Clearwater would surely lose.

But if Julia was determined to stay in London, then she ought not to be excluded from every proper entertainment but the theater. After all, despite her present position, she was a gentleman's daughter and a nobleman's sister. Not just a lady's companion, but a lady.

"O-of course," Lady Clearwater insisted, though it was abundantly clear she had intended no such thing.

At last, he had succeeded in gaining Julia's full attention. Her head snapped up, and she fixed him with a look—not quite of anger, he thought, but astonishment. As it had that afternoon, a blush darkened her cheeks, deepening the blue of her eyes.

Would her skin be soft as a rose petal? Warm to the touch?

His touch?

Would she blush so readily, so prettily at the offer of a kiss?

His kiss?

Oh, but the knowledge he wanted was dangerous, indeed.

Julia's mouth popped open, the sure prelude to a protest.

"In that case," he said, forestalling her, "I would be delighted." Then he bowed, signaling his intention to depart. "Enjoy the rest of the play."

"You're leaving?" exclaimed one of the Misses Clearwater, making very little effort to hide her disappointment.

"You won't stay to see how it ends?" pleaded the other.

"He already knows," said Julia, with a flicker of annoyance. "*Everyone* does."

"Then you must have had other reasons for coming." Lady Clearwater sounded absurdly hopeful.

"Must I?" said Graham. "Then let us say that tonight, I merely wished to assuage my curiosity."

"And have you?" Julia asked boldly. The question was accompanied by an increasingly familiar—and undeniably attractive—lift of her chin.

Had she overheard enough of his conversation with Mrs. Hayes to guess the direction of his interest?

"Not by half, Miss Addison," he answered softly.

Then he bowed again, this time to each of them, taking the Misses Clearwater together and, in defiance of good manners, saving the last for Julia. "Until the day after tomorrow."

Chapter 8

For the second day in a row, Julia woke to bright, clear skies and muddled, turbulent thoughts. The interest Lord Dunstane had shown at the theater played right into her plan to use him to learn more about the mysterious Ransom Blackadder.

But what had inspired his strange, sudden desire to learn more about her?

Whatever Lord Dunstane intended by such attention was unlikely to be either serious or proper. His granite-faced expression and proud posture as he'd surveyed his box the night before last had conveyed his disdain for those assembled there more clearly than words. He'd accepted Lady Clearwater's invitation with obvious reluctance, as if the baronet's family was unworthy of his company.

Julia knew better than to be flattered by the notice of a taciturn, mercurial man who considered himself above her touch—even after Mrs. Hayes's nattering had revealed that Julia's family connections were not so lowly after all. Julia had overheard her brother's title dropped more than once. He must realize, she was hardly friendless.

But given the present inequality of their stations, would Lord Dunstane scruple to share stories about her with Blackadder? If she were not careful, would she find herself in yet another of his awful plays, this time as a caricature of a naïve country clergyman's daughter and lady's companion?

She had no desire to be the target of the playwright's satire twice over, once as Miss on Scene and once as Miss No Sense at All.

Still, the fact remained. Something about her intrigued Lord Dunstane. And the staff of the *Magazine for Misses* was counting on her to make use of his interest, even if she would rather not.

Throwing back the coverlet, she swung her legs out of bed and inserted her feet into her waiting slippers. The day promised to be fair, but the morning air was cool—a blessing, really, when her blood was prone to boil every time a certain Scotsman intruded into her thoughts.

Before she could determine how best to behave toward him tonight—for, of course, Mrs. Hayes had accepted Lady Clearwater's grudging invitation, though the intimate gathering of friends had surely been invented on the spot to attach Lord Dunstane—she must devise some excuse for another afternoon jaunt. Lady Stalbridge had sent word that her stepson, Lord Manwaring, wished to speak with her in person about the rumors he had heard concerning Blackadder's play. They would meet her at one o'clock on Clapham Common.

As Julia dressed and arranged her hair, she racked her brain for a solution. If Lady Stalbridge and Mrs. Hayes had been acquainted, it would have been an easy enough matter. But Lady Stalbridge had spent half her life the near prisoner of her late husband, Lord Manwaring's father, and had remarried and returned to society only recently. She and Mrs. Hayes did not move in the same circles.

And a mention of Lord Manwaring's invitation to take her out for a stroll would not increase the likelihood that Mrs. Hayes would grant her her freedom for the afternoon. The young viscount was, to use the phrase she heard most often bandied about, *outré* in both appearance and manner. Everyone who was anyone disapproved of his refusal to settle to anything serious. He dressed flamboyantly and wore his hair in unfashionably long curls. Some said he spent all his time with low women. Others whispered that all the ballet dancers and opera singers were mere decoys, to disguise the fact that he preferred the company of men.

Whatever other secrets he kept, the *ton* would be most scandalized to know that the viscount wielded the pen behind the famous domestic doyenne, Mrs. Goode.

Even if Mrs. Hayes were inclined to try to marry off her companion—and thus far, she had shown no such inclination—she was not likely to throw Julia in the path of Lord Manwaring.

So, Julia would just have to concoct her own excuse. Not another trip to the theater, or the bookshop. She had visited both too recently. Daniel retrieved the post. A pity Mrs. Hayes didn't have a large dog that required regular walking. Or a pet parakeet that could conveniently "escape" every now and then.

Perhaps the apothecary? Mrs. Hayes did indulge in various remedies for her rheumatism, and Julia might be able to persuade her that the contents of one of those precious jewel-toned vials had dwindled dangerously low.

With a sigh, she rose from her dressing table, hoping that some better plan might occur to her over the course of the morning.

The next few hours were taken up, as usual, with correspondence and whatever gossip could be gleaned from the newspapers. Neither task required her full attention, which ought to have given her ample opportunity to devise a better excuse for meeting Lord Manwaring and Lady Stalbridge.

But this morning, the tasks were also insufficient to occupy Mrs. Hayes. Julia had all she could do to steer the conversation away from Lord Dunstane, where lately her own thoughts had also been all too inclined to wander.

"When he appeared in his box last night, you could have knocked me over with a feather," Mrs. Hayes said, tossing aside a letter. *He* required no further identification.

"Indeed, ma'am, it was a surprise to see his lordship there." Especially when he knew the box had already been taken.

Lord Dunstane had ascribed his presence to curiosity.

The question was, curiosity about what?

"And so attentive, too. He seemed content to hang on my every word. One hears him called standoffish, but I saw nothing of it."

Julia recalled his scowl, his ramrod-straight spine.

Perhaps Mrs. Hayes was not as perceptive as Julia sometimes gave her credit for being.

At long last, shortly past midday, Mrs. Hayes called for her usual light luncheon to be served and asked Julia to fetch the blue bottle of tonic.

Julia knew she must seize the opportunity she had been given. Reaching across the table to tipple a drop or two into Mrs. Hayes's goblet, she allowed the glass vial to slip from her hand and spill its remaining contents onto the cloth.

The apothecary around the corner would whip up another draught for his best customer on a moment's notice. So when Julia returned home from her walk on the green, she still might have to devise some explanation for a longer-than-expected absence. Perhaps, if she were lucky, he would be called away to visit a patient. Or he would have to procure some ingredient from another shop. In any case, she could tell Mrs. Hayes as much.

It was far from a brilliant excuse, but it would have to do.

"Oh, dear," she exclaimed, hurrying to soak up the puddle of liquid with her napkin so that nothing of it might be saved. "Look what I've done. I'll go right after luncheon and have Mr. Watkins put up a new bottle of the same for you."

Mrs. Hayes looked remarkably unperturbed and continued spreading butter on her bread. "'Tisn't necessary, my dear. I'm not convinced that bottle has done my rheumatism a bit of good."

This was an unforeseen complication. "Nonsense, ma'am," Julia quickly countered. "Don't you feel that our afternoons have been more pleasantly spent of late?"

"Oh, yes, dear. But it's all down to that new book, I think. You have just the right voice for it."

"You are too kind, ma'am. I date the matter somewhat differently. I noticed an improvement well before the book—from the time, in fact, that Mr. Watkins sent round the blue bottle for you to try." Julia's cheeks heated at the lie.

Mrs. Hayes tipped her head. On anyone else, Julia would have described her expression as skeptical. But Mrs. Hayes was such a trusting soul, she believed every fib Julia told. After a moment's hesitation, she nodded. "Very well. I wouldn't want to interfere with your preparations for Lady Clearwater's party, though. I'll send Daniel for the medicine."

Julia fumbled as she tried to recork the now-empty bottle. "Oh, no. It's no trouble, ma'am. I, um—if you send Daniel, he'll surely tell his mother why. Before you know it, all the servants will be wondering about the state of your health and, uh, fretting about the security of their positions."

It was a tale crafted to appeal to Mrs. Hayes's particular worries, and Julia felt more than usually guilty about deceiving the poor woman, who had been so good to her, albeit often unwittingly. Occasionally, Julia wondered whether it wouldn't be better just to tell her the truth—about her solitary adventures through London, about her work for the magazine, even about her longing not merely to review plays, but to perform onstage in them. To act.

But confessing any one of those secret desires might be scandalous enough to cost her her place as Mrs. Hayes's companion and force her to return to country life, forever under her mother or brother's watchful eye.

So she palmed the blue bottle and curtsied. "I shan't be gone long, ma'am."

Only as long as it took for Lord Manwaring to reveal what he'd learned and for the three of them to devise some plan to protect Miss on Scene and the magazine.

Clapham Common was a wedge of wilderness, surrounded on its three sides by the homes of wealthy City merchants and the Holy Trinity Church. Though it lacked the posh appeal of Hyde Park, it was often busy; on this day, when sunshine beckoned and Londoners recalled the impending approach of gloomier days, it fairly bustled. Nurses gathered in clusters to gossip while their charges ran free, chasing after balls and butterflies. Old men strolled in pairs, reliving their glory days. Near the church, a pair of modestly dressed women and a man in a battered beaver skin hat were handing out leaflets about some cause or other.

Julia ducked into the apothecary's shop, confessed that she had spilled Mrs. Hayes's tonic, and requested a replacement.

"Of course," said Mr. Watkins, as she sheepishly handed over the empty vial. "Won't take a moment. It's helping with the swelling, then?" he called over his shoulder as he retreated among his jars and bottles.

"As much as anything can, sir," she replied. "But you needn't hurry. I have another errand to run. I'll stop in for it on my way back."

Mr. Watkins waved her off, and Julia escaped into the sunshine, her eyes searching the edges of the green for Lady Stalbridge and her stepson. At last, she spotted them, not by the sight of one of Lord Manwaring's eye-popping waistcoats, as she had half expected, but because of the distinctive china-blue pelisse the countess often wore.

With hurried steps on Julia's part, and a more sedate tread on the part of Lady Stalbridge, the three of them met where two footpaths crossed near the center of the green. Lady Stalbridge inclined her head toward a nearby bench, beneath a spreading oak. "I will chaperone from there," she said with a wry sort of smile.

Lord Manwaring's answering grin was charmingly lopsided, though bracketed by surprisingly deep grooves. Fatigue had left dark smudges beneath his eyes. Evidence that he had recently passed one of his notoriously wild nights, Julia supposed. She took his offered arm with the slightest tremor of trepidation.

He seemed to guess the direction of her thoughts. "I won't bite, child."

Though his linen was remarkable, a degree of brightness and crispness achieved only by the valets of dandies, he was otherwise ordinarily dressed for a gentleman. His waistcoat was a perfectly respectable buff, a shade or two lighter than his breeches, which disappeared into riding boots that were just worn enough to convince her they had actually been used for their appointed purpose. His duster concealed nothing more ostentatious than the jeweled handle of his quizzing glass. Perhaps he was not quite as wild as he was rumored to be.

Julia was on the point of retorting that she was hardly a child, at most only a few years younger than he, when he snapped his white, even teeth together in another, more lupine smile. "Unless asked."

The flare of her eyes must have been visible to Lady Stalbridge, now sitting several feet away. "Oliver," the countess reprimanded him, her voice at once stern and amused. "Behave."

"Very well, Mamabet," he promised with an exaggerated sigh. "But if Miss Addison can't bear to be teased, I don't think she's ready to hear the sort of naughtiness Ransom Blackadder's got up to."

Julia tightened her grip on his forearm. "My lord, please. I must know."

The viscount's expression sobered, leaving behind just those traces of weariness and giving her the sudden impression that they might not be the result of debauchery after all. He looked . . . worried. "I'm afraid it's not good news, my dear. For any of us."

She had been thinking, first and foremost of her own position, and then of the fate of the magazine. She had not considered that even "Mrs. Goode" might be a target of the playwright's rancor, or the audience's rank curiosity.

All of them had something to fear from exposure.

"Mr. Blackadder's play, you mean?"

"Your review must have struck a nerve, Miss Addison. In the play currently under rehearsal, the character of Perpetua Philpot is certainly no flattering portrait of reviewers. A hack, without taste or scruple, a murderous shrew."

"*Murderous?*" she echoed. "You don't—you don't mean to say that she kills people? With . . . with . . ." Laughter bubbled in her chest, in spite of the seriousness of the situation. "She kills people with bad reviews?"

Lord Manwaring looked down at her with frank appreciation in his dark eyes and chuckled too, albeit wryly. "Only one person, actually."

"Let me guess. A scandalous playwright?"

"Oh, no. A poet. A delicate sort, according to my friend. Probably consumptive. Hence his susceptibility to Miss Philpot's poison pen. Everyone agreed he wrote awful, treacly stuff . . . no great loss to the world of literature."

A scuffed red leather ball rolled across the path in front of her. Julia's steps stumbled to a stop just in time to avoid the two lads in short pants chasing after it. "Lady Stalbridge feared the play would draw notice to my column," she said, once more struggling to make sense of the matter, "and thus to the magazine. But with what you've described, I don't see how. I'm quite sure my reviews never killed anyone."

Lord Manwaring chuckled, but the humor did not reach his eyes. "The murder, so-called, takes place early on. The trouble begins at the start of Act Two, when the poet's brother turns up, determined to discover the identity of the reviewer who blasts hopes and destroys promising careers. The brother is the clever one in the family. Though no one suspects him of penning verse, he dashes off a brilliant but shocking volume in no time, which, of course, attracts the notice of the periodicals and in particular a popular magazine for young ladies."

"Ah," Julia sighed as understanding dawned. "I suppose his initials are R.B.?"

Lord Manwaring nodded. "And he gets all the best lines, according to my informant. But Blackadder isn't satisfied with scandalizing audiences in his usual mode, or even in persuading them to doubt the authority of reviewers. His character is determined to lure Miss Philpot to her doom— and I suspect he hopes to do the same with you."

"How?"

"My friend couldn't say. He plays a fellow in the sickly poet's circle, and having no lines in Act Three, he hasn't even seen the script for it. But he did say Lord Dunstane was in attendance at rehearsals the other day and hinted that Blackadder intends to make some changes."

That's why she had seen him at the theater. Moments before their encounter, and only a few yards away, actors had been spouting the mocking lines that would expose her to audiences' censure and might spell the end of her work at the magazine— or the end of the magazine itself.

"Is it true, Miss Addison," the viscount asked as

he steered them back toward his stepmother, "that you've struck up a friendship with the Scottish earl?" His voice dropped to a mocking whisper with those words, an allusion to the way superstitious actors called *Macbeth* "the Scottish play" to avoid the witches' curse. "I've never met the man, but I've heard he's most unpleasant."

"He can be," she readily agreed. "And I certainly would not describe our brief acquaintance as a friendship. Mrs. Hayes's reserved box at Covent Garden for this Season was, in fact, Lord Dunstane's box—the box manager resold the ticket, unbeknownst to either party, and his lordship was seriously displeased to find us polluting his sanctuary. But after a bit of grousing and harumphing, he offered her the use of it on the nights when he would be seeking his entertainment elsewhere. So he is capable of something like generosity."

Though *generosity* hardly explained his curious behavior of the other night.

"Then no matter how unpleasant the company, you must seize upon that glimmer of finer feeling, Miss Addison." The earnestness with which Lord Manwaring spoke ran counter to his usually carefree air. "In the theatrical world at least, Dunstane alone has Blackadder's ear and might persuade the man to redirect his ire."

Lord Dunstane's goodwill and influence over Ransom Blackadder seemed to her rather narrow odds on which to pin all their hopes. She wanted to protest even the possibility of success.

But even she, who never gambled, knew enough

to realize that one could only play the hand one had been dealt.

She released Lord Manwaring's arm and curtsied. "I will do my best, my lord. But now, I must go. Any longer, and Mrs. Hayes will wonder what has become of me."

Lord Manwaring dipped his head, half nod of understanding, half gesture of parting. "I wish you luck, Miss Addison." Any possibility that she had misread her chances flew when he added, "I fear you'll need it."

With a shallow curtsy in Lady Stalbridge's direction, Julia turned and hurried back toward the apothecary's shop. Whether Lord Dunstane's questions for Mrs. Hayes had indicated genuine interest or idle prying, she must find a way to sway him to her cause—without revealing it was hers. And the party at Lady Clearwater's would be her next best opportunity to attach him.

Before, she had dreaded the evening ahead. Now, a mixture of apprehension and anticipation fluttered in her chest. Though far from the theater, tonight would be her acting debut. She would pretend to be charmed by everything he said. She would convince him to invite her to a rehearsal of *The Poison Pen* so she could see for herself how to redirect the playwright's wicked wit and rewrite both Miss Philpot's future and her own.

Perhaps, if she played her part very well, she might even elicit one of Lord Dunstane's elusive smiles.

Chapter 9

Graham had expected an insipid evening, and so far, his expectations had not been met.

They had been exceeded.

There was nothing striking about Sir Henry Clearwater's house on South Audley Street. It had been decorated to appease the tastes of a country squire who evidently came to Town most reluctantly, brightened here and there by touches in a light, modern style, a nod to the preferences and ambitions of his elegant, and considerably younger, wife.

Almost the whole of the first floor was taken up by a large drawing room, papered in shades of cream and gold, the row of silk draperies at the back shielding a wall of French windows that gave onto a balcony. He'd overheard one of the Misses Clearwater—he still had not learned to tell them

apart—refer to it rather grandiosely as *the ballroom,*
though tonight the space was filled with half a
dozen tables for cards.

For the first hour, Graham was partnered with a
neighbor of the Clearwaters, a white-haired General Zebadiah Scott, for a game of whist against Sir
Henry and another neighbor, Lady Dalrymple.
Mrs. Hayes was seated behind him at a different
table, with Julia at her side. He thanked his lucky
stars for the mirror above the sideboard that stood
opposite, which gave him an occasional glimpse of
her dark-brown head, bowed over Mrs. Hayes's fan
of cards as she directed that lady's play rather than
wield her own hand.

It would have been an insufferable hour, indeed, if Sir Henry had not been inclined to play
deeper than was wise, and General Scott had not
been cleverer than he appeared. Military life had
given Scott a wide acquaintance and interesting
conversation, and he inquired about Graham's
Highlands home without any trace of the superior-
ity he often detected among the English.

Nevertheless, at any given moment, half or
more of Graham's attention was given to what
passed at the table behind him. Julia offered whispered advice that Mrs. Hayes as often as not neglected, while her partner laughed good-naturedly
at her mistakes, though they were surely costing
him dear. Graham's own partner was similarly patient, as if he suspected that Sir Henry's guineas
were not what had brought Graham here tonight.

Nor were they the reasons he had been invited,
as he was forcibly reminded when, two tables over,

one of the Misses Clearwater began to beg her mother to call for a footman to clear the tables while they were at supper so that the young people—he supposed, given the company, he was to be classed among them—might dance.

Graham rarely danced. Oh, he *could*. He'd been given a gentleman's education, after all. But the prospect of standing up for even a quarter of an hour with one of the Misses Clearwater was hardly an appealing prospect. He would be expected to talk to her, and he had nothing to say that she would like to hear.

"As the guest of honor, my lord, you must choose," Lady Clearwater called across the room to him, with one of her smiles that revealed just a little too much tooth to be truly flattering. He'd seen hunters with that expression, when they had at last managed to corner some wily beast they had tracked for days. She would be the envy of her social set, the first—though also, he fully intended, the last—to secure the elusive earl's company at a dinner party, rout, or ball.

If they continued at cards after supper, then by the rotation of chairs Lady Clearwater herself had proposed at the beginning of the evening, he would be partnered with Mrs. Hayes next. And though he stood to lose the guineas he'd just won and more, he would bear it gladly for the prospect of a direct view of Julia's rosy cheeks and the swell of her bosom, set off to perfection by her pale pink gown.

If they danced instead, might he secure Julia's hand for a set?

He dared a glance at the mirror as he tossed his cards into the center of the table, curious to see if the shade of her blush would give some indication as to which course of action he ought to choose.

What he saw instead was the end of a whispered conversation between her and her employer, Julia's fingertips pressed to her temple, as if pleading a headache. And then, followed by a worried look from Mrs. Hayes, she left the room.

Without thinking, Graham pushed back his chair and stood. Because he was the gentleman of highest rank present, those around him did the same, though supper hadn't been announced and most of the card games were still in progress.

Lady Clearwater stepped to his side, ignoring Julia's exit. "If you are ready to go up, my lord, let us lead the way," she said and moved to take his arm.

He jerked away from her touch, then looked around for some convenient excuse for his odd behavior. His gaze fell on the French doors at the far end of the room. "I—I'd like a breath of fresh air first, ma'am."

"Oh—of course, my lord. If you'll—"

But he was already gone, stalking toward the wall of windows and brushing aside the draperies as he stepped into the night.

The air was damp and almost cold; the balcony was empty. Slowly, his eyesight adjusted to the dimness. Topiaries in stone pots cast eerie shadows from the feeble light of the drawing room. No one had lit the torchiers that lined the iron railing.

After dragging a few steadying breaths into his

lungs, he laid his fingers on the door handle and braced himself to return to the assembled company.

Out of the corner of his eye, he glimpsed a flare of light, a candle being lit. Another set of French doors gave onto an unknown room.

He released the door handle and walked along the balcony with more measured steps. It might be anyone, of course. And even if Julia was on the other side of that door, she might not appreciate being found. Or being found by him in particular. She might have preferred any one of the other gentlemen below the age of forty present this evening: a pair of officers in dashing red coats, a barrister whose air could only be described as cocky, and a well-to-do mercer whose business acumen had recently earned him a knighthood.

She had done nothing more to acknowledge Graham all evening than to curtsy and to offer one of her mischievous smiles. She might assume that when it came to dancing or whatever else the evening promised, one of the Misses Clearwater had the superior claim on his attention.

She would be wrong.

Slowly, silently, he turned the handle on the door to the unidentified room. A rush of cool air swirled through the drapery and caused the room's only occupant to turn swiftly toward its source.

Julia's face was a pale oval, illuminated by the candle she held. Its flame swayed and flickered with the gust of air, threatening to extinguish itself. Graham stepped inside and shut the door behind him, careful to arrange the draperies so as to leave no sign of his passing that way and to allow no gleam of light to escape.

"Miss Addison?" He did not approach. Was it his imagination, or was she watching him warily, a kitchen mouse ready to flee the unexpected arrival of the cat?

Or perhaps *library* mouse was the more appropriate description, for the room contained a large oak desk and a wall of stately bookcases, though they were only half-filled with leatherbound volumes. A library in progress, then, or one designed merely for show.

"You'll miss supper."

"I'm not hungry. I told Mrs. Hayes I had a headache."

"If you stay here, you'll miss the dancing afterward."

Her shoulders rose and fell, a shrug of indifference. "I'd rather read a book." She gestured toward the nearest shelf with the candlestick. Her hand wobbled beneath its weight—or because she was, indeed, as nervous as she appeared—bringing the flame perilously close to more than ample tinder.

"A curious occupation for someone with a headache." He stepped forward then and relieved her of the burden, setting the candlestick on the desk instead.

She wove her fingers together in front of her skirts, as she had that first night at the theater. "The truth is, I cannot dance. I never learned."

"Your father did not approve?" Some clergymen were sticklers, he knew.

"My father died," she said matter-of-factly. "After that, the expense of a dancing master was out of the question."

"Ah. I understand."

And he did. His own father's death—Graham had been just nine years old on that fateful day—had set in motion a number of changes.

Too late, Graham had discovered that a good deal more of them ought to have been of the penny-pinching variety.

She looked skeptical at his claim, though not as skeptical as he might have expected. Her lips formed a circle a long moment before any sound issued from them. "Why?" she asked at last. "I mean, why did you follow me here? Wouldn't you rather be at cards or supper or dancing with Agatha or Anna?"

He slid the candlestick farther along the desktop so that he could rest one hip against that sturdy piece of furniture. "I wouldn't. And as for why . . ." It was his turn to shrug. "You intrigue me, Miss Addison."

She blinked. Again her mouth curved into an *O*—prelude to another *why?*, he thought. But before she could speak the word, something passed over her. A sort of . . . tremor. She unfolded her hands, smoothed her skirts, squared her shoulders. What he had mistaken for a shiver was transformed into a wave of resolution. And then she lifted her chin, looked him square in the eye, licked her lips, and whispered in a voice gone slightly hoarse, "Do I, my lord?"

If he hadn't known better, he would have

thought she was trying to flirt with him. Did she intend her pose to be seductive, the question to sound sultry? Surely not.

Though, for an innocent country miss, she was doing a passable job of it. He bit down, hard, on the soft skin behind his lower lip, stifling the smile that threatened, fearful it would be misunderstood. The Misses Clearwater could only dream of being half so appealing.

"Had you found anything worth reading?" he asked when he could trust himself to speak, gesturing with his chin toward the shelf behind her. "I'm sorry for intruding on your solitude. You must get precious little of it, living with Mrs. Hayes. Perhaps that's why you go about London all on your own."

She nodded, then seemed to realize how her answer might be interpreted. "I mean, yes, the library is well stocked . . . *adequately* stocked," she corrected herself. Her eyes twinkled in the flickering candlelight. "Not much history, though. And I would never dare to complain of Mrs. Hayes's treatment of me. She has been generous and more than kind."

He was in no position to dispute the claim, though she hadn't really addressed his particular charge. He could hardly imagine anything worse than being forever at another person's beck and call, his time never his own. And he still wondered whether some part of Julia wished Mrs. Hayes more capable of holding her tongue, especially at the theater the other night.

"Your family—your brother—is not bothered by your decision to continue in service?" Graham could only wonder what he would have done if his sisters had lived and still been his responsibility at the time of his inheritance. Would they have shown a similar determination to fend for themselves, particularly in the leanest years, when he could have offered them very little alternative, certainly nothing that guaranteed a roof over their heads that did not leak?

"Why should he be?" To his surprise, she did not sound affronted by the question. "I always knew I would one day be a governess, or a lady's companion. Very few daughters of clergymen can afford to form grander expectations. My father was not the previous viscount, you see—the title came to my brother after his death, from a distant relation."

He crossed his arms over his chest and looked her up and down, taking a curious sort of pleasure in her inability to decide whether she despised his notice, or enjoyed it. "You might have married. Might yet, in fact."

Her eyes flashed, and he suspected her of blushing, though the light was insufficient to say for certain. Again, that curious sort of shiver passed through her, as if she were at war within herself, part of her eager to make some cutting retort and the rest reluctant to risk weakening his interest.

If she only knew how unlikely that was, how her occasionally wicked tongue or mischievous glance only made him more determined to know her better.

"I don't think so, my lord. For then I should have to give up my independence."

"I was not suggesting you give yourself to some brute who would crush your spirit, Miss Addison."

He pushed away from the desk and took half a step closer to her. "And I suspect even a country clergyman's daughter knows that matrimony offers other, more . . . *intimate* benefits. Not that those benefits cannot be had in other ways," he added, probing her intentions.

Instinctively she turned from his piercing look and discovered, a moment too late, that he had reached up to tuck a wayward curl behind her ear. Her heated cheek grazed his palm. Then, quickly correcting herself, she dropped her chin to avoid his gaze. Dark lashes swept over her cheeks. "What I know, my lord, is that this conversation does neither of us any credit."

From the neighboring drawing room came the rumble of furniture being moved, and someone—probably some unfortunate soul dragged up from the servants' hall—began to tune a fiddle. So, the Misses Clearwater had got their way. When the party returned from supper, there would be dancing. The fiddle began to scrape out the opening notes of a reel.

Graham trailed his fingertips over Julia's shoulder and down her arm to capture her hand, which was bare and icy cold. "Will you dance, Miss Addison?"

"I told you, my lord, I can't."

"You said you never learned. But you might still make an attempt, in the privacy of this library, with me."

Ah. There it was, the tiniest hint of a smile tugging at one corner of her mouth. "You're insufferable—did you know?"

"Aye."

He was, not to put too fine a point on it, a right prick most of the time. Bored by others' attempts at cleverness. Irritated beyond measure by almost every person he met. Hell, everyone knew he didn't like people. But he *wanted* Julia Addison—which was not at all, in his mind, the same sort of thing.

Especially not when his longing was more than half motivated by her refusal to admit, even to herself, that she wanted him too.

"There isn't room, my lord," she chided. She might not have practiced her seductive glance enough to perfect it, but evidently she had prepared for her possible future as a governess. She spoke in the sort of voice usually reserved for wayward children. "Sir Henry's study is far too small."

"So it is," he conceded, without releasing her hand. "Whatever shall we do instead?"

She half turned her head, though not far enough that he could look into her eyes. Once more, the tip of her tongue swept over her lips. "What is it you want from me, my lord?"

Raising his other hand, he grazed his knuckles beneath her chin, urging her to face him. Something glimmered deep in her eyes. Trepidation, perhaps, but not fear. In the flicker of candlelight, her mouth glistened invitingly. Slowly, not breaking her gaze until the very last moment, he lowered his mouth to hers.

She would kiss like a clergyman's daughter, he told himself. Puckered and prudish. An innocent. It would cure him of this strange malady of attraction that had afflicted him. It would surely cool the fire in his blood.

Aye, innocent.

After a moment's hesitation, she gave a sigh of surrender and stepped into his embrace, pressing her breasts against the wall of his chest. Soft and sweet, every inch of her. The tentative brush of her lips, the mere promise of heat, was everything he had never known he needed.

Oh God, oh God.

His fingertips swept along her jaw, down her throat, before firming against the back of her neck, drawing her closer still, holding her prisoner to his kiss. Her free hand settled at his waist, light as a butterfly, but making no effort to push him away.

Nay, nay, nay.

The kiss was rapidly spiraling out of his control. Rather than making him want her less, having her in his arms made him want more . . . made him want everything. Her artless but eager response made it seem as if she wanted more too.

Had she forgotten how awful he really was? Well, it was a simple enough matter to remind her. He traced the seam of her lips, then thrust his tongue between them when they parted in surprise. Nothing playful this time. Plundering. Punishing.

She stiffened in surprise, then moaned softly and opened to him. Rather than being repulsed by the invasion, she seemed to be inviting him to deepen the kiss further still. To devour her, if he wished it.

And by God, he did.

His hungry, primal kiss was little more than an invitation for her to slap his face. To make clear that he had misjudged her intentions. But he welcomed that stinging blow, anything to bring him back to his senses.

It never came.

At last, he tore his mouth from hers, and she sank back onto her heels, so that her eyes were level with his cravat. Their hands were still joined, her fingers still curled in the fabric of his coat.

"Now that you've taken what you wanted, my lord"—her breasts rose and fell, brushing against his abdomen with each rapid breath—"I have something to ask of you in return."

His eyelids fluttered down. But of course. Would she demand a proposal of marriage? He'd laid the groundwork with his questions, his kisses. Walked right into the trap.

Though, truth be told, it felt far less like a trap than he'd expected.

What might it be like, to spend every cold, dark Highland night with this woman in his arms, in his bed?

"Go on." It required no effort to sound gruff. Passion—and the promise of more yet—had rendered him almost beyond the power of speech.

"I know you're Ransom Blackadder's patron. I want you to secure permission for me to observe the rehearsals for his new play."

His eyes popped open. He tilted his head to the side like some shaggy Celtic hound, certain he must have heard her wrong. "You want to see *The Poison Pen?*"

"If it's not too much trouble."

She was trying to sound nonchalant, but failed. When she glanced upward, he saw the light in her eyes, the breathless hope that parted her lips . . .

For whatever reason, she wanted that favor quite desperately. Almost—perhaps more—than she wanted him.

A man of sense would ask why.

"That's rather a lot to ask in exchange for one kiss," he growled. It was not a favor he was inclined to grant. Launching a new play to the world on opening night was nerve-racking enough. But to share it now, when it was not yet in its final form, to invite Julia, with her sharp eyes, to scrutinize its every weakness before he had had a chance to make his revisions? That hardly seemed wise.

"Yes, I suppose it is." Her head tipped in a nod of concession, momentarily hiding her expression from him. A pause, long enough that he felt it might be safe to breathe again.

And then she said, "Name your price."

He felt certain his heartbeat must be audible to her in the otherwise-silent room. It roared so loudly in his own ears, he could hardly think. People were curious about Blackadder's plays, yes. They paid more for tickets than they ought. But this?

"I warn you, Miss Addison." He tightened his arm, cinching their bodies more firmly together, part of him—but only part—hoping the embrace would push her away. "I'm a demanding lover."

Once more, her chin jerked up. To his shock, his words did not seem to have made her more nervous. Only more intrigued. "Demanding?" she echoed, her eyes sparkling as they scanned his expression. He remembered suddenly what Mrs. Hayes had said about her companion's desires. "I do hope that's not just another word for selfish."

A fresh bolt of lust shot through him. Julia was not the sort of woman one ought to regard as an object of flirtation, to say nothing of anything more scandalous. And yet, he was more than tempted to sweep an arm across the desktop, lay her across it, and have his way with her, here and now.

But he made do with kissing her again, his mouth moving across hers more languidly this time, though sparking no less fire. "I promise you'll be satisfied," he rashly vowed. "What say you?"

"I say you'd best be on your way to supper, before someone comes looking for you," she answered, when he let her have her breath again. "I don't relish the look on Lady Clearwater's face if she catches us like this."

He could picture the bitter disappointment in the scheming woman's eyes. "I do." Nevertheless, he let Julia go, watched as she smoothed her dress and tried to repair the havoc his careless fingers had wrought to her simple coiffure. "But that's no' what I was askin'."

More Scots notes inevitably slipped into his speech when he allowed his restraint to unravel. "When is the next rehearsal?"

"Next Friday at two o'clock."

"I'll meet you at the theater." She held out her hand, in the manner of a someone striking a bargain. "We can settle on terms then."

He took her hand in his but did not shake it. Slowly, he raised her fingers to his mouth, let her feel the heat of his breath across her knuckles, held her gaze as he turned her hand over and pressed his lips to the thin skin of her wrist, where he was pleased to find her pulse thrumming at least as rapidly as his own. "'Til next Friday, then," he whispered before letting her go.

Then he strode toward the door, leaving not the way he had come, but heading deeper into the house. Supper and dancing would be even more interminable than he had foreseen.

But nothing compared to the days until he could see Julia again.

Chapter 10

Julia hadn't the faintest notion how much time had elapsed between Lord Dunstane's departure and the servant's almost-inaudible scratch at the study door. She had found her way to a chair and taken a book from the shelf, though she hadn't bothered to open it. The candle still sat on the far corner of the desk where he had shoved it, its flame too distant for her to read by—as if she could have concentrated on the printed page even if the light had been right beside her.

Name your price.

Her foolish words still seemed to echo about the room. What had she been thinking, allowing Lord Dunstane such liberties, offering . . . *herself,* in exchange for a mere peek at the play? She had intended to tempt him, it was true, to use his interest. But she had not considered how far she might have to go to get what she wanted.

And she had never imagined how tempted she might be to give him whatever he asked.

When she made no answer to the quiet knock, the door opened a few inches, and a parlor maid stuck her head into the room. "Mrs. Hayes is ready to leave."

Julia rose. "Has her carriage been ordered?"

"Yes, miss."

Heedless of the bookshelves' general air of orderliness, she stuffed the unexamined volume in the first convenient space she saw, then blew out the candle with a huff and followed the girl downstairs.

In the high-ceilinged foyer, only Mrs. Hayes, Lady Clearwater, and a footman waited.

"Ah, there you are, my dear," Mrs. Hayes called up to her when she was still half a flight of stairs away. "I didn't see much use in our staying for the dancing."

"No, ma'am."

"Are you feeling any better, Miss Addison?" asked Lady Clearwater, scrutinizing every detail of Julia's appearance. She did not look at all disappointed to see them go.

"Can't you see how flushed she is?" Mrs. Hayes chided. "I'll see to it you have one of my special tonics when we're home."

Julia wanted to protest, but when Mrs. Hayes promised it would bring with it the blessed oblivion of sleep, she nodded and let the widow take her arm and walked with her to the waiting coach.

Then again, sleep was not without its risks. It might bring dreams—dreams of the sort young ladies were not supposed to have.

In the dimness of the carriage, she pressed gloved fingertips to her mouth. Her lips felt the same as they always had, not swollen or tender as she had half expected to find them. She hadn't known there were such kisses—or rather, hadn't suspected she would enjoy them so thoroughly, particularly not from a man like Lord Dunstane: so arrogant and so cold.

No. Not cold at all.

Hot as a freshly stoked fire.

She could still hear his voice, the thickening of his brogue, as if passion unleashed some other side of him—as if her kiss had caused his mask to slip.

Friday's rehearsal would give her the opportunity to see him again. Was she willing to risk . . . *everything* to find out what another encounter might reveal?

A shiver passed through her. She was beginning to fear that the answer might be yes. In the chill evening air, she found herself longing for heat—no matter how dangerous.

When she had been wrapped in his arms, protecting the magazine had been the last thing on her mind. She had simply thrown herself head-long into the flames.

"I think you might be feverish," said Mrs. Hayes. Her expression was indecipherable in the semi-darkness, but her voice was full of concern.

Julia gnawed at her lower lip and nodded. "I think you might be right."

Back in Clapham, Mrs. Hayes called for her maid and ordered Julia straight to bed. Julia hardly had time to slip into her nightdress before

Mrs. Whyte, the housekeeper and Daniel's mother, appeared at her door.

"Warm milk," she said, proffering a pewter cup, "with two drops of Mrs. Hayes's sleeping tonic, on her orders. Rest is the best thing for you, Miss Julia."

With an unsteady hand, Julia reached for the cup and pretended to take a sip, then wiped warm foam from her upper lip with the back of her other hand. "Mmm, thank you. I'm sure I'll be right as rain in the morning," she insisted. "After a good night's sleep."

Mrs. Whyte's brows were knitted together in a frown of concern. "Drink it all, then straight to bed."

"Yes, ma'am."

As soon as the door was shut behind the housekeeper, Julia put the cup aside and stood staring out the small, square window into the darkness. Eventually she tipped her forehead against the blessedly cool glass.

Could she save Miss on Scene and Mrs. Goode without getting burned?

Gradually, from the hopeless jumble of her thoughts—memories of what had been said at the last staff meeting, of what Lord Manwaring had revealed, of Lord Dunstane's searing touch—a single note of clarity emerged.

She must fight fire with fire.

She sat down at the little dressing table, which sometimes doubled as a writing desk. The room itself was so narrow that when the stool was not tucked beneath the table, it nestled against the bed.

Withdrawing a sheet of paper from the drawer

with one hand, she dipped her pen with the other
and dashed off a few lines, pausing only to read
them through once before folding the letter and
sealing it—along with, perhaps, her fate. Then, wrapping a shawl around her shoulders, she opened
the door again and peered out into the darkened
house. From all appearances, everyone else was
abed.

With cautious, silent steps, she descended into
the kitchen. As she had hoped, Mrs. Whyte had retired after delivering the warm milk; only Daniel
was still within, banking the fire before settling in
for the night.

She cleared her throat, and he jerked about,
poker upraised, obviously startled. "Oh! It's you."
He lowered his weapon apologetically. "I expected
you'd sleep until noon, Miss Julia. That dose usually does it, even for Mrs. Hayes. You must have the
constitution of a horse. Beggin' your pardon," he
added, with a lopsided grin.

She gave a silent chuckle and lifted one shoulder. "Every body's different, I guess."

"What are you doing down here? Hungry?"
Gradually, his voice had risen from a shocked whisper to something almost conversational. With a
clatter and a clang, he thrust the poker back into
the iron cage that held the other fire tools.

She held up the letter and raised a finger to her
lips. "I need you to take this to Lady Stalbridge."

She had written a brief addendum to her latest
column and hoped it was not too late to get it to
the printer. Surely if Miss on Scene issued another
salvo at Ransom Blackadder, it would redirect his
patron's attention to the business at hand. Then,

during the rehearsal, Lord Dunstane would be focused on the play's success, not on her.

"*Now?*" Daniel mouthed the word, eyes round. But his expression was eager, too; he was always up for an adventure.

"I'd offer you a guinea for the trouble," she murmured, handing over the letter. "But at present, I haven't even a ha'penny."

"No worries, Miss Julia." He tucked the letter into the pocket of his livery coat, hanging on a peg behind him, and then shrugged into the garment. "Maybe you could find time for giving me another lesson in—what d'ya call it?—instead."

"Deportment," she supplied with a gentle smile. "And I think maybe you're ready for a few phrases in French, too."

He beamed. "Gee, thanks! But . . ." His hand clutched his breast, where the letter had been secreted. "What if the fellow who opens the door says her ladyship isn't to be disturbed and won't take it to her?"

"You will just have to be persuasive, Daniel. It's very important."

With an earnest nod, he was off.

Julia made her silent way back to her bedchamber. Once inside, she sank onto the stool of her dressing table and reached for the mug of doctored milk, now tepid rather than warm. She glanced from the frothy contents of the cup to the rumpled white linens of the bed behind her.

I promise you'll be satisfied.

Squeezing shut her eyes, she downed the milk in three noisy glugs, grimacing at its bitter aftertaste, then flung herself backward onto the mattress and prayed the sleeping draught would at least keep her from dreaming of him.

Between now and next Friday, she needed to forget what those forbidden words had made her crave, to recall that her attraction to Lord Dunstane was meant to be an act.

The following Friday morning found Graham in the blue study, seated by the window at the table where Keynes usually worked, staring at a blank sheet of paper.

Well, not quite blank. He'd pressed the tip of his pen into the page so firmly it had made a small tear, not only spoiling that page, but also allowing ink to bleed onto the page beneath. A perfect metaphor for the progress, or lack thereof, he'd made in his revisions to *The Poison Pen*.

The play had a flaw in it. Hardly visible to the naked eye . . . at first. But large enough to make a mess of things and damned difficult to repair.

It had been written in a fit of pique. Taking on the critics was biting the hands that indirectly fed him. And attacking Miss on Scene was scolding the one reviewer who had ever seemed to imagine that anything might lie beneath Blackadder's sardonic mask. The only one who had ever offered anything like praise.

With one swift movement of his hand, he snatched up the topmost two sheets and crumpled them in a ball, then tossed it angrily over his shoulder.

As luck would have it, Keynes chose that moment to enter the room, whistling an airy tune despite the morning's gray skies.

The sound from his lips stretched into one long, sinking note, miming the high-pitched whine of a cannonball as it arced through the air over the battlefield. "I didn't expect to find you here at this hour, my lord," he said as he skirted the lob and came around to the front of the table where Graham sat.

"Sorry for that." Keynes's brows rose. But Graham's apology, though grudging, was sincere. "I had a restless night."

A series of restless nights, in fact. Since that fateful kiss in Clearwater's study, he had slept only fitfully and always woke aching with frustration. He should never have kissed Julia. He should never have granted her request to watch the rehearsals of Ransom Blackadder's play. The risk was too great. And whatever she intended to offer in return for the favor was nothing he dared to accept.

No matter how much he wanted to.

"Ah." Keynes sent a sideways glance toward the coffeepot, as if he knew it was the third Graham had rung for that morning, as if its bitter contents were to blame for Graham's irritableness. "Then perhaps this should wait for another time."

He was carrying a stack of papers, as usual. Graham hardly ever saw the man without them. Correspondence, he supposed. Some pressing business from Dunstane?

"What is it?"

At least it could not be devastating news about some member of his family. The last possible letter of that sort had been received a few months ago. And it couldn't be a snarling review of a Ransom Blackadder play, either, since none was currently being performed.

With a show of reluctance, Keynes laid something atop the stack of blank paper in front of Graham. Familiar words, framed by the figures of two Greek women with enigmatic smiles, looked up at him.

MRS. GOODE'S
MAGAZINE FOR MISSES

He raised his eyes to Keynes's face, searching for an explanation.

"The latest issue, sir. Just out this morning. I thought you might wish to . . ."

Graham pushed the magazine aside and picked up his pen. "I'm busy. Too busy for frivolities, Keynes."

"Of course. My apologies. I'll just—"

As he reached to retrieve the magazine, Graham casually laid his hand atop it.

"I myself find knitting patterns quite soothing," Keynes ventured after an uncomfortable pause, withdrawing his own hand to shift the stack of paperwork that remained in his arms. "When my thoughts refuse to untangle themselves."

"Given the dreck one finds beneath this cover," Graham retorted, tapping his long forefinger against the word *Goode's*, "any random page might put a fellow right to sleep."

Keynes's answering laugh sounded a trifle uncertain, but he agreed, "Just so, sir," and turned to deposit the rest of his burden on the polished desk. "Shall I . . . ?"

With a flick of his quill, Graham gestured for his secretary to seat himself.

For a stretch of several minutes, only the ordinary sounds of work could be heard, the organizing of papers, the breaking of seals, the smoothing of pages. Graham dipped his quill, tapped it against the mouth of the glass inkwell, and then sat with its sharp tip poised above another pristine sheet, waiting . . .

Twice in rapid succession, he drummed the fingers of his left hand, each fingertip striking a tiny blow, momentarily blotting out those little faces and meaningless words like *rational* and *proper*.

At last, he tossed his pen aside and leaned back in his chair. Watched the traffic slice through the puddles on Half Moon Street. Blew out a breath. Picked up the magazine and leafed through it with casual disdain.

Sheet music. He hummed a few bars. Not a melody he had heard before. Tolerable, he supposed.

Some screed defending ladies' study of botany. Who would have guessed that allowing young women to learn about flowers was so controversial?

A recipe for syllabub. Perfectly ordinary, except for the line, intermixed with the instructions for preparation, which remarked that it was the ideal dish to serve the average suitor, who was also "cloyingly sweet, insubstantial, and full of air."

A laugh rasped in his throat before he could stop it, and out of the corner of his eye, he saw Keynes pretend not to glance his way.

And then two more pages slid past beneath his thumb, and he was struck by the words *Miss on Scene* in bold script, the mask of Tragedy to their left and Comedy to the right, the ribbons of the masks trailing to either side to form a sort of banner across the top of the page.

Beneath that banner was a review of an opera performed a few weeks past at the Haymarket, one of the most innocuous assessments of an artistic production he had ever read in any publication. Hardly worthy of the name *review* at all. It left him with the same sort of feeling one might have at biting into a last winter's mealy apple. Nothing like the review of *Othello*. Nothing into which a reader might sink his teeth.

Proof that "Miss on Scene" was merely a name, not a person? Perhaps a variety of would-be authors—men, women, young, old—submitted reviews for the magazine. He was no doubt wasting Keynes's time, having his secretary chase after a figment, a figure as flimsy as that syllabub, as papery as the fictitious "Mrs. Goode" herself.

With a wry sort of smile, something like chagrin at the credence he'd placed in a single column in a silly ladies' magazine, he returned his attention to the page. Centered beneath the toothless review was a printer's flourish that looked—he tilted his head to the side to be certain—yes, oddly like a dagger. And then, below it, a few more lines of type:

Miss on Scene is flattered to learn that her work has earned the notice of Mr. Ransom Blackadder, who seems to imagine he has cause to fear her poison pen. She wishes to reassure him that he need not be concerned for the fate of his work at her hands.

She reserves her 'deadliest' reviews for plays that are not deadly dull.

"Why, that little—!"

His final word was not quite drowned out by the sound of the magazine slamming against the tabletop. The gust of air sent his discarded pen skittering a few inches farther away, and the force of the blow made the ink in the bottle shiver.

Keynes whipped up his head. "My lord, is everything all right?"

"Perfectly," Graham snarled past clenched teeth, though he meant it. More than all right, in fact. "Ransom Blackadder would seem to have made himself an enemy, Keynes."

And Blackadder was at his best when he had someone with whom he could spar.

"Oh." Keynes pushed his wire-rimmed spectacles up his nose with the tip of his index finger. "Does that mean—?"

"It means that, after this, he can have no compunction about treating Miss on Scene as an adversary, albeit an unworthy one." He picked up his quill and twirled it between his thumb and first finger, watching the faint gray and white striations on the feather blur and swirl together. "If she shows no mercy with her weapon, she can expect none from his."

With exaggerated care, he laid the pen atop the stack of paper, closed the magazine, and pushed away from the table. "I'm sure I speak for Blackadder when I say that any revisions to *The Poison Pen* must take into account this latest sally and respond in kind."

Something twitched at one corner of Keynes's mouth. "Or unkind," he said, low enough that Graham could pretend not to have heard. "Are you off to the theater, then, sir?" he asked in his normal voice.

"I'm going to consult with Blackadder first. Advise him. This afternoon, I'll convey his instructions to the players." And in a tone that brooked no dissent. Oh, aye, there would be harsh words at Covent Garden this afternoon. Mr. Fanshawe might find himself without a part—in this play, or any other.

Well, that's what rehearsals were for. To improve matters. To tear things down so that they might be built up better, stronger. They were messy, ugly things, unfit to be seen, and for that very reason, closed to the public. At least no one would be there to witness—

"Damnation!" he muttered beneath his breath.

He'd been so focused on the irritating words of "Miss on Scene," he'd momentarily forgotten the true source of his present madness.

Julia.

"Problem, my lord?"

"Nay." Graham bit off the word with an audible *snap* of his teeth as he strode from the room. A solution, in fact. If he wanted one.

To keep himself from ravishing Miss Addison, he could simply direct his energy toward ravaging Miss on Scene.

And once Julia had seen what he was capable of, she might never step foot in the theater again.

Chapter 11

When Mrs. Hayes announced at the end of luncheon that she intended to rest that afternoon and wished to be left alone, Julia could hardly believe her luck.

Whether it was good luck, or bad, remained to be seen.

"Are you all right, ma'am?" she asked as she helped Mrs. Hayes to her feet.

"Oh, well enough, I suppose. When the weather turns this time of year, these old aches and pains fatigue me so. I hardly slept a wink last night."

Julia knew that wasn't quite the case. For one thing, Mrs. Hayes had softly snored her way through the second half of *The Iron Chest*, to which they had returned, unaccompanied, because too many evenings at home were intolerable to the widow. And while Mrs. Hayes had dozed, Julia had been at liberty to imagine what the next day would bring—if she decided to go to the rehearsal, and if she could find some excuse for going out.

Now, it was Friday at midday, rehearsals for *The Poison Pen* began in a couple of hours, and Mrs. Hayes was providing the excuse for her.

Julia knew better than to tell herself it was Fate, nudging her toward a decision to sacrifice her virtue to save the *Magazine for Misses—Mischief*, she had almost thought. Never had the mocking soubriquet seemed more apt. Papa, who had been a *good* man, was certainly not smiling down on his mischievous daughter and paving the way for her misdeeds.

No, the temptation came from quite another direction, another source.

But really, if she *did* make up her mind to let a wicked Scotsman have his way with her, would it go any worse for her immortal soul if she let herself enjoy it?

After she helped Mrs. Hayes settle into bed and drew the drapes to shut out what little light the day had provided, she brought a glass of water into which she was instructed to add a drop of the same sleeping tonic that last week had rendered Julia dead to the world for a dozen hours at least. A smaller dose would not last as long, and because Mrs. Hayes turned to it more often, it was not likely to have quite as powerful of an effect on her. But still, Julia knew that for the next few hours, she would never be missed.

Retreating from Mrs. Hayes's chamber on tiptoe, she closed the door behind her with no more sound than the faint *click* of the latch. In her own little room, she closed the curtain and arranged the bed so that if anyone chanced to peek, it might look as if she were resting too. Into her reticule, she tucked a tiny notebook with pencil attached, to jot down her observations about the play. And then she slipped downstairs without alerting anyone, even Daniel, to her departure.

Her hooded mantle protected her both from prying eyes of passersby and the chill of early November. With its windows shut tight against a drizzling rain, the interior of the hansom smelled faintly musty, and the long, jostling ride to Covent Garden offered little more to look at than a constellation of raindrops on the glass and the blur of traffic beyond. She made herself relax the fingers that were clenched around the ribbons of her reticule, watching the movement of her gloved hand as if it were a thing quite separate from herself. It would not do to behave as if she was nervous.

To say nothing of excited.

At the theater, the cab driver deposited her in a puddle and hurried away. She was left to knock at three different doors until a man in rough clothes—he either worked behind the scenes or was costumed to play the part of someone who did—let her in.

"Lord Dunstane said I might..." Her voice trailed off as the man turned away, indifferent to her explanation.

Uncertain what else to do, she climbed the stairs and slipped past the heavy curtain into the familiar box. Lights had been lit around the stage, but the large chandeliers overhead remained dark, casting all else into shadow. Empty of an audience, the theater felt enormous, the box higher and farther from the stage than it had been just the night before. She sank into the nearest chair, its blue silk upholstery cool to her touch, and watched as the actors milled about the boards, clad in ordinary clothes rather than costumes, tattered scripts still clutched in several hands. They talked and joked with one another in rather ribald fashion—her first glimpse at the coarse behavior that made actors scandalous.

"All right," called one of the men, gesturing with his own tightly rolled script like a baton. His paunch and balding head made him look older than she thought he probably was. "Places, everyone."

The actors scattered, some to the wings, two to chairs on opposite sides of the stage. The woman, seated at an elegant French escritoire, picked up a quill, tested its point, gave an exaggerated wince to suggest its sharpness, and began to write, the lavish plume dancing above the paper. She was in her thirties, Julia guessed, still beautiful in a cold, unapproachable way.

On the other side of the stage, the man who had spoken now hunched over a scarred oak table, its surface lit by the stub of a tallow candle, his quill a bedraggled feather. Once silence fell, he mimed several cross outs and corrections and at last began to speak the words he had penned.

"O fairest Muse, return to me!

I can but choose to pine for thee,

For while thou leav'st me empty-hearted,

From thither to thence my thoughts have darted—"

Evidently, he played the ill-fated poet Lord Manwaring had described. Between the first and second couplet, he broke for an ominous, though hardly convincing, cough.

When he finished, the woman paused in her scribbling to read over what she had written.

"Though empty-hearted he claims to be,
More empty-headed, 'tis plain to see.
The only rhymes he's fit to parse
I'll use for paper to wipe my—"

Julia pressed her fingertips to her lips, uncertain whether what she stifled was a gasp or a laugh. Surely Blackadder did not intend to pass that off as a witty exchange. Was that how he imagined Miss on Scene? Did he really believe her capable of writing anything so crude?

Though the character of the reviewer *was* as least as good a poet as the fellow who was now slumped over his work, soon to breathe his last, pierced to the quick by the woman's pointed words.

Julia sighed. Perhaps Blackadder hadn't yet seen the challenge she had issued in this month's issue of the magazine. Or perhaps he intended to take her advice and shield himself from criticism by making *The Poison Pen* as dull as possible.

"Nay. Stop. That'll never do."

If she hadn't known already to whom the voice must belong, the shape of that final vowel—*dae*—betrayed the speaker's Scottish origins. A man emerged from the shadows at the back of the theater with a sheet of paper in his upraised hand. It took several of his long-legged strides before the stage lights struck a coppery gleam from Lord Dunstane's hair and highlighted the seemingly permanent scowl etched into his sharp-featured face.

At the edge of the pit, he paused and, to her surprise, tore the sheet in half. "Here," he barked, thrusting each jagged-edged piece toward one of the principals, who stepped forward together with obvious reluctance and took them from his hands. "Blackadder wants you to read that instead."

The scene began again, the two performers back-to-back in their opposing corners, once more showing their characters at work. This time the poem, still expressing love for a fleeting muse, was more melancholy than maudlin. The reviewer, however, flatly rejected the poet's claim to either artistic inspiration or the love of a beautiful woman.

A chill chased down Julia's spine. With a few strokes of his pen, Blackadder had transformed the play's version of Miss on Scene from somewhat clever to downright cruel, perhaps in response to Julia's latest goading words. And Lord Dunstane looked on and nodded approvingly at the change.

Well, no. Not exactly *approvingly*, though his head did move in an oblique motion as he listened and watched, his arms folded across his chest. When the scene came to a close, with the actor playing the part of the poet splayed across his worktable, he said nothing. A moment's silence stretched into a minute or more, seeming to echo about the theater with no audience to absorb it.

"Mrs. Cole," he said at last, addressing the woman who played the reviewer, "I fear Mr. Sawyer erred in his recommendation of you for the part

of Perpetua Philpot." The actress, who had risen
to her feet when he began to speak to her, straightened her spine at that, a movement Julia mimicked in her seat, as if she could withdraw further
into the shadows, far enough not to witness the
tongue-lashing she fully expected to follow.

But Lord Dunstane spoke quietly. Only the theater's excellent acoustics made it possible for Julia
to hear him. "Perpetua is meant to be deadly, it's
true. But she must also be desirable," he went on
before the actress dared to interrupt. "What makes
the poet crave her approval? What gives her her
power? You play her as an ice queen, cool and remote. But you must think of the to-and-fro between writer and reviewer as a seduction." Julia felt
a blush heat her cheeks. Certainly she had never
considered her work in quite that manner. "If she
is to be successful at stabbing men in the back, first
those men must want to get close enough to f—"

Though unfamiliar with the final word he
spoke, Julia could not mistake its meaning. This
time, her gasp left her lips before she could prevent it. Heat flamed up from her chest, burning
across her cheeks and in the tips of her ears. Onstage, heads swiveled to find the source of the
sound, and she tried to duck behind the back of
the chair in front of her.

Not soon enough. Not before Lord Dunstane
had caught her eye.

She was meant to be a writer, and yet she knew
of no word to adequately describe the mixture of
sardonic amusement and annoyance that lined his
expression. He did not speak, only beckoned her

down to the pit with the *come-hither* curl of his forefinger before turning his attention back to the actors.

In her haste to flee from the box, she tangled her limbs in the drapery and could have sworn she heard a derisive feminine laugh from below. Once she had freed herself, she stumbled to the nearest bench in the long saloon to catch her breath and gather her wits.

She knew she ought to leave Covent Garden entirely. To display good judgment, for once. *And certainly*, she thought as she glanced around the empty saloon, *there is nothing to stop me.*

Nothing but her own curiosity. Her desire to see what was behind the curtain, to witness the machinery that made the magic of the theater. And yes, more than a little—she curled her fingers in the plush velvet upholstery—her desire to see Lord Dunstane once more.

I promise you'll be satisfied.

Pushing to her feet, she descended the staircase with measured steps and crossed the vestibule. The doors leading into the pit were tall and heavy, and she struggled to open one of them. Another sign, perhaps. Another opportunity to demonstrate good sense and leave.

At last, after using the combined strength of both arms to give the handle a determined wrench, she succeeded in opening the door just enough that she could slip inside.

The theater's horseshoe shape enveloped her, directing her footsteps down the aisle, toward the stage, where the actors and Lord Dunstane had resumed their conversation in voices that did not carry. Three more players, two men and a woman, had emerged from the wings to join them.

Lord Dunstane was standing in the second or third row of the pit. Above, on the stage, the actors towered over him, looked down at him.

And yet it could not have been more obvious that he was in command.

Though it had hardly been a silent entrance on her part, no one paid any heed to her arrival or her approach as she walked down the aisle with hesitant steps and stopped a few yards from where he stood. At last, he turned, though only enough to look over his shoulder.

"Ah. There you are. I'd begun to think you changed your mind."

She lifted her chin, rising instinctively to the challenge in his voice. "No, my lord. Nothing could be further from the truth."

"Excellent." He beckoned her closer with a wave of his arm and faced the actors again. "This is Miss . . . Hayes." The hesitation in his voice was too brief to draw attention to the falsehood he had uttered.

At first, she could not imagine why he had given her employer's surname instead of her own. A mocking reference, perhaps, to the fact that Mrs. Hayes insisted on introducing Julia as her relation when they were in company.

But it was also a measure of protection. Whatever happened, she might yet leave the theater with Miss Addison's reputation intact, and for that, she could only be grateful.

"She has asked to observe a rehearsal of *The Poison Pen*," he went on, "to which I agreed, in exchange for her—"

Please don't say it. Heat prickled her cheeks.

"Willingness to smooth my way with a certain young lady of her acquaintance."

"Skirt-chasing again, my lord?" teased one of the men who had come from the wings. He was a year or two younger than Lord Dunstane, with light-brown hair and a cleft chin, and he carried himself with confidence—like all actors, she supposed, but still, she suspected he was the one who would play the Ransom Blackadder part in Act Two.

"I hardly need to chase them, Sawyer," he corrected mildly. "And *again* implies that I ever stopped."

All of them, even the man lying face down on the table, joined in a wicked laugh.

Julia could not remember hearing a more humorless sound. Well, hadn't she suspected for some time that Lord Dunstane was a rogue?

Mr. Sawyer then turned toward her and bowed. "What do you think of the play so far, Miss Hayes?"

"Oh." She started at the address, then managed the shallowest of curtsies. "I, er . . ." Even a few moments of watching had shown her the vast difference between what an audience saw and what went on before the curtain rose, how little her experiences at the theater had prepared her to give an answer at this juncture.

Mrs. Cole fixed her with a narrow-eyed glare. At this distance, even with no stage makeup to exaggerate her features, her expression of contempt was perfectly legible. "Yes, do tell."

Julia lifted her chin a notch higher still. "After my brief observation of your rehearsal, I believe both Mr. Blackadder and his patron have it wrong."

Her words were met with a chorus of *oh-ho*s and cleared throats and the creak of two chairs as the bad poet sat up a little straighter and the barbed-tongued reviewer sat down.

Lord Dunstane regarded her with fresh interest and not, she thought, anger.

Not yet.

"The problem does not lie with Mrs. Cole's acting," she went on, focusing her gaze on a point just below the lip of the stage. "Both the lines originally given to her, and the revision, are ill-judged. They paint her as too crude, or too cruel. If Perpetua Philpot is to fool people into falling in love with her, she cannot—at least at first—seem to be either of those things."

Her assessment of the problem was met with silence. Every member of the company appeared to be waiting for Lord Dunstane to speak first. And his reply, when it at last came, was delivered as quietly as his earlier critique, his voice no less wry.

"I said nothing of *love*, Miss Hayes."

Her blush burned a degree or two hotter. What retort could she make? She did not think she had ever been more aware of the rise and fall of her breasts, how every effort to slow her breath only made it come more rapidly.

"Tell me," he went on after a pause, "what would you suggest to improve matters?"

The actor playing the sickly poet made a scoffing noise. "With all due respect, my lord, what does she know? If the little miss fancies it's so easy to play the reviewer's part, perhaps she ought to come up here and give it a try."

Julia whipped up her head. "I protest, sir. I never said—"

"An intriguing idea, Fanshawe," declared the actor who had spoken so boldly to Lord Dunstane—Mr. Sawyer, was that his name? As he spoke, he came down from the stage using a small staircase off to one side, taking the steps two at a time. His nimble movements and mischievous air would have made him an excellent choice to cast as Puck, the troublemaker in *A Midsummer Night's Dream.* When he reached the level on which the audience was usually seated, on which Julia and Lord Dunstane stood, he bowed with a flourish that could only be called theatrical. "Won't you help us, Miss Hayes?" He held out one hand to assist her in ascending to the Covent Garden stage.

She fully intended to refuse. Mr. Fanshawe's words had been intended as a taunt, not a sincere offer. Besides, some dreams were not meant to be fulfilled.

But just as she began to demur, she caught sight of Lord Dunstane, standing a few feet away with his arms once more crossed over his chest. He was regarding her with a curious expression: part intrigued, wondering whether she would rise to the challenge, she supposed. And part something she was tempted to call jealous, as if he did not like the idea that someone else had been the one to issue that challenge to her.

Slowly, he shook his head. More disapproval? Another warning?

She laid her fingers across Mr. Sawyer's palm, though her eyes were still locked with Lord Dunstane's. "Gladly."

Chapter 12

Graham knew he should put a stop to it. Tell Sawyer enough was enough. Block their way to the steps, if necessary.

But the part of him that knew what was right was rapidly losing ground to the part of him that wanted to see what Julia would make of her moment in the limelight. He wondered whether this moment, this chance, had been in her thoughts when she had asked to watch the rehearsal. Determined actresses had always found ways to catch his notice, which sometimes, yes, had involved an offer to, er, *trade favors.*

Surely that was not the case this time, however. She'd given him no sign that her interest in the theater extended to acting.

Then again, if not the chance for a moment onstage, what *had* motivated her request?

"This friend of yours," Sawyer was saying to her

as they passed, his head tipped so he could speak low in her ear, though not so low as to keep his words a secret from Graham, "the one his lordship's taken an interest in? She cannot be a good friend, if you are willing to let her associate with Dunstane."

Julia's eyes darted to the side, not quite meeting Graham's, though it was obvious to whom her next words were directed. "Is he so very bad, then?"

Sawyer laughed. "Not as bad as Blackadder, if the stories one hears are true. Then again, the two of them are like peas in a pod—"

"Dried-up, bitter peas in a rotting pod," muttered Mrs. Cole.

"Have you acted before, Miss Hayes?" Mr. Sawyer hastily continued over the interjection.

The false name startled Graham, though he had been the one to supply it. Why *did* he care what became of her reputation?

"No, never," she confessed as she reached the boards with Sawyer's hand hovering too close to her waist for Graham's comfort. "I don't suppose I shall be very good."

"No," agreed Mrs. Cole acidly. "I don't suppose you shall. But the play's shite anyway, so what does it matter?"

Graham gritted his teeth together, refusing to rise to the bait. She was a shrew, but, unlike Fanshawe, she was generally regarded as an excellent actor. She would be next to impossible to replace at the last minute. Contrary to Julia's notion of Perpetua Philpot, the part called for someone with steel in her spine and acid in her veins, not an ingenue afraid of hurting people's feelings.

"Here," Mrs. Cole said, dragging the chair back from the escritoire and motioning for Julia to sit. She jabbed her finger against the scrap of paper on which he'd scratched out the new lines. "See what you can make of it."

Julia glanced at the paper before pushing it aside and picking up the pen. "Thank you. But I have an idea of my own."

Whatever Mrs. Cole replied was rendered inaudible by Sawyer's exclamations of approval. "Excellent, Miss Hayes. Breathe some life into the part. Look sharp, Fanshawe."

Fanshawe had been following Julia's movements without seeming to watch her. At Sawyer's command, though, he glared at the other actor. "From the top," he called and began to read his dreadful poem.

Too dreadful? That was always the danger with satire—too much, too far, and audiences might not follow.

Pulling a pencil from her reticule, Julia quickly wrote something down and then struck a contemplative posture as he recited his lines, in a convincing performance of listening. When her turn came to speak, she got to her feet and began to pace behind her chair as she read her "review," occasionally pausing to twirl her quill.

She had admitted she had no experience with the theater beyond the audience. The lines she'd dashed off ought to have been terrible. Her performance ought to have brought him to his senses, made him remember what he was about.

Instead, she was a natural.

Oh, there were flaws, of course. No one had ever taught her to project her voice. But her instinctive movements brought a certain visual interest to the part. As a writer, he recognized that sense of urgency, the sometimes-futile hope that activity would stir the brain and drive some useful idea to the fore. And as for the words themselves? Well . . .

Though too quietly spoken, the newly written lines demonstrated her innate command over the situation. Over him. Her gentle innocence, so different from the older, more jaded Mrs. Cole, was compelling. Riveting.

It was the kiss all over again.

A murmur of praise passed his lips before he could stop himself. And this time, someone *was* near enough to hear.

"Oh, Miss Hayes," exclaimed Sawyer, who had dropped back a step after escorting Julia to the top of the stairs and now stood with one foot on the stage, his elbow resting on his bent knee as he watched. "Lord Dunstane approves!"

"I said nothing," Graham insisted hotly. He might have dismissed Sawyer on the spot if he had thought he could find some knave better suited to play—well, himself.

Sawyer straightened and turned to face him. "Do you deny you made a noise? A sort-of . . ." He circled one wrist in the air, searching for the word. "A hum. Sounded a damned sight more positive than any other sigh or groan that's issued from you these two weeks."

"Oh, this is preposterous," declared Mrs. Cole

from stage left, where she stood with arms akimbo. "Surely you do not mean to tell me—"

Julia, whose cheeks were positively crimson, managed an airy laugh. "I assure you he does not, ma'am. He's only humoring me to get in my good graces." She laid aside the lines she'd written as she darted a quick glance Graham's way, the first hint of uncertainty he'd glimpsed in her since she'd put her hand in Sawyer's. As if she, too, would like to know what he was about. "For my friend, you recall."

"Does this friend have a name?" Mrs. Cole narrowed her eyes as she awaited a response, clearly skeptical of Julia's ability to supply one on the spot.

"Julia," she answered with an immediacy and honesty that almost made him choke. "And I won't say more than that, so you needn't bother asking. No need to tarnish her reputation."

"Yet," Sawyer supplied with a knowing chuckle.

"I say," Fanshawe broke in peevishly. He was still seated at the writing table, now employed in scratching designs into the candle stub with the tip of his pen. "Are we done, then?"

"Somewhere you'd rather be?"

Not for the first time, Graham regretted hiring Fanshawe, who was widely regarded as past his prime. But having discovered the subject of Blackadder's new play, the fellow had pleaded for a part, no matter how small, desperate for a chance to rehabilitate his name with the critics.

Graham's question—or the tone in which he'd asked it—had the desired effect. Fanshawe sat up a little straighter, Sawyer sank onto a lower step, and Mrs. Cole's hands slipped from her hips to cross behind her skirts in a posture that was almost demure.

"No, sir," Fanshawe ground out.

"Go anyway." Graham dismissed the lot of them with the wave of one hand. "I wish a private word with Miss Hayes."

Fanshawe scuttled away, not mingling with the other actors. Sawyer sent a glance toward Julia that was almost wistful, then shrugged and went up the steps as he'd come down them, two at time, crossing the boards with long strides to catch up with the rest of the cast as they left the area around the stage.

Only Mrs. Cole remained, fussing over the papers that were spread across the escritoire, though with the exception of the torn sheet on which he had written the revised lines and the one on which Julia had penciled hers, they were meant to have nothing but nonsense scrawled on them, mere props. Once she had the pages gathered in a bundle, she laid them neatly on the center of the desk, sent a look toward Graham over her shoulder, and said to Julia in a voice intended to carry, "Watch yourself, miss."

Julia looked taken aback, as well she might. "I'm not going to steal the role from you."

"Of course not," Mrs. Cole said brusquely, as if such an outrageous notion had never crossed her mind. "Watch yourself around him."

It was as close as the woman might ever get to a sisterly gesture, those words of caution about an unscrupulous gentleman, given to a naïve younger lady headed toward danger. He couldn't very well object to them.

He was, however, increasingly convinced that Julia was less naïve—and far more dangerous—than he had at first believed.

As if to confirm him in the notion, she slanted a glance in his direction, familiar mischief twinkling in her blue eyes. "Thank you, ma'am," she said, diverting her gaze to Mrs. Cole once more and mustering a small smile. "You are too kind."

At that, Graham found himself choking back a laugh, the sound of which—poorly disguised as a cough—made Mrs. Cole spin on one foot to glare at him. "Right, then." She offered him a half-hearted curtsy. "I'll leave you to it."

As the soft scuff of Mrs. Cole's footsteps faded into silence, he stood watching Julia, who had once more lowered her eyes and resumed the project of neatening the surface of the escritoire. "How long?" he asked when he was certain they were alone. "How long have you wanted to act?"

Her chin jerked up. He expected a protest, a denial. Instead, she stepped around the corner of the desk, putting herself an arm's length closer to him.

"I was five, or a little more, when a traveling troupe stopped in our village. They stayed two days. Gave three performances on a makeshift stage on the green. I attended every one." Her head tilted further, and her eyes softened with a faraway expression. "By the end of the first scene of the first show, I'd fallen under the actors' spell." Then she stiffened almost imperceptibly and rubbed her hands together as if brushing away the memory. "By the end of the second scene, I had been told in no uncertain terms that actresses were women of low morals and ill repute. That I must never think of doing such a scandalous thing, must never speak of it, never even allow myself to dream."

"Clearly, you didn't listen."

That brought her gaze back to his face, her blue eyes cooler now. Wary. "Oh, but I did."

"Really?" He closed half the remaining distance between them with a single step. "Dreams are not usually so easy to constrain."

"Gentlemen's imaginations may be allowed to run free," she countered. "Young ladies, however, are expected to regulate their thoughts. The author of every conduct manual and sermon demands it." She spoke without rancor, though he could guess how such opinions must chafe.

The mention of sermons reminded him of the strictures that her father—his profession, as well as his death—had placed on her upbringing. "I daresay at the ripe old age of five, you were not reading conduct manuals. Who told you such things about actresses, then? Who taught you that thoughts could be penned in like so many dim-witted, docile sheep?"

The simile made one corner of her mouth twitch. "Mrs. Nathan. The wife of the local squire and the most respectable lady in Papa's parish, not even excepting Mama, who smiled too much for Mrs. Nathan's liking. She often looked after me, when Papa's spells of illness required Mama's undivided attention."

It irked him beyond reason, the notion that some interfering busybody had been allowed, perhaps encouraged, to implant such foolishness in Julia's head—though the evidence at his disposal suggested that Mrs. Nathan's lessons in propriety hadn't all stuck.

"Yet she took you to watch the players twice more?"

"Oh, no. The second time, I tagged along with my brother, Jeremy, though it kept me out past my bedtime and he had to carry me home on his shoulders. And by the next day, Papa was feeling enough better that he took me himself." Her voice grew wistful. "Afterward, he told me he hadn't spent such an enjoyable afternoon in an age. I wished Mrs. Nathan had been by to hear him say it."

"You knew her to be full of stuff and nonsense, even then, but you heeded her advice all the same."

"It's hardly 'stuff and nonsense,' my lord. Surely you do not mean to try to convince me that acting onstage in public is a respectable occupation for a young lady? That gentlemen do not regard actresses as little better than . . . *harlots*?" Her voice dropped instinctively, though there was no one to overhear.

Harsh words, but fair. The effort required to refute them would be wasted, and he wanted his energy for other things.

"You ask me to believe you have not pictured yourself here before?" He swept an arm in a gesture that took in the stage and the empty pit below. "All those nights at the theater, and you never went home and spoke lines into a mirror after Mrs. Hayes was in bed? Never told yourself you could do better if given a chance?" Pink splotches appeared on her cheeks, reminiscent of the exaggerated cosmetics of stage performers. He wondered whether, in her playacting fantasy, she had ever gone far enough to toy with the contents of a rouge pot. "Is that the reason you wanted to come to this rehearsal?"

"No, my lord. I assure you nothing could have been further from my thoughts."

"Ah, yes." One last step and the space between them was gone. He reached up to brush a tendril of hair from her temple. "Your thoughts. So easily kept from wandering where they ought not go."

"I never said it was easy, my lord."

"Nay." He trailed his fingertips across her cheekbone and traced the curve of her jaw. "You didn't."

He felt her throat bob in a swallow, but she did not retreat from his touch. Her eyes, however, shied from his face and toward the empty, shadowy pit. "Might we negotiate the terms of our arrangement somewhere less public?"

They were alone in the theater. But he understood what she meant. Standing in the middle of a stage surrounded by several thousand seats, empty though they might be, felt anything but private.

Backstage were any number of places where a tryst might take place, with no one the wiser. And Julia appeared willing to go with him, to uphold her end of the bargain.

But when he thought of those spaces—an unused dressing room, a storage closet filled with discarded props or broken furniture—he could not help but think of that distant evening, his elder brother and the actress, the agonizing moments he'd spent in the corridor, longing for somewhere to hide.

That innocent boy had long since grown into quite the rogue.

But pray God Graham knew better than to be as reckless as Iain.

He drew back his hand and put a half step between them, a few inches at most, but enough that he could breathe without being all too aware of the rise and fall of her breasts. "There's nothing to negotiate, Miss—" He couldn't do it, couldn't shape the name that wasn't hers. But what rose to his lips instead came out as little more than a desperate rasp. "Julia."

He wanted her. And not just her sweet lips and soft body pressed to his. He wanted her bright, mischievous eyes and her clever retorts and her unexpected gift for untangling the knots he'd made in his own damned script.

"You saw the rehearsal, as you wished," he went on, in something resembling his usual voice. "You even had your moment in the sun." At that, he flicked his wrist to gesture toward the enormous chandelier closest to the stage, though it was, unfortunately for his metaphor, unlit. "Now you should go."

He couldn't concentrate with her there—couldn't concentrate at all. Somehow, he had to focus his mind. Remember why he had come to London. He had to put his plan to punish Miss on Scene first.

Her lips parted on a silent *oh*, and disappointment clouded her gaze.

Disappointment over the play, he told himself. She couldn't possibly want—

Before the thought had fully formed, she rose up on tiptoe and launched herself toward him, her hands on his shoulders and her lips brushing swiftly over his cheek before pausing to whisper in his ear. "Thank you for today. I'll never forget this."

Any rogue worth his salt would have wrapped his arms around her, captured her mouth with his, and put a seal on . . . well, on whatever this was.

Graham watched her settle onto her heels, drop her hands to her sides, and blush as prettily as a rose.

Damn it.

He was utterly, hopelessly lost. He didn't just want her.

He needed her.

Damn it all.

"Come back Monday," he said. "Same time. See what Blackadder makes of your changes."

Her eyes flared, an ocean of vivid color in which a man would willingly drown. "Truly? Do you think he might approve of my suggestions?" Then she snagged her lower lip in her teeth and tilted her head. "But I suppose I ought to ask what such an indulgence will cost."

Reaching behind her, he snatched up both the scrap of paper on which he'd made his corrections and the page on which she'd written hers. The light scent of her soap, her skin, caught him off guard. No actress of his acquaintance had ever smelled so sweet and fresh, like the Highlands on the first truly warm spring day.

His heartbeat pounded in his head, his chest, his cock. Good God, but he was a fool. How could he hope to work in close proximity with her without revealing his secret?

"More than you can afford."

The words slipped out, half whisper, half growl, spoken more to himself than in answer to her question.

Then he strode offstage and into the shadows.

Chapter 13

Julia listened to his booted tread thump across the stage and down the steep, narrow steps. A moment later she heard the opening and closing of some nearer door she had not previously noticed. When she gathered the courage to turn and look behind her, he was gone.

Quickly she shuffled through the remaining papers on the desktop, some blank, some marked with lines and flourishes that would look, from a distance, like handwriting. At the very bottom of the stack lay Mrs. Cole's script.

The script whose dog-eared pages contained the fate of Perpetua Philpot—which was to say, Ransom Blackadder's plans to ruin Miss on Scene and the *Magazine for Misses*.

Knowing that someone might return at any moment, Julia picked up the script, hid it in the crook of her arm, and hurried away from the theater.

Only when she was safely ensconced in a hackney cab, summoned for her by one of the urchins who hung about Covent Garden, did she allow herself to page absently through the script as she contemplated the enormity of what had transpired that afternoon.

She had not just witnessed but participated in a rehearsal for *The Poison Pen!*

She had come only with the intention of watching, gathering information about the play, the actors, anything that might be useful in preparing a defense against the aspersions Blackadder intended to cast on Miss on Scene and the magazine.

Certainly, she had never imagined taking the stage at the Theatre Royal herself. Still less had she contemplated the possibility of speaking lines of her own invention and earning a measure of praise for them. A part of her knew she ought never to have allowed herself to get swept up in the moment. But she had longed to try her hand at acting for so long, how could she possibly have said no?

Now she had an invitation to return to the next rehearsal, not merely to observe, but to contribute. She had in her hands not just Blackadder's damning words, but also the power to change them.

And it seemed Lord Dunstane did not intend to demand anything from her in return.

How foolish it would be of her to feel anything like disappointment at such an outcome.

She recalled that moment, as his fingertips caressed her face, when she had felt far from sure about how things would end. No one who knew the man behaved as if he were above debauching a clergyman's naïve daughter. Mrs. Cole had warned her. Mr. Sawyer had all but called Dunstane a rake.

She ought to be grateful for his restraint, rather than annoyed at his presumptua in making the choice for her.

In the end, she had come away from today's rehearsal with far more than she could have hoped— even if she wasn't precisely *satisfied*, as he had promised.

Beneath her trembling fingers, the paper wrinkled and nearly tore.

"Drat these cobbled streets!" she exclaimed to no one in particular, ready to blame her agitation on the condition of the roadway, the careless cabbie, or the lack of carriage springs.

Anything to avoid confronting its true source: her ill-advised attraction to a certain Scottish nobleman.

She renewed her attention on the page in front of her. She had read plays before. Her father's library, though modest, had contained all of Shakespeare, and not the schoolboy versions with all the scandal scrubbed away and the tragic endings made happy. But she had never seen an actor's script, which was, she soon discovered, incomplete. Mrs. Cole's copy contained just Perpetua Philpot's part, with half lines from the other roles provided as cues. Here and there, Mrs. Cole or someone had penciled in a few words, a stage direction or some indication of the tone with which a line was to be spoken.

Julia wondered whether this was the ordinary

state of things, or whether it was an attempt by the playwright to control the dissemination of his work, by ensuring that none of the actors knew the whole of the play. Only Lord Dunstane seemed to be privy to all the details.

It would require more work than she had expected to sort out Blackadder's plot from such sketchy information—to say nothing of determining how best to foil it.

The words leaped as the coach jounced and jerked along, making the text doubly difficult to decipher. Eventually she closed the script and her eyes. But no sooner had she done so than her mind was flooded by memories of her strange afternoon: Mr. Sawyer's puckish grin of encouragement, the creak of the boards beneath her feet, the unexpected warmth in Lord Dunstane's light eyes.

Why had she told him about that day on the village green more than a dozen years ago? She had kept that foolish dream tucked away like a flower pressed between the pages of a book no one ever read. After all this time, it should have been brittle and faded. Instead, it had retained its freshness, its alluring scent.

She knew better than to fall under its otherworldly spell.

Once she had told Laura, the woman her brother had later married, that it wasn't fair to decry actresses' reputations and deny respectable women a place on the stage. All women played parts, she had insisted. Every young lady occasionally hid behind a costume, a well-rehearsed line, a mask.

Never had those words felt more true.

She, for instance, was accumulating new roles by the hour. Miss Hayes. Miss Philpot. Miss on Scene. *Julia.*

The memory of his rough voice as he'd all but groaned her name sent a shiver of longing through her. He could be such a disagreeable man. And she knew better than to desire his attention.

But still she found herself wishing he had kissed her once more . . .

Determined to dispel such thoughts, she rolled the script into a tube, as Mr. Fanshawe had done. But instead of gesticulating with it, she used it to peer out the window, like a pirate through a spyglass. The treetops of Clapham Common were just visible in the distance. Then, laughing at her own childishness, she smoothed the script over her knees until it lay flat again. Once she had gleaned everything she could from the document, she would have to return it, ideally without Mrs. Cole even realizing it was gone.

A few moments later, the hackney rolled to something like a stop near Mrs. Hayes's front door, and Julia leaped nimbly to the pavement. Inside, she met Mrs. Whyte escorting the apothecary, Mr. Watkins, down the stairs.

The housekeeper's ordinarily mild expression was lined with concern and darkened a bit further as she greeted Julia with a well-disguised scold. "Ah, Miss Addison. I wondered where you'd got to."

"I had an errand to run," she explained. "On behalf of Mrs. Hayes."

She told herself it wasn't quite a lie. As far as she

was concerned, every woman in London stood to suffer some degree of loss if the *Magazine for Misses* was destroyed.

"The last for a while, I daresay." Mr. Watkins placed his apothecary's bag beside his hat on the demilune table positioned against the wall near the front door, then slipped his arms into the sleeves of his greatcoat.

Julia looked from one to the other, suddenly worried. "Is everything all right?"

"A rheumatic flare," Mr. Watkins said with a sigh of compassion. "I've insisted on a fortnight's strict bed rest and left Mrs. Whyte with a poultice and instructions for bandaging her limbs, which I hope will alleviate some of her discomfort. A warmer climate for the winter really would be best, but alas, with the war . . ." He shook his head as his voice faded away. "It's good you'll be here to keep her amused, Miss Addison."

She managed to nod. "I'll go to her now, shall I?" With a quick curtsy, she hurried past Mrs. Whyte on the stairs, not waiting for an answer.

After pausing to shed her pelisse and bonnet in her room, she tapped on the door of Mrs. Hayes's chamber. One of the housemaids responded to her knock.

"Has she been asking for me, Nelly?" Julia had come armed with the French romance they had been reading and the afternoon papers.

A soft snore from the bed answered her question.

"She were that done up," the girl said. "Mr. Watkins recommended another dose of her sleeping draught to help her settle."

Julia nodded her understanding and gestured to indicate that Nelly might resume her usual duties. Once the girl was gone, Julia took up the chair positioned near the head of the bed and deposited the pile of amusements she had brought with her on the small marble-topped table beside her.

After several moments, in which Mrs. Hayes showed no sign of wakefulness, Julia twisted the chair toward the window to catch the last of the fading afternoon light and slid Mrs. Cole's script from the pile, where she had secreted it amidst the gossip sheets and the news of the day.

She had known better than to think that a few hours of unexpected freedom had been a sign. If Fate, or the guardian angel sent by her father, *were* to intervene in her life, this would surely be the form such an intervention would take: a circumstance tailor-made to ensure she would be stuck at Mrs. Hayes's bedside for at least two weeks, safe from all but the desire to return to Covent Garden and Lord Dunstane.

If she were diligent, the script would tell her what she needed to know and show her how to respond, without any further risk to her virtue or her reputation.

If she were wise, she wouldn't return to the theater until she could do so in the company of Mrs. Hayes, for a scheduled performance.

Perhaps not until the end of November, when *The Poison Pen* was set to debut.

* * *

The next morning, Nelly came to Julia's bedside. "Mrs. Hayes is askin' for ye, miss."

Julia blinked against the dawn. "She's awake?"

Mrs. Hayes had hardly stirred since the apothecary's visit. After supper, Mrs. Whyte had ordered Nelly to sit with their mistress, with every expectation that she would pass a quiet night. Julia had thus been settled comfortably in her own bed by half past ten, according to the bells of Holy Trinity Church.

But sleep had been elusive. She had heard the mournful hours of two and three ring out across Clapham Common before finally managing to quiet her restless thoughts enough to snatch a little rest. She had even caught herself wishing for the oblivion of Mrs. Hayes's sleeping draught, which had been at least temporarily effective once before at blotting out the memory of Lord Dunstane's touch.

What would Lady Stalbridge say if she knew that Julia had so thoroughly abandoned her good sense?

At least she had made the most of her one opportunity to gather information on *The Poison Pen.*

The script crinkled beneath her pillow as she pushed herself to sitting. She had read and reread as long as the daylight had held out yesterday, and though she still didn't understand how all the pieces of the plot fit together, it was clear that the poet's brother, one Reginald Briggs, managed to trick Miss Philpot into saying more than was wise and thus turned public opinion against her. Just as Ransom Blackadder hoped to do to Miss on Scene.

Now she had only to figure out how to turn the tables.

"Please tell Mrs. Hayes I'll be right there, Nelly," she said around a yawn. The girl gave a quick curtsy and left her to dress.

Not ten minutes later, Julia tapped on Mrs. Hayes's chamber door. Not being tightly latched, it swung open to reveal a surprising commotion.

Daniel stood at the end of the bed in his straightest, most footmanlike pose, the effect of which was marred only slightly by his struggle to contain a grin as his mother remonstrated with Mrs. Hayes over her breakfast order.

"Now, ma'am, Mr. Watkins was most clear about the need to abstain from coffee. And chocolate. And I don't think he'd approve of the kippers, either."

"I wouldn't need the coffee or the chocolate if he hadn't poured half a bottle of that awful sleeping tonic down my throat yesterday." Mrs. Hayes pulled a face as she twisted her mouth and stuck out her tongue. "Nasty stuff. The kippers are only to take away the taste of it. Not another drop of it, do you understand?"

"I do, ma'am," Mrs. Whyte replied in a more soothing tone as she exchanged a series of gestures with her son, who chose not to understand them. "But you may feel differently later . . ."

"I will *not*. And as for this nonsense about a fortnight abed—"

"Mrs. Hayes," Julia said, stepping into the fray. "How good it is to see you improving. Let's see, Daniel—how about poached eggs, toast, and some of your mama's wonderful gooseberry preserves. Oh, and a pot of weak tea. No one was ever harmed by a cup of tea, were they, Mrs. Whyte?" She finished with a smile for the housekeeper to quell any protest she was tempted to make.

"Certainly not, Miss Addison," Mrs. Whyte agreed, still regarding Julia with a hint of yesterday's wariness but slightly mollified by her remark about the jam. "But Mr. Watkins was most clear—"

"About the need for rest. Yes, absolutely. Mrs. Hayes ought to be disturbed as little as possible."

At that, Jess, the other housemaid, who had been vigorously fluffing the pillows behind her mistress's head and fussing over the linens, retreated a step away from the bed and dropped her hands to her sides.

"Ahh," sighed the widow as she sank against the mountain of goose down, no longer being churned by the maid's efforts. "That's more like it."

Mrs. Whyte and Jess soon left the room, and Julia returned to the chair she had occupied yesterday evening. "How do you feel, ma'am?"

Mrs. Hayes's face was still pale, and her lips pinched with pain as she shifted slightly on the plush mattress. "Like I'd been dragged through a stony field behind a team of oxen." She managed to squeeze out a smile. "But I've been worse. It'll pass. And in less than a fortnight," she added, another pointed reference to the apothecary's orders. But there was a hint of worry in her voice, the knowledge that someday, the pain might not dissipate and he might be proved right.

Pity swelled in Julia's breast, pushing aside her

own concerns. "What can I do to help you pass the time more comfortably?"

"Will you read to me?"

"Of course."

After breakfast—which Mrs. Hayes ate well, as both Julia and Mrs. Whyte were pleased to see—Julia picked up where they had left off in the French romance. Veronique's adventures, and the frequent need to repeat or translate passages when Mrs. Hayes nodded off and missed something important, occupied her for the remainder of Saturday.

On Sunday, it was a recital of the vicar's text and sermon, a description of the various bonnets in church, and the newspapers.

By Monday afternoon, Veronique's tale having twisted its torturous way to a happy end, Julia was left scrambling for something amusing. Mrs. Hayes dipped in and out of sleep. With nothing else at hand, and Mrs. Hayes to all appearances indifferent to anything but the soothing sound of her companion's voice, Julia opened the script of *The Poison Pen*.

Right at this very moment, rehearsal for the day was beginning. Would her absence be noted—by anyone? Would Lord Dunstane even remember he had issued another invitation?

Surely Mrs. Cole would be hampered by the missing script. Or perhaps not. With the performance just a few weeks away, she must have memorized most of her lines already. And with Lord Dunstane delivering regular changes from Blackadder, any printed version must be at least partly incorrect. Perhaps the version Julia held was already obsolete. Which would certainly render the task of extracting useful information from it more difficult, if not altogether pointless.

With a sigh, she flipped a page and continued reading in a soft monotone, the sort of voice intended to keep Mrs. Hayes asleep for as long as possible, so that Julia might think. Would theatergoers recognize Miss on Scene in the character of Perpetua Philpot? Would they agree with Blackadder's premise that the reviewer's identity must be exposed to put an end to her unjust power over public opinion and taste? Blackadder's last play had been sold out every night, obviously not harmed by her review in the *Magazine for Misses*.

What had she said to make him hate her so?

Could she persuade Lord Dunstane to get him to give up the fight?

In Covent Garden, it had seemed almost possible. But from Mrs. Hayes's house in Clapham . . . ?

Without realizing it, she'd stopped reading, her head too full of worry to leave room for anything else.

Beneath the quilt, Mrs. Hayes stirred. "Well?" she murmured. "Is Perpetua going to give this Briggs character a piece of her mind, or what?"

Julia jerked, and the script slid off her lap onto the floor. "I, er—I didn't realize you were listening."

"Of course, I'm listening," she insisted, never opening her eyes. "What else have I got to do?"

"I apologize. I would have chosen differently if I'd—"

"Yes, this story isn't much like our usual—other

than a certain melodramatic flair. But I'm hard-pressed to see how she and this poet fellow work things out in the end. He's insufferable, and she's a shrew. I suppose if they end up together, we can be glad they haven't ruined anyone else's happiness. What's the title?"

"It's, um . . ." She bent at the waist to retrieve the script and mumbled the answer to the carpet. "It's Ransom Blackadder's new play, out later this month. *The Poison Pen.*"

Despite Julia's efforts, Mrs. Hayes heard every word. "Blackadder? That rascal." Wincing, she pushed herself higher on the pillows and fixed Julia with a look. "However did you come by such a thing?" Julia chewed at her inner lip, trying to muster a reasonable reply. When none was forthcoming, Mrs. Hayes went on in a knowing voice. "Would it have anything to do with where you were on Friday afternoon, and why I had to fib and tell Mrs. Whyte I'd given you a half day?"

Julia recalled Mrs. Whyte's expression when she returned. Apparently, neither Mrs. Hayes's explanation nor Julia's had been very convincing. There was no disguising the inevitable blush that began to warm her cheeks.

"Or with Lord Dunstane's peculiar behavior at the Clearwaters' card party?"

Warmth became heat, rising to the tips of her ears. "What could he possibly have to do with—?"

"Because he's Blackadder's patron, isn't he?" Mrs. Hayes countered with a little *hmph* of satisfaction. "And he can't keep his fine Scottish eyes off you."

The blush grew hotter still, threatening to engulf her in flames. But at least if she were rendered nothing but a smoking pile of ashes, she wouldn't have to face another question.

She parted her lips to speak, though she hardly knew what words to frame. A lie was perfectly useless. It seemed that, after all, Mrs. Hayes did not need to have her lorgnette to hand to stare directly into Julia's soul.

"Yes," she confessed in a rush of breath. "Yes. Lord Dunstane allowed me to attend the rehearsal. At my request."

Birdlike, Mrs. Hayes tilted her head to one side. "And why would you make such a request of him?"

"Because I—" She glanced down at her lap, watched herself flick one curled corner of the script with her first fingernail. "Because I write reviews of plays for a periodical called *Mrs. Goode's Magazine for Misses.* I'm sure you haven't heard of—"

"Oh, but I have." Her knowing nod was triumphant. "*Goode's Guide to Misconduct,* people say. Lady Clearwater was just complaining about it the other night, how she'd forbidden her girls even to glance at a copy. Of course, any fool would know that's the surest way to make them desperate to read it." Her lips slanted in a crooked smile. "Then again, she's not just any fool."

In spite of herself and her present situation, Julia giggled. "It's not as scandalous and shocking as people make out. It's only that society isn't ready for young ladies to have opinions of their own."

Mrs. Hayes was eyeing her once more, a curious gaze, but not—so far as Julia could see—a disapproving or disappointed one. "How long?"

"Since the beginning. Almost a year. We meet regularly in the back room of a bookshop."

"Ah." She diverted her gaze toward the ceiling, as if she were trying to recall something. "I suppose that's why you offer to run so many errands for me—and why they all take twice as long as they should."

"Yes, ma'am," Julia agreed, embarrassed and yet relieved to have the truth out in the open. "And a good deal of the letters I claim to write are really drafts of my column, to the magazine's editor."

"I suppose you wanted to see rehearsals of the play so you could publish the first review, get the jump on your competitors?"

"Not exactly." She resumed her restless ruffling of the script's tattered corner. "It seems Ransom Blackadder took issue with my previous review of his work. *The Poison Pen* is his rejoinder. It's about—well, it's about me. And the *Magazine for Misses.* Rumor has it, he wants to turn society against us. Expose our identities, if he can." A shiver passed through her; speaking the threat aloud made it all the more real. "So I used my acquaintance with Lord Dunstane to finagle my way into a rehearsal, to see if it was true."

"And is it?"

Julia lifted her head and nodded, though the movement was uncertain. "I think so, yes. The script suggests as much. But Blackadder is still making changes to the play."

Mrs. Hayes sat up a little straighter, ignoring her pain. "He was there on Friday? You've seen him?"

"No. He sent new pages with Lord Dunstane. It was clear from the actors' reaction, it wasn't the first time he'd made changes, and it seemed unlikely to be the last. Lord Dunstane said I might come back today, and I had hoped—" She gave a little shake, driving away the idea—though not the ache of longing that had accompanied it. "It doesn't matter," she insisted, laying the script aside on the marble-topped table. Mrs. Hayes needed her. "Blackadder will do what he wants, in the end."

Silence hung between them for a moment. Then Mrs. Hayes sighed as she eased herself against the pillows once more. "Of course, it matters. You must go."

Julia caught her breath. "Ma'am? I—no." She couldn't. It would be foolish in the extreme for her to return to Covent Garden. She was in danger of losing her reputation. And—if she were honest—her heart. "It's too late, anyway. By the time I arrived, rehearsal would be over. And you need me here."

"I need *rest*. You said so yourself. When's the next rehearsal?"

"Wednesday, I believe."

"Ah. Well, then. We have time to think up a proper excuse to give Mrs. Whyte for your going out. A pity about today, but Lord Dunstane must know that a lady's companion is sometimes at the whim of her crotchety old employer and unable to get away."

"Go out?" She couldn't disguise the incredulity in her voice. "Surely you don't mean to allow . . . ?"

Though truth be told, *encourage* might be the better word.

"Allow what?" As Julia watched, the shrewdness

faded from Mrs. Hayes's expression, leaving her looking positively feeble. "How can an old lady possibly be expected to be aware of everything that goes on beneath her roof, all the comings and goings?" And then she winked, and the spark returned to her eyes. "Just ask my niece."

While ostensibly serving as her aunt's companion, Laura had often sneaked out to play a dangerous role, acting as an avenging angel for mistreated young women. Laura still believed she had succeeded in pulling the wool over her aunt's eyes about those escapades.

Julia gasped. "You knew?"

Mrs. Hayes shrugged, as if to excuse herself. "I know what it is to love the theater, the donning of costumes, the playing of parts. I also know what freedom tastes like. A nibble now and again is never enough. And I've always thought it a pity that women are so rarely afforded a chance to do as they wish until"—she paused to pluck at the linens, puckering the fabric here and there—"they are too old and feeble to do much of anything."

Julia sent a sidelong glance at the tattered script. "What if someone finds out?"

The discovery that she, a young lady—paid companion or not—had spent time unchaperoned in the company of actors . . . and Lord Dunstane . . . What a scandal! Even if nothing happened between them, her reputation might be tarnished. And if something did happen?

Then things would go worse for her still. Her family would insist she leave London forever.

If they didn't disown her entirely.

Mrs. Hayes now smoothed one gnarled hand over the quilt, as if wiping away the wrinkles in their plan. "You must see that no one does."

Julia leaped to her feet and wrapped the frail woman in a careful hug. "Thank you, ma'am!" she breathed.

"Just be careful not to lose sight of what's important, my dear," Mrs. Hayes said, returning Julia's embrace with surprising strength. "This *Guide to Misconduct* must go on giving young ladies a voice— no, teaching them they have a voice of their own. And one more thing—"

"Ma'am?" She pulled back enough that she could see Mrs. Hayes's face.

"I do wish you would call me Aunt Mildred."

Chapter 14

Monday's rehearsal had been the worst yet. Mrs. Cole had misplaced her script. Fanshawe had whinged interminably about having to learn new lines. And Graham had known, even before the words were spoken, that the scenes he had labored for the better part of three days to rewrite were swill.

They lacked Julia's deftness, her lightness of touch. Once he had read her suggestions, nothing in Blackadder's ordinary style sounded quite right.

For the first hour he had sat in the back of the theater, ready to assist her with the door. He had divided his gaze between his box, lest she had decided to observe from a distance, and the stage, where he imagined her bright eyes and mischievous smile as Perpetua Philpot brought a poor poet to the brink of despair and made the audience half in love with her for it.

When it became clear she had no intention of coming his rescue, he had reminded himself that fascination with the clever critic was to be expected. After all, had he not once been almost seduced by Miss on Scene's compliments? Then she had delivered the death blow—that snide remark about pity—and now she would be justly punished in the end.

Not long into the second hour, he had stridden to the foot of the stage, told the actors of Blackadder's disappointment at their efforts in no uncertain terms, and gone back to Half Moon Street to berate Keynes about his lack of progress in discovering the identity of Miss on Scene.

On Tuesday, when no rehearsal had been called, he ordered his curricle and set out in a southerly direction. Over the Thames. In the general vicinity of Clapham, as it happened. Not that he had any intention of stopping. He certainly didn't wonder which of the stately, modern houses belonged to the Widow Hayes. He was just passing through into the country for a longer drive. The horses wanted the exercise. And he needed fresh air, somewhere away from Mayfair.

Far away from the theater and everything—everyone—associated with it.

Only when Clapham Common was far behind him did he loosen his grip on the reins, allow himself to take in his surroundings. To either side of a narrow lane lay rolling fields, some fallow for the impending winter, others awaiting a final harvest of grain, all of them constrained by brown, scraggly hedgerows.

Except for the sheep dotting a distant pasture,

none of it reminded him of the Highlands. Too flat, too cultivated, too . . . English. But something about the countryside made him think with longing of Dunstane. Despite the pains and travails associated with the place, when all was said and done, it was still his home.

He wanted, quite suddenly, to write. Not the painstaking—and, he feared, ultimately pointless—revisions to *The Poison Pen*, which required too much coffee to begin and too much whisky to continue. Something fresh. Something with a bit more heart and a bit less rancor.

Something that probably wouldn't sell a single ticket.

He tried to push away the peculiar mood. He could hardly afford such an indulgence. But he hadn't quite succeeded in dismissing the idea when his gaze fell upon a house—a cottage, really, with stone walls and a slate roof. It sat alone amidst fields whose crops had already been taken in, at the end of a straight drive whose tracks showed little sign of recent wear. No smoke rose from the chimney.

He slowed his horses enough to take a cursory inspection of the place. Too well-kept to have been abandoned, he judged. But clearly uninhabited at present. Though rarely given to romance, his mind began to concoct a story about the owner, some star-eyed but sturdy fellow who had set out on an adventure and left his sensible neighbors shaking their heads.

A mile farther on, he came to a village. Thirsty enough to bear conversation with strangers, he went into the pub to ask for a pint and something to eat. The beamed ceiling of the Spindle and Plow was low enough that he had to stoop. Both his entrance and his question to the barman about the solitary cottage were met with chary looks.

"Belongs to Squire Brereton, like everythin' else in these parts," the man said, turning toward a nearby cask.

"He's away for the winter?"

A foaming mug of ale was his only answer.

The girl who brought his food was more talkative. "You're Scottish, ain't ye?" she demanded as she laid before him a trencher of pale-yellow cheese, cold mutton, and crusty bread.

Graham fished for a coin and slid it across the rough-hewn table to her. "Aye."

"I heard ye ask himself about Brereton Cottage." At Graham's encouraging nod, she went on. "The squire had it fixed up for his second son and the girl he was to marry. Then the boy announced he were going off to war—said it were his duty. Guess his girl didn't agree. She packed up and left in the middle of the night not a week later."

"Alone?"

The girl's knowing grin revealed a missing tooth. "You look like a clever fellow. What d'ye think?"

So much for his imagined tale of noble adventure; the tawdry truth was far more suited to Blackadder's usual fare.

He nodded again, more curtly this time, and picked up his knife, grateful when the girl took those for signs of dismissal.

The Spindle and Plow's scattering of patrons showed little interest in him, though he overheard a few words exchanged about his curricle that made him smile behind his bread and cheese. Once he'd drained his mug, he steeled himself for the return to Town, the playhouse, and the problems that awaited him there, so far removed from young Mr. Brereton's bravery and betrayal.

A shadow fell across the table. He dragged his gaze upward to find a man standing there this time, a fellow somewhere between thirty and forty years of age, clad in dark garments.

"Tetley," he said, thrusting out a hand. "I'm the curate here. But I also handle matters of business for Squire Brereton when he's away."

The double duty made some sense, Graham supposed. Tetley was surely the most literate man in the village, and his profession doubtless gave him a reputation for trustworthiness, though whether that reputation was deserved or not was another question.

Reluctantly, Graham shook his offered hand. "McKay."

His surname no longer rose more naturally to his tongue than his title. But here—in what felt like the middle of nowhere, despite being at most a dozen miles from London—he was determined to cling to something like anonymity.

Uninvited, the curate slipped into the chair opposite. "Kitty tells me you're interested in Brereton Cottage."

Regretting his decision to stop at the little pub, Graham made no answer.

But Tetley was undaunted. "I can offer it to you on very reasonable terms."

Astonished, Graham made a scoffing noise in

his throat as he shook his head. He opened his mouth to decline in no uncertain terms. But from somewhere came the words, "How much?"

He didn't need another house. At such an extravagance, Keynes would peer at him disapprovingly over the tops of his spectacles. He might even dare to mutter something critical beneath his breath.

But the appeal of a place with no connection to Graham's past or even to the rest of his present life was too strong.

"How much to rent the cottage until next quarter day?" he clarified. Once the play was over, he would return to Dunstane. He might never come this way again.

Tetley couldn't hide his disappointment; clearly, he had hoped for more than a month. But he named a number that wasn't unreasonable.

Graham countered nonetheless; what sort of Scotsman wouldn't try to drive a bargain? "And I will expect to take possession straightaway."

After a moment's hesitation, Tetley nodded and signaled to the barman. "Have another pint, sir. I'll have Mrs. Tetley freshen up the place for you."

His mother? Graham wondered. *Or his wife?*

"No need," he declared, unfolding himself from the chair as he reached into his breast pocket for a pair of banknotes. "That should be enough to trust me with the key."

"Of course, sir." Tetley stood. "I'll just—I won't be a moment."

Graham met the curate again in the inn yard a few minutes later, where a lad—the barman's son, to all appearances—stood holding the reins of his curricle and handed them over with a sigh of envy.

Breathless from having hurried off somewhere and back again, Tetley extended a heavy iron key. "You're sure you wouldn't—"

"Nay." It hardly mattered what the man had been about to suggest. Graham was too eager to examine the cottage, to seize this strange urge to take on something new.

He arrived at Brereton Cottage certain he'd made a mistake. A house, empty for months—*years*, for all he knew. He imagined the dust, the damp air. No provisions. No kindling. Christ, but he was a fool. Tetley would be sniggering into his tea as he regaled the evening crowd at the Spindle and Plow with the tale of the daft Scotsman who'd paid twice what the place was worth.

Fitting the heavy key to the lock, he pushed the door inward on surprisingly silent hinges. Ghostly shapes greeted him: the furniture, hidden away beneath holland covers. He strode across the sitting room to open a window. A fresh autumn breeze soon cleared the stale air. He dragged the cover off a chair near the fireplace, then another from a low table. The furnishings were old-fashioned but of a respectable quality. Squire Brereton had obviously wanted good things for his second son.

Upstairs he found two bedchambers, almost identical. Both beds were unmade. Impossible to determine which had been intended for the poor couple's marital bower.

He found sheets in a chest, perfectly clean and dry and scented with sprigs of lavender. With some effort, he managed to cover one of the plump, wool-stuffed mattresses. Then he hung his coat on a peg, rolled up his sleeves, and went downstairs to tend to the horses and draw water from the well.

The labor felt like more honest work than any he had done for some time. Not that he was entirely a stranger to working with his hands. Though improved now, for many years, conditions at Dunstane had been such that he could not afford simply to sit behind a desk. Such physical demands had also provided a much-needed outlet for his frustrations.

But even as he fetched and carried, his head buzzed with ideas, characters who demanded their story be told. Once the horses were settled, he went inside, lit a fire, and cursed himself for not having brought anything to write on.

Even that, however, the little house provided. In the drawer of a table, he found pencils and a few sheets of letter paper. Perhaps the would-be Mrs. Brereton had left a note when she'd flown.

But why should he assume that *she* had been in the wrong? Perhaps she was to be married to the farmer's son against her wishes. Perhaps young Brereton would have treated her ill.

A rap at the back door startled him into renewed awareness of his surroundings. He was already several pages deep in notes for . . . something. A new play? He wasn't quite sure. Not a satire, in any case. A story that still held out some hope.

Sunlight was rapidly fading from the sky, and the air coming through the still-open window had turned cold. He stopped to close it before going to the door.

Outside stood the girl from the pub—he didn't remember her name—with a shawl wrapped around her head and shoulders and a basket hanging from one arm. "Mrs. Tetley thought you'd be wantin' dinner," she explained, gesturing with the basket. "And I offered to bring it. Save her the trip."

"Most kind of you." He took the laden basket from the girl with one hand and fished in his waistcoat pocket for a coin with the other.

She shook her head. "No need for that, sir. I, er . . ." She swept a toe across the ground in front of her. "If you'd like me to come in, I'd be lief to light a fire for you and straighten up the place," she suggested, as if certain that a gentleman would be incapable of either task.

It was not all she intended to offer, he could guess, though she was hardly half his age and no one with whom he wished to dally. He turned to one side just enough that she could see past him into the room, lit by the glowing hearth. "I've managed on my own, thank you," he said, pressing the coins into her work-roughened palm. Sensing defeat, her protests faded, and he closed the door between them.

I've always *managed on my own.*

Well, not always. He'd had help from time to time. Simon Keynes, for one, had done much to help him save Dunstane—both the title and the estate—from ruin. But for the most part, solitude had been his lot since he'd started at school. He'd never minded it. Fewer demands, fewer expectations. His own thoughts were usually good company.

Though there were times, of course, when a man wanted something else. Something more.

He placed the basket on the kitchen table and began to unpack its contents: a piping-hot earthenware crock filled with some sort of stew, a loaf of bread, a bottle of wine, more of the same cheese he'd had earlier in the day, and a few fresh apples. What would Mrs. Tetley say if he knew she'd sent such simple fare to a peer of the realm? Though, truth be told, he preferred it, even when it ran counter to his London chef's notions of consequence.

After ladling some of the stew into a bowl and pouring a glass of wine, he broke off a hunk of the bread and carried everything into the sitting room, where he had spent the afternoon scribbling down every wild idea that had popped into his head. At the risk of spoiling his appetite, he should review what he'd written, to see if there was anything of substance there.

Instead, he sat back in his chair, sipped at the wine, and let his thoughts wander to Julia.

He knew better than to be surprised by her absence from Monday's rehearsal. It was, in one sense, what he'd wanted—to push her away, to keep himself from getting closer. An entanglement was the very last thing he desired.

All the same, if that strange moment in the empty theater had been the end of things, he regretted not giving in to his urge to kiss her.

Perhaps, if he'd kissed her, she would have come back.

Now, in the twilight of the day, with a glass of

wine in his belly and his mind drained of the ideas that had harried him all afternoon, he could relax enough to admit she had been the force behind today's drive into the country, to this empty, isolated house.

He had chased a wild hare, half to tamp down his need for her, to remind himself of the pleasures, the necessity, of being alone.

And half because she, with her bright eyes and mischievous smile and way with a pen, had reignited a joy in wordplay that he had all but lost.

She would laugh to see him here. Not in the malicious fashion of audiences at a Blackadder play. She would be amused by his impulsiveness. *Bemused*, he corrected himself, remembering her expression the day he'd dropped her at Porter's Bookshop. She didn't know what to make of him, of his gruff, taciturn ways.

And she didn't like wanting him, any more than he liked wanting her.

Draining his glass, he pushed himself more upright in the chair, forced himself to eat the bowl of Mrs. Tetley's good stew and a few bites of bread, then carried everything back into the kitchen. After storing the food, he shrugged into his greatcoat and grabbed an apple, munching away at its tart crispness as he strode to the outbuilding to check on the horses. Fallon whickered softly; Findlay nosed the apple core out of his palm. A sleek tabby cat wound around his ankles but refused an offer to be petted.

Finding everything secure and settled, he returned to the house, banked the fire, and went upstairs, though it was hours earlier than he usually retired for the night. Nonetheless, he found himself drained by the events of the day.

In a room lit only by the moon, he stripped off his clothes and slipped into bed. When he'd started out as a writer, the best ideas for his plays had come to him in those hazy moments between waking and sleep.

But tonight, what came to him were more thoughts of Julia.

Decidedly improper thoughts.

If his strange fatigue weren't enough, the chill in the air ought to have put a stop to them. He rolled onto his belly, hoping the rough, cold sheets against his bare skin would have the desired effect.

A few moments later, he caught himself grinding his hips into the mattress as he relived their first kiss in his mind: her hot, soft mouth and eager groan.

You're no' a randy lad anymore, he chided himself, flopping onto his back again. Though admittedly, schoolboy Graham would have been impressed by the way his cockstand tented the bed linens.

It would be tawdry and desperate to frig himself. But his body didn't seem to care. He slid his palm down his belly and cupped his aching bollocks before taking his cock in a firm grip and jerking at his flesh almost frantically.

He would scratch the itch and be done with it.

Stave off this foolish need.

In any case, she would never know about this place. This night.

She would never know—

He would never—

"Ah, God," he groaned into the darkness as his legs went rigid and his spine bowed against his impending climax. He was worse than a randy lad, spending almost as soon as he'd begun, and ending something less than satisfied.

What if he never saw her again?

When the sun rose Wednesday morning, he contemplated the prospect of another day in Brereton Cottage, surrounded by silence. A few more hours with only his own thoughts for company might yet do him some good—provided he could keep those thoughts in check.

Rehearsals for *The Poison Pen* would go on without him. Perhaps Fanshawe and the rest would perform better without Blackadder's patron looming over them, correcting their every breath.

But in the end, he dragged himself out of bed to eat cold stew, hitched up the horses, and returned to Town. Unshaven and unkempt, dressed in yesterday's clothes, he arrived at Covent Garden at half past two. Hailing the most responsible-looking of the ragged boys who hung about the theater, he handed over the reins of his curricle, squared his shoulders, and went inside.

Chapter 15

When the massive door at the back of the theater swung open, Julia refused to turn and look. It would be someone who painted scenery, or another actor. She would not allow herself to appear either eager or disappointed.

Even if she *had* been foolish enough to imagine that Lord Dunstane attended every rehearsal.

She was here to discover the inner workings of the play, to protect her name, to save the magazine. She had not come for him.

And she would remind herself of that until she believed it.

When she had arrived, Mr. Fanshawe and Mrs. Cole had exchanged words—about her, she could guess. But they seemed to have agreed she must have Lord Dunstane's permission to attend the rehearsal. When Julia had quietly slipped into her present seat, three rows back from the stage, and made it clear that she intended to observe in silence, they shrugged and largely ignored her.

Without the critical eye and tongue of Blackadder's patron, the actors relaxed into their roles. In their skilled hands—and when they weren't being questioned at every turn, they were indeed skilled—the characters came alive. Details of the story, disjointed on the page, now fit neatly together in her mind.

And as she listened, she noted a few significant changes, too, which only made her task more difficult. How could she possibly prepare a defense when the battle lines kept shifting? She would have to write to Lady Stalbridge this evening and—

"Rough night, m'lord?" Mr. Sawyer called out with a laugh, breaking character—though only slightly. The poet's brother was witty and wicked. Audiences would love him, precisely because they knew they shouldn't.

Julia refused to look over her shoulder. Not even when the answer to Mr. Sawyer's question was delivered in a soft Scottish brogue.

"Aye, rough." A few rows behind her, a bench creaked as he sat down. "Just the way I like it."

I'm a demanding lover.

The words, both the memory of those from the past and the echo of those in the present, set something aquiver inside her, made her curl her fingers around the front edge of her seat.

"Let us hope the lady's wishes were also taken into account," said Mrs. Cole with a huff of disapproval.

"Oh, aye," Lord Dunstane answered coolly—

though his voice made Julia flush. "Never you fear about that."

From the side of the stage, Mr. Fanshawe cleared his throat. "May we continue? With your permission, of course, my lord." The mulish set of his jaw made clear how little he appreciated having to ask.

Lord Dunstane must have granted his permission with a nod or a gesture, for the rehearsal resumed a moment later, the two principals once more back-to-back at their desks, Mrs. Cole reading with great satisfaction of the poet's death while Mr. Sawyer looked over his brother's papers and plotted his revenge.

"Better," declared Lord Dunstane when they came to a stop, not disguising his surprise. "Livelier." A long pause followed, and from the expressions on the actors' faces, she could imagine his contemplative pose. "Hearing the second act, I wonder now whether it wouldn't improve matters further to shorten the first? Get to the heart of the conflict."

Mr. Fanshawe bristled. "I beg your pardon, sir. If you cut my lines, how will the audience grasp the source of the animosity between the younger Mr. Briggs and Miss Philpot?"

"I think they might feel more sympathy for your character, Georgie," said Sawyer, rocking back onto the hind legs of his chair, "if they heard less of his doggerel."

Mr. Fanshawe's eyes flashed defensively, as if he had written the awful poetry himself.

"What say you?"

No mistaking that Lord Dunstane's quiet question was intended for her. She had not heard him move, but he was closer now, nonetheless—close enough that the actors couldn't overhear what he'd asked her.

At last, she dared a backward glance and found him standing just over her right shoulder. He did indeed look as if he'd tumbled out of bed at two o'clock in the afternoon. Hardly unheard of for a lord, she supposed. His linen lacked its usual crispness. His coppery hair was mussed.

Somehow, his disheveled state made him handsomer still.

She turned back toward the stage and pushed to her feet. "The problem," she announced in a voice that carried, "isn't Mr. Fanshawe's poetry. The problem is Perpetua Philpot's motivation."

That got Mrs. Cole's attention. Lord Dunstane murmured, "Go on."

"We're asked to believe she writes these heartless reviews because she's been jilted by a poet. But it's quite clear she's a poet herself—and a good one, not some mere poetess." In popular parlance, the feminine version of anything was always the lesser. The term was bitter on her tongue. "If Mr. Blackadder would help us see her instead as a thwarted artist—"

"Audiences might have some sympathy for her, too," finished Mrs. Cole with a nod of something like solidarity for Julia.

"But I forgot," added Julia, tilting her chin to direct her words to Lord Dunstane, though she did not meet his eye. "The playwright doesn't require such a complex emotional response from those of us in the seats. It might interfere with our willingness to view her only as an object to f—"

Whether she possessed the courage to utter that shocking word remained unknown. Lord Dunstane spoke over her.

"Thank you for your insight, Miss Ah—*Hayes.*"

He'd almost addressed her as Miss Addison. *An honest slip,* she told herself—but also a stark reminder that he had the power to ruin her if he chose.

She must learn to disguise her frustration.

"That's enough for today." Lord Dunstane dismissed the actors, chipping away still more at Mr. Fanshawe's role. "Blackadder will be pleased to learn of your progress," he called after them as they filed out through the back of the stage as before, talking and joking with one another. Mr. Sawyer tried to put his arm around Mrs. Cole's waist; she slapped his hand away, though without rancor.

When they were gone, Lord Dunstane stepped into the aisle. "You weren't here on Monday," he chided as he gestured for her to accompany him out.

"No." The climb toward the door was steeper than she remembered, but he did not offer his arm. "My aunt needed me."

"Your . . . *aunt.*" She heard a thread of amusement in his voice. Clearly, he recalled having been corrected on that very matter the night they met.

But today, she wanted him to remember she wasn't alone in the world.

They passed into the vestibule in silence. The bustle of preparation for tonight's show had already begun. A tall, thin man with a beaky nose inspected floral arrangements, while maids tidied and swept around him; ticket sellers hurried to their posts at the snap of the new box manager's fingers.

On the pavement, Lord Dunstane signaled for a hackney. When a cab rolled to a stop before them, he opened the door and helped her in, holding her hand a moment longer than was strictly necessary. Uncertain, she swept her gaze over his face, taking in the sharp angle of his jaw, hardly softened by a scruff of reddish-brown beard, and his moss-green eyes, underlined by shadow.

"Make whatever excuse to Mrs. Hayes you think best, Julia," he said. "But be here the day after tomorrow, with a draft of those edits you suggested. The play needs you."

What had looked in the dimly lit theater like rakishness, the mercilessly gray afternoon revealed to be weariness. Worry. Over *The Poison Pen*?

He must have wagered a great deal on Blackadder's success.

At last, he released her, closed the carriage door between them, and slapped his palm against the roof to signal the cabbie to depart.

She looked back at him through the dirty glass as he watched her go, her heart in her throat. *The play needs you*, he had said.

Was it her imagination, or had he meant, "*I* need you"?

I have him right where I want him, she wrote to Lady Stalbridge the next evening, after pointing out to Lord Dunstane that the loss of a loved one would likely dampen Reginald Briggs's creative output. He'd responded by trimming a few of Mr. Sawyer's harshest lines.

She didn't dare tell the countess, or Aunt Mildred, the whole truth.

How Lord Dunstane's stricken expression when she'd spoken of grief had made her want to gather him to her breast and soothe the hurt that she was beginning to suspect hid behind the cold, hard mask he wore.

How she had begun to wonder whether the bond between him and Ransom Blackadder might be more than patron and playwright. Brothers, as the script suggested?

Whatever drove him, she felt certain it was more than a return on his investment.

The following week, he'd called for daily rehearsals as opening night drew nearer. Monday and Tuesday the cast went through the entirety of the first two acts, with a rationally softened Perpetua and a marginally less arrogant Briggs, thanks to a combination of Blackadder's edits and Julia's. Julia was no longer certain her changes always made the play better—some of its humor had gone hand in hand with its sting. But she couldn't worry about that, couldn't worry about anything but saving the magazine.

Certainly, she couldn't worry about Lord Dunstane or wonder what he'd meant by those whispered words, why his thoughts were often far away.

Wednesday began rehearsals for Act Three, which, according to the script she had read, called for the critic's exposure and eventual destruction.

Undercutting its message would take some doing. On the first day, she did nothing but listen and plan.

On Thursday, however, she arrived with her script marked up with new ideas.

"Up you get." With no more fanfare than a flick of his wrist, Lord Dunstane ordered her to the stage. "Watch her," he said to Mrs. Cole, who had given up protesting Julia's incursions.

When Mr. Fanshawe called the scene, she spoke the lines as originally written.

"Again," said Lord Dunstane in his quiet but forceful way as he stood and walked to the end of the row where he'd been seated for the past half an hour.

This time, she dared to incorporate a few of her changes.

"See," he said to Mrs. Cole when the scene was done. "Sweet, not sour."

Mr. Sawyer made a show of licking his lips, to the amusement of the men standing just offstage.

Lord Dunstane bounded up the steps. She thought, for a moment, that he would reprimand Mr. Sawyer's bawdy behavior. But he stopped beside Mr. Fanshawe in the wings and explained away his decision to move by rubbing his neck with one hand, evidently easing the stiffness brought on by sitting below and looking up at the stage. "Again."

Julia returned to Perpetua's mark, drew a breath as if about to utter her lines, and then hesitated. "I've been thinking," she said. "I wonder if it wouldn't work better to—"

"Jesus." Mr. Fanshawe tossed his script to the ground. "I signed on for a play by Ransom Black-adder, not Miss Hayes."

Lord Dunstane swept the tattered paper aside with his foot, sending some of the pages fluttering into the pit. "Perhaps you'd rather not act at all. In this play, or any other."

"Nay, m'lord," Mr. Fanshawe ground out as he set about collecting his script. "Apologies. I only meant—"

"I know what you meant. Go on," he said to Julia, jerking his chin as he crossed his arms over his chest. "Let's hear it."

She quailed beneath his cool regard and nearly lost her courage. Had he too grown tired of her interference?

"The first rehearsal I attended, you said that everyone ought to want to—" She willed herself not to blush. "That they ought to desire Perpetua Philpot. That if they did, it would make it easier for her to stab them in the backs."

He regarded her with wry amusement—she'd still never seen a genuine smile. "Aye. I did say . . . *something* to that effect."

"Well," she said, forging bravely—or foolishly—ahead. "Shouldn't Reginald Briggs want her too?"

"What makes you so certain he doesn't?"

"He says the most awful things about her, in his poetry."

"That's how some men declare themselves, Miss Hayes," said Mr. Sawyer, chuckling darkly as she tried to block out the memory of his conversations about women with Lord Dunstane, the rakish exchange about his *rough night* in particular. "Some men can't show their feelings any other way."

"In some cases"—Lord Dunstane pushed away from the proscenium and began to walk across the stage, tossing the words over his shoulder to Sawyer as he passed between the man and Julia—"not even when they are being paid to act. Scene."

He spoke the direction so quietly that she didn't immediately realize what he meant. Not until she saw that he'd stepped to Mr. Sawyer's mark did she understand that he intended to act the part of Briggs.

One of the unusual—sometimes, she was tempted to say *remarkable*—things about *The Poison Pen* was that the principals never actually met, though they were onstage together throughout, verbally sparring with another. But they spoke to one another only through their writing, from opposite sides of a stage divided, as it were, by a partition, albeit an invisible one. They lived in two worlds—even the scenery was split between the artist's garret and the lady's boudoir—worlds that had no point of overlap, save for his poetry and her reviews.

"'You squander your gift on the masses.'" Julia read Perpetua's line from the script. She could not meet Lord Dunstane's steady gaze.

"'Your only talent is to call forth the mob,'" he recited in his turn. He knew everyone's lines by heart.

His commanding presence served him well onstage. She wondered whether he had acted before. Though his voice was still quiet, she suspected he could be heard in the farthest seats.

Back and forth the exchange went, the two of them speaking to one another, past one another, over one another, coming ever closer to the invisible wall that divided them. She tried to invest Perpetua's words with anguish, and sometimes with heat. Perpetua didn't really despise the poet, she had decided. Or at least, not for his poetry. She envied his popularity, his creativity. His freedom.

As the scene wound to a close, Julia drew herself up to her full height, a meager attempt to counterbalance Lord Dunstane's imposing stature—Mr. Sawyer was not nearly so tall—and tossed her head defiantly. "'You claim I can't even read—'"

Lord Dunstane took one final step toward the center of the stage. "'You say I'm not worth the printer's ink—'"

They were standing so close now that when his chest rose on those words, his cravat nearly brushed her upturned chin.

Then the shared line, spoken together, that ended the scene and cemented their tangled fates: "'Yet we both know, you write for me alone.'"

For a moment, they held their positions, no movement but their breathing, the imaginary wall between them thin as a pane of glass. No, thinner. A skim of ice at the edge of a quiet pool as winter turned to spring. It would melt away at the slightest touch—if either of them dared to reach out a hand.

Mr. Sawyer broke the spell with mocking applause. "Very instructive, sir. I see now what you mean. They think they want to kill one another." He had gone to stand beside Mr. Fanshawe and now jostled him with an elbow, much to the other actor's annoyance. "But really, they'd rather kiss."

Julia turned sharply away under the guise of returning the script to the desk.

When it came to disguising her growing feelings for Lord Dunstane, she'd turned out to be a terrible actress.

"Now you know what that looks like," sniped Mrs. Cole, "maybe next time you'll make a more convincing job of it."

"That's enough for today." Lord Dunstane put an end to their bickering. "Go home. All of you."

Julia trudged off the stage with the rest of the actors, they to the dressing rooms below, she to the entrance of the theater. At the door, she paused to glance back.

Indifferent as to whether his command had been obeyed, he had seated himself at Briggs's desk and was swiftly scrawling something across one of the prop scraps of paper.

Probably more suggested revisions. Though part of her wished it might be a letter to Blackadder, resigning from his commission as the playwright's go-between and washing his hands of the whole production.

As much as she wanted to put a stop to Blackadder, she needed to know that the play wasn't the only thing drawing her and Lord Dunstane together.

The next afternoon, Friday, she was settling Mrs. Hayes for her afternoon nap as usual, when a rap sounded at the front door. She heard Daniel open it, the muffled exchange of masculine voices.

In another moment, the boy appeared on the threshold.

"There's a gentleman downstairs, asking for you."

"For me?"

"Yes, miss. A Scotsman, with the grandest rig I ever saw!"

Her heart had already begun to pound, even before he'd added those unmistakable details. Slipping past Daniel, she hurried down the stairs, then paused at the landing to collect herself.

Lord Dunstane stood, hat in hand, his tall, lean frame almost filling the narrow hall. "Today's rehearsal has been canceled. I thought you should know."

"Thank you." She dipped into a curtsy, in part to hide her bafflement. "But you hardly needed to come all this way. You might simply have sent word."

"Aye," he agreed.

"I wrote out those revisions I suggested yesterday," she began.

"Later." He waved her words away. "Since we're free, I thought we might go for that drive." His expression—she hardly knew how to read it.

Or perhaps she knew exactly how to read it. She'd seen it in his eyes before. The intensity of his gray-green gaze drove away every thought of the play, the magazine, Aunt Mildred's caution that she must be discreet.

She could only recall how it felt to be close to him.

His as-yet-unfulfilled promise of satisfaction.

She nodded. "Just let me get my things."

Chapter 16

Beyond Clapham Common, Graham gave the horses their heads. Findlay and Fallon knew the way well enough by now. They'd made the trip to Brereton Cottage half a dozen times since Tetley had given him the key.

Beside him, Julia gasped. The wind whipped the rose-colored ribbons of her bonnet. One small hand slipped from beneath the heavy woolen lap blanket he'd tucked around her, protection against the bite of the November air. For a moment, it seemed as if she meant to urge him to slow down. He considered telling her she was in no danger.

But that wouldn't entirely be true.

Her gloved fingertips settled lightly on his forearm, tracing the subtle movement of his bones and sinews, as if seeking a share of the power that flowed up through the reins.

He recalled their conversation about racing curricles the first time he'd driven her. She had come today of her own free will.

Perhaps she didn't want to be perfectly safe.

Shifting the reins into his left hand, he wrapped his right arm around her shoulders, snugging their bodies closer still. Curving his fingers over hers, he pressed the reins into her hands. "Take them."

She glanced up at his face. Astonishment flared in her eyes. But she didn't refuse.

Once her grip was secure, he released her hands, though he kept his arm around her. Sensing the change in command, the horses shifted their pace. The reins slackened in her grasp.

"Oh," she breathed, the sound hardly audible above the clatter of hooves and the rattle of wheels. But he'd heard that soft gasp of disappointment before, on the night they had met.

And he never wanted to hear it again.

"Did you wish them to run away with you?" he teased.

"Yes, please."

Despite the chill wind, heat surged through him. "Then hold tight."

With the toe of his boot, he rattled the whip, still in its socket on the dash. Fallon started, Findlay leaned into the bit, and the pair were off, running against nothing but the cloud-lowered sky.

Fields flew past, and soon the stone cottage appeared on the horizon. Taking her hands in his once more, he eased the horses to a trot.

"Are they tired?" she asked.

Findlay and Fallon touched noses—laughing together, he imagined. "Nay," he said as he steered them onto the drive.

"Then why are we stopping?"

"Too many questions. You'll have to be patient for the answers."

The answering wrinkle that appeared between her brows revealed that patience was not one of her many virtues—as if he had not already guessed as much.

The horses slowed to a walk as they rounded the corner of the cottage and came to stand in front of the barn. He swung down, then lifted her from the curricle and nodded for her to take a seat on a nearby stump.

"Where are the servants?" she mused as he unhitched the pair and began to wipe the foam from their flanks. The tabby barn cat had emerged from one of its hiding spots, and she was trying to coax it closer, seemingly paying Graham little mind. But when he strode to the well to get fresh water, he knew that her gaze followed, as if she were intrigued by watching him work.

At last, he held out an elbow to escort her inside. As she came to her feet, she tilted her head, still inquisitive. "Aren't you at least going to tell me whose house this is?"

He laid a hand over hers where it rested against his forearm, pinning her to his side, as much to keep himself steady as to keep her from flight. "I decided it was high time you met Ransom Blackadder."

He had determined on this course of action a few minutes before the end of yesterday's rehearsal, when he'd at long last allowed himself to get close enough to truly see Julia. To risk being seen. When he'd discovered that the yearning inside him was matched by the yearning written on her face. The moment when wanting her had overtaken every other thought—even the success of *The Poison Pen.*

For years, he had built walls: between Castle Dunstane and the London stage, between Perpetua Philpot and Ransom Briggs, around his own heart. But it was time for those walls to come down. And he must be the one to dismantle them.

This play would be the end of Blackadder. And, if Julia were willing, the beginning of something new.

But would she be willing, once she knew the truth?

"Notorious rake and ne'er-do-well Random Blackadder lives in a country cottage?" she demanded, incredulous.

Slipping free, she charged up the pair of oak plank steps, through the back door, and into the kitchen, where they were greeted by well-stocked cupboards and a clean-swept hearth. He shrugged out of his greatcoat and hung it on a peg. Everything was neat as a pin, not because he had left here the last time with any notion of returning with company, but because he wouldn't have it otherwise.

He'd had enough messiness for a lifetime.

With the sweep of one arm, he waved her through to the sitting room. "I'll make tea."

While he lit the spirit lamp to boil the kettle and prepared a plate of bread and butter, he watched out of the corner of one eye as she tossed her bonnet and pelisse over the arm of a chair and began to inspect her surroundings, the questions continuing thick and fast.

"But isn't he Scottish? Why would he take a place in Surrey? Do you visit him here often? Where is he now? Wasn't he expecting you today?"

Just before he went in with the tray, she finally fell silent. He found her seated on the horsehair sofa, staring fixedly at the sheaf of notes on the low table in front of her. She might recognize the hand, he supposed; she'd seen the revisions he'd claimed to be delivering on behalf of Blackadder.

But these papers were pinned in place by a crystal paperweight in the design of a thistle, superimposed with the letter *D*—Dunstane's seal, and the one ornament he'd brought from the house in Half Moon Street.

"Oh. How silly of me." She darted a glance in his direction, then focused once more on the paperweight, which magnified the words beneath it. "*You're*—"

"Yes."

"I thought . . . perhaps . . . brothers . . ."

Ah. Like Reginald Briggs and his hapless sibling. But why should he be surprised that she'd worked it out thus? He'd known from the start that she was clever.

"I haven't any brothers." He filled a cup with steaming brew and passed it to her. "At least, not anymore."

The cup rattled in its saucer as she accepted it from him. "Wh-why are you telling me this?"

He couldn't say what reaction he'd expected to his revelation. Anger, perhaps. But not this. Not

something that might too easily be mistaken for . . .
fear?

"Because once I'd entrusted you with my play, it
seemed a rather pointless secret to go on keeping."

"Eh-en-entrusted me?" She struggled to frame
the word, then tried to disguise her bewilderment
by taking a sip of tea. She gasped as it scalded her
throat.

He sat down beside her on the sofa, lifting the
saucer from her trembling fingers and returning it
to the tray. "Surely you've noticed that I didn't
allow Fanshawe or the others to have their way
with the script."

She gnawed on her lower lip, then nodded.

"And how did you explain such unaccountable
behavior to yourself?"

"I, uh," she rasped, then swallowed and squared
her shoulders and met his eyes with a steadier
gaze. "I assumed at first it was a sort of . . . flirtation. Because you believed I would be flattered
and let you have your way with *me* in turn."

She wasn't far wrong. Turning slightly, he
stretched his arm along the back of the sofa without touching her. "Why 'at first'? Do you imagine
my motives have changed?"

"Haven't they?" She jerked her gaze to the far
corner of the room. "After the first rehearsal,
when I . . . but you didn't—"

"Kiss you?"

"I decided I had misunderstood."

He slid his hand down the sofa's slick back. At
the nape of her neck, a single dark curl had
sprung from her coiffure, teased loose by the wind

perhaps. He twined it around his first finger. "I would no' have wanted to stop at kisses. And Covent Garden is no place to—"

"Speaking from experience, I suppose." She spoke over him, turning back to face him even as she tried to slip free from his touch.

But the lock of hair only wound tighter. "Aye," he agreed with a leering grin.

Her whole body went still, and the spark in her eyes was suddenly cold, ice rather than fire. "So. You've brought me all this way because 'Ransom Blackadder' wants to make a conquest of me. I take it you've decided that 'The Playwright and the Actress' will draw bigger audiences than 'The Poor Lady's Companion and the Earl.' "

"Julia," he chided, releasing the curl. "I would never—"

"You would," she countered, her dark brows dipping into a frown. "You *have*. Perpetua Philpot is modeled after an actual critic of your plays."

"That's hardly the same."

"Is it not?" She jutted out her chin, narrowing the scant distance between them. The posture reminded him of the night they'd met, when what he'd taken for apprehension had been quickly replaced by audacity.

"You take a keen interest in the fate of some anonymous hack."

"*Anonymous hack?* That's rich, coming from—"

He silenced her the best way he knew how, by covering her mouth with his. She gave no sign of resistance to his kiss. But neither did she relent. Her posture remained perfectly straight, her lips pliant but still.

When he pulled back, he met her wounded gaze. "The whole world knows Blackadder is cruel and heartless," she said flatly. "The more fool I for hoping you might be the better man."

Those words brought him to his feet. "I'm sorry."

Sorry for kissing you against your will. Sorry I cannot be the one you need.

Desperate for something to do with himself, he plucked up her outer garments from the chair where she'd casually discarded them and carried them into the kitchen to hang beside his. "I revealed something to you I've never told another soul. What more do you want from me, Julia?"

"I told myself I was coming here today because I wanted the satisfaction I'd been promised." She was staring straight ahead, into the empty hearth, perhaps recalling their exchange in Clearwater's study. "But the truth is . . . I would be satisfied with a genuine smile. Some hint . . . some proof that the man you really are, the man inside, isn't colder and harder yet."

He tipped his forehead against the glass door of a nearby cabinet and found it blessedly cool, a balm to his sudden fever. He'd thought himself prepared to be honest with her.

But his truths weren't the sort a fellow delivered with a smile on his face—and they certainly didn't inspire smiles in return.

Pushing away from the wall, he lurched back toward the sitting room, uncertain where else in the little cottage to go. She gave no sign of noticing when he threw himself into the chair closest to the fireplace.

"I wasn't meant to be Earl of Dunstane." He hoisted himself more upright, just enough to pour more tea, then dashed the contents of the delicate little cup down his throat, wishing it were whisky. "But if I'd never become the earl, 'tis likely I'd never have become Blackadder, either."

Her posture stiffened still more. "You presume I care about your sordid past, my lord."

"Aye," he agreed. "I think you do. Leastways, no other woman has ever fussed over whether the smile I had for her was *genuine*."

Their interest in his mouth had been far less innocent.

Her only response was a slight pursing of her lips.

"Iain was the eldest, the heir, and very like our father he was, too, though I had no notion how much at the time. Father was an old man when he married, older still when I was born, and it wasn't until many years later that I had cause to discover what a rogue he'd been in his younger days, late to wed because he'd been reluctant to settle down.

"But old as he was, he fathered six children, the last of whom took my mother to the grave with her. She'd lost two wee girls already, sisters I cannot even remember. And though my father never seemed to miss them, so long as he had sons and to spare, the sorrow of it had left her weak.

"For a year, it was the four of us: my father; Iain; my younger brother, Rory; and me. Father hadn't a prayer of keeping three boys in check, though, truth be told, he rarely tried. I was nine when he died of a heart complaint. Rory was a lad of five.

And Iain was all of eighteen when he became the new earl."

She blinked, twice. He went on. "Another year saw Iain off to—well, Oxford, he told his guardians and trustees, though it was London where he spent all his time. And I was sent to Harrow—to face the unending torment of my peers."

"Why?"

Her quiet question—the first she'd asked in some time—was nearly lost beneath the sound of her movement as she rose and went to the window overlooking the drive.

"Why Harrow? Because my father had insisted upon it. Or do you mean to ask why they tormented me? Well, then, you may take your choice. Because I was a lanky, awkward lad, never one for a game or gossip." He shrugged. "Or, more often, because I have red hair, a brogue when I'm not careful, a quick tongue, and an even quicker temper. I rose to the flimsiest bait, much to their delight. I fought—and nearly got myself expelled. Then one day, Iain took me with him to Drury Lane to see a play—Molière, it was—and I came to understand that words could do far more damage than fists. After that, instead of fighting, I wrote in secret. Fine speeches, bawdy poems—anything to make fools of the boys who had tried to make a fool of me."

Her shoulders rose and fell on what he presumed to be a silent, wry laugh. "Ah. So that's how Ransom Blackadder got his start."

"Not exactly. That *is* when I first began to sharpen my wit. But Blackadder himself came along later. When I was one and twenty and Iain

the age I am now, he was killed in a duel." He
paused to pour a second cup of tea and sipped
from it more slowly, though it was now almost
cold. "From my perspective as a younger brother,
he'd always seemed a grand fellow. But from the
perspective of a young man who now had the responsibilities of an earldom unexpectedly thrust
upon his shoulders, Iain's raking and whoring and
drinking and gambling took on a decidedly different cast.

"After many years away from Dunstane, I returned to discover it in shambles. Iain had inherited an estate on the edge of ruin and had
gleefully given it a shove. The title had been be-
smirched, the property mortgaged to the hilt.
Thanks to feckless guardians, he'd squandered
Rory's tuition and allowance and left our little
brother to fend for himself. The castle my ances-
tors had defended from invaders was crumbling
away. In a moment of utter despair, searching for
anything that might save us, I was rummaging
through old papers and found those schoolboy
scribbles. I remembered the power I'd felt when
I'd held the pen, how writing had honed my anger
like a blade. And, oh, I was angry. Angrier than I'd
ever been in my life. So I wrote, intending to make
men—myself included—see themselves for the
knaves and fools they are. I invented Ransom
Blackadder."

Julia stood, staring outward, shoulders hunched
inward and hands gripping her upper arms as if
cold. He returned his cup to the table, heaved
himself from the chair, and knelt to light a fire.

"I hadn't any notion at first of making any

money by playwriting," he went on after a few moments, watching the flames devour the kindling and lick along the wood. "Certainly not sufficient funds to dig us out of the hole Iain had left. But it seems I'd underestimated English theatergoers' eagerness to be mocked." Getting to his feet, he returned to his chair. Julia turned at last and held out her hands to the hearth, though she was surely too far away to feel its warmth. "The first play's profits were enough to shore up Castle Dunstane. The second and third paid down the worst of Iain's debts. A few careful investments in other productions brought in still more. And the receipts from *Vice Is Its Own Reward* were to have brought Rory home."

Having no prospects, Rory had joined the army and gone off to fight. Without the means even to buy his brother an officer's commission, Graham hadn't been able to stop him.

"I saw that play," Julia said. "People came in droves." Her reassurance—if indeed it was intended as such—was conveyed with a heavy dose of skepticism at the audience's taste.

"Yes, it did well enough—it made Ransom Blackadder a wealthy man. But the earnings check arrived too late: a week after the letter from Rory's commanding officer, telling me he'd lost his life in some pointless skirmish in this endless war. *An honorable death for king and country,* the officer had the nerve to write."

Whose king? Graham had shouted, the words bouncing from the cold stone walls surrounding him. *Whose country?*

Words were powerful—he'd proven as much, time and time again.

But they hadn't the power to bring his brother back.

Graham had been left utterly alone, with not even a picture to remember his brother by, Rory having been born after the only family portrait had been painted.

A cool hand caressed his cheek. He glanced upward. When had Julia crossed the room and come to stand before him?

"I'm sorry," she whispered. "So very sorry."

The pad of her thumb brushed along his cheekbone, the gesture of one wiping away a tear, though he knew he hadn't shed any. He'd been dry-eyed since the arrival of that letter, the day the last remaining bit of softness in him had turned to stone.

"Nay, lass." He cupped her hand in his, turning hers slightly to press a kiss into her palm. "No Scotsman wants aught to do with pity. I only sought to help you understand how things came to be as they are."

She gazed down at him, the slightest furrow between her dark brows. "Is that when you began writing *The Poison Pen*?"

"Aye—with poison flowing through my veins." He gave her fingers a squeeze, still clinging to her as her hand slid from his face. "That's why it's no' very good."

"And this place?" she asked, glancing around.

"About a week ago, in a fit of frustration—"

"Over the play?"

He swept his eyes over her face. Was that a hint of mischief he saw there?

"Partly," he answered, stretching out one leg so that she now stood between his knees. "Anyway, I went for a drive. I stumbled upon this cottage. And I decided to . . . write." He gestured toward the papers on the table with a motion of his chin. "I set aside *The Poison Pen*, Blackadder, all of it. I let myself remember how it felt to make something new. I'd been so focused on the power writing gave me, I'd forgotten how humbling it could be." Absently, he brushed his thumb over the thin skin of her inner wrist. "I'd been so caught up in my pain, I'd almost forgotten about life's pleasures."

Her expression solemn, she nodded as if she understood. "It's a lovely, quiet spot," she said, glancing about the room before returning her gaze to his face. "Perfect for starting fresh."

"Aye. I've never liked London. Too many people. Too much noise."

She tipped her head to the side, and her eyes twinkled. "But if you hadn't come to London, you would never have met me."

"Aye. That's true."

"So, what happens now?"

He managed a ragged breath. "Well, come opening night, I think Blackadder's done for."

Her brows rose. "Surely your adoring public will forgive one less-than-perfect play."

"Perhaps. But I'm ready to be free of him. Especially if it means I could have—"

You.

One gentle tug of her hand pulled her off balance and sent her tumbling into his lap.

Rather than protest, as he had half expected, she slid her arms around his neck, her fingers toying with his hair where it fell over his collar.

And then she pressed her lips to his.

Chapter 17

Julia found it far easier to imagine that he'd brought her here to seduce her than that he'd intended to lay his life's history at her feet.

Though the two things were not unrelated, for her heart, already susceptible, had become entirely his once he'd opened up about his past.

On occasion, she had caught herself thinking, even hoping, that all his glowering and hard words were naught but a mere papier-mâché mask, disguising the real man beneath. But the metaphor had been truer than she had known. Every tragedy, every trauma in his life had been another sticky, messy layer, clinging to him; he'd smoothed and shaped them around his soul as best he could, until the mask and the man were one and the same.

Now that rough, heavy mask had a crack in it,

made when he'd revealed his biggest secret to her. She trailed her fingers around the sharp angle of his jaw. Here, in this simple cottage, he'd shown her his determination to peel away the broken pieces of his past. He was trying to set himself free.

But if she in turn revealed her biggest secret to him—that she was the reviewer who had so disdainfully spoken of pity, little imagining how it had added to his pain—it would only plaster over that sliver of a crack, sealing off that glimmer of hope forever.

So, she went on kissing him instead.

One of his big hands came up to cup the back of her head. Ah, but she did not think she would ever tire of the sensation of his mouth on hers, soft and firm at once. It made her forget all about the magazine and her dilemma.

"I suppose you tell this story to all the women you bring here?" she teased, when he let her have her breath again.

He drew back, and his brows dove downward. "I've never told this story to another soul."

"What of the girl Mr. Sawyer teased you about the other day? When you came to rehearsal rather . . . rumpled."

"Sawyer." Beneath her, she felt the muscles of his abdomen ripple in a huff of annoyance. "There've been no others since I met you, Julia." His gray-green eyes held hers. "The day I was late to rehearsal, I'd come straight from here, it's true. But if I looked as if I hadn't slept, it's because I laid awake half the night, thinking of you."

"Oh." Perhaps such honeyed words shouldn't

please her, but they did. She shifted her hips against his groin, deliberately provocative. "Only half the night?"

One corner of his mouth twitched—almost a smile. "Naughty lass. What am I going to do with you?"

The answer, it seemed, was to kiss her senseless again. After learning every curve of her lips, he nibbled his way along her jaw to murmur against her ear. "Dare I ask—did you ever lie awake thinking of me?"

Before she could answer, he traced the shell of her ear with the tip of his tongue. "I t-tried not to," she insisted, aware for the first time how little the notion of *a wicked tongue* had to do with words.

"I'll take that as a *yes*." Sharp teeth nipped at her earlobe and made her gasp. "Now, tell me, did you give in to temptation and touch yourself too?"

"T-touch myself?" His lips against her throat were doing strange things to her pulse. "Where?"

A low laugh hummed against her neck. "Wherever gives you pleasure. Here, perhaps." His fingertips slid from her hair and down the path his mouth had taken, brushing along the edge of her bodice, then slipping just beneath to tease the tops of her breasts. One thumb swept over her nipple, bringing it to an aching peak. "Or between your legs."

His touch alone would have been enough to set her aflame. But when combined with the smolder in his voice? Heat rushed through her—no mere blush this time, but a roaring inferno of desire.

"No," she confessed on a needy sob. To have

done such a thing would have been to admit to herself how much she wanted him.

Though now, as she lay panting in his arms, she wondered how she ever could have denied it.

"I was saving that honor for you."

Between thumb and forefinger, he pinched the nipple he'd roused, firmly but not to the point of pain. Something like an electric charge zinged from her breast to that secret place at the joining of her thighs, leaving behind a delicious ache. "And what an honor it will be."

It was evidently not, however, an honor he intended immediately to bestow. He went on kissing her, stealing her breath as his hot mouth searched every inch of bare skin it could reach—her lips, her throat, her chest. Nor did the hand at her breast cease its playful torment, kneading and teasing until she began to squirm.

"Have mercy," he groaned against her hair before shifting her in his lap with a flex of his hips, as if she weighed nothing at all. "I'll give you what you need."

His left arm cradled her as the right swept down her body, his palm leaving a path of longing in its wake—waist, hip, thigh. Long fingers encircled her ankle, then followed the pattern of her clockwork stocking up her calf. He resumed kissing her as he toyed with her garter.

"I can feel the heat of you from here."

Her cheeks prickled. "I think you've made every inch of me blush."

"Let's just see, shall we?" One twitch of his forearm bared her to the tops of her stockings. "Open your legs."

The dark note of command in his voice was difficult to resist, though she tried to sound saucy as she retorted, "Yes, my lord."

"*Graham*," he corrected swiftly, sternly.

Of course, he would have a name that was little more than a growl. The sound of it reverberating through his chest made something inside her vibrate like a plucked harp string.

"Graham," she repeated, half acquiescence, half plea, as she slid her knees apart.

"Good lass."

To her shock, a sense of pride suffused her at those gravelly words. Sprawled in the lap of a man, with his hand up her skirts, surely she ought to have felt shame? But somehow, knowing how stinting he was with praise made her crave it all the more.

His thumb swept over the delicate skin of her upper thigh. "Lift your skirts the rest of the way."

She fumbled to hike the light woolen dress to her waist, wishing suddenly she could shed it entirely and be bare to his gaze.

"Very pretty." He watched himself brush a finger along the seam of her sex. "Aye, and rosy as your cheeks."

Though tempted to look for herself, she squeezed shut her eyes, the better to lose herself to the building sensations as his fingertip danced over her folds, dipped into her entrance, then slid higher to tease her already swollen pearl. She'd never done more than toy with her private curls or press the heel of her hand against the spot that ached. But with a touch both gentle and sure, he seemed determined to learn what pleased her most.

She heard with amazement the sound of her own wetness and the greedy groan its discovery dragged from his chest. "It pleases you?" she murmured against his questing mouth.

"Only one thing could please me more." His tongue surged inside her mouth, and below, one finger mimicked the motion, easing into her tight channel. His thumb pressed against the little bundle of nerves at the top of her sex. Together, the sensations were almost overwhelming.

When he slid his finger out, she whimpered, and he thrust forward again. He began to make maddening little circles with his thumb. A second finger joined the first, stretching her, filling her, driving her toward some unknown crisis. The throbbing ache became a tingle. Light sparkled behind her eyelids.

"Aye, that's it," he crooned. "Come for me."

Instinctively, she lifted her hips to his hand as something burst inside her, radiating in circles from her core.

Lightly, he stroked her mound, easing her past the peak, murmuring against her brow, "That's my lass."

My lass. Oh, how could she, who had only ever wanted her independence, thrill to the thought of being possessed by a man? But she could not deny the appeal of hearing Graham call her his.

At long last, she opened her eyes to find him watching her. The room had grown surprisingly dim. "Did I sleep?" She scrambled awkwardly to sit up, making him wince.

"Nay," he reassured her, glancing toward the window. "There's a storm approaching." At just that moment, rain began to lash the glass. "Not exactly curricle weather. I'm sure it'll blow over after a while." He dropped his gaze to her face again. "Fortunately, I can think of a few ways to pass the time."

A moment before, she had felt perfectly sated. Now her pulse leapt. "I'm sure you can." She studied the sculpted angles of his face from beneath her lashes. "How many of them involve me, er, *deepening my acquaintance* with the fearfully hard thing that's been pressing into my backside for the last half an hour?"

A shocked laugh rippled through him, appearing at last on his lips as a sardonic smile. "You've seen too many Blackadder plays." One russet brow arced in a delicious scold. "But as it happens"— scooping his arms beneath her shoulders and knees, he rose with her in one swift motion, making her squeal—"all of them."

A playwright hadn't any cause to be so strong. But having observed the deftness with which he had tended the horses and drawn water from the well, she could guess experience and circumstance had made him familiar with labor of the sort that ordinarily did not fall to the lot of earls.

Why, he'd probably even split the logs for the fire!

He carried her up the stairs without showing the least sign of strain, though the delight of being cradled against his broad chest had left her breathless.

At the nudge of his toe, a door swung inward. Once swift glance took in the small, slant-ceilinged room and its contents: a ladder-back chair, a chest of drawers that doubled as a washstand, and a bed. *His* bed.

Just over the threshold, he lowered her feet to the floor, then slid a finger under her chin to tip her face to his when she would have lowered her gaze. "The, ah, *degree of acquaintance* is entirely up to you, Julia," he insisted, searching her eyes with an intensity that made her knees weak. "If you wish to rest for an hour, I'll leave you in peace. If, however, you have . . . other desires, I can more comfortably fulfill them here."

An hour.

When that hour was up, no matter what had transpired in this little cottage, in this little room, they would have to return to Clapham. She would once more be a mere lady's companion, and he the earl. And, for at least a few days more, he would wield the pen of Ransom Blackadder, while she was expected to take up that of Miss on Scene.

She didn't know how those other stories would end. She could only take charge of the one playing out in the here and now, in which she was Julia and he was . . .

"Graham," she breathed, closing the slight distance between them to lay her cheek against his breastbone. "Make me yours."

Slowly, his arms came around her, his embrace both tender and strong. He pressed a kiss to her crown and breathed deep. "A man such as I does no' deserve such sweetness."

"That's wrong. Think what sugar can do for lemons, or a cup of over-steeped tea." She rose on tiptoe to press her lips to the edge of his jaw, prickly with the day's growth of beard. "Take what you need."

She hadn't been fully prepared for the hunger those words would unleash. He raised his hands to either side of her face, driving his fingers into her hair and scattering her hairpins. Her heavy brown locks tumbled over her shoulders as his mouth crashed over hers, devouring her inhibitions. Against her belly, she could feel the evidence of his arousal.

"I want you bare," he insisted, as his hands slid down her back to undo her dress.

For answer, she began to fumble with the buttons of his waistcoat. "I want that too."

In another moment, she stepped out of the puddle of her gown, and a few quick tugs of the laces set her free of her corset. She stood before him in nothing but shift and stockings, having made little progress in her turn, nothing more than pushing his coat askew and disheveling his cravat. A little hiss of frustration escaped her lips.

One corner of his mouth kicked up—half a smile, at least. "Go stand by the bed," he told her.

Clinging to one bedpost for support, she watched as he shed his coat and waistcoat and laid them over the chair, then picked up her dress from the floor and shook it out before draping it over his clothes.

It both amused her and ratcheted up her frustration. "Are gentlemen always so particular about wrinkles at a time like this?"

"Habit," he said with a shrug that conveyed something more than indifference. He tugged loose the knot of his cravat, slid it from his collar, and wound it neatly around his hand before laying it aside. "I couldn't always afford to be careless. But I suppose the truth of the matter is, it was a way of maintaining control when everything around me had gone mad."

"And now, do you"—she slipped one shoulder from her shift—"do you ever just let yourself go?"

"You may fancy you want me t' say *aye*." He pulled the hems of his shirt from his breeches and dragged the garment over his head in one swift motion, revealing the brawn that she had only before suspected, the size of his arms, the wall of muscle that made up his chest. He'd spoken of shoring up Castle Dunstane—had he hewn stone and laid it with his own hands? Her mouth went dry as he tossed the shirt onto the chair and took another step closer to her. "But best be mindful what you wish for, lass."

She wasn't frightened of him. A bit apprehensive, perhaps, as she'd heard that being bedded inevitably involved pain. But nothing about what she'd seen, or what he'd said, made her wish to change her mind.

Pushing away from the bedpost, she walked toward him, grasping the sides of her shift and slowly raising it. When she came within arm's length of him, he reached out, covered her hands with his, and helped her lift the garment over her head.

He sucked in a breath. "I imagined you thus," he said darkly, "the very night we met." With one fingertip, he pushed aside a strand of hair that had fallen over her breast, teasing her nipple with the curl. "But my imagination didn't do you justice."

"Will you let me see you, too?" she asked as she stretched out a hand to him.

His arms fell to his sides, so that nothing stood in her way as she dared to brush her fingertip over his shoulder and down his biceps. Her own imaginings had been severely hampered by a lack of information. She'd seen statues of naked men before, but they were mere marble, and while Graham's muscles were almost as hard, his skin was anything but cold. And as for those so-called works of art, well, she could guess that whatever they hid behind their little fig leaves would not compare to what tented the front of his trousers.

Her hand moved lower, one finger snagging his waistband and slipping free the first button of his fall. Then another. And another.

"It's hardly fair," she cried after working half a dozen buttons loose. She'd meant to tease, but her voice sounded fretful. "My skirts hampered your desires not at all."

"If I'd known, I would have worn a kilt for you."

"How would that help?"

"Well, for one thing, there are no buttons." He winked. "And for another, a true Scot wears nothing at all beneath."

With that, he at last came to her aid, making short work of the remaining buttons and pushing his trousers over his hips. His member sprang free, ruddy and just as gloriously powerful as the rest of him.

Oh. She wanted to touch him, be touched by him, everything, all at once. Flailing one arm behind her, she reached for the edge of the bed and took a stumbling step backward.

He followed, grasping her shoulders, easing her onto the mattress, then lowering his mouth, first to suck the sensitive spot at the base of her throat, then to nuzzle her breast before capturing her nipple between his lips.

"Graham," she gasped, arching her back and curling her fingers in the linens as his hands swept to her hips, caressing her skin and spreading her legs so that he stood between them, his erection hot and heavy where it pressed into her belly. She writhed as his ravening mouth moved to her other breast, then traveled lower, lower. His tongue swept along the crease at the top of her thigh. Surely, he wasn't going to put his mouth—

Her whole body jolted as his hot breath stirred her thatch of curls and he began to kiss her mound. When his tongue began to tease the same sensitive spots that his fingers had found earlier, she cried out and would have closed her legs if not prevented by the breadth of his shoulders. "Nay." The thrum of his deep voice against her aching flesh was the most extraordinary torment. "You must come for me again." She drove her fingers into his coppery hair and once more gave in to his command.

Aftershocks were still rippling through her when he rose, lifting her higher on the bed. Setting his knee to the mattress, he caught her hand and brought it to his member. Her eager fingertips encircled his flesh, so hot and so smooth.

"Your skin is like silk," she marveled, watching herself stroke him.

"And so is yours," he said, as he curved his hand

around hers to help her guide him to her slick entrance.

Her body was pliant, but still it was a stretch to take him. He eased forward gently, patiently, filling her. Then he caged her body with his, surrounding her with his strength, his heat, his scent.

"This, *this* is how it feels to be mine."

She understood, now, why his ability to maintain control was so important. But a part of her still longed to know what it would feel like if his control began to fray. Impaled, pinned to the mattress by the wonderful weight of him, she could do nothing more than drag her tongue over the hollow at the base of his throat, tasting salt.

He shuddered and drew back. "No—Oh!" she gasped when he thrust his hips forward, driving into her again.

"No?"

"No. I mean, yes." She tossed her head from side to side, her hair scrubbing against the sheets. "Don't stop."

He didn't. He set a steady pace of advance and retreat, the movements of a primal dance whose motions came to her as naturally as breathing. She began to rock her hips upward to meet his, feeling a now-familiar sensation begin to build once more. As another climax overtook her, he thrust and held himself deep within her, his neck and arms corded with desire. Then, as the pulses of her own body began to fade, he pulled free and rutted once, twice, against her belly. She felt his seed spurt in hot jets across her skin.

She might have dozed then, but not for long. She knew when he rose, listened to him pad across the room, heard the splash of water being poured from a pitcher into the bowl that sat atop the chest of drawers. A moment later, she started as he wiped away the evidence of his passion with a wet handkerchief.

"That's c-cold," she protested.

When he was satisfied, he helped her to sit up. She watched as he returned to the washbasin, admiring the taut muscles of his backside. He rinsed the handkerchief, then wiped himself clean. The white linen cloth came away faintly stained with pink. "Did I hurt you?"

"No."

He sent a stern, skeptical glance over his shoulder, demanding the truth.

"It's a pleasant kind of soreness," she insisted. Already she could feel the twinge of previously unknown muscles in her thighs.

That softened his expression just a bit. "Ah. The kind that comes from a good day's work," he teased, coming toward her. "The kind that makes you eager to do as much again."

They sank down to the mattress together, bodies relaxed and twined together, his kisses leisurely, as if they had all the time in the world.

Though they didn't, of course. And he knew it too. "The rain has stopped," he remarked with a sigh as he rolled away from her, onto his back. "I should take you home."

"I suppose so, yes." Aunt Mildred would fuss if she were gone much longer. She propped herself on one elbow for a last look at him, sprawled in naked splendor. "But thank you for bringing me here. I wish I could stay."

His chest rose and fell on an almost-silent breath. "You could . . . if I made you mine in earnest."

"That wasn't *in earnest?*" she asked with a playful smile, dragging a fingertip down his arm. "My goodness."

But he was perfectly serious, it seemed. He turned his head to face her. There was a rawness, a vulnerability to his expression greater even than she had seen downstairs, as if more of the mask had been chipped away by their lovemaking.

"I could make you my wife."

Her breath caught. "You're only saying that because of what we've done, because you think it's the honorable thing to do."

He shook his head, his hair bright against the pale sheet. "I'm saying it because I need you." Then he sat up, so that she could no longer see his face. "I'd hoped you needed me too."

This wasn't at all what she'd imagined when she'd vowed to use his interest in her to save the magazine.

Then again, almost everything that had happened since that day had been beyond her wildest dreams.

What might happen if she dared to push the boundaries of her happiness beyond the back room of Porter's Bookshop, beyond this cottage, even beyond the Covent Garden stage? This would be writing a new ending, indeed.

"Graham." She slid her hand along the sheet and tangled her fingers with his. "I do."

Chapter 18

Julia woke with a start at another knock on her chamber door. Blinking awake, she took in her narrow bed in her narrow room in Mrs. Hayes's house.

Had yesterday been a dream?

But no. The pleasant twinges that greeted her when she lifted her head from the pillow were more than ample proof of what had transpired the day before.

"Come in," she called, dashing one knuckle across her lips to wipe away a smile.

It was Jess this time. "Do come quick, Miss Addison. She won't listen to reason."

Julia scrambled from her bed, snatched up her dressing gown, and hurried after the maid. After what had happened last evening, she could only imagine Aunt Mildred's state.

Graham had returned her to Clapham a little

bedraggled and damp, thanks to another spate of cold rain, and later than intended, because he had insisted on making love to her again—so gently, so tenderly, his powerful body had trembled with restrained desire. Julia trembled again at the memory.

Daniel had been waiting for them at the door. The boy hadn't even bothered with a greeting. "Mistress wants to see you," he'd reported. Julia had already had one foot on the stairs when he'd added, "You too, sir."

It little mattered that Mildred Hayes was a small, sickly, old woman, propped up on pillows and confined to her bed. The moment the two of them had crossed the threshold of her chamber, she had launched into such a tongue-lashing, punctuating her words by jabbing her folded lorgnette at each of them in turn.

"Daniel—curricle—Scotsman—gone for *hours*— surely recognized—gossip—reputation—"

"My apologies for distressing you, ma'am," Graham had interjected smoothly when she had finally paused to draw breath. "Your niece has consented to make me the happiest of men."

The hackneyed expression was doubly ridiculous from a man Julia knew to be gifted with language, and who kept his emotions under such strict regulation.

But on Aunt Mildred, the words had worked like a magic charm.

Her choleric color had faded to girlish pink, and tears of joy had sprung into her eyes. "My Julia, married, to an earl?"

Graham had left soon after, with a kiss on the

hand for Mrs. Hayes and one on the cheek of his betrothed. Julia was left to settle and soothe Aunt Mildred, who had at least been wise enough not to ask questions for which she did not really want answers.

"And to think, it's all down to that mix-up with my theater box," she'd said, just before drifting off to sleep. "You really must invite Mr. Pope to the wedding."

Julia couldn't guess what this morning's renewed agitation might portend.

She found her sitting on the side of her bed, her wrapped legs dangling over the edge of the mattress, with her walking stick in one hand and Mrs. Whyte at her other elbow, urging her to lie down again.

"I'm perfectly capable of sitting at a table for a quarter of an hour," Aunt Mildred was insisting. "There's correspondence that demands my attention."

"I can write for you," Julia said, hurrying to the bedside.

"Not on your life." She thunked the tip of the walking stick onto the carpet for emphasis, narrowly missing Julia's bare toes. "Dunstane will write to your brother, of course—has written already, I daresay. Last night, he had a certain look in his eye—the look of a man who wanted to be doing something, anything to move matters along." She shuffled forward, until her feet brushed the floor. "But I am determined that your mother will hear the news that her daughter is to be the Countess of Dunstane from my own hand."

There was little to do, then, but help her to a

chair—the chair in which Julia usually sat, fortunately just a step away from the bed. Between the three of them, Mrs. Whyte, Jess, and Julia managed to drag the mahogany pedestal table from across the room and arrange it in front of her.

"I'll fetch pen and paper," Julia said and went down to the sitting room.

Daniel met her on the stairs. "A message for you, miss." He'd even remembered the salver—though he gave her the folded missive with one hand while balancing the tray on the other.

"Thank you, Daniel," she said, tucking it into the pocket of her dressing gown for safekeeping. Who but Graham would have written to her? And his words would be for her alone.

Once Aunt Mildred was busy with her letter, Julia decided it would be safe for her to enjoy hers. Stepping closer to the window, with her back almost to the table, she fished the letter from her pocket and slid her finger beneath the disc of wax. He'd been in such a hurry, he hadn't even bothered with his thistle seal.

But the hand was strange, and the message stranger still.

> *Urgent meeting of the Misses. In the usual*
> *place, at noon.*
> *—Mrs. G.*

"A love letter?" Aunt Mildred tilted her head, the better to spy on Julia's expression.

Julia started. "No, Aunt. It's a—" Something about the message made the skin along her spine prickle. Better to spare Aunt Mildred further anxi-

THE LADY PLAYS WITH FIRE   249

ety. "It's a notice from the bookshop. That new novel I ordered for us has come in. I'll just go and fetch it after breakfast, shall I?"

Mrs. Hayes dipped her quill and resumed writing. "And how will I explain your absence to his lordship when he calls on you?"

Before leaving, Graham had mentioned a matter of business to which he must attend the next day. "I don't expect him, ma'am," Julia said. "But if he does come, tell him . . ." She sent another frowning glance at the paper in her hand and then mustered a smile. "Tell him it was urgent— we'd run out of Hume."

Julia arrived at the bookshop with a quarter of an hour to spare 'til the clock struck midday, but the others had still arrived before her. All but Lady Stalbridge, that was.

Lady Clarissa Sutliffe, Miss Theodosia Nelson, and Miss Contantia Cooper were all seated around the table, in the center of which lay three identical letters. Julia sank into a chair and slid her letter across the scarred and stained wood to join the rest.

"I wonder why Lady Stalbridge needs to see us on such little notice? I had to say that Thomas, my cat, had run away—even though the poor old thing is asleep under my bed." Lady Clarissa's eyes were wider than usual, fixed on the pile of paper. "Papa let me join some of the servants in a search for him. I gave two footmen the slip and came here. I figured, it worked for Daphne," she said with a shrug, a reference to the feline misadven-

ture that had brought Daphne Burke, now Lady
Deveraux, to join the magazine last spring.

"I had been wishing for another meeting," confessed Miss Nelson, "so I could tell you all that I'm
to have an article published in the *Times*."

"Theo, that's marvelous," declared Clarissa,
reaching out to squeeze her hand. "I knew you
could do it."

Constantia fidgeted with her pencil, though for
once, she did not draw. "I've submitted a water-
color to an exhibition," she said, speaking to no
one in particular. "Anonymously, of course."

"Excellent news," said Theo.

Julia knotted and unknotted her fingers in her
lap.

The mood in the room was strange. Nervousness—they'd never been summoned by Lady Stalbridge in such a fashion before. And all these
declarations—as if they might never have another
chance to speak. It reminded her, oddly, of the
sense of anticipation she'd felt in Graham's cottage as she'd waited for tea. The feeling that something important, something life-changing, was
about to be revealed.

Beneath the table, she pushed her damp palms
down the front her skirt. "I'm going to marry Lord
Dunstane."

Three sets of eyes—hazel, brown, and violet—
bored into her, full of astonishment. But before
anyone could say anything, Lady Stalbridge arrived.

"Oh." She glanced around the room at each of
them, looking crestfallen to find them there. "I
had hoped . . ." Then her gaze landed on the pile

of papers in the center of the table. With a sharp sigh, she opened her reticule, withdrew two letters, and with a flick of her wrist, sent them to join the rest. "Lord Manwaring received one as well."

"Oh. I thought perhaps that he . . . *You* didn't send them, then?" Lady Clarissa's golden brows still had a hopeful lift. "As a . . . as a sort of . . . joke?"

Lady Stalbridge demurred. "I did not."

"But—but this means, someone else knows who we all are, even where we live!"

At Theo's words, Constantia pushed back from the table, her chair scraping noisily across the floor. "You'll excuse me, please," she said with a nod and a curtsy. The door shut softly behind her.

She'd left her sketches strewn across the table.

"It's worse than that, I fear," said Lady Stalbridge, retrieving another letter from her small, beaded bag. "This was enclosed with the first." She unfolded the note, spread it smooth with her palm, and scooted it first toward Julia.

> *You're not as clever as you thought you were, or it wouldn't have been so easy for me to learn the identities of Mrs. Goode, Miss on Scene, and the rest.*
> *Next week, at opening night of my new play, you'll see what I've done with this valuable information. Soon, <u>everyone</u> will know.*
> *—R. B.*

Julia shut her eyes and pushed the paper toward Theo.

"Ransom Blackadder." Theodosia spat out the

name as she reached the end of the second letter. "How did he find out?"

"I don't know yet," Lady Stalbridge admitted. "I suppose it really doesn't matter. I'm afraid this is goodbye to the magazine. I'd hoped we'd at least last out the year." She reached out a hand and covered Julia's where it lay on the table. "I'm sorry, my dear. It seems all your efforts with Lord Dunstane were for naught."

Graham grumbled beneath his breath as he pushed open the shop door and ducked inside. Above his head—but only barely—a little brass bell tinkled to announce his arrival.

After hours of searching, he'd left the bright, polished storefronts of Bond and Oxford Streets behind.

That's rather an old-fashioned style, sir. I'm afraid we've nothing like it here.

No, my lord. I've seen nothing to match that description in years.

Surely, you'd rather choose something grander, more suited to grace the hand of the Countess of Dunstane?

This dingy little jewelry shop was his last hope. Or at least, his last attempt before he surrendered to the consolations of a glass of whisky and one of the gaudy pieces that had been pressed upon him earlier in the day.

"How can I assist you, sir?" said the man behind the counter, tucking away a dusty rag that needed to be put to more frequent use. He was sixty if he was a day, white-haired, with small, square-rimmed spectacles perched on his forehead, whose existence he appeared to have forgotten some time ago.

But none of that was what struck Graham first. "You're a Scot?"

"Aye, sir. That I am. Hamish Armstrong of Dundee, at your service."

It was an omen, if ever he had heard one. He'd searched the town through for a man who would understand.

"I need a ring for a lass," he began.

The man gave a knowing smile. "Your lass?"

"Aye." *His.* "She's sweet as the honey made from spring heather."

"But I'll wager she's got a twinkle in her eye, too." Hamish looked him up and down. "She'll need it, if she's to take up with a man the likes of you."

"Aye, that she does," Graham agreed with a soft chuckle.

Then he set about describing a ring that existed only in the haziest reaches of his memory, the betrothal ring his mother had worn, set round with pearls and some purplish gem.

"Amethyst," the jeweler supplied with another smile. "Go on."

There were no McKay family jewels left. No McKay family left. As Blackadder, he had spent years tearing down everything that carried even a whiff of sentiment. But now Graham had been given an unexpected chance to rebuild what he'd lost, with Julia at his side.

After a few more questions, Hamish disappeared into a back room and returned with a delicate ring held up between forefinger and thumb. "This."

It wasn't a question. Graham had to clench his jaw to fight its sudden inclination to wobble.

He would have been willing to swear it was his mother's ring.

"Aye," he managed at last.

Hamish put it in a little box and gave it to Graham in exchange for far fewer banknotes than the ring was worth—at least, to him.

"My brother, Tavish, owns just such a shop as this," the jeweler called after him as he stepped to the door with his prize. "In Edinburgh. If you have need of aught when you're home."

Home.

He imagined dancing her around his bedchamber at Dunstane, clad in nothing but jewels.

But first, the ring. That, he would present to her on Monday, after rehearsal. And he'd do it properly too. Fully clothed. Down on one knee. *Would you do me the honor . . .* and all that.

As he trotted up the steps of the house on Half Moon Street, he patted his breast pocket in almost boyish delight. A footman bowed and, at Graham's nod, opened the door to the study. He had a letter to write, to Julia's brother.

But he found his secretary at the desk with his usual array of papers before him.

"Good afternoon, Keynes," he said, tossing aside his hat.

The man looked up and adjusted his glasses, as if afraid Graham's good mood was a trick of the light. Graham hadn't told anyone the source of his present happiness, deciding it was better to wait until he'd spoken to her family and a formal announcement had been made.

Keynes moved to stand. Graham tried to wave him back to his chair, but the man insisted. "I have some news, sir. Something I think you'll be glad to hear."

"Oh?" Graham couldn't imagine anything capable of improving his already buoyant mood.

"I've completed my mission, sir. I've discovered the name of the person who writes as Miss on Scene."

The whole scandal felt remote, now. The review. Even his response in *The Poison Pen*. He was ready to wash his hands of all of it and move on to the next part of his life, his new writing project, his . . . *wife*. The thought, the memory of what had transpired at the cottage, made one corner of his mouth kick up.

He settled into a chair, picked up a stack of letters, and began to leaf through them. "Hmm. And how did you manage that?"

Keynes drew himself up proudly. "As it happens, the *Magazine for Misses* leases a room from a bookshop for their meetings. The shop's chief clerk knew something about the arrangement, of course. Then he was caught stealing from the till and had to be let go. And, of course, a disgruntled former employee can no longer be counted on to keep a secret—particularly not when he's pockets to let and someone offers a reward for information."

Graham didn't look up from the post. "No, I suppose not. Well," he asked absently, all but indifferent to the answer, "who was it, then?"

"You'll never believe it, sir. Do you remember that woman, the one who'd mistakenly been sold the ticket to your box at Covent Garden?"

Graham's ears began to buzz, making Keynes's voice sound as if it came from another room.

"Mrs. Hayes?" The widow was even feistier than he'd imagined, it was true. Last evening's display of temper had been something of a revelation. But to think of her composing scathing reviews of plays for a scandalous periodical?

"The very one, sir," Keynes confirmed. "It seems she's been employing Miss on Scene as her companion, though I doubt the poor widow knew anything of her double life. A young lady by the name of—" He paused and made a show of looking through his notes.

"Julia Addison."

"Oh." Keynes looked up, somewhat deflated by having his triumph swept away so unceremoniously. "Do you know her, sir?"

The ring was a leaden weight resting on Graham's heart. "Apparently not."

Chapter 19

Aunt Mildred made excuses for Lord Dun-stane's failure to appear in Clapham on Sunday: the weather was poor; gentlemen had many demands on their time.

Julia, however, understood what his absence meant.

Somehow he had discovered that she was Miss on Scene. Perhaps he had known for some time. Had he orchestrated all of it—the sweet little cottage, the stories of his tragic childhood, the revelation of his secret identity, the proposal—to humiliate her? To ruin her?

Surely he might have been satisfied with mocking the magazine, even revealing her name and exposing her to censure and ridicule.

Did he also have to break her heart?

Well, even if it were true that all her efforts to soften him had been for naught, she still had no

intention of letting him have the last word. He had
a surprise in store for him at Monday's rehearsal of
The Poison Pen.

She hadn't told the others at the magazine that
Graham was Ransom Blackadder. She had wanted
to leave them with a sliver of hope that she still had
the power to make things right. Though surprised
by Julia's request, Lady Stalbridge had allowed her
to keep the second note that had been sent to her.
It crinkled now in her reticule as she prepared to
set out.

Aunt Mildred, at least, had continued to improve and had even summoned Mr. Watkins to
demonstrate how much. She had managed, with
assistance, to descend to the sitting room and was
awaiting her caller there now—wrapped up against
any possibility of a chill in the air, with her feet
propped up on cushions, it was true, but nonetheless, much better than anyone had expected and
in half the time the apothecary had predicted.

From below, Julia heard a knock and smiled to
think of Mr. Watkins's astonishment. Then, as she
was buttoning her spencer, Nelly appeared at her
door. "A gentleman to see you, miss."

Julia's hand—body, heart—twitched at the unexpected news. *Graham?* Threads popped, and a
button came away in her hand.

"Oh, dear, miss," Nelly said. "Best give it to me.
I'll have it fixed in a minute. They're waiting for
you below."

Torn between flying down the stairs—she did
not wish to seem eager, but every moment gave
Aunt Mildred more opportunity to say something

ridiculous—or appearing in a state of cool and righteous fury, with her chin in the air, she stumbled and nearly fell on the steps.

A dark head appeared in the doorway of the sitting room. "Julia, are you all right?"

"Jeremy!"

She launched herself into her brother's arms and might have let herself snivel against the shoulder of his coat if his next words had not been, "I understand felicitations are in order?"

"Oh, well—" She drew back enough to peer into the room behind him and saw his wife, Laura; their mother; and Mama's husband, Mr. Remington, looking at her with expectant faces. "How lovely of you—all of you—to come all this way to deliver them in person."

The others beamed. Jeremy gave her a fierce squeeze before releasing her. "My little sister—a countess!"

"I shall insist on at least one scraping bow from you, brother dear," she managed to tease.

Her mother came forward with hands extended. "I'm so happy for you. When shall we meet this Lord Dunstane?"

"I, uh—"

"He's a busy fellow—"

"—more interested in how Julia met *him*—"

Beneath the cover of a cacophony of voices, everyone speaking and no one listening, Julia took a chair in front of the window, hoping the light at her back would make her expression more difficult to read. With a wave of her arm, she invited the others to sit down.

"His lordship is patron to some of the most noted playwrights of our day," Aunt Mildred was explaining to Mr. Remington, a description that made Julia's belly do an uneasy flip.

One playwright in particular. And notorious *might be the better word.*

"Though he hardly ever leaves Scotland, you said." Mama's soft blue eyes looked worried. "I do hope his coming to Town this Season marks a change of sentiment on the matter. I hate to think of my daughter so far away."

You say that now, Mama, but when I'm disgraced . . .

"We'll visit the Highlands," her husband reassured her. "Lovely spot."

"You know I'm no stickler," Jeremy interjected, a statement greeted by a wry lift of his wife's lips, "and I have every confidence in Julia's decision, but I do think the man might have written to me."

"I'm sure he told me he would," said Aunt Mildred, still determined to believe the best of Lord Dunstane's intentions.

"We've discussed this." Laura soothed both her husband and her aunt with a gently admonishing shake of her head, setting her short, red-gold curls abob. "You were so eager to get here, Jeremy, you wouldn't wait for the post. His letter and our coach must have crossed on the road."

"Yes, my dear. I'm sure you're right." Jeremy reached for his wife's hand. "As you say, what matters is that this Dunstane sounds a decent fellow and our Julia is happy."

At that, Julia popped to her feet. "To call my present feelings *happiness* hardly does them justice, brother dear." She pressed her lips together and stretched them into something she hoped would pass for a smile. "Shall I ring for some refreshments?"

"If I know Mrs. Whyte, she'll be in a flurry with such an unexpected houseful," Laura said, rising. "Why don't we go down together and speak with her?" She looped an arm through Julia's and guided her toward the corridor and the stairs.

As soon as they were out of earshot of the others, she repeated her husband's question. "*Is* everything all right?"

Julia made some noncommittal noise.

"You seem . . . forgive me . . . not quite yourself. Watching you, I began to fear that Aunt Mildred might have been confused, or—or exaggerated the nature of this Lord Dunstane's attentions?"

"Oh, no. He told your aunt in no uncertain terms that I was to make him the happiest of men."

Just not, as it came to pass, in the ordinary way.

But she had little doubt he was delighted by his triumph over Miss on Scene.

The door of the kitchen swung outward, and Nelly appeared. "La, miss!" she exclaimed, clearly surprised to find them there. "And milady," she added, dropping into a curtsy. "I never meant you should have to come looking for me. Here you be." She held out the mended spencer, which Julia did not immediately take from her.

"Were you going out?" Laura asked. Her eyes glittered, sharp and knowing, even in the dimness of the basement corridor. "An assignation with your betrothed, perhaps?"

Julia hesitated for a moment before nodding. "We have an urgent matter to discuss, yes."

"Oh?" Laura's voice turned cool. Experience had given her an abiding suspicion of every nobleman who wasn't her husband.

Julia sent her a pleading look. "There's something I must settle with Lord Dunstane before my brother hears of it."

For a moment, Laura appeared to weigh how to proceed; given her history, Julia wouldn't have been surprised if she had insisted on going in Julia's stead and putting Graham in his place. "All right," she conceded at last. "Go—but try not to be away for long. I have some news I believe will keep everyone occupied for a time." She smoothed her palm over the front of her skirts to reveal the slightest rounding of her figure.

"A baby?" Julia gasped, throwing her arms around her sister-in-law's neck. Jeremy and Laura had been awaiting the blessing of a child for quite some time.

"Yes, you shall be *Aunt Julia* at last."

Scandalous Aunt Julia, more like. She imagined her future nieces and nephews whispering among themselves, stories of the aunt who had once written for a daring ladies' magazine and then allowed herself to be seduced and ruined by a Scotsman bent on revenge—if she were permitted to be mentioned in the family at all.

"Hurry," Laura urged. "It's a juicy tidbit, but it can only sate them for a while. Eventually the others will notice you've gone."

When Julia arrived at the theater, rehearsal was already underway. But to her surprise, Graham

was nowhere to be seen. Perhaps he had anticipated that she would come and was avoiding her.

Immersed in their characters, the actors paid
no attention as she slipped into her usual seat. Several rows from the stage, she watched as Mr. Sawyer and Mrs. Cole worked their way through the
scene she and Graham had acted out just a few
days before. The tension, the physical closeness—
audiences could not but see the exchange for what
it was, two sworn enemies battling their desire for
one another. When Mr. Fanshawe called a halt,
Mrs. Cole was pink-cheeked and Mr. Sawyer was
breathing as if he'd just run a footrace.

After a brief pause, during which stagehands re-
arranged some of the furnishings, Mr. Fanshawe
directed them to begin Act Three. Julia had read
Perpetua's lines, of course, but seeing them performed was worse than she had imagined. As Reginald Briggs's power grew, he tamped down his
inconvenient attraction to the woman he blamed
for his brother's death. He began to wield the sort
of control over the public that he had previously
accused Miss Philpot of abusing. The circulation
of her reviews declined, driving her to heat her
now-miserable room with a paltry fire made by
burning unsold copies of the magazine for which
she wrote. Julia realized with a start that even the
desks had been changed. The scene ended with
Briggs now seated at an escritoire with elegant
turned legs, while Perpetua slumped over a battered deal table.

"That'll do," Mr. Fanshawe called from the
wings, before the final scene. "Good work, every-

one. I believe even his lordship might've been pleased with that."

"That'll be the day," said Mrs. Cole.

The actors chuckled doubtfully, knowingly, as they cleared the stage.

Julia sat for several minutes after everyone was gone, struggling to collect her thoughts. She wasn't sure whether Ransom Blackadder possessed sufficient influence over audiences to prompt them to punish critics in general.

But it was quite clear how Graham meant to use the knowledge he'd acquired specifically to damage her and the *Magazine for Misses*.

She pushed to her feet. But rather than leave, she ascended the small staircase to the stage one last time. She stood in the center, sliding the tip of her first finger over the edge of one desk, and then the other. The silence of the empty theater was oppressive. In that cavernous space, she felt very alone, indeed.

"Plotting the next victim of your poison pen?"

When Graham spoke from the wings, opposite where Mr. Fanshawe had stood, she couldn't contain her shriek of surprise. It echoed as he strolled across the boards as if he owned them.

Julia gathered her courage and met his hard look with a defiant one of her own, gripping the rail of Perpetua's chair, the better to hide her trembling hands. "I leave such despicable tricks to you, my lord."

He stopped with the table between them and tossed something onto it. She glanced down to see a copy of the last issue of the magazine, open to her column.

"I told you *everything*," he said. His voice was ragged, raw. "You might at least have mentioned this."

"As if you didn't already know," she replied with a glare. "Why couldn't you be satisfied with taking down the rich and powerful in your plays, those who could stand to be knocked down a peg? But no—you couldn't bear to be criticized. You said you wanted Perpetua to get close to Briggs, to lure him in. It's clear to me now, however, just who stabs whom in the end. Well, do your worst." She spun on one heel, deliberately turning her back to him as she prepared to leave. "I'm not afraid of you."

Out of the corner of one eye, she saw his hand shoot out—to stay her, she thought. She expected to feel his iron grip on her arm.

But his fingertips settled light as a feather on the pulse point throbbing at the base of her throat. "You're a liar."

It wasn't fear that made her heart race, however. His fingers slipped along the sharp angle of her collarbone, sparking in her a most unwelcome memory of their shared passion only days before and eliciting from him a soft groan.

When he spoke again, his voice was thick with a mixture of regret and longing. "And I'm a fool."

With gentle but inexorable pressure on her shoulder, he turned her to face him, and she made no effort to resist.

"I didn't tell you," she said, "because I didn't want to hurt you."

"Hurt me?" he scoffed, though pain gleamed in his eyes like unshed tears. If anything, the crack in his mask had widened in the days since she had seen him. But he seemed determined to cling to whatever protection the remaining fragments afforded. "All that I've been through, all that I've suffered, and you thought one review—one anonymous reviewer—could hurt me?"

"*Yes*," she insisted in a voice hardly above a whisper. "And I'm sorry."

He shoved the table aside and pulled her into his arms.

"How did you find out?" she asked against the soft wool of his coat, dragging in a lungful of his intoxicating scent.

"I put my secretary to investigating the identity of Miss on Scene several weeks ago. I intended to invite her to the opening performance of *The Poison Pen*. I wish . . ."

Chastened, she nodded her understanding. "You wish I had been the one to tell you the truth."

"Nay," he corrected, "I wish I'd never made such a ridiculous demand of him. Or that Keynes weren't such a persistent man."

Her answering laugh might have been mistaken for a sniffle. "I wanted to tell you at the cottage. But once I finally understood the reason you wrote in such anger—and I realized the state you must have been in when you read my review, so soon after your brother's death—I feared if I revealed I was Miss on Scene, you would only push me away. And I couldn't bear that. So I convinced myself that since you'd already had a change of heart about *The Poison Pen*, it was better for me to say nothing. I decided, rather than giving you my secret"—she paused, chewing on the inside of her lip—"I would give you myself instead."

"*Julia . . .*" he half scolded, half sighed against her hair, the warmth of his breath making her scalp tingle.

"Oh, Graham. I understand why you're upset with me, and I know pain makes people do terrible things." She lifted her chin just enough to look into his face. "But I also know you're a better man than this. Please, don't use the play to ruin Mrs. Goode and the others. Say what you like of me, just spare the magazine."

A wrinkle of confusion darted across his brow. "Are you referring to the ending?"

She extricated herself from his embrace, opened her reticule, and held out the letter. "I'm referring to this."

He read it through, and his frown deepened. "What is this?" He turned the paper over, but of course it bore no direction, having been sealed inside the other note. "How did you come by it?"

"On Saturday morning, each of us—the editor of the *Magazine for Misses* and every young lady who writes for it—received your letter—"

"*My* letter?" He snapped his wrist, making the paper rattle. "This isn't my hand."

"Well, R.B.'s letter, then." Still, he looked uncomprehending. "Didn't you—? I, er—I assumed you had disguised your writing to protect your identity."

"Why would I do such a thing when you already knew the truth?"

A new sense of alarm jolted through her. She'd

wanted to deny it could be Graham, but everything had seemed to be against him, everyone had been so certain . . .

If he had not written it, then who?

"Perhaps your secretary?" she suggested, even as she recalled the man's precise copperplate from the letter he'd sent about the ticket to Lord Dunstane's box.

Graham's expression hovered somewhere between amusement and affront. "Keynes issue threats? Certainly not."

"Then who would?"

"Keynes told me he bribed a former clerk from a bookshop—Porter's, I assume?" he added as an aside, cocking one brow—"to reveal what he knew. Perhaps my secretary wasn't the only one the fellow told."

"Perhaps. But we're clearly meant to assume the letters came from Ransom Blackadder."

"Yes." He had resumed studying the much-folded note from every angle, testing the weight of the paper and examining the ink. "Someone who expects to command an audience at my play."

"It could be anyone. Someone could pay the boys on the street to hand out leaflets," she cried, then glanced around at the boxes. "Or someone might stand up in the middle of a scene and shout."

But Graham, who was looking about the stage, shook his head. "Neither of those things is likely to get the sort of attention this person seems to desire. May I keep this?"

She nodded, and he began to refold it. "Do you think it could be a reference to what happens in the play itself?" she asked. From what she'd seen, things still went badly for Perpetua in the final act.

"If so, this person's plans can still be thwarted," he insisted, "because the play can still be changed."

"But you've only a few more rehearsals before opening night!"

He waved a hand to dismiss her concerns. "Why not send Blackadder out with a flourish?"

"You still mean for this to be the end of him?" she asked, thinking back to what he'd told her at the cottage.

"Yes." He slipped the letter into his breast pocket, but did not immediately withdraw his hand, as if reaching for something else. "I'm more certain than ever that Blackadder must give way to make room for a new beginning."

"A new beginning . . ." she echoed. "I've been thinking. About what else you said at the cottage. Your proposal." The movement of his hand inside his coat stilled. Unable to meet his eye, she dropped her gaze, focusing instead on the table and the copy of the magazine. "It was made under false pretenses, before you knew the whole truth about me. You might regret—"

"Do *you*?"

His voice was strange, harsh. Hopeful? He was too much of a gentleman to jilt her. But *she* might yet call off the engagement. Surely, in spite of what had transpired between them, it would be the right thing to do.

Why, though, if freedom was the thing she had always wanted most, did the prospect of freeing herself from him make her heart ache anew?

She parted her lips, but he spoke before her

words came. "Don't answer that." He caught her hand, and she watched as he dragged his thumb across the back of her knuckles, unable to lift her eyes to his face. "For the next week, I'm going to be very busy with revisions and rehearsals—and these, I must handle myself. But on opening night, after you've seen the play, when all this is behind us, I'll ask you again. You can give me your answer—your *real* answer—then."

She managed a stiff nod, fighting the impulse to launch herself into his arms instead.

He released her hand and picked up the magazine, evidently having followed the direction of her gaze. "In the meantime, it seems I'll be devoting myself to saving . . . what did Keynes say everyone calls this blessed thing? Ah, yes," he said, holding it out to her. "*Mrs. Goode's Guide to Misconduct.*"

As she reached out to take it from him, she looked up at last to search his face.

The familiar mockery was there, perhaps, in the curve of his lips. But his eyes were clear and warm, his gaze as intense as she had ever seen it.

"Don't look so surprised, lass."

They were not the eyes of a man who intended to let her go.

Nor had he released his end of the folded periodical. "I won't let aught happen to it." *To you*, his eyes added as they stood together, not touching one another but linked by what had once divided them, what only moments before she had believed would be the last issue of the magazine. "I'm too eager to read your next review."

Chapter 20

Graham squared the small box where it sat on the corner of his blotter, reached for a penknife to sharpen a quill, then picked up the box instead. A flick of his thumb revealed the ring in all its quaint perfection. The purple of Highlands heather, encircled with creamy pearls that seemed to capture all the variegated hues of clouds in a summer sky.

Would Julia accept it? Accept him?

Or would he be torturing himself thus forever?

He snapped shut the box and slid it away from him, though not far enough that he was spared glimpses of it in the corner of his vision as he spread his papers across the desktop and picked up his pen.

Yesterday evening's tweaks to the opening of the play had been easy enough. But this morning, he intended to write the entire third act anew. The actors would be fit to be tied when he presented them with more last-minute changes this afternoon. He could hear Fanshawe grousing already, could picture the roll of Mrs. Cole's eyes.

But there was nothing for it. He had to give the play an ending that would undercut the damage he'd set out to do so long ago, as well as whatever devilry that anonymous letter writer had planned.

With his first two fingers, he slipped the damning note from beneath the blotter. Something about it niggled at him, something about the hand or the scrap of foolscap on which it had been written—or perhaps it was merely that he'd looked at it so many times now, it could not help but strike him as familiar.

In truth, the hundredth inspection of it told him nothing more than the first.

"Enough," he muttered to himself, tucking the note away again. He could not afford to let himself be distracted further.

He had work to do if he meant to win Julia's doubtful heart.

The quiet *tink-tink* of his quill against the ink bottle was drowned out by a *tap-tap-tap* at his study door. He sent a scowl across the room. What now? He had sent Keynes away not a quarter of an hour ago, to find the clerk from Porter's and discover whom else the fellow had spoken to. And he had told the servants he did not wish to be disturbed.

Determined to ignore the interruption, he dipped his quill again. Once more the knock intruded on his thoughts. Louder, this time. More insistent.

"I should have gone to the cottage," he groused

beneath his breath, then tossed aside the pen and growled out, "Enter."

The footman who opened the door was visibly reluctant to do so. "Forgive me, my lord. But the gentleman was most insistent about needing to speak with you."

"Who?"

"Lord Sterling is the name he gave."

Before Graham could answer, almost before he could remember where he had heard the name before, that gentleman stepped around the harried footman and into the room.

Julia's brother.

Even without the information Mrs. Hayes had revealed about Julia's family, he might have guessed the two were related. They had the same dark hair, though his was a shade closer to black, and the same intelligent blue eyes. The same high color streaked across his cheeks as so often appeared in Julia's.

Though in Sterling's case, he suspected that the color owed something to the reflection of his red coat.

Graham recalled Mrs. Hayes remarking with some incredulity that her nephew by marriage preferred to be addressed as *Captain Addison*. Not by everyone, of course. He'd asked the footman to introduce him with his title.

Nonetheless, he had come decked out in his officer's uniform, complete with gleaming sword.

Graham pushed to his feet. "Sterling."

"Dunstane," the other man said, tucking his hat beneath his arm and snapping into a bow. "A word, if you please."

Graham wasn't sure he had much choice. With a nod, he dismissed the footman and then waved his arm for Julia's brother to take a seat.

It was too early in the day for a social call. And far too early to offer his guest anything other than coffee for refreshment. Though perhaps the proprieties could be overlooked on such an occasion.

Sterling looked as if he could use a drink.

For a few moments, however, it seemed as if he intended to refuse even the offer of a chair. At last, he sat down where Graham had indicated, fingering the hilt of his sword. An attempt at intimidation?

Well, Graham didn't intend to go out as his brother Iain had, in some bloody duel.

Or rather, if he were challenged, he didn't intend to lose.

Then again, what would victory look like? Killing or maiming Julia's brother hardly seemed likely to win her hand.

Graham started to return to his seat behind his desk, thought better of it, and came around to take the chair opposite Sterling's. Better to meet him on equal ground. They were, after all, two men with much in common. Similar in age as well as in circumstance, each one having inherited a title he had not been raised to expect.

And united, he hoped, by a shared concern over what was best for Julia.

"You've come because of your sister."

Sterling's answering nod was sharp. "Since you did not see fit to come to me."

The uniform made it less immediately obvious that the other man was slighter of build and shorter of stature than Graham. It also made it easier to forget that his father had been a clergyman, that if circumstances had been different, Captain Addison might have followed the same peaceful path.

It was, above all, a visible reminder of his willingness to fight for what he believed to be honorable and right.

Graham weighed whether to offer some explanation for his conduct, even an apology. He'd intended to write, had even started a letter. But the revelation about Miss on Scene and yesterday's conversation with Julia had made him hesitate. Better to wait until he had her answer before approaching her brother for his consent.

Not that he was particularly worried about acquiring it. If Julia said yes, then if necessary, he would take her back to Scotland, where she could do as she pleased.

"She's a grown woman," he pointed out. "The decision of whom, or whether, to wed ought to be hers."

To his surprise, Sterling gave another nod of agreement. "And I would be thought a fool if I refused to grant my permission for her to marry a gentleman of rank and fortune." As he spoke, his gaze traveled around the well-appointed room before settling again on Graham. "But I am her brother. I wanted some reassurance that you're the man to make her happy."

Graham fixed his eyes on a point over Sterling's shoulder. Across the wallpaper, the frolicking figures of maidens and swains made sheep's eyes at one another; their expressions still set his teeth on edge.

He understood, even admired, her brother's protective impulse.

But how could he promise Julia happiness when he'd known so little of it himself?

"Then, as I made my way here," Sterling continued, a new, slightly self-deprecating note in his voice, "I thought of what she would say if she discovered I'd made such a demand on her behalf. She has a bit of an independent streak, as you may have discovered."

Graham bit back an incredulous snort.

Would that be the same independent streak that had taken her to Covent Garden alone? Taken on Shakespeare? Taken charge of his racing curricle?

Taken hold of his heart.

"Still," Sterling went on, "since I've come all this way . . ." He leaned back in his chair. Graham braced himself for a military-style interrogation.

But the first question wasn't even a question. "Mrs. Hayes tells me it was a mutual interest in the theater that brought you together."

Graham thought of Miss on Scene's review. Of the first time he'd seen Julia, that night in his box. Of the light in her eyes as she'd ascended to the Covent Garden stage. "Aye. That's fair to say."

"Julia explained something about your connection to—to this playwright fellow—a satirical sort, or so I've heard . . ." Sterling circled a hand, searching for the name.

"Ransom Blackadder," Graham supplied, more reluctantly. Blackadder certainly had never been a source of happiness. Only an outlet for misery.

"Exactly. His patron, she called you. And unfortunately, it seems we've caught you just as his next play is set to begin. The business of it demands your attention," Sterling went on, sounding almost regretful for the intrusion. "That's why we've not seen you or heard from you since our arrival in Town, she says."

Julia might have said nothing, offered no explanation at all. Certainly, she would have been within her rights to express reservations about his intentions or their future together, to prepare her family for the possibility of their engagement being called off.

But evidently she hadn't. At least, not yet.

In spite of himself, hope swelled in Graham's chest. "You'll come, I hope? All of you," he offered rashly. "On opening night. You're welcome to the use of my box."

"Very generous of you." Sterling's face eased into a smile. "It will be like old times. I've taken my sister to a good many performances over the years, you know." Memory softened his expression further, making Graham think he recalled the long-ago outing to see the actors on the village green with the same fondness she did. "And watched her recite lines from the plays she's seen without me— nothing like amateur theatricals to pass a winter's evening, eh?"

Finding such a scene easy to picture, Graham nodded. But what would Sterling say to the discovery that those evenings at home had been preparation for the Covent Garden stage, albeit in the privacy of closed rehearsals?

"Yes," her brother continued, his gaze still far

away, "it seems she's always loved a play—the farce, especially."

"As do I," Graham confessed. The admission would astonish Julia, who imagined him incapable of a smile.

But the spark of a forgotten emotion had flared to life in his chest and now began to emit a steady glow, a hint of warmth.

He did love the theater, though he hadn't always known it. Certainly, he hadn't always shown it.

He loved to hear peals of laughter coming from the audience—not wry or cynical, but . . . well, *genuine.*

Most important of all, he loved Julia.

He was not yet prepared to make that confession aloud, however; at least, not to her brother. Instead, he rose to his feet. "You say you wish your sister's happiness—"

"I do." Her brother stood, too, and looked Graham up and down with a clear eye and a firmly set jaw. "Though no doubt you think that to ask it of a man with your history is unpardonably naïve of me."

Graham jerked back as if struck. "What do you know of my history?"

"Enough. I know that your title was no blessing to you, coming as it did. And I know you lost a brother to this damned war, and I'm heartily sorry for it."

The mention of Rory caught him by surprise, and he stiffened, his bow of acknowledgment for Sterling's words of condolence little more than a jerk of his chin. "Julia told you as much?"

"No. I learned of it just this morning. I had a meeting with my commanding officer." At Graham's look of puzzlement, he added, "I take it Julia didn't mention that I'm an intelligence officer? Under the command of General Zebadiah Scott."

It took Graham a moment to recall the gentleman with whom he had played cards at the Clearwaters'. And another moment to reflect on the possibility that people had been investigating him, perhaps on Julia's behalf, for some time.

"No, she didn't."

"Don't bandy that about, of course," Sterling added in a lower tone. "But since you're to be one of the family, I don't see any harm in you knowing."

Was it possible that this visit, the one he'd first seen as a threat or a warning, had, in fact, been a gesture of trust?

"The truth is . . ." Sterling gave a rueful smile and ran a finger beneath his collar, as if the uniform chafed. "I'm much more suited to such weapons as those"—he nodded toward the littered desktop—"than this sword."

"The pen is said to be the deadliest weapon of all," Graham offered, and the two men shared a glance that could only be called one of understanding.

A slightly awkward silence followed, which Sterling attempted to fill by gruffly clearing his throat. "Well," he went on, after another glance around the room, "I should leave you to your business. There will be time for getting acquainted and settling matters and planning a wedding when the play is over."

"Yes," Graham agreed. "My time then will be a great deal more my own."

Which was to say, *hers*—if she meant to have him.

Together, they strode across the room, their booted treads muffled by the plush wool carpet. At the door, Sterling thrust out his hand.

Graham hesitated only for a moment before taking it in a firm grasp and clapping Sterling on one epaulet-covered shoulder. "You are right to say that happiness has not always been my lot, Sterling. But you may rest assured, I will do my best to make it Julia's."

"I could not ask for more." He started across the threshold, then paused. "Well, one thing more. I would appreciate it if you didn't say anything about this visit to—"

"Your sister." Graham nodded, almost conspiratorially.

Sterling laughed. "Actually, I was going to say 'my wife.' Her spirit is even more, ah, *independent* than Julia's. She does not approve of interference—unless she's the one causing it," he added with a wink. "And if she is, then heaven help you."

Graham remembered that Mrs. Hayes had said something about "Lady Sterling" being in all the papers. Perhaps he would have Keynes look into that little mystery next. "I look forward to meeting her. She sounds an interesting woman."

Part compliment, part commiseration.

One corner of Sterling's mouth kicked up. "She is that, indeed."

When he left, Graham returned to his desk, more determined than ever to set things right. He had known already that marriage to Julia would bring a thousand blessings.

Until this morning, however, he had never considered that one of them might be a brother.

Chapter 21

Julia approached Covent Garden on opening night of *The Poison Pen* with the same anticipation she had approached it on the first night of the Season.

No, *greater* anticipation.

In fact, she wasn't even sure *anticipation* was the proper word to describe the emotions currently at war within her. Her stomach was twisted in knots, and so were her fingers—both, thankfully, invisible to Aunt Mildred. Surely, though, she could feel Julia's leg, bouncing nervously beneath her skirts.

As evidence that her state of agitation had not entirely escaped notice, when the carriage turned onto Bow Street, Aunt Mildred admonished Julia with the same words she used every time: "Settle yourself, my dear. We're nearly there."

Nearly there did nothing at all for Julia's nerves.

Against Graham's insistence that he would pro-

pose again after the play, she balanced the fact
that she had heard nothing from him for a week.
True, he had evidently sent word to Aunt Mildred—
or at least, she had made the announcement over
dinner—that they were to have the use of his box
on opening night. But there were six of them: Mama,
Mr. Remington, Jeremy, Laura, Aunt Mildred, and
her. And only six seats in the box. Which meant
that Graham would not be joining them tonight,
either.

Had he succeeded in revising the play suffi-
ciently to keep her and the rest of the *Magazine for
Misses* out of danger?

Or had he changed his mind? Was this the invitation to Miss on Scene he'd always intended to
send?

Oh, if only she could have a look or a word from
him before the play began. If only he could be
seated beside her and, when everyone else was focused on the stage, reach out and give her fingers
a squeeze of reassurance.

The four ladies had traveled in Aunt Mildred's
barouche, while Jeremy and Mr. Remington had
elected to call for a hackney. When Julia stepped
onto the pavement, she could not determine which
of the cabs waiting in the long line of carriages in
front of the theater might contain her brother and
stepfather.

With Laura's assistance, she helped Aunt Mildred from the coach. Though improved even more
from what she had been a week before, she still
moved slowly and stiffly. A jouncing ride across the
city had rendered her pale beneath her rouge. But
there was a familiar twinkle in her eyes as they

joined other theatergoers in the vestibule and waited to be reunited with the rest of their party.

The crush was breathtaking—quiet literally. Fashionably dressed people pressed in on them from all sides. The staircase ascending to the long saloon flowed like a waterfall of humanity, and Julia could imagine that the benches in the pit would be crowded past capacity tonight. Rumor had it even the Prince of Wales intended to make an appearance in his father's box.

She could not help but think of what Graham had said, about English theatergoers' eagerness to be mocked. What accounted for their enthusiasm?

Or had they heard rumors about the target of tonight's satire? The *Magazine for Misses* certainly had its detractors. Had some number of these people come to join in the mockery at her expense?

Was the person who had sent those awful notes among them?

Julia glanced from one person to the next, from silk gown to quizzing glass, from balding head to elegant coiffure. Which of them had claimed to be R.B.?

Finally, she caught sight of Jeremy straining to search above the crowd. Heedless of propriety, she thrust a hand into the air to signal them. Beside her, and much to her amusement, Laura did the same. Mama sent them both a gently chiding glance, but Julia also noted the eagerness of her expression as Mr. Remington pressed through the throng to appear at her side. The two of them had first met many years ago, before Mama's marriage to Papa, but circumstances and an ocean had come between them and kept them apart for almost thirty years.

Mama's face made clear that she did not intend to lose sight of him again.

"About time," Aunt Mildred grumbled, not quite under her breath, as the six of them formed a phalanx to tackle the stairs.

The curtain to Lord Dunstane's box stood open, anticipating their arrival. Six empty chairs with blue upholstery awaited them, as always. Julia bit back her disappointment. She had been hoping one of the ushers had been ordered to squeeze in a seventh chair, as was sometimes done. She had been hoping Graham would join them, as a surprise.

After some discussion, Laura, Mama, and Aunt Mildred took the seats in the front. Jeremy and Mr. Remington sat behind their wives, and Julia took the chair behind Aunt Mildred, despite that lady's objection.

"You won't be able to see as well," she insisted. "And worse yet, you won't be seen."

But Julia didn't mind the relative obscurity, tucked behind Aunt Mildred's turban and almost against the silk-covered wall dividing their box from the next. She could see perfectly fine. Or well enough, at least. And the curtain at her back promised the possibility of escape, if all did not go as planned.

In a box across the way sat the Marquess and Marchioness of Estley and their daughter, Lady Clarissa, who had inherited her father's golden good looks and her mother's gift of music. Clarissa caught Julia's eye; she, too, looked faintly queasy. With a surreptitious tilt of her head, she directed Julia's gaze to a box closer to the stage, where sat Lord and Lady Stalbridge with her stepson, Lord Manwaring.

Tonight, there was no mistaking that young man for anything but a dandy, in a russet velvet coat paired with a purple- and green-striped waistcoat, a jewel-encrusted quizzing glass, and artfully mussed brown curls. It was a costume that invited even the most jaded theatergoers to stare.

If the world was to discover tonight that he was the famous Mrs. Goode, he appeared to be ready for the attention, prepared to defy their anticipated scorn.

Half past six o'clock came and went. Twice, Mr. Remington pulled out his pocket watch and showed it to all the ladies. In a most uncharacteristic gesture, Jeremy reached out and covered her hand where it lay clenched in her lap. The noise around them rose and fell in waves of speculative chatter and anticipatory hush. At long last, the curtains on the stage moved and finally parted enough for a single person to step through.

Graham appeared, and Julia's breath caught in her throat.

Even alone on the stage, dwarfed by the gilded proscenium, he cut an imposing figure. The light from the chandelier struck fire from his hair. And he was wearing a kilt! Heat rushed into Julia's cheeks at the sight of his legs, the memory of his teasing words at the cottage, and the possibility—nay, the certainty—that he had done it for her.

Someone in the audience—Julia felt sure it was Lord Manwaring—whistled.

Graham bowed in acknowledgment, but his stern features did not crack. Against the murmur that began to ripple through the crowd, he raised a hand until silence fell once more.

"On behalf of the playwright and the actors, allow me to offer my thanks for your patience. We have all been waiting eagerly for some time to bring you *The Poison Pen.* Unfortunately—"

At that word, noise from the audience swelled again, whispered speculations, murmurs of disappointment. Julia leaned forward, gripping the edge of her seat with her free hand, wishing she had the power to make them all hush.

Graham stood, saying nothing more until he was sure he would be heard.

When the uproar had settled, amid reprimands from various spots about the theater for "Quiet!" he crossed his arms behind his back, dipped his head, and began again. "Unfortunately, we will be unable to bring you tonight's performance, as we find ourselves without our leading lady, Mrs. Cole, who plays the part of Perpetua Philpot."

Mutters of disappointment surged, fans snapped open, and a few people stood to depart.

Julia's heart pounded. Had this been Graham's plan all along, not to go through with the play? But no, she could not imagine he would have allowed the theater to fill with people who were now poised to leave, even more disgruntled than if they'd sat for two hours having their taste criticized and their flaws made ridiculous.

Had Mrs. Cole refused to go on after all the last-minute changes?

Or had Graham discovered that she had something to do with the notes? Might she be the mysterious person who had signed herself R.B.?

Then again, it could simply be bad luck. A head cold or sore throat might make it impossible for her to perform, and Julia could not remember having heard any mention of an understudy.

And if that were the case . . .

"Wait!" she called down, scrambling to her feet. Jeremy's hand gripped hers, urging her back to her seat. She slipped free of his grasp and stepped to the front rail of the box. "Wait."

Throughout the audience, heads began to turn. Ladies whispered behind fans and gentleman pointed discreetly. Quiet, though not silence, returned to the theater. Most of the people who had stood up sat down again. Graham tipped his head to one side, his expression that familiar mixture of disapproval and bemusement. "Aye?"

She held up a finger, asking for a moment, and then turned to leave the box.

Jeremy stepped between her and the curtain. "What do you intend to do?"

"Julia, Julia," Mama sighed. "You're making a scene."

"Is there a better place for it than the theater?"

That voice belonged to Aunt Mildred, who had turned partly in her seat, the better to favor Julia with a sly wink. "Let her go."

When that command was not immediately heeded, she struck the floor with her walking stick to reinforce it. With the closest thing to a glower

Julia had ever seen, Jeremy reached out a hand and drew back the curtain at the rear of the box. "I hope you know what you're about," he said in a low voice as she passed.

She didn't. Or at least, not entirely. But her slippered feet carried her swiftly down the staircase and through the vestibule. Two ushers guarded the heavy double doors into the theater. Startled, one of them reached for a handle so as not to impede her progress. In another moment, she was at the foot of the stage, looking up at Graham. The little staircase had been taken away.

Graham squatted at the edge of the stage and said in a low voice, "What is it I'm waiting for?" His bare knees above his stockings were a distraction.

"Let me help."

One brow arced. "Help?"

"I can play Perpetua Philpot."

The expression that crossed his face was only slightly less doubtful than the one he had worn during rehearsal when she had first taken the stage. "Aren't you worried about your good name?"

She wasn't certain whether he'd *intended* the play on words—*good* and *Goode*, her "Goode name" being the name under which she wrote for the magazine. Still, she returned a mischievous smile. "I thought you might be more worried about yours."

Blackadder's name, that was. But also the name he'd offered to share with her.

His lips quirked in answer. Then he motioned to her right with a nod of his head.

"*Psst!*"

She turned to see Mr. Sawyer gesturing to her

through the crack of what would otherwise have been a hidden door.

"This way," he directed, urging her through.

Julia slipped past the actor into a narrow corridor, and as the door shut behind her, she heard Graham say to the audience, "If we may beg your indulgence for a few more moments, it seems the show will go on after all."

"What happened?" she demanded of Sawyer who was already hurrying back along the corridor, which ran below and along the right side of the stage. "Where's Mrs. Cole?"

"No one knows," he answered without a backward glance. "Not like her to be late. Dunstane even sent a boy to her rooms. No sign of her anywhere. Here." He pushed open another door, where she found a room full of costumes. "Be ready in five minutes."

"Five minutes?" Julia echoed. "But I—"

The dresser, a girl a few years younger than Julia, her light brown hair covered by a kerchief, looked her up and down in patent disbelief and said, "Who're you?"

"I'm Miss—" she hesitated over her choice of answers, then shook her head. "Doesn't matter. Tonight, I'm Perpetua Philpot. Will you help me please?"

Though the girl shook her head, she jerked her thumb to point behind a screen. "Let's get you dressed, then. Can you do your own paint?"

No lady's maid had ever got her mistress out of one gown and into another with the efficiency of a theatrical dresser, who even had time to complain about the work she had done tailoring the costumes to the more statuesque figure of Mrs. Cole. "All for naught," she grumbled around a mouthful of pins. "All right. That'll do. Sit down at the dressing table."

Julia did as she had been bid, her eyes sweeping over a bewildering array of cosmetics as the girl fussed over a selection of hairpieces, none of which matched her hair.

"Never mind it."

Glancing into the looking glass, Julia met Graham's eyes over her shoulder. He was standing just inside the doorway to the dressing room. Impatience had been added to the mixture of expressions he had been wearing a few moments before.

And something that looked like worry.

"You're certain about this?" he asked.

"I am," she told his reflection, then she spun on the stool to address him directly. "Unless you think I'll make things worse."

"I'm not sure that's possible," he answered dryly. "The papers on Perpetua's desk are pages from the script now. You can read most of the lines directly from them and make it look as if you're reading from your notes. When you get to the third act—"

"Places, everyone," a voice called down the corridor. "Curtain going up!"

"Go on, then," Graham said, stepping away from the door so that she could slip past.

"But the third act?" she cried.

"But her face?" cried the dresser. She snatched up a pot from the table. "At least let me dab on a bit of rouge."

"Allow me," Graham said, taking Julia's hand to

pull her onto her feet and into a swift kiss. As always, color rushed to her cheeks. "I dinnae ken whether you're a brave lass or a foolish one," he whispered into her ear, no longer attempting to restrain the Scots in his voice. "But I love you, all the same."

Before she could even react to those words, he practically pushed her down the corridor, at the far end of which Mr. Sawyer stood, motioning for her to hurry. "Up you get," he said, handing her up another set of wooden stairs, almost a ladder, that led to the back of the stage. "Fanshawe's already in place. And for God's sake," he called after her as she scurried toward Perpetua's writing desk, "speak up!"

"You?" Mr. Fanshawe sneered as he motioned for the stagehands to draw the curtain. Then he picked up his pen and squared himself to his own table. "Perfect."

A packed theater was nothing like an empty one, she quickly discovered. It buzzed with a sort of electricity—and with conversation, as speculation over her identity passed in whispers behind fans and hands. Fanshawe had some trouble making himself heard over the noise.

She wanted to glance up at her family in the box but didn't dare. Instead, she picked up the extravagant quill, bowed her head over the escritoire, and pretended to write on a page already filled with the lines she was shortly to speak. Lines which bore a remarkable similarity to the words she had jotted down at her first rehearsal. A sensible critique from a writer who was twice the poet as sickly Robert Briggs.

And when she stood to deliver Perpetua's first speech, she forgot to be nervous. Forgot to wonder what changes were in store for the third act. Forgot everything but what Graham had said right before she stepped onstage.

She wished she had had time to tell him she loved him too.

But for the next hour, her performance would have to speak for her. She was determined to earn his praise.

Chapter 22

Graham dragged in a deep breath of the familiar scents of the theater—greasepaint, sweat, and sawdust—and held it. Waiting.

The noise was terrific. Even Fanshawe, who had come up through the music halls and penny shows, struggled to make himself heard over the crowd. Graham considered whether to signal for the curtain to be dropped, to put the play out of its misery at last.

Then Julia stood, paper in one hand, quill in the other, and an unexpected hush fell over the audience.

Less out of respect than morbid curiosity, he feared. Theatergoers found entertainment in spectacle, even in failure. He should never have agreed to this, should never have let Julia go on.

By Christ, she was brave, though. Her posture revealed no hint of nervousness. She looked every inch the clever, confident reviewer whose judgment deserved to be heeded.

Oh, but she was foolish, too—foolish in her determination to rescue this play. After tonight, she would be the subject of whispers wherever she went, and for longer than he cared to imagine.

And he loved her for all of it, for her spirit and her heart and her strength. She would meet society's scorn with a twinkle in her eye—*and pray God*, he added, pressing the ring box in his pocket against his ribs, *with me at her side*.

The hope and love that had flickered to life last week during Sterling's visit were now burning brightly in his chest. For Julia hadn't just stepped onstage intending to save *The Poison Pen*, or even the *Magazine for Misses*.

He understood that she was doing everything in her power to save him, as well—not Blackadder, but *him*. The man he had once been. The man he could be again.

Fingers plucked at his sleeve, and he glanced down to see Sawyer urging him to move. "You can't stand there, my lord." He pointed above their heads.

Graham followed his gesture to a network of ropes and pulleys, connecting the poles from which hung the heavy painted backdrops, anchored by pendulous sandbags. Being struck by any one of the objects dangling above them would at the very least render a man unconscious. Stagehands crouched high above on rough-hewn boards, waiting to drop the scenery on cue and trusting that anyone backstage would know better than to be in the way.

"Else you'll be leaving your brains on the boards, as well as your heart," Sawyer finished, with a sideways glance toward Julia, who was at present struggling to disguise a laugh as Fanshawe plodded his way through another verse.

"That obvious, am I?"

"I daresay, since Blackadder trusts you, you must know something about the theater," Sawyer conceded. Even behind the painted-on brows of the sardonic Reginald Briggs, his expression was teasing. "But an actor you'll never be."

Sawyer was a cleverer fellow than many, but Graham wondered whether he was the only member of the cast who had worked out Lord Dunstane's feelings for the young woman he had introduced to them as "Miss Hayes."

"Now then, my lord," Sawyer continued, tugging at his arm. "Haven't you got a box to watch from?"

He did, of course. And by his calculation, that box now held one empty seat, if not more. He had visions of ushers in the vestibule struggling to keep an outraged Lord Sterling—or perhaps Mrs. Hayes, brandishing her ebony walking stick—from storming the stage.

Even aside from the cold reception he anticipated, though, tonight his box wasn't the proper place for him. He did not want to hold himself aloof and apart. He could not bear to be so far away from Julia.

So, he made do with withdrawing farther into the wings, into the shadows, watching as she moved with striking confidence through the scene and breathed life into his words.

To his utter amazement, the audience laughed—right where he'd hoped they would, and with less bitterness than a Blackadder script usually inspired. Fanshawe even managed to play up his own death for comic effect, done in in the end not by Perpetua's review but by his own terrible verse.

The curtain swept down at the end of the scene. Fanshawe sat up, gathered the various papers strewn across both desks, and used them to prod Julia to exit the far side of the stage. While the dresser fussed over the pins in her costume, Julia pored over the script pages, her lips moving in silence as she tried to familiarize herself with the changes that had been made. Graham took a single step toward her, wanting to offer both praise and encouragement.

Once more, Sawyer grabbed his arm as a new backdrop came whizzing down from the rafters to replace the first. With a shake of his head, Sawyer stepped to his mark as the curtain rose again on a new scene. Half of the stage was now Reginald Briggs's quarters, less dreary than his brother's, and the other half had become the sitting room where Perpetua Philpot would receive the editor of her magazine.

Graham retreated once more into the shadows, leaning against a battered wardrobe where costumes were stored for quick changes between scenes. Briggs launched into a speech about his poor brother and the dastardly critic.

"'She killed him,'" Sawyer-as-Briggs explained to his manservant, "'with her poison pen. I daresay she stirs up some witches' brew of poets' tears and novelists' sighs, speaks some dreadful incantation to harden her heart, then dips in her quill and the words begin to flow, an evil spell that blinds her readers to everything good.'"

When the audience laughed, Graham eased a sigh of relief. The changes were working. Everyone in the theater had heard for themselves how terrible the brother's poetry was. Then, to cement their perception that Briggs was in the wrong, Sawyer picked up the slim volume of his brother's poetry as he finished his speech and began to read it, obviously for the first time. The mischievous contortions of his face, his inability even to sit still as he paged through the poems, only increased the audience's amusement.

The lines also served to create a sharp contrast between the Perpetua of Briggs's imagination and the Perpetua the audience had come to know for themselves. As Briggs accused her of witchcraft, she arranged flowers in her sitting room and paused to listen to birdsong. In Mrs. Cole's experienced hands, the revised character had begun to show the requisite softness and gentleness; Julia's genuine innocence and sincerity—the lack of makeup had turned out to be a stroke of brilliance—only amplified those traits. Just as Graham had planned from the beginning, everyone was falling in love with her.

Or . . . well, something like that.

By the end of the next scene, Briggs would be among them, and the play's transformation from satiric tragedy to romantic comedy would be complete.

A muffled *thump* distracted him from the action on the stage. He sent a chiding glance to a nearby stagehand, who shrugged his shoulders and spread his hands to indicate that he had done nothing to make the noise. Graham tried to ignore it, in favor of the debate between Perpetua and her editor, who was demanding more cutting critiques to encourage circulation of his magazine.

"'The public's taste cannot be trusted. You must teach them what to think.'"

"'But if what I tell them isn't true, they will no longer trust me.'" Julia gestured with what might have been a draft of Perpetua's next column. She was doing a masterful job of disguising the fact that she was reading most of her lines.

Fanshawe, who had crossed underneath the stage and come up to stand near Graham, nodded. "Yes, that's it," he whispered in a tone of astonishing encouragement.

Thump-thump! Thump!

This time, Graham felt the commotion as well as heard it. Beneath his shoulder, the sturdy piece of furniture rattled. What on earth? Next, they would be beset by rumors of a malevolent ghost.

He tried to open the wardrobe door and found it locked. "Have you a key?" he demanded of Fanshawe in a whisper.

"No, sir. The property manager—I'll fetch him." Fanshawe walked away as Graham dropped onto one knee, trying to peer through the keyhole.

It would be as well if he didn't watch the scene between Briggs and Perpetua, when they spoke directly to one another through their work, coming ever closer though still meant to be in separate rooms in different parts of the city. It was the scene he had acted out with Julia not so very long ago, the scene that had made him realize that it was useless to deny his feelings for her. He'd made few changes to it, since it had obviously worked so well to communicate the forbidden spark between writer and critic.

He glanced over one shoulder to judge the progress of both the scene and Fanshawe. Onstage, the actors grew ever more intimate. He felt a familiar surge of jealousy as Sawyer's hand rose, almost touching Julia's upturned face. Beyond them, the audience seemed to hold its breath.

He both couldn't bear to watch and didn't want to tear his eyes away. Damn it! Fanshawe was taking his own sweet time. What had got trapped inside the wardrobe? An animal, perhaps? He had seen cats hanging around the alley behind the theater, looking for mice. One might have sneaked its way inside the building, he supposed, and fancied that the open wardrobe looked like an inviting spot for a nap.

But no matter how alarmed such a creature might have been to awake and find itself locked in, Graham doubted that three or four those scrawny strays together would be capable of making the heavy wardrobe shudder. Perhaps one of the urchins who hung about had thought to play a prank and found himself stuck instead?

At last, Fanshawe returned bearing a ring of keys that would have done the chatelaine of the castle proud. It would take an eternity to sort through them. "Sorry, sir."

Graham snatched them from the man's grasp and began to search for one that looked like it might fit the wardrobe lock. Too big. Too small.

Fanshawe was no help; his attention was, at long last, all on the play. Finally, Graham fitted the proper key into the keyhole.

"Oh, brava, Miss Addison," murmured Fanshawe as the scene drew toward its conclusion and the doors to the wardrobe sprang open.

Mrs. Cole rolled out and onto the floor.

She was bound at wrist and ankle with rope, her mouth stuffed with a dirty rag. Terror flared in her eyes as she stared up at Graham.

"My God! Who did this?" he exclaimed as he pulled free the gag.

She tried to speak, but no sound came from her parched tongue. Fanshawe, who now crouched beside Graham though his gaze was still locked on the stage, shrugged helplessly. A stagehand reached into his pocket and handed over a flask. Though its contents smelled strong enough to peel paint, Graham tipped it to Mrs. Cole's lips, and she drank greedily and gratefully.

"I don't—ahh!" she gasped as Graham fumbled with the knots at her wrists, revealing angry abrasions. "I don't know. I never saw. I was in my dressing room, looking over those new lines for the final act, when someone came in. The screen hid my view of the door. He must've . . . ooh." As soon as her hands were free, she reached up to prod a tender spot on the back of her head.

"He struck you," Graham said. "And then tied you up. But who—?"

Applause broke, drowning out his words as the scene playing out behind them ended. The curtain swept down again, and for a moment, all was dim. Sawyer hurried over to them.

"What's happened?" he said, shrugging out of his coat and accepting another from the dresser, this one more flamboyant, suited to the style of a successful poet—a success he owed in no small measure to Perpetua's reviews.

"Mrs. Cole was attacked in her dressing room, then bound and gagged and locked in here," Graham explained. "Clearly, someone didn't want her to take the stage tonight."

"But it makes no sense," she insisted, sitting up and rubbing her rope-burned ankles. "I'd just got the pages you sent, that dramatic confrontation scene, and I—"

"Pages *I* sent?" Graham echoed, absently winding the rope into a coil as he crouched beside her.

"Well, I assumed they came from you, my lord. You've delivered all his other changes, and these had a note pinned to them signed *R.B.*"

"R.B.?" Sawyer pulled a face. "I say, that's strange. I didn't get any—"

Graham leaped to his feet without hearing him. "Fanshawe!" he shouted, heedless of the fact that his voice would carry beyond the curtain. He realized now why the paper on which the threatening letter had been written felt so familiar. And the words the actor had spoken moments earlier had finally penetrated his brain. "Did I hear you call her Miss Addison?" He spun, searching for him.

His realization had come a moment too late.

Fanshawe stood with his back to the curtain, a knife in one hand, the other elbow wrapped around Julia's throat. She clawed fruitlessly at his forearm as he dragged her away from the others, toward the center of the stage. Just as Graham lunged toward them, the curtain rose.

The audience gasped in unison, then nervous giggles and uncertain whispers began to erupt around the theater.

"Isn't that fellow meant to be dead?"

"Perhaps it's a ghost story."

"But that's Lord Dunstane! Is he taking on a role too?"

And from above, the tremulous voice of Mrs. Hayes. *"J-Julia?"*

Fanshawe laughed. "This is working out even better than I planned, my lord. I thought that if I got rid of Mrs. Cole, then the show would be canceled." He continued to retreat from Graham, dragging Julia with him across the stage, until Perpetua's writing desk was at his back. A gleeful, mad smile stretched across his face. "It was beyond my wildest dreams to think that Miss Addison here might step into the part and make things even worse."

The man did not seem to have been watching the same performance as Graham.

"Why?" he asked in a softer voice, slowly approaching the pair. "Why would you want the play to be ruined?"

"Isn't it obvious? Blackadder's lost his touch. His plays used to cut like a steel blade." He twisted his weapon, making it gleam in the light. "But this one's got less tooth than an old whore."

"You pleaded for a part in it," Graham pointed out, taking another step.

"That's close enough," Fanshawe said, turning

the knifepoint toward Julia. "I didn't used to have to go begging for parts, you know. Not until the reviewers got their teeth in me. But what do they know? What gives 'em the right? Muckin' about with a man's livelihood, and some of 'em no more than girls." He spat. "When I heard Blackadder had it in for *Miss on Scene*, I wanted in. Knew I could count on him to do what had to be done, teach the critics a lesson once and for all. Then this girl showed up, wanted to turn things all soft, like. Didn't seem to understand that Perpetua Philpot was the villain of the piece. And you—" Here the knife flicked toward Graham. "The high and mighty patron didn't put a stop to it—you went all dewy-eyed and let her have her way with you, the play, all of us! I decided I'd have to take care of Miss on Scene and her ilk myself."

Graham didn't dare risk a glance over his shoulder to see whether Sawyer or anyone else was prepared to back him up if he made a move to rescue Julia. The audience sat, stunned into silence, listening to her panting, rasping breaths, as she struggled ineffectually against Fanshawe's choke hold. To think, Graham had promised to look after her happiness.

He should have vowed to keep her from harm.

"Stroke of luck," Fanshawe continued, giving Julia a silencing shake, "that I happened to be in the same pub as the clerk from Porter's, overheard him crying into his ale about M-M-Mrs. Goode's m-m-magazine." He pulled a face and made his jaw wobble in mocking imitation of the man. The story jibed with what Keynes had been able to learn from the clerk, who had tried to drown his sorrows at his loss of employment and couldn't recall to whom he might have spoken. "Now I know who's behind it all." He sent a leering glance toward the theatergoers around him. "And soon you will too. I mean to end it, if you won't." Those last words were directly squarely at Graham.

"But the notes you sent were signed 'R.B.' "

"That's right. For Robert Briggs," he said, naming his character. "Though I knew those silly girls at the magazine would think it was Blackadder who'd done it. Even you must have wondered—must have feared he'd found out at last that you were destroying his play and with it, his name."

"Actually, no."

Graham calculated frantically. Would it work? Could he catch Fanshawe off guard, open him to an attack?

"You see . . ." Graham raised his voice to make certain that every one of the thousands present could hear him. "I'm Blackadder."

At that, the audience gasped as one, just as he had hoped. The sound of their surprise, or perhaps the revelation itself, startled Fanshawe just enough that he relaxed his hold, and Julia was able to slip free of his grasp.

Fanshawe snarled. "Damn me. I might've known it." He kicked at her, but she had already scrambled out of his reach, behind the writing desk. Deciding to ignore her, Fanshawe instead stepped toward Graham, blade first. "Just another nob, toying with the lives of honest working men like we," he said, with a sweep of his other arm that took in everyone on the stage and behind the scenes. "Well, no more."

He started to lunge at Graham, then seemed to catch a flash of movement out of the corner of his eye and twisted his body at the last minute. Julia stood behind him, the brass candlestick from the desk in her upraised hands, prepared to bash his skull. The arm holding the blade curved toward her instead, toward the defenseless expanse of her rib cage—and beneath that, her liver, her lungs, and her precious, precious heart.

Graham leaped for the knife, pulling the man's eyes toward him as she brought the candlestick down on Fanshawe's head. The actor collapsed to the stage like a dummy filled with sand.

But not before his knife connected with flesh, piercing the center of Graham's palm, its tip reemerging through the back of his right hand.

Chapter 23

Silence hung in the theater for what felt like an hour, though it was surely no more than half a moment. Transfixed by Graham's gruesome wound, Julia let the candlestick slip from her suddenly nerveless fingers. The heavy brass ornament struck the boards with a resounding crash, and that seemed to be the general signal for chaos to break loose.

Graham stumbled backward to sit in the chair at Briggs's writing table, clutching the injured hand in his lap, the better to support the weight of the knife, his features distorted in agony, though he made no sound. A woman in the audience screamed, and then another and another took up the cry. A stampede of footsteps followed as seats and boxes emptied, most to the exits. But a goodly number rushed to the stage. At her feet, Fanshawe groaned, roused by the clamor. Sidestepping him, she hurried to Graham's side.

"Don't touch it!" ordered a voice from below. She stopped herself, but not before her fingers were stained with his blood. "Name's Essex. I'm a physician. And pulling out the knife might make matters worse." Two other gentlemen helped to hoist the doctor onto the stage, and he dropped onto one knee beside Graham. "If I may, your lordship."

His jaw set in a firm line and his face paler than usual, Graham allowed the doctor to examine the blade's entry point as well as its exit.

"Well?" he demanded.

The doctor shook his head. "Difficult to say. The knife may be the only thing preventing a significant loss of blood, and removing it could . . ." The physician's expression told clearly enough how that would end.

Graham swore beneath his breath. "So, then? I can't verra well go about like this, can I?"

"No, my lord. But it is not a procedure I wish to undertake here, before an audience."

Julia glanced around at the theater. Some still stood near their seats, unable or unwilling to leave, while others crowded around the exits. Various groups littered the stage: a pair of men who'd rolled Fanshawe onto his stomach and bound his arms with a length of rope; Mr. Sawyer ministering to Mrs. Cole by chafing the feeling back into her hands and feet; other actors and stagehands looking on in shock. Why should a medical man be reluctant to do his duty in front of any of them?

When she turned back to the doctor, though,

she realized from the tilt of his head, silently directing Graham's notice, that he'd been referring only to her.

"Go to your family," Graham told her. "I'll send word when all is well."

"No, Graham. No." She threw her arms around his neck. Clung to him. "I won't leave you."

His left hand curved around the back of her head, pressing her momentarily closer before pushing her away. "You must."

"Julia." Jeremy's voice. He spoke low, the better to be heard beneath the noise around them. She glanced upward to find him standing over them, though she hadn't any notion how he'd managed to get there so quickly. She wouldn't have put it past him to have swung down to the stage from the box.

Though, since Mr. Remington, who was considerably older, was also with him, such a maneuver seemed less likely.

Less likely, but not impossible.

"If I may, sir," Mr. Remington said, "I have some experience with such injuries, both the treatment of them and the recovery afterward."

He had once been a soldier and then a manservant to a notorious rogue, and when he said such things, it made Julia wonder how many other lives he had lived.

Graham's brow wrinkled, a mixture of pain and confusion. "And you are?"

"My stepfather," Julia explained. "Arthur Remington."

"Much obliged to you, sir," Graham said then. "Right now, the only thing I have need of is someone to take Julia away from here. It wouldn't do for her to see me . . . faint."

It wouldn't do for her to see me die.

Julia knew exactly what he had been thinking, perhaps what he had been on the point of saying. She sent a desperate, prayerful glance upward.

Her gaze came to rest on Aunt Mildred, still seated in the box. Mama and Laura were gone— on Jeremy's orders, she supposed, given Laura's delicate condition. He would want to guard her from any shocks. But the older woman could not walk away without assistance.

"What nonsense," she called down in a carrying voice. "A hale and hearty fellow such as yourself has no cause to concern himself with such things. And besides, I should think you already understood that our Julia is brave."

"And stubborn," Jeremy added, shaking his head.

"Aye," Graham agreed in a gravelly voice.

The physician's gaze darted among all the involved parties. "How do you wish me to proceed, my lord?"

Graham jerked his chin once toward his hand. "Get on with it."

Every man nearby surrendered a handkerchief at the doctor's request. "I advise you to look elsewhere," he told Graham.

She expected him to refuse out of some misguided sense of toughness, but he turned his head to the side and locked eyes with her. Then again, perhaps that was as much to keep Julia from watching the removal of the blade than anything else.

"Wait," she whispered as the doctor grasped the

hilt. "Just in case you . . . *faint*, Graham, I want you to know that I love you too."

"My dearest lass. This isn't quite as I'd planned it"—he tipped his chin toward his chest—"but reach into my pocket."

Despite a rumble of disapproval from her brother, Julia slid one hand across Graham's chest and inside his coat. Her fingers closed around a little box.

"Open it."

Beneath the brilliant lights of the chandeliers, the amethyst gleamed like a sunrise. A betrothal ring. Without hesitation, she slipped it onto her finger. "Oh, Graham. Yes. The answer has always been yes."

He blinked as if in disbelief, his gray-green eyes hazy with pain. Her name escaped his lips on a breath.

And then, taking advantage of his patient's distraction, the doctor pulled the knife free.

The string of oaths that followed—not spoken under his breath this time—flooded her cheeks with heat, even as the remaining color leached from his.

But the doctor made a satisfied sound. "Not as bad as I'd feared." He applied half of the stack of handkerchiefs to either side of the wound and bound them in place with his own cravat. "Still, an infection might yet cost you the hand. And even if you keep it, it may be of very little use to you— once injured thus, the sinews of the hand do not always recover their strength and flexibility," he warned. "If you gentlemen could help me take Lord Dunstane back to my practice," he said to Jeremy and Mr. Remington, "I'll do what I can to improve matters."

Julia ceded her place to her brother, who helped Graham to his feet. "Go to Aunt Mildred," Jeremy said. "We'll talk about the rest of this business"—he glanced around the stage, pausing at Fanshawe's still-prone form, then looked Julia up and down—"when I get home."

After maneuvering through throngs of curious theatergoers, Julia was at last reunited with Aunt Mildred in the long saloon behind the boxes. "Well, my dear," the older woman said, her lorgnette half raised to her eyes, "that was quite the theatrical debut."

Tears sprang to Julia's eyes—shock, fatigue, and a hundred more emotions that she could not name. "Oh, Aunt. This will teach me to be careful what I wish for."

"Come, now," Aunt Mildred said, looping her arm through Julia's. "It's not like you to give up so easily. And who knows what may happen, now that you're to be married to the most notorious playwright of the age?"

She'd almost forgotten that Graham had revealed his secret identity to the world—to forestall Fanshawe, who had come perilously close to revealing hers.

"Jeremy is fit to be tied by it all. He may yet refuse his consent."

They reached the lower level, walked through the vestibule, and emerged into the chilly evening, where the line of carriages had begun to thin. Aunt Mildred pointed with her walking stick toward the barouche, directing Julia's footsteps. "Your brother has enough to concern himself with, just now. Scolding the future Countess of Dunstane can wait. Half Moon Street," she called up to the driver when they were within earshot.

"Aunt Mildred?" Julia asked uncertainly. It was not a direction she recognized, and it would hardly be proper to hope.

"Dunstane will have need of a nursemaid," the other woman explained with a wink, the movement almost lost in shadow if not for the twinkle of her eye. "It's only right for me to send him the best."

Graham arrived in Half Moon Street at nearly midnight, exhausted as much by the tumult of his emotions as the pain in his hand, the expenditure of nervous energy draining him more than the loss of blood.

Climbing wearily from the hackney, he struggled up the steps and into the house. No doubt the cabbie thought him a sot. Once inside, a footman reached to help him off with his greatcoat. Graham merely shrugged, and his coat and greatcoat came away together; the physician, Essex, had only draped them over his shoulders after bandaging Graham's hand and strapping his arm into a sling to discourage its use.

"My lord?" the footman began. Graham's shirt was streaked with blood.

Graham waved him off with his good hand. "See that I'm not disturbed." Then he trudged up another two flights of stairs to his bedchamber and swung open the door, expecting to have to fend off his valet. Just a dozen steps more to his bed.

To his surprise, Harcourt was not within. Nevertheless, he or someone had prepared the room for an invalid. The bedcoverings had been turned back and the pillows fluffed. A roaring fire crackled in the hearth.

The firelight painted a glow across the sleeping figure of Julia, curled in an oversized leather chair, hair down about her shoulders, still clad in the costume of Perpetua Philpot. His ring glittered on her finger. He blinked twice, trying to clear the vision.

"Lass."

He'd meant it for a scold, but the word eased from him with what sounded suspiciously like relief. She jerked awake and to her feet. "Graham." Her bright eyes swept over him, as if checking to make sure he was still whole. "You're here."

"Aye. And you shouldn't be."

A toss of her head sent unexpected sparks of red and gold scattering from her dark locks. "It's no use sounding all gruff and telling me I have to go. I'm here to nurse you back to health, on Aunt Mildred's orders." With gentle pressure, she guided him to sit in the chair she'd just vacated.

He sank down to find the leather warmed by the fire and her body. He was too tired to argue, though he knew he ought. "How did you get in?" he asked instead, attempting to toe off his shoes.

"Let me," she insisted, kneeling before him and slipping the shoes off his feet, then setting them neatly aside. "When the footman opened the door, I simply wouldn't let him say no."

Suddenly Graham understood that what he'd taken for the manservant's expression of concern had more likely been an attempt at a warning.

"Though he did fetch someone else. Your secretary, I believe, who—"

"Never say Keynes let you wait in my bedchamber?" He could picture the man's goggling eyes and determined, though obviously ineffectual, protests.

"I didn't exactly ask permission," she admitted, glancing up at him with a mischievous smile and waggling her hand to make the ring sparkle. "And he seemed to run out of arguments when I told him I was your betrothed."

He started to shake his head in patent disbelief. Had her work at the magazine encouraged such shocking "miss conduct," or had she always been prone to it?

But when he looked into her glowing, upturned face, he forgot to be disapproving. "When I think of what might have happened tonight, the harm that might have come to you . . . I should never—"

"I stepped onto that stage most willingly," she reminded him. "Though I do believe I'm now well and truly cured of my longing to act."

"You were brilliant," he insisted. "From the first scene to the last."

"You may tell me *that* as many times as you wish." Her kiss was swift, more a buss in passing as she got to her feet. "But first you need your rest."

She wasn't wrong, though he would not have balked at a more thorough kiss.

He stood, slipped off the sling, and half stumbled toward the bed.

"Ought I to help you with that, first?" She gestured with the waggle of a finger toward his lower half.

It took a long moment for him to realize she was referring to removing his kilt. "Nay." He climbed onto the mattress and slid beneath the cool linens as another wave of fatigue washed over him. "I'll just . . ."

Sleep—and whatever the physician had given him for the pain—weighed on his eyelids, dragging them lower. She smiled as she drew the covers over him and then turned away, as if intending to return to the chair. With his good hand, he patted the empty expanse of bed beside him.

"Graham," she chided. "I couldn't possibly. You need your rest."

"And I'll have it," he vowed. "But I'll rest better if you're here, rather than all the way over there."

She shook her head, her mobile mouth caught between disapproval and amusement. Then, with a sharp sigh, as if she couldn't quite believe her own actions, she pulled a few pins from her gown—"wouldn't want to be poked"—and clambered onto the bed to curl up at his side. "Now, go to sleep."

He didn't need to be told twice.

He woke again as the first gray hint of dawn was streaking the sky, both surprised and relieved to find that Julia was still tucked against him, in the shelter of his good arm. Her dark locks hid her face and tickled his chin; her left arm was flung across his torso and her fingers spread possessively

over his heart. Just as he'd hoped—nay, dreamed—
the delicate ring perfectly suited her hand.

He dragged in a deep breath, unable to recall
the last time he'd awoken feeling so content. As if
all was right with the world. His hand still throbbed,
it was true. And a good night's sleep hadn't
cleared his thoughts of the doctor's grim warnings
about the threat of infection and permanent dis-
ability.

It had increased his determination to triumph
over his injury, however. He tried to waggle his fingers and sucked in a breath at the pain even that
slight movement produced.

But pain, he reasoned, was better than no feeling at all.

"Graham?" Julia stirred against his shoulder,
swiped her hair away from her face, and looked up
at him with heavy-lidded eyes. "Are you all right?"

"Aye. I will be. And so will you—and all of Mrs.
Goode's Misses, thanks to that timely knock on
Fanshawe's head, and whatever additional punishment your brother and stepfather managed to
exact after they consigned me to the physician."

Confusion flickered across her eyes. "That's
good news, isn't it? Yet you look a trifle . . . disappointed."

"Aye, well. A Scotsman likes to be the one to save
his lass."

Her head tilted in a charming scold. "Graham.
That madman had a knife at my throat. You *are* the
one who saved me. And not just through your
brave actions, but through even braver words. For
my sake, you revealed one of your most deeply
held secrets to all of London society."

"One?" He arched a brow. "Are there others?"

She nodded. "Who would have suspected the caring man you really are, beneath that scowling mask." Then, sliding higher along his body, she pressed a string of kisses along his jaw. "Thank you. Thank you. Thank you."

He turned and captured her mouth with his, seeking the kiss she'd denied him last night. Lips softly parted, she surrendered to his demand.

Or perhaps *surrendered* wasn't quite the right word. Pressing her hand more firmly against his chest, she rose above him, her tongue stroking eagerly into his mouth, her hair tumbling around them like a curtain of brown silk.

"My love?" She drew back, nibbling her lower lip uncertainly as she rubbed her breasts against him with a becoming urgency. "Are you in a great deal of pain?"

"Oh, aye," he teased, his breath already ragged.

She pushed herself fully upright, until she was kneeling beside him on the bed. Her blue gaze flickered to his bandages, to the bloodstained shirt he still wore.

"I didn't mean my hand," he tried to explain, feeling a fool. "I'm sorry. That joke was unworthy even of Blackadder."

Though her lips curved slightly, an acknowledgment of his feeble attempt at humor, her eyes darted to his bandaged hand, and a notch formed between her brows. "Will you still be able to write?"

Essex had said a loss of dexterity was likely. Graham dragged in a breath and reached up with his uninjured hand to brush her hair behind her shoulder. "I don't know."

Sensing the moment for playfulness had passed, he planted one foot against the mattress to join her in sitting up. Her eyes followed the movement as the linens slipped to bare his leg, the hem of his kilt hiked to mid-thigh.

With one tentative fingertip, she brushed the dusting of coarse hair just above his knee. "I could hold your pen."

Bawdy wordplay? Or the promise of a new writing venture beyond anything he had imagined? Either way, he hardly dared hope.

Her fingertip slid higher up his leg.

"And would you write exactly what I told you?" he growled.

She shot him a look of mock disbelief. "Certainly not. I was not offering to take dictation. A woman with my knowledge of the theater, not to mention my experience on the stage"—her fingertip abandoned his leg in favor of tracing the edge of her bodice; the oversized gown had slipped lower while she slept, leaving Perpetua Philpot with a delightfully daring decolletage—"ought to be considered an equal partner in this venture."

"I agree," he said, reaching up to wrap his hand around her neck and draw her down for a kiss. "But until I'm healed, you'll have to do a bit more of the work."

Thankfully, this time, she understood exactly what he meant. In a matter of moments, she had peeled off her clothing, tossed aside the coverings, and climbed back into the bed, straddling one of his knees.

"Does this mean I finally get to see what's under your kilt?"

He groaned as her hands swept beneath the plaid, one on either thigh, to his groin. The brush of her fingers against his cock was the sweetest agony as she bared him to her gaze in the early morning light. "You already know."

Still, the eager flare of her eyes was flattering. And he admired the sight of her slender hand, adorned with his ring and curled around his ruddy shaft, more than a gentleman ought.

Still less should he have enjoyed it when she leaned forward and brushed a gentle kiss across his crown. Another groan rumbled through him as her hands pushed up his shirt and her mouth moved higher, her tongue teasing the ridged muscles of his abdomen, his flat nipples, the hollow at the base of his throat.

Meanwhile, he caressed her breast with his left hand—less nimble, perhaps, than his right, but hardly useless—then reached down to cup her already slick mound. "Take me inside you, Julia."

With eager, uncertain motions, she shuffled her hips higher, her knees spreading wide around his body, and led him to her entrance. Slowly, inch by inch, she sank down on his cock.

"That's right," he urged as she shifted her position until a shuddering gasp of pleasure burst from her lips. She lifted her hips once, experimentally, then slid down again. "Ride me."

Prone, he gave himself over to her pleasure, guiding her with his hand on one hip, then sliding his fingers across her belly to circle her bud with his thumb. The sweet, hot clasp of her sex was exquisite, her passion like nothing he had ever known.

"Graham!" Her voice was almost a sob, her rhythm already beginning to fray. "I'm going to—"

"Yes!" Someday, he would teach her patience. But not today. Because he was already on the edge of climax, too. And in his position, withdrawal was out of the question. After this, she would be truly his.

He thrust upward as she ground her pelvis against him, the pulsing of her channel calling forth his seed.

Both spent, they collapsed together, damp with sweat though the room was cool.

Around them, morning crept ever closer, and with it the arrival of servants to sweep the hearth and newspapers containing columns about the shocking events at the Theatre Royal and almost certainly one brother in high dudgeon about where his sister had spent the night. Carefully, he wrapped both arms around her, a shield against the day to come.

Pray God Keynes knew the ins and outs of acquiring a special license.

Because Graham meant never to wake up alone again.

Chapter 24

Half a day to acquire a special license.

Two days, at Mrs. Whyte's insistence, to prepare for the wedding breakfast.

Another day on top of that for the modiste to finish the new dress.

Julia tapped her toe impatiently, making the scalloped hem of her gown ripple.

"Only a few minutes more," the modiste insisted around a mouthful of pins. "I'm almost done."

With a frustrated sigh, Julia stopped moving her foot and folded her arms across her chest instead—which earned her a gentle scold from Mama. "Stand up straight, dear. You're going to be a countess!"

I don't give a fig about that, she wanted to retort, but didn't.

Because it wasn't entirely true.

She understood that with the title came awe-inspiring responsibilities and a very different sort of life, far away from this one.

It was lovely to think of being addressed as Lady Dunstane.

If a bit strange to think that she would never again be Miss on Scene.

Immediately after the wedding breakfast, she and Graham would leave for Scotland and might not return for some time. The plays at Covent Garden, Haymarket, and the rest of the London theaters would be out of her reach.

She had explained her reasoning for stepping down from the magazine to Lady Stalbridge when she delivered her final column.

"Do not say *final*, my dear," Lady Stalbridge had replied. "Miss Burke—Lady Deveraux—continues to contribute, for example."

It was one thing to pen an advice column in Hertfordshire, Julia had pointed out. Quite another to review performances on the metropolitan stage from the Highlands.

But she could not muster much regret at the change in her circumstances. Once, she had viewed country life, and the consequent loss of her favorite amusement, as a sort of punishment. But she knew now that life anywhere with Graham could never be dull.

Lady Stalbridge's reply had been accompanied by the sly smile of a woman who understood a great deal more than most people imagined. "Distance is an obstacle, Miss Addison. But you have too much to say to be forever silent."

That conversation had only increased Julia's excitement to discover what Graham might have meant by sharing the pen with her.

A new playwriting identity? Something else entirely?

But in the days since he'd said it, it had begun to feel as if she might never find out.

Since the lovely morning in which she had woken up in Half Moon Street, wrapped in his arms, everyone seemed to have acquired a sudden obsession with propriety. She had been allowed to see him exactly twice, and only in company. And each time, his scowl had been carved so deeply into his face, she despaired of ever seeing anything else written there.

The first visit had been to announce his possession of the special license. "Now, as to the matter of when and where the ceremony will take place—"

Graham's choice, whatever it might have been, had gone unheard.

Mama had spoken in favor of adjourning to Jeremy's estate in Wiltshire for a family celebration. Aunt Mildred had countered with a plea—in that feeble voice both Julia and Laura knew to be false, though remarkably effective at wheedling others into granting her wishes—that Julia be allowed to marry "from home," which was to say, the Hayes home. Jeremy, alive to the delicacy of his sister's reputation given all that had transpired, had spoken in favor of whatever was closer.

Clearly, he had meant "wherever the marriage could be solemnized with the most expediency." In any number of London churches, they might have been married yet that day, without delay. And *without delay* she had understood to be Graham's wish as well. Certainly, it was hers.

But Aunt Mildred had clapped her hands in glee and declared, "Holy Trinity it is." Thus, the matter was decided in favor of Clapham, and the date was set—upon consultation with the rector, Mrs. Whyte, and the dressmaker—for Friday morning. Graham had departed with a bow—and two new furrows in his brow.

The only other time she had seen him in the past four days had been at dinner on Wednesday. The evening had begun well enough. Graham had brought with him the good news that Mr. Essex had changed the dressings on his hand that morning and had seen no sign of infection.

Then, after dinner, when the ladies had withdrawn so that the gentlemen might enjoy their port, raised voices could be heard from the dining room. "There's some slight disagreement over the marriage settlements," Laura had confided. "Jeremy wouldn't tell me anything more."

That was a detail guaranteed to alarm Julia, particularly when Graham had left shortly thereafter, his frown lifting only slightly as he wished her good night.

"Really, miss," the modiste pleaded.

Julia glanced down to discover she had crossed her arms and resumed tapping her toe. Friday would surely never come. And if it did, she was beginning to feel nervous about how it might end.

Friday did come, however, and exactly when it was expected. Julia awoke to see the modiste's completed handiwork hanging on the back of the door to her little bedroom. From below wafted the delicious scents of baking, proof that the final stages of Mrs. Whyte's labors were already underway. This chilly, gray last day of November would end with Julia in Graham's arms at last.

Jess was the first to arrive, with a canister of steaming water and an offer to help her dress. Julia, who was almost afraid to touch the delicate white muslin, was grateful for the assistance. The gown floated over her head and down her arms, its puffed sleeves and shallow bodice trimmed by silk ribbon of palest lilac, chosen to match her ring. White silk embroidery and tiny pearls had been stitched into a subtle pattern over the narrow skirts.

The fabric and trimmings had been frightfully dear, but Aunt Mildred had insisted on purchasing them and waved away every protest. "Only the best for my niece," she had insisted, with a wink and a hug.

Laura was the next to arrive, with a paper of pearl-headed pins that had belonged to her grandmother. "They'll look lovely in your dark hair." With a quick curtsy, Jess took over the arrangement of Julia's heavy locks, while Laura perched on the edge of the bed to watch.

The smallest bedchamber in the house was already rather crowded when Mama appeared on the threshold, nervously pleating a lace-edged handkerchief. "Oh. I hadn't expected . . ." She cleared her throat, a delicate *ahem.* "It is usual, my dear, on such an occasion, for mothers and daughters to talk privately about . . . certain matters—"

At once, Julia's cheeks were aflame with mortification. "It isn't necessary, Mama, for you to distress yourse—"

But her mother pressed on with the speech she had obviously rehearsed. "Well. Marriage can be the source of new enjoyments—"

Even Laura, who'd been wed two years, began to squirm. Jess was struggling to contain a laugh.

"Though, of course, a gentleman may feel a sense of reserve with his bride, and a lady will naturally be reluctant to—"

Julia refrained from pointing out that she was not really a lady. Perhaps, depending on whom one asked, by birth, but certainly not by inclination. And she already had ample proof that Graham was not always a gentleman.

"Really, Julia," Mama scolded. "I should think you might approach the event with a bit more decorum."

"Yes, Mama." She managed to choke out the words. "But I—I only wished to spare you the trouble. Because . . . well, as it happens, I haven't any need of a lecture on . . . mechanics."

"Mechanics?" It was her mother's turn to blush, and as she was as fair as her children were dark, the color was visible to the roots of her hair. "My dear, I'm not a fool. But I did think that, well . . . Lord Dunstane seems a very stern gentleman, and I thought perhaps you might be worried that in marrying him, all your girlish amusements would be at an end. But he is a *good* man—the right one for you, of that I'm certain, even after just a few brief meetings. And the happiness you'll make together, well . . . I assure you, nothing can compare."

Her blue eyes were soft, the corners wrinkled with a gentle smile. "I married a stern gentleman, too, you know."

"Mr. Remington?" He could, on occasion, call forth a certain stiffness of posture, a certain stuffiness that belied his humble origins—part sergeant, part valet. But *stern*?

"No, dear. I was referring to your papa. Of course, you do not remember him as stern, because by the time you knew him, he had softened. He had you, and your brother—a family—love—"

All the things Graham had so long been denied.

Tears stung Julia's eyes as she contemplated the transformation. "Thank you, Mama. I believe you are right. Lord Dunstane and I shall make one another very happy."

Jess's lips were wobbly, and Laura dabbed surreptitiously at the end of her nose, which was pink. When Nelly arrived on the scene a moment later, bearing a large box tied with a ribbon, alarm at all their tears showed plainly on her face. "Is aught amiss?" Only partly reassured by four rather snuffly denials, she laid the package on the bed. "This just arrived for you."

"Thank you, Nelly," Julia said.

The girl curtsied and retreated to the doorway with obvious reluctance, muttering something about Mrs. Whyte having need of her in the kitchen.

"Stay a moment. You must be curious about what's inside." Julia certainly was. Untying the ribbon and lifting the lid, she revealed a hooded cloak of purple velvet, trimmed in soft gray fur. "Oh, my," she cried gathering its richness into her arms.

Laura peered into the box. "There's no note. Just a pair of fur-lined gloves to match," she said, holding them aloft with a mischievous smile. "But there's no mystery as to who sent this. Someone doesn't want his bride to catch a chill on that long carriage ride north."

Julia smiled softly to herself, rubbing her heated cheek against the luxurious softness. How could she ever be cold with a fiery Scotsman at her side?

A half an hour later found her crossing the corner of Clapham Common, the frostbitten grass crisp beneath her feet, her hand looped through her brother's arm. Aunt Mildred walked a few steps ahead of them, supported between Daniel and Mr. Remington, while all the others followed behind.

"I hope, Jeremy, you can find it in your heart to wish me well."

His dark brows arced in astonishment. "What else would I wish you?"

"I never imagined I would marry such a man," she confessed in a voice almost too low for him to hear, thinking of what their mother had said about Graham's sternness, and the number of times she herself had thought him unpleasant and cold.

"Really? He's exactly the sort I pictured would suit you—always blathering on about some play, and stubborn as the day is long."

She couldn't decide whether he was teasing. "You don't approve of the match, then. I know the two of you had words about something . . ."

"We did," Jeremy admitted mournfully, shaking his head. "Not sure he'll ever forgive me for being the one to make sure Fanshawe understood what would become of him if he didn't hold his tongue—in prison, or out of it. But I saw no reason not to put my military connections to good use. As to our argument, well . . . Dunstane positively refused to accept a dowry. It took a great deal of arm-twisting even to get him to agree to settle the money on your children." Then his eyes twinkled down at her. "Have you seen the size of the fellow's arms?"

"As it happens, brother dear," she answered with a naughty smile, "I have. Oh, Jeremy, I do love him, you know."

"And I haven't the slightest doubt that he loves you." They were at the doors of the church now. Jeremy slid her hand from his arm and raised it to his lips. "Papa is smiling down on you today. Be happy, little one."

Why, oh why, had everyone conspired to turn her into a watering pot on her wedding day?

The handful of congregants were dwarfed by the large, modern church, where Wilberforce and the other firebrands of the Clapham Sect often met and worshiped. Mrs. Hayes and Julia's family were seated in the box pews near the front, while a scattering of others—Mrs. Whyte and the servants; Graham's secretary, Mr. Keynes; and a gentleman she had thought never to see again—occupied the benches in the balcony that ran along either side.

And at the front of the church, standing beside the rector, stood Graham, handsome as ever. He was clad in a dark-blue coat, the perfect contrast to his coppery hair, paired once more with his kilt. At the sight of him, heat prickled her cheeks.

A high arch separated the nave from the altar. *Almost like a stage*, she thought. Which was probably sacrilege. But the lines she would speak today were, indeed, scripted, and her elegant new dress might certainly qualify as a costume.

The only difference was that she had long since stopped acting a part where Graham was concerned.

He turned and scanned the assembly. Despite the length of the church separating them, she knew exactly when his gaze settled on her.

His lips curved, almost shyly at first, as if the movement were unfamiliar to him. Then his face was transformed by a genuine smile.

Her heart fluttered, and she had to blink away more tears to make sure her eyes were not playing tricks on her. But no, it was true. He was smiling at her. The mask was gone. Not a hint of wryness or even slyness. Only delight.

And, perhaps, just a hint of relief, as if he, too, had begun to think this moment would never come to pass.

What followed was a blur: the exchange of vows, the pledging of troths, the clasping of hands. And then, finally, they were husband and wife, never to be parted again.

Under cover of their family and friends' expressions of joy, she nodded toward the balcony and whispered to Graham, "Are you the reason Mr. Pope is here?"

Graham looked chagrined at having been caught out. "As I'd invited my secretary, it seemed only fitting to invite my new manager as well."

"'Manager'?"

"He'll be handling theatrical matters on behalf

of Ransom Blackadder, while I'm away from London."

She couldn't disguise her surprise. "That's showing him a great deal of confidence."

"Yes, well." Gruffly, he cleared his throat. "He's obviously a shrewd fellow. And it seemed to me that he deserved a second chance."

It was Julia's turn to smile.

When it came time to sign the register, the pen trembled in her fingers as she wrote her new name. "Perhaps I ought to have practiced," she said. "But it didn't feel right—or real—until now."

With another of those extraordinary smiles, Graham took the quill from her. "It's both, my dear. Real. And oh, so right." Using his left hand—the other was still bandaged and bound in a sling—he wrote with painstaking slowness beneath her signature: *Dunstane.* Then he gave a self-deprecating shake of his head at the almost-childish scrawl his efforts had produced. "And to think, I practiced for hours."

She laughed and looped her arm through his, gazing admiringly at the page. "I think it looks marvelous, indeed, my lord."

"As do you, my lady." As he passed the pen on to Jeremy, a hint of wickedness crept into the curve of his lips, and he added, low enough that only she could hear, "My lass."

The sound of his voice would never cease to send a shiver of delight through her.

Afterward, they returned to Aunt Mildred's house, to find a table groaning beneath a wedding feast fit for an earl and his countess, capped off with cake and champagne.

And then, the passage of time grown suddenly swift after so long a wait, it was the hour for good-byes. Talk turned to the remaining daylight, how far along the journey they expected to travel today, and how long it would be before they would see one another again. A cold rain had begun to fall, so the whole party crowded into the little entry hall. Mama and Laura and Jeremy took turns hugging Julia, none of them quite ready, it seemed, to let her go so far or so soon.

"Oh," said Aunt Mildred with a dismissive wave. "They'll be back before we can miss them. I'll wager you do not find England quite so unappealing as you once did, eh, Dunstane?" she asked him with a sly look. "I predict that box at Covent Garden won't stay empty forever."

"You must consider that box yours, ma'am," he answered, bending low to kiss her gnarled hand. "But I hope you will save a seat for me and my wife."

"Just one seat for the two of you?" she retorted with a twinkle in her eye as she tapped his arm with her folded lorgnette. "You Scottish rogue. But then, I thought from the first time you laid eyes on Julia, you'd be happy enough to share."

They all laughed, and before the mood could turn somber again, Graham ushered Julia out the door. A dash between the icy raindrops, and they were secure in his traveling coach, waving through the glass as the wheels began to roll.

Seated beside him on the forward-facing bench, wrapped in his arm and her new velvet cloak, Julia paid no attention to anything but her husband for several minutes. Only when she reached across him to draw down the shade, preferring not to have half the eyes of London gawking at their wedded bliss, did she realize they were surrounded by nothing but fields.

"Graham," she gasped. "This isn't the way to the Great North Road." They ought to be crossing the Thames, toward the bustle of Smithfield.

"Isn't it?" he asked lazily, tracing her ear with the tip of his tongue.

"No. In fact, we're headed . . . south."

That piece of information was met with a string of kisses along her throat that almost made her forget to care. Still . . . she laid a palm against his chest, putting a scant few inches between them. "May I ask where we're going?"

"Scotland," he assured her, his eyes already dark with desire. "Starting first thing tomorrow. But tonight, I thought you might prefer somewhere more private than an inn. Somewhere no one can find us." Each sentence was punctuated with a lingering kiss. "Somewhere we won't be disturbed."

"Brereton Cottage," she breathed, taking one final glance out the window before closing her eyes and giving herself over to his lips.

Leave it to a scandalous playwright to pick the perfect setting for the first scene of their new life together.

Epilogue

Castle Dunstane, Scotland
Christmas Eve, 1810

"It's snowing. It never snows on Christmas."

"It rarely snows in the south of England on Christmas," Graham corrected, pausing to look up from his desk so he might watch Julia wander in wide-eyed amazement from one window of his study to the next. Snowflakes had already begun to collect in the corners of the leaded windowpanes. "The Highlands are another world."

"A beautiful one," she said, praising the stark landscape spread before her, as yet only lightly disguised beneath the snowfall.

"Aye," he agreed, with eyes only for her. "Now, come here and tell me what this word is." In just a few weeks, she'd become expert at deciphering his left-handed scrawl. He'd worked to strengthen the fingers of his right, but the dexterity required for wielding a pen with it still eluded him and perhaps always would.

He was surprised by how little it mattered.

Particularly not when Julia perched on his knee, giving him a rather tantalizing view down her bodice. She peered at the pages of the manuscript they'd been working on together, lines and scenes that were half her invention, half his.

"I might be able to make it out," she mock-scolded, "if you wouldn't insist on squeezing your bits in between mine."

Now, *that* sounded appealing, indeed.

"Never you mind about those pages, lass," he told her in the gruff voice that pleased her so, chasing away her studious frown with a kiss.

They were interrupted by the sound of Keynes clearing his throat. "I beg your pardon, my lord. My lady." He bowed, his arms full of papers, as always. As he did, his spectacles, which had been perched on the top of his head, tumbled onto the floor.

"Oh, dear," exclaimed Julia, leaping to her feet to retrieve them, much to the secretary's mortification. A high stickler his countess would never be.

"You look well, Keynes," Graham said, accepting the stack of papers he held out to him. The man was still thin, but some of the grayness had left his complexion since they had returned home.

"Th-thank you, sir. I do believe it's the fresh Highlands air."

Graham suspected Keynes's improvement ought to be chalked up to something other than the brutally cold wind that occasionally swept through

Castle Dunstane despite the mason's best efforts. The fact that his employer no longer barked unreasonable orders at him, for instance. Or the permanent reprieve from scouring the papers for reviews of Blackadder's plays.

Once Keynes had gone, Graham turned his attention to sorting through the post. "Ah, my love. Here's an invitation to a ball on Hogmanay." He would enjoy the chance to show her off.

"Hmm?"

He looked up to find her fully absorbed by something that must have been addressed to her. Between her fingers he spied a familiar Grecian figure.

"The latest issue of the *Magazine for Misses*?"

"Hm, yes," came the distracted reply. She was still thumbing through the pages. "I began to think it might never arrive."

He had wondered whether the mysterious Mrs. Goode might yet close up shop. Though Fanshawe hadn't succeeded in exposing any of the other women involved, it could not be easy for them to dismiss the danger they'd been in.

"Odd," she said.

"What is?"

"No 'Unfashionable Plates' this month." She flipped from front to back, as if still in disbelief. "No illustrations at all."

"Perhaps Miss C. took a holiday," he suggested, mildly curious about what that might involve. Mrs. Goode, Miss C., and the rest were still as much a mystery as they had ever been. Julia had offered to reveal the secret identities behind the magazine to him, but he had declined. Those women had a right to protect their names, just as he had done, and to reveal them only when and if they were ready.

"Perhaps." She sounded dubious. "Anyway, there's this." As she approached his desk, she creased open the magazine to a page near the middle and laid it before him. *Miss on Scene*, the bold banner across the top proclaimed.

"You wrote this?" he asked, picking up the magazine. "When did you find the time?"

"You mean, in between dress fittings and wedding planning and—?"

"Play rehearsals," he supplied, then added with a sidelong glance, "And, er, nursing me back to health."

"Just read it," she urged.

It, he quickly discovered, was a review of *The Poison Pen*.

"I went back to see it the next night," she explained. "With Aunt Mildred."

The next night? What extraordinary bravery it must have required to return to Covent Garden at all, to say nothing of doing so hard on the heels of near disaster. More courage than he seemed to possess, even now. Instinctively, he shied away from the words before him. He knew, of course, that the play had gone on, with Mrs. Cole restored to her role and Sawyer, in a wig and spectacles, taking on Fanshawe's part, in addition to his own. But as far as Graham was concerned, it would be better never to think about Perpetua Philpot or the Briggs brothers again.

Seeming to read his thoughts, Julia shrugged her explanation. "I had to find out how it ended somehow." Then, with playful fingers, she brushed a piece of hair from his temple. When she spoke again, her voice was a soft plea. "Read it."

If you came to this page expecting to learn the grisly details of the opening night of The Poison Pen, *or to discover the fate of the actor who is said to have intended to stopper the inkpots of theater critics everywhere, and to silence this reviewer especially, you will be sadly disappointed. As luck would have it, Miss on Scene was not at liberty to be in the audience that night and so cannot speak to the particulars of the infamous performance for which the entire* ton *is rumored to have been in attendance. Whether her luck was bad or good, she leaves for others to determine.*

Whatever those in that first audience saw, it seems to have lured many of them back the following night, for the theater on this occasion was as crowded as this critic has ever seen it. Fortunately, a seat in the box belonging to a friend was yet unclaimed.

And so, it is with something of surprise and more of delight, that this Miss can report Ransom Blackadder has claimed his proper throne at last— not as the disdainful emperor of satire, but as the prince of more amusing pleasures, telling the story of a creative but fiery man who learned to value the wit of a clever young woman.

He had. Oh, indeed, he had.

Graham's eyes began to skim over the page in his haste to take it all in—her words of praise for Mrs. Cole, Mr. Sawyer, the unusual use of the stage. At last, he came to her description of the final act.

*It will, I hope, spoil no one's enjoyment to reveal
that in the end, our two protagonists—both writers—come to understand that their work unites,
rather than divides them. Ultimately, of course,
their love of words takes second place to their love
for one another.*

*N.B. This reviewer is surprised Mr. Blackadder
did not call his play* The <u>Passionate</u> Pen
*instead—proof, one may surmise, that even the
best playwrights cannot think of everything on
their own and must, on occasion, turn to their
critics for proper inspiration.*
Miss on Scene expects some credit in the revival.

When she seemed certain he had done, Julia
reached out a hand and closed the magazine. One
fingertip traced over the caryatids. "My final contribution."

"For now."

She lifted her gaze to his face, her blue eyes unusually sober. A wrinkle formed in her brow, and
her lips shaped a question, though she did not
speak.

Graham explained. "I've been meaning to suggest you might send in a few of the dialogues you've
written. The conversation between the girl and
her governess about the need to study history, for
instance. Mrs. Goode seems to have an eye for orig-
inal work, particularly on subjects of interest to
her readers."

"Oh. I—I didn't realize you'd read that piece. It
was just a—a, well, an exercise, I suppose you
might say. I never considered . . ."

"And I see no reason why Miss on Scene should not resume reviewing at least occasionally when we return to London next season." He slid some of the pages of the manuscript on which they'd been working over the magazine. "For example, the debut of a brilliant new playwright, who will be known to have the support of a well-regarded patron of the dramatic arts."

"I—" Her teeth sank into her lower lip. "Do you really think our play could be ready to perform within a year?"

"I do," he said, catching her by the waist and pulling her into his lap. "Though it would require us to focus on work. Fewer . . . distractions."

"Ensuring an heir to the Earl of Dunstane is hardly a distraction, my lord," she retorted primly, pretending to be immune to the gravelly suggestiveness of his voice, or the brush of his fingers beneath the curve of her breast.

His heart began to knock against his ribs. He cared little enough for heirs and earldoms—but a child? a family? "Is that what we've been doing, my lady?" he rasped.

"Well . . ." Her cheeks pinked, and that marvelously mischievous glint shone in her eyes. "Some of the time." She picked up the quill and sat up a little straighter; the movement slid the curve of her bottom suggestively over his cock.

"You're inspiring this playwright right now," he said, nipping at the place where her neck and shoulder joined. "Though I wouldn't call it *proper* inspiration."

"Graham," she scolded, tickling the feather over

his nose. "Focus, remember? Now, have you given any thought to what name we'll use?"

"I have, actually. What say you to Addison McKay?"

She glanced over her shoulder to see if he was serious. "Won't people suspect?"

"I'm counting on it. Their curiosity will draw them to the theater."

Though there was surprise and delight in her gaze, there was merriment in her voice when she replied, "That's quite brilliant, actually."

"Careful, lass. Too much praise will go to my head."

With a smile, she turned back to the papers strewn across the desk, trailing the end of the quill over her lips. "Now, then. About this exchange between the suitor and the soldier. I really don't think—oh!" She shuffled back a few pages. "Ardor."

"Pardon?"

"*Ardor*—that's the word you wrote. The one I couldn't make out earlier."

He shifted her more securely onto his knee— since she seemed determined to work, rather than play—and directed his attention to the scribble she had underlined with the ink-stained nail of her first finger. Truth be told, he wasn't sure he'd ever in his life written the word *ardor*.

But he was quite sure it was the perfect word to capture the love he felt for his bride, his partner, the leading lady of his life.

Keep Reading for the special bonus novella

Nice Earls Do

To readers of her popular book *Mrs. Goode's Guide to Homekeeping*, "Mrs. Goode" is an expert in all domestic matters. Household management, home décor, entertainment . . . there is nothing about which she lacks an opinion. Who better to assist the Earl of Stalbridge, newly appointed guardian to his niece and nephew, in turning his house into a home?

The widowed Lady Manwaring is the furthest thing from a domestic doyenne, so when asked to pose as Mrs. Goode on behalf of the book's true author, she warily agrees. On arrival, she's surprised to discover that Lord Stalbridge is actually her childhood friend Kit Killigrew. Tabetha might be an imposter, but her attraction to Kit is all too real . . .

After years separated from the woman of his dreams, Kit's eager to do more than play house. Will Tabetha's big reveal ruin everything, or lay the foundation for true love?

Nice Earls Do

a novella
by Susanna Craig

To Brad,
my hero

Acknowledgments

As I kick off this new series, I am grateful for the support I've had throughout my writing career: my agent, Jill Marsal; the fabulous team at Kensington (Alex, Lauren, Jane, and all the folks in production and art); and especially my editors, Esi Sogah, who helped turn this dream into reality, and Liz May, who carried the ball over the finish line. I also owe huge thanks to my author friends in the Drawing Room historical romance group: to Amy, for listening, reading, and everything else; to my mom, daughter, and especially husband both for their steadfast encouragement of my dreams and for carrying on when my schedule turned things upside down; and of course, to my readers.

Chapter 1

Kit had already read the letter a dozen times at least. Looking at it again would tell him nothing new—not least because he'd left his reading spectacles downstairs. Nevertheless, restless, he withdrew the paper from his breast pocket and unfolded it.

The blur of indistinguishable words might just as easily have belonged to another, similarly life-changing letter, one he'd received almost a year ago, announcing his younger brother's death.

That news hadn't come as a surprise, by any means. A lifetime of rebellion and risk-taking was not likely to lead to any other outcome. Nevertheless, Kit had mourned, was still mourning, his loss. The world's loss. Edmund's gifts might have been turned to better uses. Kit found himself now, as then, grateful his parents had not lived to see what had become of their favorite.

Amid the clatter of his thoughts, he hadn't heard Mrs. Rushworth's footsteps.

"Lord Stalbridge?" the housekeeper prompted, a hint of worry in her voice.

Kit folded the letter, returned it to his pocket, and glanced toward her before surveying the boxes and crates that surrounded them, the sundry relics of another man's life. "I want this room cleaned out, thoroughly scrubbed, and set to rights, Mrs. Rushworth."

"Of course, my lord," she replied, inclining her head. But she did not immediately turn and go. He had not really expected it of her. "May a body ask why?"

The previous earl, a distant cousin Kit had never met, had been a noted traveler and a collector. The uppermost floor of Ferncliffe had been devoted to storage of his treasures. In the four years since his unexpected inheritance, Kit had focused his attention on other parts of the estate and spared little thought for the house itself, and even less for this particular room. He had had no need for the space. Until now.

"Because, Mrs. Rushworth, the nursery is soon to be occupied."

"Oh?" A note of speculative interest replaced the previous concern in Mrs. Rushworth's voice.

"Edmund's children will be arriving by the end of the month," he explained.

Silence hung on the air, mingling lazily with the dust motes. "Beggin' your pardon, my lord," she said at last, "but I never knew your brother had taken a bride."

Kit cleared his throat. The housekeeper's respectability fit her even more neatly than the char-coal-colored woolen dress she wore. If he weren't careful in his reply, she'd tender her resignation—or at least leave him to clean out the nursery by himself.

"Oh, yes," he told her, though he, too, had his doubts. The wedding ceremony had probably been conducted under the watchful eye of some poor girl's father—or at the end of his hunting rifle, or the point of his sword.

"The children and their mother were living with Edmund in Sicily. She contracted his fever while nursing him, it seems, and died some months after," he said, patting the letter inside his coat. "But her friends did not initially know to whom the children ought to be sent." The only marvel, really, was how much time had elapsed before someone had asked him to clean up another—and hopefully the last—of his brother's messes.

To his surprise, Mrs. Rushworth sighed. "Then the poor things are *orphans*."

"Yes." He surveyed the dismal, dirty attic. "I'd like to arrange a suitable welcome for my niece and nephew, Mrs. Rushworth."

"Of course, sir," she said, though the enormity of the task had stripped away some of her usual confidence. And his.

How could a man of forty-five, with no wife of his own and no intention of acquiring one, no ex-perience with children, and a house in which even he did not feel welcome, ever hope to give two young children the home they needed?

"You need Mrs. Goode," the housekeeper de-clared.

Was this another of Mrs. Rushworth's match-making schemes? Since he'd come into the title, the housekeeper had hinted mercilessly about the need for a Lady Stalbridge.

Kit, who had sworn off marriage twenty years before when the girl he loved had married another, had learned to smile and nod and politely ignore her. This time, however, he blurted out, "I beg your pardon?"

"Mrs. Goode," she repeated, as if the woman's identity must be self-evident. "Of *Mrs. Goode's Guide to Homekeeping*," she added by way of explanation, though clearly incredulous at the necessity of providing it. Finally, his baffled expression forced her to concede defeat. "It's a book, my lord. Very popular. Indispensable advice on how to design, decorate, and prepare the household for any guest or occasion."

"Ah. A pity this Mrs. Goode cannot come to us in person," he joked, then sobered as he looked once more about the room. "We need all the help we can get."

Mrs. Rushworth made a noise in her throat, the meaning of which was indecipherable to him. "I'll get right to it, sir." With a curtsy, she bustled away.

Though wintry wind whistled through the cracked window, chilling the air around him, Kit remained behind, thinking not of the work that lay ahead but of Edmund and the adventures they would have had in such a room when they were little boys, when guarding his brother from cuts, torn clothes, and splinters was the biggest challenge he faced.

People had always thought of Kit Killigrew—he

thought of himself—as a serious, predictable, or-derly sort of man.

Why then had nothing in his life turned out as he had planned?

Tabetha Holt Cantwell, Dowager Viscountess Man-waring, stared down at the gray pavement three stories below and sighed. London in November tried her patience. Her friends had long since de-camped for the autumn entertainments of the countryside, and the promised amusements of the Christmas season were still weeks away. She was in danger of succumbing to ennui.

Truth be told, she was beginning to find it equally difficult to fend off boredom in the other eleven months of the year.

Early in her widowhood, London had held an allure nothing could match. Her late husband's country estate, in which she'd been immured for the better part of twenty years, hadn't even had much of a library. In London, she'd found plays and lectures and books and people. She'd de-voured the town's pleasures like a starving woman presented with a plate of cream puffs.

And now she had a stomachache.

From the opposite end of the room, her stepson Oliver, Lord Manwaring, echoed her sigh. Or per-haps it would be more accurate to call the noise he'd made a gasp. Oliver had a tendency toward the dramatic, to be sure, but when she'd gone to the window, he'd been lazily leafing through his correspondence, and he was not the sort of young man who generally exclaimed over the post.

In any case, the sound made her turn. His posture, usually teetering on the brink of indolence, was as rigid as she had ever seen it, though his head was bent over his letter. No, *two* letters, one in each hand. As she watched, he shoved the papers together in one fist and pushed the shaking fingers of the other hand through his dark brown curls.

She began to hurry toward him, then forced her steps to a more sedate pace. She'd been Oliver's protector for so long, first from his father and later from the world, that the impulse to smooth his hair from his brow and solve his problems was second nature. Sometimes she forgot he was a grown man and might no longer appreciate the interference.

"What is it, dear?"

She had to repeat the question before he looked up from the papers, and when he did, his brown eyes verged on wild. "It seems I've landed in a spot of trouble, Mamabet," he said, twisting his lips into a self-deprecating smile. He'd chosen the name for her on the second evening of their acquaintance, combining the address upon which his father had insisted with a lisped version of what she'd always been called by family and friends, which she'd told Oliver he might use in private.

She laid a hand along the curved back of a green-and-gold striped chair. "What sort of trouble?"

"The 'detrimental to the name of Manwaring' sort, I'm afraid." He punctuated the sentence with a humorless laugh.

Detrimental to the name of Manwaring. His father's

phrase—they'd both heard it often enough. Applied variously to Oliver's mannerisms, to his lack of athletic prowess and distaste for shooting a rifle, and most recently to his failure to choose a bride and "do his duty by the title," Oliver's own desires and future happiness be damned.

The late Lord Manwaring had not been an ideal husband, by any means, but he'd been a truly awful father to Oliver.

She'd entered the marriage in possession of all the desirable accomplishments a young lady might acquire—dancing, drawing, modern languages— and with a clear understanding of what was expected of her.

Or so she'd thought.

As it had turned out, she'd been better prepared by the books on philosophy she'd sneaked from her father's library and by the childhood games of hide-and-seek she'd played with the boys next door. The old viscount had married her for one reason: to produce a second, more acceptable, son. Tabetha, who liked children very much and who had looked forward to motherhood, had not mourned her inability to give her husband what he most wanted. When he'd died, she had made the proper observances, but she had not mourned him in her heart.

Oliver sank back in his chair, the partner to the one against which Tabetha now leaned, and flung one leg over the rolled arm, in something approximating his usual relaxed pose. Only his death grip on the letters betrayed him.

"You've heard, I suppose, of *Mrs. Goode's Guide to Homekeeping?*" he asked, not quite meeting her eye.

Tabetha was the sort of person who happily left decisions about the weekly menu to her housekeeper. She preferred the role of guest to that of hostess. And she had given carte blanche to Oliver when it came to redecorating the townhouse they shared.

But one would have to have taken up residence under a rock not to have heard of *Mrs. Goode's Guide*, not only because of its ubiquity but because of the controversy it had engendered by making the secrets of elegant design and epicurean delights accessible to anyone who could afford the book; six shillings in paper, ten and sixpence bound.

Who would have suspected that homekeeping could inspire such passion?

She nodded, and though Oliver was not really looking at her, he seemed to have anticipated her answer.

"Well, *this*," he said, shifting his thumb to push the uppermost letter forward slightly, "is from a devoted reader, the housekeeper of a bachelor gentleman who has recently been named guardian to the children of his dearly departed brother. He would benefit from Mrs. Goode's assistance in the preparation of his nursery, she says."

"And what, may I ask, has that to do with you?" As she spoke, Tabetha stepped around to the front of the chair and sat down, fearing Oliver's answer might require it.

He favored her with a lopsided smile and lifted one shoulder. "I'm Mrs. Goode."

Her mouth popped open, as if the hinge of her jaw were powered by a spring beyond her control.

But no words came. Only a strangled noise of astonishment in her throat.

"That is to say," he went on smoothly, ignoring the fact that she was gaping at him like a fish floundering on dry land, "I wrote the *Guide to Homekeeping.*"

Still wide-eyed, Tabetha glanced around the room. Four years ago, following her husband's death, both she and her stepson had been eager for a change. Oliver had suggested the rarely used family townhouse in Berkeley Square and promised to make it ready for them to inhabit by the time her mourning ended. He'd always had a flair for colors and textiles, for arranging things *just so*—much to his father's chagrin. Tabetha had agreed to remain in the country while Oliver chose every finish, every fabric. He'd overseen the workmen. And he'd recorded the adventure in a series of amusing letters to her that had made a long, dreary winter bearable.

Perhaps his revelation about the book should not have surprised her as much as it did.

"Does anyone else know?" she asked, dragging her gaze back to her stepson.

His lips quirked in a chiding smile that carved a dimple into one cheek, as if he suspected she must already know the answer. "Not even my publisher. We've been negotiating plans for a companion volume, you see." He held out the two letters to her. "And before those plans are finalized, they're insisting Mrs. Goode go to Hertfordshire. They believe it will be excellent publicity."

Tabetha scanned the letters. The threat—for

what else could it be called—wasn't explicit. But clearly the publisher's willingness to purchase Oliver's future work depended upon Mrs. Goode's compliance with this, this . . . *request*. She suspected it was at least in part a ploy to find out the identity of Mrs. Goode. But the publisher wouldn't be happy with what their little scheme uncovered.

Oh, it wasn't just that *Mrs. Goode's Guide* had been written by a man. Gentlemen were forever involving themselves in ladies' affairs, telling them what to do or wear or buy. That a man would proffer a book of advice on such topics was unremarkable. But gentlemen weren't actually supposed to be *interested* in such feminine trifles as home décor, recipes, and furbelows. If word got out that Oliver had written *Mrs. Goode's Guide* from a place of genuine enthusiasm for its subject matter, he could expect ridicule, scorn, or worse. He would be driven to set aside yet another of his passions to keep someone else's peace.

"What will you do?"

He shrugged, as if the matter were of complete indifference to him. As if a measure of his happiness didn't hang in the balance.

She'd seen that shrug before.

"I'll go in your stead," she offered rashly. "I can pretend to be Mrs. Goode."

One eyebrow shot skyward. "You know I love you, Mamabet. But no, you cannot."

Did he hesitate for her sake or his own? Was he reluctant to participate in a deception that might damage his stepmother's character? Or fearful her taste was so execrable that Mrs. Goode's good name would be ruined?

"We could come up with some pretext for you to accompany me," she suggested. "That way, you could still make all the important decisions, while I simply play the public part."

"If I were able and inclined to disguise myself as a lady's maid," he scoffed, "I daresay I could also manage a passable Mrs. Goode."

"Not as my *maid*," she said, pushing to her feet and beginning to pace. "As my . . . my groom?"

His lips pursed, and distaste shuddered through his lithe frame.

"My manservant, then. Or—oh, I know! My secretary. Surely someone as successful as Mrs. Goode would have a secretary?"

She held her breath, waiting for his reaction. After an impossibly long moment, his long leg slid down from the arm of the chair, and his glossy boot settled on the floor beside its mate. "Go on . . ."

"We will travel to Hertfordshire and present ourselves to . . . to . . ." She sat down and scanned the letter again. "To this Lord Stalbridge's housekeeper as the esteemed Mrs. Goode and her secretary, Mr. Oliver. A day or two of discussion and sketches should be sufficient, wouldn't you say? Surely your publisher cannot expect more. And then we'll be free to return to town. You can make all the actual arrangements for the nursery renovation from here, in the name of Mrs. Goode, and no one will be the wiser."

Oliver leaned toward her. "You would do that? For me?"

"Can you doubt it?" The hurt in her voice was not put on.

Certainly she wasn't doing it for Lord Stalbridge,

whoever he might be. She'd heard the title but could put no face to it. Under ordinary circumstances, her curiosity might have been piqued, particularly when she had so little to occupy her at present. But now, her irritation outweighed her interest. Being a bachelor gentleman did not excuse a total inattention to matters of household management.

Oliver snatched up her hands, heedless of the papers crumpling between them, pulled her to her feet, and planted a smacking kiss on her cheek. "Bless you, Mamabet. I'll see to everything," he promised before departing in a whirlwind.

A house in mourning, buried in the country, undergoing improvements, and soon to be filled with the noise of children, was not exactly the cure for the doldrums she'd been hoping for. But she would go gladly, just to help Oliver.

And perhaps for the added pleasure of giving this Lord Stalbridge a piece of her—or rather, the indomitable Mrs. Goode's—mind.

Not quite a week later, Kit looked up from the account ledger he'd been reviewing to find Mrs. Rushworth standing in the doorway of his study, her starched linen handkerchief stark white against her dark dress. He had to peer over the tops of his spectacles to see her expression clearly, a mixture of apprehension and surprise.

"Is everything all right?" he asked. For a moment, she didn't answer, leaving him to picture any number of catastrophes. "Something in the attic?" Perhaps, against all odds, one of the late earl's crates had contained something interesting, even shocking.

"No, my lord. That is, everything is fine. It's naught to do with anything upstairs . . . exactly."

He closed the ledger, laid his spectacles aside, and folded his hands on the desktop. "Then what, *exactly*, is the matter?"

"It's Mrs. Goode, sir." Mrs. Rushworth's mouth moved oddly; he suspected her of chewing on the inside of her lip. Her voice dropped. "She's here."

His brain suddenly felt as thick and impenetrable as the crust of an overdone plum pudding. Her whispered words could not seem to pierce it. *Mrs. Goode?* He'd assumed the name was nothing more than a polite fiction, manufactured to sell books.

Before he could muster even simple questions—*How? Why?*—Mrs. Rushworth went on. "I wrote, you see, to her publisher. It was you, my lord, who put the notion into my mind. I thought perhaps, if she weren't too busy, she might offer a little free advice. But I never dreamed . . ." Now she began to twist her handkerchief with agitated hands.

"She's here." In his stuttering attempt at comprehension, the words came out half-statement, half-question.

"Yes, sir. With her secretary, Mr. Oliver. To help us," she finished, brightening. "Shall I show them in?"

He didn't think he'd answered her. He still didn't think Mrs. Goode was real. But the housekeeper turned from the room with a purposeful stride, and he found himself unfolding his hands, laying them flat on the desktop, and pushing to his feet, just in case.

A moment later, he heard steps along the corridor. Mrs. Rushworth reappeared and curtsied. "Mrs. Goode to see you, my lord."

A lady entered behind her. A flesh-and-blood lady, clad in a china-blue pelisse. More, he could not say, for her head was turned in such a way that he could see nothing beyond the brim of her bonnet, not a glimpse of her profile, not even the color of her hair.

She was speaking low to someone behind her: her secretary, he presumed. He could not make out her words. But the voice . . . Its huskiness sent a spark along his spine, like the sensation of a touch tracing the contours of each vertebra. *A familiar touch . . .*

He kept his hands planted firmly on his desk, suddenly conscious that if he lifted them, he would reveal two perfect prints, the sweat of his palms dark against the leather blotter.

The secretary, Mr. Oliver, entered behind Mrs. Goode. He was a tall, slender young man with a veritable mop of curly dark brown hair, his coat and greatcoat gaping open to reveal the flash of a pink-and-green checked waistcoat. One of Mrs. Goode's gloved hands rose to brush a few raindrops from Mr. Oliver's shoulder, a surprisingly intimate gesture between a lady and her secretary.

Before Kit had succeeded in tamping down a rush of jealousy, to say nothing of examining the absurdity of such a reaction, the woman turned, and his brain—moments before, as solid and impervious as a kiln-fired brick—turned to mush.

Beth—unmistakably *his* Beth, though twenty years had passed since his parting look at her—was stepping toward him.

She extended that same hand in greeting, and though her steady blue gaze appeared to be focused on him, he could tell she hadn't really *seen* him. Not yet.

He knew precisely the moment she did. The flicker of recognition. The flash of disbelief. Her cheeks paled, then pinked, and the outstretched hand drew back and fluttered to the base of her throat. "Lord Stalbridge?"

The necessity of coming forward and helping her to a chair prevented him from giving in to the temptation to sink into one himself. He curled his hand beneath her elbow and eased her to a seat, bending close enough that he could smell her perfume, an inviting mixture of pear blossoms and vanilla.

"Are you quite well . . . Mrs. Goode?" She had never been far from his thoughts, but the address was strange on his lips. *Manwaring* had been the fellow's title, the dour old hermit her father had insisted she marry, all so he could hear his only daughter addressed as "my lady."

She didn't answer, merely searched his face, her eyes wide with aching wonder. Then her gaze dropped to his hand, which had slid up from her elbow to curve around her upper arm, a forward gesture, even in spite of their history. He tried to marshal his mind—more custard than pudding, more mortar than brick—to order his fingers to relax their grip.

But every instinct told him never to let her go again.

Chapter 2

Kit Killigrew.
Tabetha curled her fingers into the arms of
the chair to keep from lifting her hands to caress
his face, just to prove to herself he was real. How
was it possible? Here? After all this time? And . . .
Lord Stalbridge?

Both Oliver and Mrs. Rushworth had hurried
forward and now stood, one at either side of the
chair to which Kit had helped her. "Is ought amiss,
ma'am?" asked the housekeeper, while Oliver's
brow furrowed with worry.

"I—I'm fine," she insisted, though unconvinc-
ingly. "Just a sudden spate of dizziness. I am prone
to carriage sickness, you know."

Oliver must have recognized it for the lie it was,
an excuse fabricated to explain her sudden faint-
ness; his expression shifted into puzzlement. His
curious glance toward Kit's hand, still wrapped

warmly around her arm, made Kit at last release her. He pushed himself backward a few steps to lean against the front of his desk, as if he, too, were not quite steady on his feet.

"I'll fetch tea, shall I?" Mrs. Rushworth offered.

"That won't be necessary," said Kit—Lord Stalbridge—abruptly. "If you would take Mr. Oliver to the attic—er, nursery, Mrs. Rushworth, I daresay he might begin by, um . . ."

"Taking measurements?" Tabetha suggested. Though it really should not have been a question. Someone with Mrs. Goode's experience ought to know exactly how to proceed. "His lordship and I will follow you up momentarily. I'm almost recovered."

She wasn't. Her heart was pounding so hard, she feared it might burst free of her chest. But *why*? Yes, it was a surprise to find Kit Killigrew at Ferncliffe. And yes, she was pleased to be reunited with a dear childhood friend, as anyone might. But neither surprise nor friendship was an adequate explanation for the fact that her insides seemed to be performing pirouettes.

"Of course, Mrs. Goode," Oliver said. "Whatever you wish."

She watched his glance travel skeptically, protectively, between Tabetha and Kit before he followed the housekeeper from the room.

Once the others had gone, neither she nor Kit seemed to know what to say. Without taking his eyes from her, as if fearful she might disappear if he did, he fished for the decanter sitting on a tray on one corner of the desk and nearly knocked it over. "I think I could use a splash of something stronger than tea," he said at last, laughing as he snagged the heavy crystal stopper between his first two fingers and reached for a tumbler with the other hand. "How about you?"

"Please," she managed to whisper, gratefully accepting the glass he handed her, which contained a scant swallow of some amber-colored liquid. His own glass, she noted, contained rather more. She lifted the drink to her lips and tasted brandy.

Kit took a deep gulp from his glass before setting it aside. "I hardly know which question to ask first. I, uh"—another laugh, incredulous—"I did not believe Mrs. Goode to be an actual person."

"It is an assumed name," she explained, feeling safe to confess that much. As a girl, Tabetha had never managed to keep secrets from Kit—at least not for very long. But Oliver's situation demanded her circumspection.

"You—" He hesitated. "You are still Lady Manwaring, then."

"By courtesy," she answered, after a moment's reflection as to what could or could not be said. "My stepson holds the title now. I was widowed four years ago."

Kit's expression softened. "I'm sorry. I didn't know."

"Why should you?"

"Surely such old friends may take an interest in one another's lives?"

It surprised her to discover she'd been in his thoughts. Then again, when news of Kit or his family had made its way to her over the years, she'd been glad enough to get it. And if she had ever thought to herself that it might be strange, even unseemly, for a married woman to follow the affairs of another man, she had told herself it was merely because they were old friends, just as Kit had said.

"But it just so happens that four years ago, I was distracted." A bitter smile stretched around the rim of his glass. A second swallow drained it. "You see, I'd just inherited . . . all this." With the hand holding the now-empty glass, he gestured wide enough to take in his new title, the manor house, and the estate beyond.

She focused her attention on the room in which they sat, with its warm, masculine furnishings and overfilled bookcases. Its comfortableness reflected the man who sat before her in buckskin breeches, a coat softened with years of wear, and an unstarched cravat—a gentleman at home, indifferent to fashion. It was the sort of ensemble that made Oliver twitch, but it suited Kit perfectly.

And much to Tabetha's surprise, seeing Kit in it suited her.

The years had been gentle with him, despite the signs that he'd been spending a great deal of time outdoors. His golden-brown hair had always betrayed hints of copper after a day in the sun; now it was also sprinkled with silver. His shoulders were as broad and solid as they had ever been, if anything strengthened by the weight of the responsibilities he had been made to bear while still a young man: his widowed mother, his—

"Oh, Kit." Her wavering breath was loud in the silent study. "I'm sorry too." She'd just recalled the reason Mrs. Goode had been summoned to Hertfordshire. "Poor Edmund . . ."

Tabetha didn't even realize she'd stretched out her hand, but she suddenly found her fingers clasped in Kit's, which were as warm and steady as she remembered. She wanted to stand and wrap her arms around him, to comfort her friend as she would have done without a second thought, so long ago.

But the very idea made her heart resume its erratic thumping, and she decided it would be safest to stay in her seat.

"I've been told he didn't suffer," Kit said—meaning, she supposed, to reassure her. But his voice was at once weary and sharp, a reminder that others had suffered, and would go on suffering, in Edmund's place. "And you? I gather . . ." He seemed not to know how to frame the sentence he wished to speak. Finally, it tumbled from his lips with surprising bluntness: "Did you decide to take up writing after your husband's death?"

Tabetha had read through the *Guide to Homekeeping* twice in the past week, to familiarize herself with the part she was to play. In it, Oliver had been careful to reveal very few particulars of Mrs. Goode's domestic life, the better to allow readers to identify with her. What would he say to the idea of her as a genteel but impoverished widow, forced to pick up a pen to support herself?

Not, of course, that Manwaring had left her poor—at least, not by any conventional definition of the word.

"That is to say," Kit went on, "I don't remember you being particularly interested in housekeeping matters. Before."

Tabetha managed to disguise her chuckle of

agreement by taking another sip of her drink. As a young girl, she'd been notoriously indifferent to anything that smacked of domesticity, preferring rough-and-tumble games with Kit and Edmund to playing with dolls or stitching her sampler. Marriage to a staid viscount had restrained, but not necessarily reformed, her. There had been no *Mrs. Goode's Guide* for her life.

"People change," she said, making herself look him square in the eye as she added, "Lord Stalbridge."

"In some ways, yes," he agreed with a wry sort of smile that made fine wrinkles form at the corners of his gray-green eyes. "In others, not at all."

His expression did nothing at all to quiet her erratic pulse. Or perhaps she should blame the gentle pressure of his fingers . . . ?

Freeing her hand from Kit's, she rose, placed her glass on the desktop, and smoothed her skirts, determined to behave in a businesslike manner from this point forward. She had come to Ferncliffe for Oliver's sake, and she would do well to remember it.

"I'm perfectly recovered now. Shall we go upstairs?"

Was it ever ungentlemanly to offer one's arm to a lady?

Certainly, if the offer was made to someone who didn't require assistance, purely to court her touch.

Nevertheless, Kit offered.

After an almost imperceptible hesitation, Beth laid a gloved hand along his forearm. He didn't know what fascinated him more—the ways she had changed or the ways she hadn't. She had always had a pertness, even a hardness, about her. Time, or circumstance, had sharpened her edges even further. But her figure was softer, her curves more generous. And twenty years had not lessened his desire to trace those curves with his eyes . . . his fingertips . . . his lips.

Some friend he was.

"May I see some of the rest of the house on our way?" she asked. "It will help me to understand what's wanted upstairs."

"I . . . yes. Yes, of course." Ferncliffe was one of the showpieces of Hertfordshire.

So why then did he feel a sense of dread at the prospect of showing it to her?

When she said nothing else, he focused on the sound of her footsteps—a brisk, ominous *tick-tick-tick* against marble; more hollow on wood; muffled almost to silence where carpets had been laid—as they passed from room to room. Most were cold, dim; dark curtains drawn even against the feeble winter sun, the furniture strange ghostly shapes between holland cloth.

"I haven't had much occasion to use a ballroom," he explained sheepishly, "or a dining room that seats twenty."

The brim of her bonnet tilted in acknowledgment. "But surely in four years' time, you might have redecorated a bit. Made the place your own."

"I suppose," he acknowledged. "But I have preferred to spend my time and effort out of doors. The last earl was not as careful of the rest of the estate as he might have been. The house is . . . well, as you see it. But the farms, the village . . ." *The peo-ple.* "I inherited just in time to rescue that stream you must have driven over. The landscape archi-tect he had hired wanted to redirect it to be visible from the house. No one involved seemed to have considered that it would be more difficult to raise crops on the south farms without water."

Good Lord. He was babbling worse than a brook. And about water conservation. He needed some-one to redirect *him.*

Beth only nodded. "How fortunate, then, that you came when you did. Still . . ." Her voice dropped lower; he found himself leaning toward her to catch her words. "It would be nice to see something of *you* in these rooms, as there is in the study."

A curious sort of pleasure bloomed in his chest. "Oh? I always imagined you thought of me as being precisely like this drawing room: stuffy and old-fashioned."

She laughed, then slowly shook her head. "Not stuffy. Cautious. Careful—car*ing*, I suppose I should say. You certainly came to Edmund's rescue many times." Another laugh, more rueful. "And mine."

Yes, he had. Except when it had mattered most. But he'd had little prospect of preventing her wed-ding to Manwaring. Her father had been deter-mined to marry his only daughter to a title and a fortune, and until four years ago, Kit had had nei-ther. Even knowing how she'd dreaded the match, Kit wasn't convinced she would have had him in-stead.

"You never married," she said, still quiet.

It wasn't precisely a question, at least not one

Kit had to answer. He took some grim comfort in the fact that her thoughts had been traveling a similar path to his.

He had never told Beth how much he loved her; perhaps he hadn't really known himself until it was too late to do anything more than dream of what might have been. But he'd never seriously contemplated marrying someone else. How could he fairly and honestly pledge himself to another when his heart would always be hers?

"Well," she went on more briskly, steering them away from the drawing room as she spoke, "it's clear you need a lady's advice." The brim of her bonnet pointed the way to the final set of stairs.

"So Mrs. Rushworth has often told me. I suppose that's why she wrote to Mrs. Goode without telling me—she knew I would have dismissed the idea out of hand. I am sorry to have dragged you all this way," he said, though he knew he did not sound regretful.

Her shoulders rose and fell, making the puffed sleeve of her pelisse brush against his arm. "It's a welcome change of scenery. At this time of year especially, London can be dreadfully dull."

Kit smiled to himself, absurdly glad to think that, in her eyes at least, he was not *dreadfully* dull.

He still could not quite believe it: her story, his luck—any of it.

But he was willing to overlook the improbabilities if it meant another glimpse of her face.

They entered the would-be nursery with her fingers still resting lightly on his sleeve. One speculative glance from young Mr. Oliver—Kit could not ever remember taking such an instant dislike to a person—and her hand fell away. Its absence came with recompense, however. As she looked around the room, she tugged off her gloves, unbuttoned her pelisse, and at last reached up to remove her bonnet.

Free of the bonnet's shadow, her eyes glittered, a well-remembered spring-sky shade of blue. Her hair, still dark as a raven's wing, had been artfully arranged not to disguise but to highlight a streak of silver. And her face? Even prettier than he remembered, despite the dismay presently coursing through it.

He forced himself to drag his gaze away from her to the room she was surveying. Footmen and maids had been hard at work for days, clearing out crates and brushing away cobwebs. The windows had been scoured clean—all but the cracked one, which had been boarded over until a new pane of glass could be ordered. The room was warmer as a result, but at the moment, Kit would have welcomed a breath of fresh air.

Though gray, the afternoon light streamed through the remaining windows, reaching into every corner and crevice, disguising nothing. Somehow, Kit thought as he looked around him, things had actually gotten *worse.* The nursery was bright, yes, but utterly cheerless and comfortless—much like the rest of the house.

Mr. Oliver called Beth to his side with a tut-tutting noise, and they bent their heads together to discuss their plans. Kit could not help but recall how the Tabetha of his youth would have disdained concerns over paint color and drapery fabric.

Though Mr. Oliver seemed to be the one making all the decisions . . .

The approach of Mrs. Rushworth momentarily redirected Kit's thoughts.

"Mrs. Goode's secretary says she will inspect today, devise a plan tomorrow morning, and then return to London in the afternoon."

"So soon?"

Both Beth and Mr. Oliver turned toward him, as if the clatter of his heart were audible from across the room.

"I—I am . . . astonished that you can be done with your work so quickly."

"Mrs. Goode will write to you if any questions arise," the secretary explained, "and I will order the necessary materials and furniture to be delivered. Everything will be completed before the children arrive."

Kit managed a nod. "I hope you will use local workmen whenever possible."

Mr. Oliver looked down at his papers, but Beth continued to study Kit carefully. "Certainly, if you wish it, my lord," she promised.

With a few words, Kit sent Mrs. Rushworth on her way to arrange for rooms for their guests. When he turned back, Beth had tipped her head close to Mr. Oliver's to read some notes the latter had made.

It was a pose that spoke of their familiarity, to be sure. Once more, Kit tried to reason away his jealousy at the sight of it. Two people who worked together as closely as "Mrs. Goode" and her secretary must, of necessity, develop a degree of intimacy, and Kit was pleased Beth had at last found something fulfilling—if a bit puzzled by her uncharacteristic choice.

But he was still envious. Envious of one who spent his days in her company, one who was making better decisions at five and twenty than Kit had, to be sure.

"Lord Stalbridge?"

At the sound of his name, he came to himself with a start and discovered Beth watching him again, spots of color on her cheeks. Mr. Oliver had looked up too, and his dark brows were knitted together in a scowl. Kit must have been staring, like some besotted fool.

After twenty years apart, what hope had they of being what they had once been to one another? To say nothing of more . . .

"Excuse me." His bow was even stiffer than usual. "I'm clearly in the way here. I'll leave you to it."

Chapter 3

To his credit, Oliver waited until the sound of Kit's footsteps had faded before skewering her with a glance. "I take it you and Lord Stalbridge have some prior acquaintance?"

"Don't look at me like that." She moved to the nearest window. A misty rain blanketed the scenery. Her thoughts were no clearer. "He and I were . . . friends, long ago. When we were children."

Not only children.

He'd been four and twenty the last time she had seen him, and she on the cusp of her twentieth year, soon to be a wife. A man and a woman, each absorbed by their individual griefs—the death of his father, the death of her innocence—but reaching out to offer the other comfort.

But how was it possible, after all this time, for her body to call up the memory of his embrace?

How hard and lean he'd been after a summer's walking tour, how she'd clung to him a moment longer than was wise and let herself wonder what it might be like to marry him instead . . .

She tipped her forehead against the glass, grateful for its chill.

"He was the elder son of my father's steward. Papa told me once that Mr. Killigrew belonged to a branch of an old, noble family, but I never dreamed Kit stood to inherit all this . . ." She peered down onto what might have been a terrace, its stone walls and urns shrouded in gray. "I don't think Kit knew, either. His brother Edmund and I were the same age, and endless trouble to him. Then I married. And now, Edmund's . . . gone."

Oliver's hand settled on her shoulder. "I'm sorry, Mamabet."

Tabetha's breath huffed from her lungs, part sigh, part knowing laugh. "My mama once scolded me for asking what a *scoundrel* was, and when she wanted to know how I had even heard such a word, I had to confess I'd been listening to two of the housemaids discussing Edmund. He couldn't have been more than seven at the time. Oh, Edmund . . . And poor Kit, always left to see things put right." She glanced around the freshly scrubbed nursery. "I've been thinking about all that's changed, but I guess some things never do."

"No," Oliver agreed. "They don't." His observant gaze was still focused on her, rather than the room, and she had the strangest sensation his words referred to something other than Edmund Killigrew's peccadillos.

"So." She levered herself away from the glass

and forced a briskness into her voice. "What are Mrs. Goode's plans for this place?"

One dark brow curved fractionally higher, but Oliver's answering nod was similarly brisk. Pointing with the end of his pencil, he launched into a dissertation on light and color, the best use of space, and current theories about children's need for active play and opportunities to exercise their imaginations.

Fascinating and impressive though it was, Tabetha's mind began to drift and eddy like the fog outside, swirling into the other neglected corners of the house, and wondering why Kit had never . . .

"I'm sorry," she said, jerking herself back to the present place and time. "Did you—did you say you were thinking of painting a mural of the fall of the Bastille along this wall and framing the doorway to resemble a guillotine?"

"The blade would be rubber, of course," Oliver explained earnestly. Then his lips quirked. "I wanted to see if you were paying attention."

Chagrined, she nevertheless pressed her mouth into what she hoped would pass for a maternal scold.

"Perhaps you should go rest," he suggested. "Recover from your . . . what was it again? Carriage sickness?"

Despite the obvious teasing, he was offering her an avenue of escape, and she seized it. "I'm not really much use to you up here anyway."

Oliver didn't disagree. But when she stepped to the door, he called after her. "Mind you don't tell him *all* Mrs. Goode's secrets."

. Tell . . . *him?* Did Oliver imagine she was going to seek out Kit?

She spun back to face him, to chide him, to correct him. Silhouetted by the window behind him, Oliver's posture was that of a confident young man. But in his voice, she'd heard the echoes of the unsure, misunderstood boy he had once been. *Don't tell . . .*

She'd kept his secrets even from his father, her husband.

What could be more difficult than that?

She nodded solemnly. "You have my word."

Certain that Kit would have returned to his study, she directed her steps in quite another direction, toward the floor they'd skipped entirely in their earlier tour of the house and on which she assumed, by process of elimination, she would find the guest chambers. She wasn't tired—or carriage sick—but it was somewhere to go, somewhere she could be alone to think. Surely after she'd freshened up, she would feel more herself.

She'd expected to be guided by the bustle of servants. What she found was a corridor of closed doors, save one. All was dim, quiet. Perhaps she'd mistaken her way. Curious, she followed the light coming from the solitary open door.

What lay beyond it was not, as she'd expected, another corridor, or a stairwell, or even a bedchamber, but a large sitting room. Too large to be called cozy, despite the fire in the hearth. Its crackle was inviting, though its warmth stood little chance of penetrating the high-ceilinged room. Half a dozen tall windows ought to have made the space bright and airy, but whoever had decorated the room had framed them in draperies they'd probably called *tobacco* or *chocolate* or *bronze*. In Tabetha's vocabulary, they were merely brown.

Kit was sprawled in a chair before the fireplace, holding a book but not reading it; with his other hand, he twirled a pair of spectacles by one ear-piece, and his gaze was focused on the dancing flames.

She really should leave him to ruminate in peace.

Squaring her shoulders, she crossed the threshold.

At the sound of her steps, Kit scrambled to his feet, tossed the spectacles aside, and dropped the book onto the chair's seat. "Beth! I didn't expect—come in! Please, join me." She followed his gaze to a tea tray on a nearby table. "Or perhaps you've already . . . ?"

Tabetha shook her head.

"No, no—of course. When Mrs. Rushworth brought this, I asked her to send a tray to the nursery as well. But there hasn't been time. Let me ring for another cup, then, or—or better yet, you take this one." He picked up the lone saucer and held it out to her as she sat down on the chair across from his—a chair in which, she gathered by its unforgiving frame, no one had ever sprawled. "I haven't touched it. You'll want to add your lumps."

Their fingertips could not help but brush as she accepted the cup of tea from him. "You—"

His eyes were searching hers.

"You still remember that I like my tea sweet?"

Something flashed across his face too quickly to name; a moment more and she would have been tempted to call it yearning. It was whisked away by a self-deprecating laugh. "Oh, I—wouldn't that be odd if I did, after all this time?" He turned to reach for the sugar bowl, then proffered it to her. "But most people take sugar, don't they?"

"I suppose so." How silly of her to be disappointed by his explanation, or to fancy she'd glimpsed something significant in his expression. She took up the tongs and dropped in more lumps than was wise.

After returning the bowl to the tea tray, he sat down again. Then, grimacing, he fished beneath himself for the forgotten book.

She disguised her smile by taking a sip of tea, which was still surprisingly hot. "What were you reading?"

He turned the book this way and that in the firelight, as if searching for the answer to her question, before giving up and balancing the volume on one knee. His well-worn buckskin breeches revealed legs just as tautly muscled as she remembered. Evidently, he was still a horseman. "It's a travelogue about Sicily. I was imagining the children playing in front of a cozy cottage, surrounded by blue: the perpetually sunny skies, the sparkling waters of the Mediterranean." Again, the ghost of a wry smile turned up the corners of his mouth; his gaze was far away. "For all his failings, Edmund would've been the sort of father children adore, don't you think?" The smile flattened, then gradually curved downward as he went on. "It's a small sort of blessing, I suppose, that they're so young. In time, the memories will fade . . . They'll forget their mother's smile, Edmund's laugh. They'll forget the home they had to give up to come"—he glanced despairingly, disparagingly around the room before settling his pained gaze on her—"here."

"Ferncliffe is magnificent," she tried to reassure him.

He tossed the book onto the table beside the previously discarded spectacles. "It's a mausoleum."

Would Ferncliffe's somber grandeur feel oppressive to two small children? *Perhaps,* she thought, looking about her again. Still, she was certain Kit had not been worrying himself over the appearance of the house. Rather, the seriousness of the charge of serving as a surrogate father to his niece and nephew had shaken his confidence. In all the years she had known him, he had never once shirked his responsibilities. But, of course, that did not mean he had always been eager or felt ready to bear them.

And then Kit said, "It's my fault he's gone."

Words caught in her throat, and it was a moment before she managed to stutter out, "H-how can you say such a thing?"

"I drove him away. I had all I could do to support Mama as her health declined, and he'd been flitting from one thing to another for years, always with his hand out. The church was his first choice, he claimed, though I think we both knew it was incompatible with his character. And then he was sure he'd prefer the law, like his brother. Soon enough, he came to tell me that the law didn't really suit him either, all that time locked away with dusty old books, and couldn't I help him to something that let him see the sun from time to time? So I—" Kit's fingers had been nestled together before him, his elbows resting on his knees. She watched his grip tighten, his knuckles whiten. "I agreed to purchase a commission for him—but that would be it, I vowed. I told him he was a grown man, and I washed my hands of responsibility for him."

Tabetha's indrawn breath was sharp but silent. England had been at war for what seemed like forever now. A young man might be drawn to the imagined heroism of life as an army officer, but Kit at least would have understood the risks.

"I had in mind a militia regiment in the north," Kit went on. "Something to instill a little discipline. But he insisted on the regulars and was soon sent to India. He was stricken by some tropical fever before he even arrived. It's a wonder he made it home again. The disorder settled into his lungs. The physicians insisted he needed a drier, warmer climate if he were to have any chance of recovering."

"Ah." She glanced toward the discarded travelogue. "Sicily."

"I offered to arrange his passage, of course, but even as weak as he was, he refused my help. That was the last I saw of him. Almost the last I heard from him, for almost ten years. I—I didn't know how he got on—knew nothing of his life there, his wife, their children—until he was gone . . . And I cannot help but doubt whether this"—with effort, he pried free one of his hands to gesture around the room before circling back to lay his fist against his breastbone, as if pressing against a pain there— "was what he wanted for them."

"Edmund's children will see a bit of their papa in their uncle Kit's face," she said, hoping against hope that those words would reassure him. No one could deny he and his brother shared a resemblance. Kit nodded heavily. "And when they do, they will understand they are safe here. You are providing a welcoming haven for them in the nursery. And in time, I'm sure the rest of the house can be—"

"Yes, yes," he spoke across her, his voice artificially hearty. "Past time to make the place my own, just as you said earlier—but it needs a woman's touch. So, Mrs. Goode, what would you recommend for this room, as a start?"

Taken aback at least as much by his tone and choice of address as by the question, she could not immediately focus her attention on the room. When she did, she found it much the same as the other rooms she'd seen—which was to say, needlessly formal and fine, as if some previous Earl of Stalbridge had required perpetual reminders of his wealth and grandeur.

Given its location near the bedchambers, it had evidently been intended as a private family parlor, though it was difficult to imagine feeling comfortable in such a space, laughing or playing games or reclining on the sofa for a nap. It reminded her a bit of Manwaring's estate and how cold she'd felt in that house, cold from the day she'd arrived to the day she'd left.

"I'm not sure . . ." she began, trying to buy a little time to consider the matter.

Oliver would probably begin by ripping down those mud-brown curtains, perhaps with his own hands, and then ordering the removal of most of the gilt-edged mirrors and marble-topped tables.

But she hadn't the faintest notion of what would be best to replace them. Inwardly, she battled a smile, thinking of his ridiculous joke about the nursery guillotine. He was such a clever, creative soul, while she . . . Well, when it came to matters of hearth and home, she was little more than a fraud.

"Beth?" Kit had been watching her survey the room. Now, one of his brows cocked in a familiar arch. Had her hesitation alone been enough to make him suspect she hadn't been telling the truth?

At that curious yet knowing look, she was sixteen again, trying and failing to concoct some story to save Edmund's hide. As a boy, Kit had rarely troubled himself to argue with her. But on that particular occasion, the Kit who had returned from university with a self-satisfied gleam in his eye—mind sharpened by endless battles of wits among his peers, shoulders broadened by punting the Cam—was having none of it. The conversation had begun with them on opposite sides of the room. Every lie from her lips had brought him one dangerous step closer, and she . . . she'd gone right on lying to him, taunting him, wanting . . . wanting things she hadn't fully understood.

Now, heart pounding and palms slick with sweat, she leaped to her feet. "No one's called me Beth in years." *I'm not the girl I was.* "Except my stepson, in his way—and never in his father's hearing."

"Beth." Softer now and tinged with sorrow. "I didn't know. I'm sorry . . ."

How like Kit to take responsibility for mistakes not of his making. Unable to face him, she turned as if to study the chair she'd so abruptly vacated. "More comfortable furniture would be an excellent place to start. Something with a bit more cushion. But sturdy upholstery, you know, because children—"

"Beth." Chiding, this time. Almost reproachful. He stood too—and stepped between her and the door.

If she tried to slip past him, he wasn't the sort of man who would lay a hand on her to stop her.

Even if she wanted to feel his fingers curled possessively around her arm again, as they had been in his study. Even if she wanted—

Helpless to do otherwise, she dragged her gaze from the seat of the chair to the unpolished toes of his boots. Over supple leather and snug buckskin and soft wool. *When I get to his face and see his expression, that will put an end to this nonsense.* The stern set of his jaw. The notch of a frown.

"Kit." The sound of that familiar name on her lips was hardly worthy to be called a whisper.

Twenty years older. An earl.

And still, somehow, exactly who he'd always been.

Yes, the notch was there, between his brows—though it reflected more puzzlement than disapproval. "About this 'Mrs. Goode' business . . ." he began.

Drawing a sharp breath, she rose up on her toes and pressed her mouth to his—anything, anything to stop the question he'd been about to ask.

She'd neglected to consider that kissing him might raise new questions. For instance, had he always smelled so marvelous—of woodsmoke and leather and bergamot? Had his lips always been so soft, so hungry, so . . . skilled?

Forty-one years she'd lived without the pleasure of a toe-curling kiss. She squeezed her eyes shut, the better to imprint the moment on her memory. And the better to deny the reality of her present situation: it was her dear old friend Kit's chest against which she was rubbing the aching tips of her breasts, and Kit's callused hands that were cupping her face, and Kit's scorching kiss that was causing little whimpering moans to form in her throat.

Oh, she needed to be careful, *careful* . . . and all she wanted to do was throw caution to the wind.

With his fingertips against the base of her skull, he tipped her head slightly and slanted his mouth over hers, kissing first her upper lip, and then the lower, stealing her breath, as if he could never get enough of her.

Behind them, the fire crackled and hissed. Kit's hands slipped down to her shoulders, and the pad of one thumb swept over her throat, seeming to take the measure of her pounding pulse. The pressure of his mouth grew less insistent, a nibble here, a brush of lips there, as if he were trying to rein himself in. Reluctantly, she sank back onto her heels, breaking the kiss entirely.

When she looked up, she could see by his expression—the slightly glazed look in his lust-darkened eyes—that the kiss had done its work. He was no longer thinking about the décor of Ferncliffe's family parlor. Or Mrs. Goode.

"That was . . ." His warm breath stirred the hair on the crown of her head and made her scalp tingle.

"Yes," she said, though whatever word he had intended to choose would surely have been inadequate to the purpose. His kiss had very nearly turned her inside out.

"I should go," she said, and he let her, as if he, too, recognized that to linger longer in this embrace would be unwise. But before she slipped entirely free from the circle of his arms, he tipped forward and pressed one last kiss to her forehead. Her eyelids fluttered down. Would it be so very wrong to stay?

Of course it would.

As the last half an hour had proven all too well, every private moment between her and Kit had the potential to turn dangerous. She'd been charged with keeping a secret, and she would do it.

But now she also understood she'd been keeping a secret from herself.

Chapter 4

Kit had never before known his valet to hum while he worked. But there they were, the steady but muted notes of a melody, punctuated by the rhythmic stropping of a razor. Curious, Kit stepped to the door of his dressing room during a break in the tune and found the man testing the blade against his thumb, a smile curling his lips.

"Should I be nervous, Winston?" Kit joked, nodding toward the lethal-looking implement.

"Forgive me, sir. I did not hear you come in." He laid the sharpened razor aside. "Will you dress for dinner now?"

As Kit removed his clothes, Winston shook them out and laid them aside, then poured steaming water from a cannister into the washbasin and began to work the shaving soap into a lather, humming all the while. Perhaps what Kit had thought of as sparing his manservant unnecessary labor had in fact been depriving him of pride and pleasure in a job well done.

Then again, the ordinarily unflappable Mrs. Rushworth had been visibly daunted by the prospect of preparing rooms and meals to impress their famous houseguest.

The Tabetha he'd known wouldn't have cared one iota for such details. And he was beginning to suspect she still didn't—if that look of near panic on her face when he'd asked about refurbishing the family parlor had been any indication.

He hadn't the faintest idea what had inspired her to dub herself "Mrs. Goode" and pretend enough interest in home décor and entertainment to write a book about it. Frankly, he didn't much care. She might call herself whatever she liked and decorate Ferncliffe's nursery as she pleased.

His mind was focused on one detail: there had been no pretense in Beth's kiss.

No young man's fantasy, nothing to do with friendship, but real and passionate and stronger than the barriers that had kept them apart for so long. After twenty years, she was free, and no one could say he wasn't worthy of her.

Winston's tune must have been contagious. Kit left his chambers whistling it under his breath—and why not? He had every reason to hope. In a matter of moments, their gazes would meet across the dining room table, and he might glimpse in her eyes what he had felt in her lips, in her body, and he would know that he had not waited in vain.

But why wait a moment longer to see what was in her eyes—even, perhaps, her heart? He would knock on her chamber door, offer to escort her down. He turned toward the corridor where he'd directed Mrs. Rushworth to place their guests.

As he rounded the corner, the song on his lips died. Mr. Oliver was there before him.

Of course. Mrs. Goode's secretary was a gentlemanlike sort of fellow. Of course he would be joining them for dinner. Even at this distance, Kit could see the young man was elegantly, impeccably dressed. Kit's best waistcoat suddenly felt dull and just a bit too snug.

Mr. Oliver held out his elbow. Beth laughed up at him, at something witty he had said. And then her slender hand rose, not to rest on his arm but to brush a stray curl from his brow.

At that lover-like gesture, Kit retreated silently into the shadows.

Perhaps the intimacy of which he had caught glimpses was *not* merely a result of her close working relationship with Mr. Oliver. Kit would not be so petty as to begrudge Beth's need for, er, *companionship* of the sort a handsome young man might provide. Above all things, he wanted her to be happy, and he doubted she had known much happiness in her marriage.

But earlier, in the parlor, he'd begun to hope that *he* might be the one to make her happy.

What a fool he'd been, to read so much into a single kiss.

For once, he could not make himself do the expected, responsible thing and join the pair for dinner, pretending all was well. Instead of torturing himself further, he disappeared to his study.

Tucked away in a corner of the ground floor,

the small, plainly furnished room had probably once been the steward's office; perhaps that was why he found it comfortable. Ferncliffe had rooms aplenty for gentlemanly occupation: a library, a billiard room, a gun room. But his study was the only place he never felt himself in the shadow of the late earl, a man with whom he had nothing in common—except the title.

For the second time that day, he unstoppered the decanter of brandy on his desk and poured himself a drink. With a groan, he threw himself into a chair before the cold hearth and lifted the glass to his lips, then set it aside untouched. *Good God.* Was he truly no wiser than he'd been at twenty?

When he'd returned from university, he'd found Beth grown from a girl into a woman, and his own feelings not one whit changed by the time apart. Inevitably, they'd argued over . . . something. Probably Edmund. He no longer remembered what they'd said, only the flash in her eyes and the color on her cheeks. He'd very nearly persuaded himself then that she at last thought of him as something more than a friend.

But at least on that occasion, he'd only *almost* overstepped.

He had no notion of how much time had passed when he heard footsteps in the corridor. Mrs. Rushworth appeared on the threshold. He hadn't bothered to close the door.

"I beg your pardon, my lord—"

"Mrs. Goode and Mr. Oliver are waiting for me in the dining room, I suppose?"

The housekeeper's head moved in something that might have been intended as a nod. "I dare-say, sir. It's gone past six. But I—"

They would be smiling and laughing at one another across the table, content in their own company. Perhaps they hadn't even noted his absence. "Tell them, please, to go on without me. I find I haven't any appetite this evening."

"Of course, sir. Right away. Only . . ." She stepped forward, and he could see a letter clutched in her hand. "A message has come for you, my lord."

From the way she held it, he could guess the sort of information she feared it must contain. Hadn't he had enough bad news for a lifetime?

"Well?"

Reluctantly, she held the folded paper out to him. He took it and broke the seal.

Only a few sentences, with nothing of flair or flourish. Still, he fished his spectacles from his pocket and read the note twice over, just to be certain he'd understood.

"It's from Mr. Fleming." He looked over the top rim of his spectacles at a worried Mrs. Rushworth. "Captain of the *Seaflower*."

"The ship on which Mr. Edmund's children are to sail?"

"The very same. Only it seems there was some misunderstanding—perhaps a mistranslation in the letter I received. The *Seaflower* is not *to sail*. It *has sailed* and is in fact presently anchored in Gravesend, with two small children among the passengers who disembarked. When I did not arrive to meet them, the captain himself generously undertook to bring my niece and nephew the rest of the journey to Ferncliffe." He laid the letter on the table beside him and contemplated taking up the tumbler of brandy once more. "They will be here tomorrow."

Mrs. Rushworth's steady exhalation of relief turned into a gasp. "Tomorrow?"

"Indeed." Screwing shut his eyes, he reached beneath his spectacles to pinch the bridge of his nose. The empty nursery rose in his imagination.

No, not empty. Beth stood there. Smiling.

In the arms of the dashing Mr. Oliver.

"Shall I tell Mrs. Goode?"

The sound of Mrs. Rushworth's voice made him start. Every castle he'd built in the air seemed to have come crashing down about him all at once. Such was the use of dreams. "Please tell her that under the circumstances, her assistance is no longer required."

"Sir?" The housekeeper's eyes were round as saucers.

No time left now to worry about paint and decoration. "We shall manage very well without her," he insisted—hoping with those words he might also at last convince himself.

From her seat at the table, Tabetha watched Oliver stroll about the dining room. They were alone; the liveried footman had helped her to her chair, poured the wine, and left them to wait for Lord Stalbridge. Oliver first stopped to survey an oversized landscape in the style of Claude Lorrain.

Then he paused to rub the fabric of one dark blue drapery panel between his fingers and thumb before tsking and shaking his head.

She admired her stepson's incisiveness, his ability to see past the surface, his refusal to bow to another's tastes. When she looked about, she saw only too much gilt and too many mirrors—and a room somehow still so dark she'd been tempted to ask for more candles. After just half a day, she was inclined to agree with Kit: Ferncliffe's grandeur was far from an improvement on the happy but considerably more humble home in which he and Edmund had been raised.

She was not surprised that Kit had been reluctant to spend—before reading Mrs. Goode's thoughts on the matter, she might have said *waste*—time and money on the house when there was really nothing wrong with it. No peeling plaster or leaking roofs. Simply a difference of taste from the previous earl.

But as Oliver had been at pains to explain in his letters about the renovations of the townhouse, taste mattered. A home ought to be a reflection of the people who lived in it. And at heart, Kit was a man who cared for people, who wanted them to be comfortable, who was happiest just being himself.

About this "Mrs. Goode" business . . .

When she'd agreed to spend a few days in Hertfordshire calling herself Mrs. Goode, she certainly had not anticipated the project would involve so much self-reflection. But being around Kit had a curious effect on her, making her think about the girl she had been, the young woman everyone had expected her to be, the person she was now.

And Kit's kiss had left her questioning what was yet to come.

They'd shared a past, but did they dare look forward to a future?

Did he want her—or the fabulous Mrs. Goode?

"It's not entirely hopeless," Oliver declared, spinning back to face her. The curtain behind him rippled with the movement.

"It isn't?" she asked, before realizing that he had been referring to the house and not her feelings about its owner.

Oliver took a step closer to the table, curling his long fingers around the carved finials of a chair that would not have looked out of place in a Tudor throne room. But he made no move to sit down. Instead, he tilted his head and studied her with the same keen eye he'd applied to the painting. "Where would we be without hope?" he said. And she knew he had divined the direction of her thoughts when his next words were, "Strange, isn't it, that Lord Stalbridge never married?"

"Well, he wasn't Lord Stalbridge until recently," she reminded him. "His prospects before the inheritance weren't exactly grand. He was responsible for his widowed mother—"

"And his wastrel brother—"

Tabetha sent him a chiding glance. "His entire family, yes. At one point, he planned to go in for the law as a way of supporting them. I daresay he never had much ready money."

His expression grew skeptical. "So he took a vow of chastity as well as poverty?"

"Oliver!"

Settling one forearm along the back of the chair, he leaned toward her and retorted in a mocking whisper, "Mamabet!"

She sent a glance over her shoulder and dropped her voice. "I don't think you should call me that where others might overhear."

He made a dismissive gesture with his hand but conceded enough to draw the chair back and sit down in it so that they could converse more easily. "What did the two of you discuss this afternoon?"

"What makes you think we spoke?"

"If you don't wish to talk about it, then we won't," he replied with a little *humph.*

"How did you know?" She dropped her voice lower still.

"I wasn't *sure* . . . until now," he teased with a triumphant grin. Then his expression softened. "Let us say that something in your voice when you spoke of him—and something in his eye when he looked at you—made me think it likely you would seek out an opportunity to converse with one another. Reminisce about old times, that sort of thing."

"Mostly we talked about the children," she confessed at last. "This house. He . . . he wondered what Mrs. Goode would recommend to make it warmer and more welcoming. I—I didn't really know what to say."

Oliver picked up his goblet, took a sip, then smacked his lips appraisingly before shrugging and downing the rest. "I wonder," he said, looking contemplatively at the empty glass, "whether we have the present Lord Stalbridge to blame for this appalling vintage, or whether the fault lies with his predecessor."

"You *must* know I didn't tell him the truth," she insisted, leaning over the table. "When he seemed surprised by my inability to suggest improvements to the family parlor, I"—her whisper became something barely audible in the vastness of the room—"distracted him with a kiss."

"Ah. How clever." Oliver twisted the stem of his goblet between his fingers, his gaze focused on the gleaming tableware, his smile more than a little wry. "But what, pray tell, will you do the next time the subject comes up?"

She sucked in a breath. "That remark is unworthy of you, Oliver," she said primly, despite the fact that she'd been wondering much the same thing. "And uncalled for. I suppose I've grown so accustomed to thinking of you as a friend, that I—I neglected to consider . . . Perhaps you find my behavior disloyal to the memory of your father, or—"

"Detrimental to the name of Manwaring?" His lips quirked. Then, disregarding her prior admonition, he murmured, "*Mamabet* . . ." and reached across the table for her hand. "I find it difficult to believe there's a man on this earth who's worthy of your affection. Certainly my father was not. But perhaps this Lord Stalbridge . . ." His shoulder rose and fell in a characteristic shrug, making their joined hands twist slightly against the table-cloth. "For once in your life, do what makes *you* happy. Tell him how you feel. Tell him the truth. Tell him . . . everything, if you must."

Reveal Oliver's secret? "But you—your publisher, your book—"

"Forgive me." He squeezed her hand before releasing it and sliding back into his chair. The high, straight back made his usual pose of indifference impossible to assume. "But I never really thought this harebrained scheme of yours would work. I will survive—even if Mrs. Goode does not."

Tabetha had to bite her lips to keep them from trembling. "Thank you, Oliver dear. But I won't sacrifice you for an illusion." He opened his mouth to protest, but she spoke over him. "Oh, Kit is a good man. A dear friend. And an excellent kisser, as it turns out," she added with a quiet laugh, as heat spread across her cheeks. "But I daresay he's painted a false picture of me in his imagination. In the end, I'm sure he'd be happier with someone more . . . domestically inclined."

"A 'Mrs. Goode' type?"

"Exactly."

For once, Oliver did not say whatever was on his mind, though he did cast her another skeptical look.

"Besides," she went on, "you told me to do what makes me happy. Shouldn't I make certain what that is, first?" She glanced around the room. She'd already endured one drafty old pile in the country—though to be fair, Ferncliffe wasn't drafty. "I'm not sure this is the life I want."

"Then what is?"

For several silent moments, she did not attempt

an answer, though some variation of the question had been swirling among her thoughts for days—no, years. She was a woman of means, a widow with a significant measure of independence. What did she intend to do with her good fortune?

"I've been thinking . . ."

Oliver fished inside his coat and retrieved the little notebook and pencil he kept tucked in his breast pocket. Lists had always been a preoccupation of his, a way of working through problems. After moistening the tip of the pencil against his tongue, he held it poised above the paper. "Yes?"

"Now that I've read it, I do appreciate how *Mrs. Goode's Guide to Homekeeping* celebrates the value of women's domestic contributions to society, while still making it clear that so-called women's work is indeed *work*, and not always a labor of love. I wish . . ." She paused, hoping not to wound with her next words. "I wish I had been possessed of such a manual twenty years ago."

Oliver only nodded without looking up and wrote two words at the top of the blank page.

"Or rather, I wish I had had something to reassure me that it was perfectly natural for a lady to want—oh, I don't know—to be heard on political matters, and not just smile and nod at her husband's opinions. Or to study economics, and not merely sufficient arithmetic to balance the household accounts. To dance, yes, but also to run and swim and . . ." She waved a hand, searching for something outrageous and snatching from the air a golden childhood memory. "Even play cricket if she chooses."

"Sort of the opposite of a conduct manual, it sounds like." He jotted down a few more words.

"Yes, I suppose so," she agreed with a laugh. "But really, I haven't any ambition to write books—and who would buy such a thing, if I did? Young ladies are the ones who need to hear such advice, and their reading is strictly monitored."

Oliver tapped the end of the pencil against his lips, looking thoughtful, and then wrote down something else. "Something less expensive, then. Something easily paid for with pin money and just as easily passed from friend to friend. Perhaps a periodical."

"You mean, some sort of ladies' magazine?" Oliver was scribbling furiously. She sighed. Such publications were filled with fashion plates and advice that only perpetuated the problem of female dependence. "No, no. That's not at all what I—"

Before she could finish the thought, crisp footsteps sounded in the corridor. Her heart began to hammer, thinking they must belong to Kit.

Mrs. Rushworth appeared in the doorway and curtsied. "I do beg your pardon for the delay, ma'am. Mr. Oliver. I'll have your dinner brought in right away."

"What of Lord Stalbridge? Won't he be joining us?"

"I'm afraid not, Mrs. Goode. I just spoke with him, and he asked me to give you a message." She paused and thrust her shoulders back to deliver the speech she'd evidently rehearsed on her way to the dining room. "As it happens, the children are now set to arrive tomorrow, and His Lordship says we won't be needing your assistance after all."

"Tomorrow?" Tabetha echoed, incredulous. "Then I should think his need for assistance would be all the greater. Why—?"

"Now, now, Mrs. Goode." Oliver pushed to his feet, tapping on the table's edge with his pencil. "As you've always told me, we must respect the client's wishes. I'm sure you'll agree that Lord Stalbridge has had a trying day. Perhaps he'll think better of his decision in the morning."

"Mayhap," agreed Mrs. Rushworth doubtfully. "Anyway, I'll see to your dinner."

"I've lost my appetite," Tabetha said, rising. Something else must have happened to change Kit's mind so abruptly. She needed to find him, to reassure him, to explain . . . as best she could . . .

"Mrs. Rushworth," Oliver said, "I'm worried about this good lady. She hasn't really been herself all day." Turning his head to evade the housekeeper's line of sight, he sent Tabetha a conspiratorial wink.

Bewildered, she narrowly managed to disguise her huff of disbelief as a cough.

"You poor dear," Mrs. Rushworth crooned, then barked out, "John!" The footman sprang into view. "Fetch a supper tray to Mrs. Goode's room. Make sure there's tea."

"Might I be so bold as to suggest a warm bath might also be of benefit?"

"Mr. Oliver!" Tabetha protested. So much unnecessary work for the servants. And she'd be trapped in her room an hour, at least.

The footman, who seemed to share at least one of Tabetha's reservations, sent a sidelong glance toward the housekeeper for confirmation.

"A capital idea. Go on, then," urged Mrs. Rushworth. John hurried away.

"Now, allow me—oh, dear." Oliver, who had rounded the end of the table and held out his arm to escort her from the room, broke off abruptly and patted his chest instead. "I've just remembered, I left Mrs. Goode's notes in the nursery. So careless of me." Both she and Mrs. Rushworth looked pointedly at the notebook, still lying on the table. "Oh, not these," he insisted, reaching across the table to snatch it up and tucking it away. "I should really run up and fetch them before I forget again."

Tabetha couldn't help but frown. What on earth was Oliver up to?

"I'll be glad to see you to your room, ma'am," Mrs. Rushworth offered.

"Excellent, excellent," Oliver exclaimed, looping Tabetha's arm around the crook of the housekeeper's elbow, as if she were suddenly too feeble to ascend the stairs without assistance. "I entrust her to your care."

"There now," Mrs. Rushworth said, firming her arm and covering the back of Tabetha's hand with her own. Tabetha hadn't a prayer of slipping free. "You can be sure if Lord Stalbridge knew how things were, he wouldn't be in any hurry to send you on your way."

"In that, ma'am," said Oliver, bowing them from the room, "we are in perfect agreement."

Suddenly, Tabetha knew exactly what he meant to do.

You mustn't, she mouthed over her shoulder, fixing him with a pleading look. She couldn't bear it if he sacrificed his happiness for hers.

But Oliver only gave her one of his knowing smiles and hurried off in the opposite direction.

Chapter 5

Though he heard a sound behind him, Kit did not turn away from the nursery window. It did not matter that it had long since grown too dark to see anything beyond his own reflection. His eyes were focused on the freshly scrubbed floor, from which rose the sharp scent of pine.

The footsteps came no closer; the person to whom they belonged did not speak. Kit clung as long as he could to the hope that Beth had sought him out to demand an explanation. Eventually, however, he would have to face the reality that it was the housekeeper or another servant. As he lifted his gaze to the glass, his resigned sigh fogged the windowpane, blurring but not disguising the reflection of the person standing behind him.

"I thought I'd find you here," said Mr. Oliver.

"The question," Kit said, after he'd recovered from his surprise at the identity of his visitor, "is what prompted you to look. Did not Mrs. Rush-worth convey my message?"

"She did."

"Then you should be relieved. You and . . . Mrs. Goode are free to return to your lives in town."

Mr. Oliver shifted his weight. "Lady Manwaring, you mean." The mirror version of his face was oddly misshapen, impossible to read. "She told me you knew—that you'd known one another for-ever."

"Did she?" But of course she had. The pair of them had probably enjoyed a good laugh over the idea of a grown man still clinging to childish dreams.

"Come, come, Stalbridge."

The familiarity of his address rankled. Kit jerked about to face the younger man. "What is it you want, sir?"

Mr. Oliver looked remarkably unperturbed. "The chance to make things plain. Tomorrow will see the arrival of your niece and nephew and, if you don't look sharp, the departure of the person best able to make your dreadful old house into a home."

"I suppose now you're referring to Mrs. Goode?" Kit had had enough. He took three steps across the floor, prepared to push past Mr. Oliver if he must. "I grow weary of this conversation, sir. I'll bid you good night."

"Oh, dear. Perhaps I've misjudged," he said, in the mocking voice of a man who fancied himself never wrong. "But your affection for the lady seemed quite genuine to me."

"I've loved Tabetha Holt for as long as I can remember," Kit growled, grabbing the younger man by his perfectly starched, elaborately knotted cravat and pinning him to the door jamb. "And I'll love her, and her alone, till the day I die. Don't try to claim you can say the same, Mr. Oliver."

"Actually," he replied with a smirk Kit was tempted to wipe away with his fist, "it's Manwaring."

In spite of himself, Kit's grip slackened, allowing his prisoner to slide free.

"And I believe I *can* say the same," he went on. With a few fastidious flicks of his wrist, he straightened his coat and fluffed his rumpled linen. "Well, perhaps not the 'her alone' bit. A young man must be allowed to sow his wild oats." He winked, then sobered. "But rest assured, I do love her."

"Manwaring." The name on Kit's lips sounded garbled, like he'd had one too many pints at the village pub or taken a shot to the jaw. "As in . . ."

"Comma, sixth viscount. Yes. Pleased to meet you, Stalbridge." He extended a hand with a flourish, and Kit was too bewildered to do anything but shake it. "And yes, Lady Manwaring is my stepmama, a part she has performed admirably for, oh . . ." He made a show of calculating, first in his head and then on his fingers. "Twenty-one years, seven months."

"Your stepmother. Not your—"

"Paramour?" He gave a rueful chuckle. "You did a poor job of disguising your suspicion, Stalbridge. But after Mrs. Rushworth conveyed your unceremonious dismissal, I grew convinced your reservations about my stepmother had been compounded by another matter. Either misplaced jealousy, or . . ."

"The Mrs. Goode charade."

For the first time in their brief acquaintance, Kit saw a spark in the other man's eyes, a hint that behind the façade of indifference and insolence lay something else entirely, something about which he cared a great deal. "It isn't a *charade*. Mrs. Goode is a testament to the true importance of what is so often dismissed as women's work. Men bloviate about politics and business, oblivious to the very stuff that holds the fabric of our society together, the dinners over which wars are begun and contracts negotiated, the balls at which dynasties are formed or broken, the homes to which we all long to retreat at the end of the day. Her book is an acknowledgment that homekeeping is both art and science, proof that its skills can be taught, and a reminder that such knowledge ought not to be the province of only a few."

"Well said." Kit's grudging nod of respect sent a flare of surprise across Manwaring's face. "But that sounds a great deal to put on the shoulders of one woman."

Manwaring hesitated. "Mrs. Goode is . . . more an idea than a person, I suppose you might say."

"Books don't write themselves."

"No, well, of course there's *someone* behind the name . . ."

Not Beth. Kit felt sure of it. Not because he thought her incapable of changing the world. But he'd been skeptical from the first that she would have chosen this particular way of doing it. When he thought back to her supposed secretary's behavior, however, how swiftly and surely the young man had taken charge of the nursery project . . .

"The person behind the name is not who the world expects," Kit suggested. *Nor what the world accepts.* "But . . ." he began, gradually piecing the situation together, "when Mrs. Rushworth wrote, and the book's publisher intervened, you found you needed someone, a lady, to embody those high ideals. And Beth agreed—"

"Volunteered," Manwaring corrected.

"In hopes of sparing the reputation of someone dear to her."

The younger man shot Kit a wary look but did not deny it.

"Then," Kit concluded, "through simple bad luck, she ended up here, with someone to whom she was previously known."

Manwaring's brows rose. "Whether it was *bad* luck remains to be seen."

Kit considered that reply for a long moment. Earlier, Manwaring had mentioned *the person best able to make your dreadful old house into a home.* Kit had taken it for a reference to Mrs. Goode. For so long, he'd focused his misgivings about Ferncliffe on superficial matters, the sort of things a noted expert in design could fix.

"Beth has no idea what to do with the nursery, has she?"

"If you refer to paint colors and wallpaper and furniture, no. Certainly not." The younger man's curl-covered head tilted as he looked Kit up and down. "Does it matter?"

Kit looked around the barren space. It needed a lot of work, to be sure. But the emptiness in his life couldn't be filled by redecorating a few rooms. Only love could complete the transformation.

And that, he suspected, was the real secret of *Mrs. Goode's Guide to Homekeeping*.

"To me?" he said. "Not a jot."

Manwaring gave a crisp nod. "Well, well. I begin to think you *might* be capable of appreciating what else she has to offer."

"Now I just have to persuade her to stay," he said.

To his credit, Manwaring did not try to tell him it would be easy. Instead, he reached into his breast pocket, removed a little notebook, tore out a sheet of paper covered with writing, and handed it to him. "That might help."

Without his spectacles, the words were indecipherable, a jumble, just like his thoughts. "I—" Was there a chance? Hope was once more fluttering its wings against his chest in a ticklish dance, and all he could manage to say was, "Thanks. And I—I'm sorry about your neckcloth."

Manwaring waved off the apology. "You don't imagine I wore my best linen to travel into the wilds of Hertfordshire, do you?"

With a somewhat baffled half smile and a shake of his head, Kit tucked away the note and turned toward the door.

"I'll stay a bit longer," Manwaring said, still behind him. Kit paused to send a questioning glance around the empty room. "Whatever happens, you'll still need this nursery put right," the younger man explained. "And Mrs. Goode does have a reputation to consider."

Kit gave another, heartier smile, nodded his thanks, and stepped to the stairs. Fortune—good fortune—had brought the one he loved back into his life.

Now to help Beth see it in the same light.

Assuming that the quiet rap of knuckles against her bedchamber door was a signal from Oliver, Tabetha readily opened it, eager for an explanation of what had transpired.

Instead, she found Kit standing there, one arm propped against the doorframe.

"May I?"

Following her bath, she'd donned only a dressing gown, and damp tendrils of hair still clung to her neck. As his gaze traveled down her body, he seemed to forget whatever he'd been about to say. His words trailed away, and the smile slipped from his expression, to be replaced by something considerably more intense.

She encircled his wrist with her fingers and tugged him into the room.

"You can't be spotted standing there," she reasoned. It would be shockingly improper for the master of the house to be seen conversing with a lady guest in dishabille.

After an impossibly long moment, Kit nodded. "I wanted to see you—though, of course, I hadn't any notion I'd see quite so much . . ." With a twitch of his upper body, as if the movement required effort, he shifted his focus to something on the far side of the room. "My apologies."

"I take it you've spoken with Oliver."

"I have."

Though she'd been expecting the answer, those two words still sent little spikes of pain into her heart. Now he knew she'd been deceiving him; no wonder he was acting so strange. "I'm sorry, Kit. Please believe, I never meant to—I've been his protector for twenty years. I had to do this for him. But I never imagined that keeping him from harm would hurt . . . *you*. Oliver and I will go, just as you asked. At first light. You needn't—"

"Twenty-one years, seven months," he murmured, still not looking at her.

"I beg your pardon?"

"Twenty-one years, seven months: that's what he said. The precision of it struck me. I had the distinct feeling he could have rattled off the tally, right down to the day. But until just now, I didn't fully understand the significance." His shoulders tautened beneath his coat. "From what, exactly, did he need your protection?"

She had to moisten her lips to reply. "His father. Oliver was a grave disappointment to him. As was I, in my way. I never managed to give him another son, you see. Worse, I insisted on standing up for the one he had."

Kit nodded heavily, a gesture that conveyed understanding rather than agreement. "My God, Beth," he breathed, and despite the despair in his voice, she relished the sound of her name on his lips. "I was appalled when your father insisted on your marrying Manwaring. But I never imagined . . . If only I'd—"

"What could you have done?" she protested, trying to reassure him. "We were young—and I, at least, was foolish. I convinced myself Papa was right: it *would* be charming to be addressed as Lady Manwaring. I—I never stopped to think it might mean the end of *Beth.*"

"Twenty-one years, seven months," he repeated incredulously. "It must have seemed an eternity." At last his gaze snapped to her, and a self-deprecating laugh gusted from his chest. "But it's still only a fraction of the time I've spent hopelessly in love with you."

The *pop!* of her mouth flying open was audible in the stillness of the room. The sudden pounding of her heart seemed to get in the way of thought, of words. Eventually, she got enough control over the muscles of her jaw to whisper, "Hopelessly?"

"Yes, and there's no sense in you denying it. You thought of me as a bothersome older brother, always spoiling your fun. I was nobody, the son of the steward. No match for Miss Holt. I could never have convinced you, or your father—"

"No," she agreed. "You're right. It *was* perfectly hopeless." Oh, how she longed to step closer to him, to soften the blow of those words, but she feared her legs might not hold her up. "It does not therefore follow that the situation is still without hope."

Kit sucked in a ragged breath, like a drowning man starved for air and saved in the nick of time. "Beth?" he rasped.

"This afternoon, when I kissed you, I made an unexpected discovery. The seed must have been planted so long ago, buried so deep, I never even knew it was here"—she laid her hand over her heart—"waiting . . ."

Kit closed the few steps that separated them and settled his hand over hers. "That's how you keep a seed safe until it's ready to bloom."

She searched his face, his eyes, such a curious, wonderful mix of the familiar and the new. "I'm afraid I'll wake up and all this will have been a dream. I—I'm afraid you'll discover I'm not really the woman you need. I'm no Mrs. Goode, after all."

"I don't want Mrs. Goode. I want you, Beth. Will you marry me? Let me spend the rest of my life being what *you* need?"

Do what makes you happy, Oliver had said. She had been shying away from thoughts of marriage and domesticity and a house in the country because she'd been so miserable before. But the problem hadn't been with those things; the problem had been her late husband.

How different the prospect of such a life looked now, when she imagined Kit beside her.

"Oh, Kit." Freeing her hand, she flung herself against his chest. "Yes. *Yes.*"

And then her mouth was on his, communicating what words could not.

His answering kiss was both a reminder that he had always known her and a quest to learn more. While he pressed his palms to either side of her head and skated his fingertips along her scalp, she rose up on her toes to bring them closer, to help him plumb her depths.

Earlier that day, wrapped in his arms, she'd been aware of the solidity of his body, the heat of him, even through layers of clothing. But now, dressed in almost nothing, she could think of little else but the moment when there would be even less between them. Slipping her fingers beneath his coat, she slid the garment over his shoulders. A satisfied grin curled her lips when he shook it free of his arms and she heard it settle against the carpet with a soft *whump*.

One of his hands trailed from her cheek, along her throat, and over her collarbone, tracing the valley between her breasts to tangle in the silk tie at her waist.

"Am I moving too fast, Beth?" he murmured against her lips. "I don't want to rush this—rush you."

Her chest was heaving as if she'd just run up three flights of stairs. "We've waited more than twenty years. I don't think anyone could describe that as rushing."

She felt his smile. "No. I suppose not." With the slightest movement of his fingers, the tie, already loose, gave up all pretense of holding the sides of the dressing gown closed.

When he took a step backward, the better to take in what had been revealed, she had to close her eyes against his stark expression, carved like granite by the firelight. Her body at forty-one wasn't what her body had been at twenty, all coltish long legs and pert breasts. "Not quite what you'd imagined?" she whispered.

"No." The sudden gruffness of his voice made her shiver. "So much better. My God, Beth." The hand at her waist smoothed over the curve of her lower belly before settling on one round hip. "So soft and plush and"—he closed the slight distance he'd put between them and brought his mouth to the curve of her jaw—"kissable. I hardly know where to begin."

The tip of his tongue against her throat, the tiniest of movements, set off a series of progressively larger explosions in her breasts, her belly, the place between her legs. Though it was cool in the room, so far from the hearth, her skin was on fire. One shrug of her shoulders sent the dressing gown to the floor, baring her entirely to the night air. To him. "Anywhere," she told him. "Everywhere. Just—I need you, Kit. I've always needed you. If only I'd realized—"

"Hush," he commanded, nipping sharply at her earlobe. "None of that. This is a moment for looking forward, not looking back."

"All right," she agreed, emboldened by the heat of his breath. "Then tell me, what have you most looked forward to?"

"Learning the taste of you." The boldness of his answer made her whimper, the eager sound caught in her throat. "Hearing you cry out in ecstasy." The hand cupping her head dropped to her breast, his callused thumb brushing across her nipple, and the unexpected pleasure of the sensation drove the whimper from her throat and past her lips as a gasp. "I fantasized about spending hours sampling each delight. But now that the moment's finally here, I—" The hand at her hip tightened convulsively, snugging her against his erection. "I want to—"

"Yes," she hissed. "Make me yours."

Releasing her with a nudge toward the bed, he shucked off his remaining clothes, tossing them aside with the sort of carefree abandon she'd somehow thought Kit incapable of. Boots, breeches, waistcoat, each one flying in a different direction, a spectacle of lust, but she had eyes only for him. His shoulders were as broad as she remembered, the muscles of his legs as finely hewn as she'd suspected. And then he lifted his arms above his head to strip off his last remaining item of clothing, and the long tails of his shirt rose high enough to reveal—well.

Twenty years ago, perhaps, his stomach had been tauter, the hair on his chest a shade or two nearer to brown. But it was impossible to imagine his cock had ever been more impressive than it was at this moment: thick and hard and straining toward what it wanted, straining toward her. She fumbled behind her for the edge of the bed, sank down on the mattress, and parted her legs in blatant invitation.

"You want this, Beth," he said as he stalked toward her. "You want me."

Was he asking her? Or trying to persuade her? But she did not need convincing. She held out her hands, encircling his erection the moment it was within her reach.

He hissed at her touch, the searing heat of his flesh making her own feel comparatively cool. One of his hands settled heavily on her shoulder, pushing her onto the mattress, while the other slipped between her legs. She was wet already, eager, but he teased her nonetheless, stroking first one and then another finger inside her, circling her nub with his thumb.

Already, her climax tingled at the base of her spine. Could he sense it? "Come inside me," she pleaded, brushing the head of his cock against her damp curls, nudging his fingers away. Her need shocked her. All her married life, sex had been a chore, and pleasure something reserved for moments when she was alone. But this . . . this must be why some called it lovemaking, the joining of both bodies and hearts. "*Please.*"

He obliged. One deep, perfect thrust of his hips that made her cry out with the rightness of it. "Mine," he grunted, pinning her to the bed with his weight, and yes. Yes! She was Kit's. Some part of her had always been Kit's, and now he was finally hers, filling her, each stroke driving her further along the road to release.

She wrapped her legs around his pelvis and held him to her as she shattered. Then, as she lay pliant and open beneath him, he changed both the angle and tempo of his thrusts, urging her to gather up the pieces of her soul and come for him again. "Yes, again," he whispered against her hair, his thumb once more seeking out that little bundle of nerves and coaxing her toward another climax. "Come *with* me."

And she did, her inner muscles rippling in time with the hot spurts of his seed.

With another, sleepier grunt, he clambered over her, dragging her into the bed with him, their limbs a wonderous, sticky tangle.

"I love you, Kit Killigrew," she said, the words muffled against his shoulder. Then, with what strength she had left, she curled her hands around his back, clinging to something that had almost slipped through her fingers.

Chapter 6

Even before he opened his eyes, Kit smiled. Or perhaps it would be more accurate to describe his expression as a grin. Despite a few sore muscles and a largely sleepless night, he could not remember a morning in which he'd awoken so satisfied.

Beth lay curled against his side, snoring softly. The realness of it made his heart squeeze. Their lovemaking had been beyond his wildest imaginings. But this—the sort of comfortable, ordinary, everyday thing that came with sharing a life with another person—was somehow even better.

His deep satisfaction with the present moment did not entirely erase the desire to rouse her with kisses and pleasure her again, however. Something slow and easy this time, with the morning sun streaming across the bed, across her body, and the—

He blinked toward the window. Morning sun,

yes. Not terribly bright; it was, after all, still November, no matter that spring had sprung in his heart. And the angle of the windows here was less familiar to him than in his own bedchamber. But if he had to guess, by both the quality and quantity of light, it must be . . .

Good God. Midmorning, at least. The only possible explanation for their not having been found out by some poor housemaid sent to sweep the hearth and light a fire was that Mrs. Rushworth had declared Mrs. Goode's room off limits. Had she suspected something? Certainly, the housekeeper would have had the staff up and at their tasks at the crack of dawn on such an auspicious day.

His niece and nephew could arrive any moment. And nothing was ready for them. Especially not their uncle.

Carefully, he extricated himself from Beth's arms, from her bed, and scurried about gathering up his clothes. He dressed hurriedly, dropped a kiss on her bare shoulder before drawing the bed coverings more snugly over her, and slipped out of the room after a quick scan of the corridor.

His own chamber was also suspiciously empty of servants. But the valet's earlier presence was marked by a basin of water and a pot of coffee, both now tepid. The door between the dressing room and bedroom stood open, and although the curtains were still closed, it was amply clear the bed hadn't been slept in. Kit stripped off his shirt and washed with cold water, thankful not to have to look a whistling Winston in the eye.

Not that he was ashamed of having spent the

night with Beth. Far from it. In fact, he intended to spend every night of the rest of his life similarly situated. But for a host of reasons—not the least of which was the previously spotless reputation of that paragon of domesticity, Mrs. Goode—he ought to have been more circumspect in his comings and goings.

Just as he finished knotting his cravat, he heard a tap on the bedchamber door.

"Come," he said, hoping against hope that the visitor was Beth.

A footman stepped into the room, his face impassive. "Captain Fleming has arrived, my lord."

So soon? He'd expected to have hours yet. Struggling to maintain his own exterior calm, he nodded. "Thank you." The footman, taking his words for dismissal, bowed and turned to go. Kit stopped him with another question. "Have you seen Mrs. Goode this morning?"

He'd left her sound asleep. But he wanted to be able to judge the sort of gossip flying among the staff.

More important, he did not want to have to meet the children alone.

"No, my lord. I don't believe she's risen yet." The footman's expression betrayed nothing.

Kit's second nod was crisper, unambiguous. The footman bowed again and was gone. He slid his arms into the coat he'd worn the night before, considering his comfort at present more important than a few wrinkles, though Winston would surely disagree. On the washstand, he spied his spectacles; the valet had a gift for rescuing them from whatever corner of the house in which Kit had laid them aside. As he tucked them into his breast pocket, his fingertips brushed the note Manwaring had handed him. No time to read it now. Kit drew a steadying breath and made his way downstairs.

Two children of about four or five years of age and dressed in traveling clothes awaited him in the entry hall. The boy was looking up at the painted ceiling, a cloying scene of cavorting cherubs against a blue sky the likes of which England had never seen. But the girl's eyes were focused on his descent. She was the elder, Kit thought, though they were nearly the same height. She had the boy's hand in a firm, almost painful grip. He knew that pose. Someone had told her to keep watch over her brother.

He found himself wondering if she'd ever once dared to release that hand over the course of their voyage.

At what Kit suspected was a firm tug from his sister, the boy redirected his attention to him. There was something of Edmund in the lad's face, though not enough to make the recognition painful. He had loved his brother, even though Edmund had surely had occasion to doubt it.

Their somber appearances aside, however, he could not help but wonder whether either or both of the children might have inherited their father's exuberance and mischievousness—the very qualities Kit had tried for years to stamp out of Edmund, thinking it was for the best.

Kit only hoped he had learned enough in the ensuing years to keep from making the same mistakes again.

"Good morning," he said. "I am your uncle."

Neither child spoke, only regarded him with wide eyes.

Captain Fleming, who had been standing off to the side examining a bronze sculpture of a salmon in the claws of some bird of prey, approached and bowed. "Good morning, Lord Stalbridge." He was a barrel-chested man with sunburnt skin and hair like straw, and he spoke with a soft Scottish burr. "We had fine roads for our journey and made excellent time."

"I am glad to hear it. It was kind of you to bring the children all this way."

"Think nothing of it. They've been no trouble. Hardly said a word since we left Palermo."

"Is it any wonder, sir?" Beth spoke unexpectedly behind him, and more sharply than was her wont.

Still, her presence was a balm. He might have managed perfectly well without her, but he would always prefer to have her by his side. "I'm glad you're here," he whispered.

"They are no doubt terrified, and still grieving besides," she said to the captain, but her fingertip trailed over Kit's arm as she brushed past him and dropped down to her knees to be eye level with the little girl. *"Buon giorno, cara. Come ti chiami?"*

"Isabella," the girl replied softly, laying her free hand on her chest. Beth asked another question, which elicited a longer answer. Beth nodded as she listened.

Kit wasn't surprised, exactly, to discover that she spoke Italian. It was the sort of accomplishment her parents would have cultivated. Speaking nothing of the language himself, he could not judge her fluency. The girl spoke more rapidly, to be sure, the words like music on her lips. But they seemed to understand one another well enough.

"I've spent my fair share of time in the Mediterranean," said Captain Fleming, "but I never picked up the lingo. It's grand that Lady Stalbridge can understand them."

Kit didn't bother to correct him over the matter of names. As soon as possible, he intended it to be the truth. He was watching as the two conversed, thinking about what Beth had said last night—about what he needed, and what she wanted. They could have it all, if they let go of the past, let go of old assumptions, and reached for something new—together.

She must have asked Isabella for her brother's name next, for the boy piped up, "Luca!"

"After your father, do you suppose?" Beth said, darting a glance toward Kit.

Bending, he reached out a hand to Luke Killigrew's grandson. The boy considered the offer before laying his palm across his uncle's, not in a handshake but in a childlike gesture of trust. Kit gripped harder and did not let go.

Soon thereafter, Captain Fleming took his leave, explaining that the children's trunks had already been unloaded. "Your servant said he'd see they were taken to the nursery."

The nursery. Once the door closed behind the captain, Kit let a sigh escape his lips. Isabella posed some question and, her cadence more halting, Beth answered. "She wonders if she might see her room," Beth explained to him.

"I haven't even spoken with Mrs. Rushworth

about where the children will sleep." He spoke low, suspecting the children must know at least a few words of English, unless Edmund had simply cast off everything that connected him to family and home.

Beth appeared to give the matter some thought. "I believe we should take them upstairs and show them what *will* be theirs. Children have marvelous imaginations, and if their trunks are already there, that will be something familiar. They can at least change out of their traveling clothes."

Luca had resumed staring about the entry hall with wonder, but he had not loosened his grip on Kit's hand. "All right," Kit agreed. Whatever her reservations to the contrary, he trusted Beth's judgment.

And so, as a foursome, Luca's hands clasped in Kit's and his sister's, and Isabella's other hand in Beth's, they turned and ascended the wide, polished stairs. He'd dreamed some variation of this scene many times: he and Beth, together, a family at Ferncliffe manor. Even unsure what they'd find when at the top of the stairs, he once more found the reality better than anything his imagination had fashioned.

By the time they reached the top floor—the children vacillating between awed quiet and anticipatory chatter—Kit's heart was hammering, and not from exertion. He should have insisted on taking them somewhere else. The awful, empty nursery would be no welcome for Isabella and Luca. When Beth reached for the door, he almost begged her not to open it.

Before he could speak, however, she swung the door wide. Isabella gasped.

"Tell her," he began, "tell them we hadn't time to—no, tell them we wanted them to be able to choose . . ."

But Beth wasn't listening. She was following Isabella through the doorway—well, being dragged along behind, more accurately. Luca went next, almost pulling free of Kit's hand. What choice had he but to go along?

A few steps more and he stopped abruptly. Blinked. Twice, three times.

The room had been transformed. Panels of blue silk, into which tiny holes had been cut, swagged over one end of the room, creating the illusion of a starry night sky. Beneath that tent lay two plump mattresses, mounded with pillows and blankets. More stars, these crafted from paper, hung from the ceiling. Beneath one window, a table had been placed, its carved legs sawn off to make it a more comfortable height for little ones; instead of rigid chairs, its sides were surrounded by a trio of cushioned footstools, collected from various rooms around the house. And over the bare walls had been sketched the outline of an expansive scene, one which transitioned seemingly without effort from the Mediterranean Sea and Mount Vesuvius to Ferncliffe, nestled among the rolling hills of Hertfordshire—in other words, tracing the journey from one home to another.

Luca squirmed free of both Kit's and his sister's hands and scampered over to investigate the tent. Isabella, still attached to Beth, focused her attention on the mural, her questions and observations intelligible to him through their enthusiastic intonation. He watched Beth, her dark head bowed to catch every syllable, and wondered what she was thinking.

Eventually, Isabella was persuaded by her brother's repeated summons to join him in admiring the silk version of the night sky. They lay side by side on one of the low beds, looking upward and nattering to one another, a contented murmur of sound punctuated occasionally by a giggle.

"I think it would take very little encouragement for them to fall asleep," Beth said softly, stepping closer to him. Already, the stream of conversation was broken by stretches of silence. "They must be exhausted by their travels, by all the disruptions and uncertainties. Now they feel safe, just as I told you they would."

Something burned in his chest, a sudden rush of love for these two children, though strangers. And for Beth, his dearest friend.

She was looking around at the room, not up at him. "Oliver must've stayed up all night."

Kit nodded. "It appears he commandeered the draperies from the dining room."

"Oh dear," she said, sounding at once horrified and amused. "Well, Oliver has never played by the rules."

Kit nodded. This was not at all what he'd had in mind for the nursery, nothing anyone he knew would consider appropriate for the niece and nephew of the Earl of Stalbridge. "Thank God," he murmured, never in his life so happy to be wrong. "He took something I thought of as hopelessly dull and made it magical. I underestimated him, even after that grand speech he gave me last night, about the true value of the kinds of domestic work so many are prone to dismiss."

"Including me," she confessed with a low laugh. "But you see now why I was determined to protect 'Mrs. Goode.' "

Kit fished for her hand. "I also see the person who encouraged his creativity, who inspired him." Raising her fingers to his mouth, he brushed his lips over her knuckles. She watched him do it, wide-eyed, but not protesting. "You were his mentor, his first teacher—oh, maybe not in the skills needed to transform an empty room into the stuff of childhood fantasies. But in something more important. You taught him those dreams were worth having, that he didn't have to stuff them into a box and tuck them away in the attic just to satisfy someone else's notion of what his life should be."

There were tears in her eyes, more than she could blink away. "Did I?"

"Look around, Beth," he urged. The children had at last fallen silent, safe and cozy in their makeshift beds. "You may not be Mrs. Goode. But none of this would have been possible without you."

She still looked dubious. "Does that mean I shouldn't regret marrying Manwaring?"

Kit considered his answer. "I will not go so far as pretending to be happy about a marriage I would have prevented if I could. But I think the present Lord Manwaring has reason to be glad of his father's choice. And if your parents hadn't been determined you'd marry well all those years ago and had you educated accordingly, you might not have been able to speak words of comfort to Isabella and Luca today."

"I suppose that's true. I hadn't really looked at things in quite that light before. Perhaps there is some use in a young lady's accomplishments. But I'll still never be a paragon of domesticity."

By the hand he still held, he led her over to the low table and helped her to one of the footstools before sinking onto another himself. He would worry about how to get up from it later. "Rest assured, I'll never ask you to be anything other than who you are—and who you want to be."

"So," she asked, in the manner of one posing a test, "you won't mind if I do not wish to spend all my time in the country?"

"No, though of course I can't abandon the estate entirely. And after so much time apart, I would prefer to avoid lengthy separations, with you in Town and me here." She nodded. "But I like London too, and it's past time for me to take up my responsibilities in the House of Lords."

She let out a breath and dragged in another, as if relief of one worry only made room for the next. "What about . . . children?"

"Luca and Isabella, you mean? You are not eager to be known as their wise and fun-loving aunt?"

Her answering smile was weak. "*Your* children, I meant. I can't give you a son."

"I have no need of a son. I have an heir."

"You would leave all this . . ." Her gaze wandered to the window, and he had the distinct feeling she was remembering as much as seeing. ". . . to Edmund's son?"

"The earldom does not begin to make up for driving my brother away." He twined their fingers more tightly together. "And it doesn't matter more to me than you do."

Her breathing grew easier, her blue eyes less stormy. "Thank you, Kit."

"So that's settled? We'll return to London, acquire a special license, and marry before Christmas?"

She didn't hesitate. "Yes."

"And come January? I've often found it a dull, lonely month," he confessed. "Though also an excellent time to resolve to make a fresh start on something, or to begin improvements one has been putting off. Perhaps I'll work on brightening up the rest of Ferncliffe," he suggested, glancing around. "How about you? Any projects you'd like to undertake?"

"I'm not . . . sure. I mean, yes. There's something I want to do. But I don't know exactly what it is—and doesn't that sound perfectly ridiculous?" Her laugh was pained, humorless.

With his free hand, Kit reached into his breast pocket for the slip of paper Manwaring had given him. "Your stepson seemed to think this would help."

"Oliver's notes?" She turned the paper toward her and made a scoffing noise. "How?"

"Well, let's see." Releasing her hand, he retrieved his spectacles and threaded them over his ears, bringing the swooping print on the tiny sheet of paper into focus, though no clearer. "Something about Mrs. Goode and a conduct manual—no, magazine?" It didn't sound much like Beth.

"Oh, I told him I wished I'd had a *Mrs. Goode's Guide* when I was a young woman. *Before* I became a bride, in fact." She lifted her gaze from the notes to Kit's face. "Something that would have helped me make better—wiser choices."

"But not a conduct manual?" He knew the sorts of books that fell into such a category, with their narrow view of what was proper for young ladies.

"No. More of a—" Her lips quirked, and then she giggled, the same merry sound he'd heard at some point last night, when he'd found an unexpectedly ticklish spot. "A *mis*conduct manual."

He lifted his eyebrows. Now he began to see a glimmer of his Beth in the project. "Ah."

"Not *serious* misconduct, you understand. But real advice—not just to marry to satisfy their families. Perhaps reviews of the kinds of books they *want* to read, not merely what some stuffy old rector deems they *should* read. But as I told Oliver, no one would buy such a thing. Not even as a tuppenny magazine. Buyers would be expecting to find the latest fashions and stern lectures about the dangers of too much dancing. And if it didn't contain those things, it would never be deemed acceptable for the young women I most hope to reach."

He puzzled over the problem, studying each word Manwaring had jotted down as if it were a code to be cracked. "What if . . . what if your magazine appeared to be just what was expected on the

surface, a sort of . . . false front? A disguise, if you
will? Perhaps you could even find a way to borrow
a bit of Mrs. Goode's prestige," he suggested, noting the words upmost on the paper. "The casual
observer would see nothing to raise any alarms. And
once parents and governesses and well-meaning
maiden aunts were satisfied no harm would come to
their charges, young ladies would be free to be . . .
well, *free.*"

"Could that work?" Beth looked skeptical but
thoughtful. "People *are* more than willing to dismiss anything specified as being for young women.
So long as we could get the young women themselves on board . . ." Her fingertips drummed on
the tabletop. "And of course, I'm no writer."

"Hire young women to do the writing. You can
be the publisher and editor in chief."

She liked the idea. He could see it plainly written on her face. But her eyes narrowed. "As Lady
Stalbridge?"

"Why not as Mrs. Goode?" Manwaring sauntered
into the room, his curls dark with damp and his
clothes uncharacteristically rumpled, as if he'd
still been wearing them while snatching what little
sleep he'd managed. Kit pressed a finger to his lips
and then pointed toward the sleeping children.
"Ah," he said, softening his voice. "I'm sorry I missed
their arrival."

"The place is a marvel," Kit said. "I'm not sure
how you pulled it off."

Manwaring's shoulders lifted in a shrug that
wasn't quite modest. "Wasn't sure what you'd make
of it."

"The children love it, and that's all that matters. Now," Kit said, picking up the note, "what were you saying about Mrs. Goode?"

"I can't go on pretending to be her," Beth insisted. "Particularly not after we're married . . ." She sent a surprisingly shy glance toward Kit.

"Ah, you worked things out last night, then? Excellent." Manwaring grinned mischievously as he looked between them. "Perhaps you ought to call your magazine *Mrs. Goode's Guide to Being Bad.*"

"Oliver, be serious. What we have in mind could besmirch Mrs. Goode's reputation." Briefly, she told him Kit's idea for a magazine aimed at young ladies and challenging society's rules.

He looked unconcerned. "And you're to be editor? Well, you've always been a marvelous manager, Mamabet. Seems like just the sort of thing Mrs. Goode would want to lend her name to. Perhaps she'll even contribute a regular column."

"Would you?" She jumped to her feet—Kit admired her nimbleness—and threw her arms around her stepson.

"Nothing would give me greater pleasure," he reassured her. "Except, perhaps, the notion of you using your jointure from my father to fund such a thing."

Their combined laughter roused the napping children, who came with shy smiles to be introduced to their cousin Oliver, the architect of their marvelous retreat. Manwaring, too, as it turned out, could manage at least a few phrases in Italian. "Six misspent months with an opera singer," he explained to Kit in a low voice. "So, when do we return to London?"

"Soon," said Beth before conveying the news to the children in Italian.

"Ah, excellent. And you'll stay until summer?"

"*We* will," Kit said, laying one hand atop Isabella's head, while encircling Beth's waist with the other. "I expect *you* will want to come back here and get started on the rest of the renovations."

Manwaring blanched. Everyone else laughed, even the children, though they could not have understood why. Afterward, Manwaring lifted Luca on his shoulders to allow him to inspect some detail of the mural. Kit picked up the little sheet of paper to study the notes once more, but Beth plucked off his spectacles and laid them on the table before leaning in to whisper warningly, "You may live to regret this."

"Never," he said, pulling her down onto his lap. "Because I love *you*, Beth. With all due respect, I never wanted Mrs. Goode. Those high ideals may be admirable, but I prefer a flesh-and-blood woman. Who would choose the perfect house or the perfect hostess, when he could have a home, and a life, with his best friend?"

At just that moment, Isabella tried to clamber onto Beth's lap, and the whole precarious arrangement gave way, with Kit tumbling off the footstool and Beth and Isabella landing in a giggling heap on top of him.

"Who indeed?" Beth laughed and kissed him.

Visit our website at
KensingtonBooks.com
to sign up for our newsletters, read
more from your favorite authors, see
books by series, view reading group
guides, and more!

BOOK **CLUB**
BETWEEN THE CHAPTERS

Become a Part of Our
Between the Chapters Book Club
Community and Join the Conversation

Betweenthechapters.net

Submit your book review for a chance to win exclusive
Between the Chapters swag you can't get anywhere else!
https://www.kensingtonbooks.com/pages/review/